The French Lieutenant and the King of Rome

—ᗰ—

A historical romantic novel set in the German occupation of France during WWII

Jay Macey Rosenblum

ABOUT THE COVER:
Directing your attention to the flag pole and the flags displayed on it; the eagle is the Nazi standard eagle used on uniforms and on buildings and it is essential that the head be turned to the right and that the wings be flattened as they are here. The eagle clutches a wreath in its talons which is attached as the symbol at the top of the flag pole. The first flag displays the escutcheon (similar to the form of a medieval shield) representing the panzar divisions of the German Army and were usually attached as a decal to their equipment. Or it could be utilized on flags attached to front fenders of their staff vehicles instead of the swastika. The panzar divisions were the conquerors of France in the approximate two week race to defeat the French in 1940. This flag and the eagle symbolizes the German victory. The lower flag appears here as small and very subordinate to the victors flag. The second flag is the flag of the State of France as created by the Germans and is referred to as Vichy. It was in fact the actual flag of Marshall Petain who was chosen by the Germans to lead and maintain the Puppet State of Vichy and constituted, at the most, one third of the old proud French State. His French flag displayed his baton and seven gold stars beneath it. The seven stars were worn by Marshalls of France, on their sleeves to represent their rank which was essentially honorary and not necessarily a matter of authority. Thus the cover is meant to display the overwhelming victory of the Germans and the insignificant residue of France as a puppet of Hitler and his German State. The cover, is thus intended to be a pure display of irony.

Copyright © 2014 Jay Macey Rosenblum

All rights reserved.

ISBN-10: 149595627X
ISBN-13: 9781495956270

Library of Congress Control Number: 2014903387
CreateSpace Independent Publishing Platform
North Charleston, South Carolina

Dedication

To the memory of my daughter Leslie Karen Rosenblum
1958–2013
So long as I shall live so shall you.

Preface

THE AUTHOR HAS woven the fictional characters and their story into the woof and the warp that constituted the fabric of their time and place—that of France and particularly Paris from the years 1938 to early 1941. Their lives and their story line have been integrated into the relevant historical events as presented through the narrative of the novel. The historical characters who are thus an integral part of the novel are, for the most part, military figures of both France and England, along with the significant political leaders and cabinet members relevant to the period of the collapse of France and its occupation by its hereditary enemy, Germany.

The "King of Rome" bore this title created by Napoleon for his successor as the ruler of his empire. After the fall of Napoleon and his imperial creation, the child was taken by his maternal Hapsburg grandfather to the Austrian Palace of Schonbrun in Vienna, where he was renamed the Duc de Reichstadt and, on his death at age twenty-one, was interred in a bronze casket in the undercroft of the Capuchin Church, which had been created in the sixteenth century specifically to receive the remains of the Hapsburg family.

Acknowledgments

I WISH TO thank both Monsieur Bendjebbar, of the Musee de l' Armiee, Hotel National des Invalides, Paris, and Monsieur M. L. Pretrini, of the Service Culturel de Pedagogique of the Musee de l' Armee, Hotel National des Invalides, Paris, for their cooperation in searching the library records of the Musee de l' Armee for information and articles concerning the return of the casket and contents of "l' Aiglon," or, in English, "The Eaglet," the name by which Napoleon II, the son of Napoleon, was commonly known. There was, of course, his formal title, created by his father and under which he rests in Les Invalides in Paris, "The King of Rome."

I must credit the outstanding authority on the subject of France during WWII who has even been decorated by the French government with the Officier, Legion d' Honneur in acknowledgment of his scrupulous examination and analysis of every aspect of this horrendous time. He is Professor Robert Paxton, BA., Washington and Lee University, MA., Oxford University (Rhodes Scholar) and PhD., at Harvard University. He has written several authoritarian works concerning this subject matter and most recently taught at Princeton University. I had the distinct pleasure of examining his two volume thesis for his PhD., at Harvard in the Harvard University Archives. This constituted one of the more than one hundred reference sources which I consulted in writing this book

I wish to also make known my immense gratitude to my life's companion, Mary Jo Singleton, for her long time patience and assistance in the production of the final product and also to my dear friend Marvin M. Early, PhD, for knowledge that he graciously

Jay Macey Rosenblum

shared concerning technical questions and advice needed to simplify the "computer world" for me. I also wish to express my gratitude for the generous information and guidance in completing the publication of the book by Joel Goldman, a friend and well-known contemporary author of mystery novels.

I

HE STEPPED OFF the curb with the intention of cutting the crosswalk short but looked up and noticed two SS men on the opposite corner, evaluating the passing crowd as it surged around them; the Parisians steadfastly refused to acknowledge their existence, while consciously avoiding any bodily contact that might arouse their ire or interest.

He immediately recouped his position on the curb by retracting his foot, but it was not as easy for him to smooth the alarming jolt to his composure of spirit. He found himself to be less abstruse then he believed, still composed but more direct and prone to "flight or fight." Not that he had been forced to do either, yet, but he knew the moments were waiting around every corner for him.

St. Germain was always bustling at four o'clock, a time when he felt safe moving about the Left Bank. His only constant concern was in being noticed by one of the judges or a colleague who might, intentionally or otherwise, highlight his existence to French people of fascist persuasion or the Germans, who seemed to live only to process their obsession with the Jews and their possessions.

He had not appeared in court since his return from combat, as he knew the Germans would force the French Ministry of Justice to invoke their Nuremberg Laws, which included the wearing of the Star of David on judges' and lawyers' robes. Lawyers could represent only Jews, and judges would be eliminated. He felt he had no choice but to abandon clients, his chambers, and all.

The sidewalk café was to his left, and the nearest table was empty, but he had lost his desire for an aperitif with the realization that the two Germans could cross the street and "work" the tables much more easily than the moving crowd that was surging around them across from the sidewalk cafe.

Instead, he turned to his left and walked toward Giselle's apartment, which was close to the river but on the Right Bank of the Seine. She had repeatedly warned him of her fear, which he regarded as morbid, that he would be apprehended by the Germans on one of his forays from the apartment. He refused to be cocooned anymore. He was mad with rage that a swaggering bully of a German could invade his country and reduce him, Giles Lambert, advocate and master, a Frenchman of highly respected status, to an animal with a price on its pelt.

But he was working on a plan.

Animal-like, he felt the immediate need of his "den" to create the intricacies of his plan. The busyness of the streets and sidewalks provided the anonymous moving belt of people he needed for protection from potentially hostile eyes; but this would be so only so long as he moved along at the same pace as those moving around him. The darkening haze of the approaching evening would provide him the shelter he sought.

He felt safe in following St. Germain to the Henri IV bridge and then crossing over to the Right Bank and traveling along to the Place de la Bastille, turning up Rue du la Fauborg to the apartment with "Elle"—Giselle, that is. She was to him "tout la monde des femmes," or in English, "all the female world" (except of course for his mother, whom he adored).

He reminisced about the first time he fell in love; he mused over that new passion for a particular girl that was a great deal more than a primal urge. A yearning for closeness and sharing, a sense of generosity of spirit seemed to pervade his identity. The period after a "breakup" was filled with gut-wrenching loneliness until he was love struck again. It seemed to him that a properly "mothered" boy would always need a mate—not a boutonniere, to be worn to enhance his image, but a mate to somehow meld into a unified portion of "we two," thus sharing the one as a whole.

Far too romantic and demanding, he thought, and far too parsing of a female who could share both his passion and their intellects to his satisfaction. Well, compromise was something he dealt with as a lawyer day to day, and he could adapt it for all things in life, he felt certain. Like holding the hilt of a fencing saber, if one attempts to grip it too tightly, it will fly from the hand when struck sharply and properly. Smothering your chosen could gain the same adverse results. This was an axiom he had sworn to abide by in any future romantic endeavors.

II

GISELLE AND GILES first met at a "pause" in an alumni soccer game between HIV and LLG, the two most highly regarded public lycées in Paris, both tuition-free, but in which only the most privileged and/or brilliant could matriculate. The schools, Henri IV and Louis-le-Grand, were on the Left Bank in the academic area containing the Ecole Normal, the Sorbonne, and the College of France. The area is known as "the Latin Quarter," and these two schools provided the eventual leaders of France in all of its principal areas. The secondary years were from ages ten to fourteen and concluded with a "Brevet de College," followed by high school (ages fifteen to eighteen) and the baccalaureate degree, both from one of the several lycées in Paris or elsewhere. Thereafter one pursued the "classes preparatoire" for one or two years, to enter one of the "Grand Ecole" or law or medical schools. A master's, or "maitre," in law took about five years, beginning to end. Medical school and specialties would take more.

On this particular June day in 1938, the weather was spectacular, and the hostess—the great Parisian park, the Bois de Bologne itself—was dressed in flourishing, luxuriant green and stridently perfect for the occasion.

Alumni classes and their "old-boy" soccer teams were marking their anniversaries and school rivalries as part of their seventh-year graduation celebration. A multitude of guests and families were also there, where an informal soccer field and goals were arranged by the players.

Our soon-to-be lovers met, of course, purely by chance, at the brief half in the game, by a refreshment table provided by the alums of both schools. Both teams were in high spirits, as was the crowd, which was ambling about or seated on fenders, or some in their opened-door cars, which had been pulled up on the grass of the Bois. Others were seated on fold up chairs or polo-style cane seats in the grass around the imaginary edge of the soccer field. Giles was a "back" on his team, as was his closest childhood friend and classmate, Ettienne Picard. Ettienne, an orphan, had been raised by his uncle, a present bishop and the incipient archbishop of Paris. Giles was about to be called up for reserve training as a second lieutenant in the infantry, to the Pau area in southern France, nearly on the Pyrenees border with Spain. He had trained as a cavalry officer, but horses were going to be dispensed with shortly, and he didn't like the smell of oil nor the clank of tank treads. Both young men were, of course, alums of Henri IV.

The teams were busy cajoling each other and joking among themselves, as young men will do as they relive their still recent juvenile years. Giselle found herself and her friend caught up in an eddy of players, and she was almost "grounded," having lost her balance because of the jostling. She was quickly righted by Giles, who had been part of the jostling, for which he embarrassedly apologized to her and her companion, who was the wife of one of Elle's medical colleagues at the hospital.

Elle had decided to go because her colleague, who was an alum of LLG, thought it would be a good break from work for the three of them. Giles barely heard her medical title, being too stunned by her persona to process her full name—justly so because of the stir of the encounter through which they met.

Now that the two elegant young women were clearly in the sights of the immediate young men about them, there ensued a "feeding frenzy" of attention rendered to these two—and all due to the inappropriate high heels worn by Giselle. The women were flirted with, flatteringly complemented, greatly celebrated for their beauty, and politely prodded with underlying sexual innuendos, all of which was more in the American fraternity style than the manner common to this group of French elite males. Elle's medical colleague was a knot or two of people away from the women and could only wonder about what caused the bustle and noise that came from where he had last tracked them.

Suddenly, they stood facing each other, confronting each other, frozen in time. Her high-heeled patent-leather pumps made her, at five feet six, eye to eye with Giles, who stood five feet nine. The impact of their eye contact was a lightning strike, at high velocity. The simple words exchanged between them belied the smashing collision of their eyes, now riveted, his to hers. A sudden, magnetized field materialized, and between total strangers, not permeable by others—strangers, drawn like moths to light in pitch darkness, destined to be devoted lovers.

The shock from the impact of their eyes meeting seemed to subside as he found his ability to speak. Her beautiful green eyes seemed to be monitoring each of his words as well as her responses. The combination of her eyes and blondish hair appeared to dictate her genealogy, as likely to be Frankish; but her nearly olive complexion spoke of the "Langue d'Oc," the Gallo-Roman country south of the Loire River. Her essence even suggested the "languor" of Provence.

His avocational interest in fine art demanded that he consider beauty objectively. She was "a thing of beauty and a joy forever," to quote the poet, and quite something to see and admire. She bore the epic mark of facial beauty, the perfect isosceles triangle: the eyes, each in the right angles of the two equal sides, with the two sides of the triangle descending from the outer edges of the eyes, till those two sides conjoined, touching together, at the base of the chin. A classic nose and brows and full lips—all specially ordered from Praxiteles, to be precisely in balance, per his special rules of proportion. In short, she was perfect, and he had not even chanced a look below the neck, as they were standing almost toe-to-toe.

Feeling numb or worse, he exerted maximum effort at suavity in his manner and smile, which were projected as smooth, facile, and debonair. He mouthed warm and welcoming words and complemented her on her remarkable beauty. In truth he hoped for a great deal more. He aspired to welcome her into his private life!

He had stumbled upon a pirates' treasure, without the esoteric, requisite treasure map: an olive-skinned human statue, bedecked in natures' finery: a humanoid goddess, beyond compare. She wore her breathtaking beauty as other women wore precious gems, to enhance their assets or to distract the observer from their lack of them. Any jewelry she would wear would be a redundant gilding of a perfect lily. He had only himself to offer her in exchange for her treasure trove.

However, he thought amusedly, he had his mother's repetitious assurances, unsought but proudly given by her, endlessly, that "any proper bourgeoisie girl would be lucky to snare" him: her inference being that he was the finest stag, with the largest rack in the forest, and any Artemis of top quality, fleeting through the woods and glades to snare and truss him, in order to triumphantly bring him home to Olympus. Now, dear Mother, he thought, ironically, smiling to himself, we shall see whether or not "the proof of the pudding is in the eating."

III

THEY CHATTED TOGETHER as they wandered over again to the refreshment table. As they did so, they managed to shed themselves of the others. And he managed to crassly, but subtly, take stock of her anatomy. Her hour-glass shape was attached to Petty Girl legs. Yes, she was exactly the long-legged, American-type model foldout for the American magazine *Esquire*, any edition, 1939, or thinking classically, a model for Aphrodite. He thought, if he were Paris, Prince of Troy, he would have chosen Giselle (if available) instead of Helen, avoided adultery, the justified anger of Menelaus and Sparta, and the world would have missed the Trojan War—and some Homeric tales.

There were no angles or rough edges to her. Brazenly, boldly, he stepped back a pace or two to sweep his eyes over her. He understood how Pygmalion had fallen in love with the marble statue he chiseled and wrested from his obsessed brain, willing it to life, by the hand of Aphrodite, to be his missing half, his Galatea. He prayed silently: let it be she!

"I did get your name in that maelstrom we were part of—Giselle? Correct?"

"Yes, Giselle d'Hozier."

"Quite an unusual last name, no!"

"Yes. From some very ancient, very, very distant nobles! Some few did survive the 1790s. My few made it!"

"So, Madame, you are a prized specimen in more ways even than you appear!"

"Yes, perhaps, but of a very mixed breed, even more so than the ordinary person whose ancestors had no choices other than their own social strata and locale."

"How interesting! Shall I bow, with a sweeping gesture of my right hand (as I have no hat available)?"

"Skip the causticity and the wit—the titles were lost with the necks that carried them. I'm a total nonevent with the Count of Paris. I'm sure a caustic wit such as you knows that he is the descendant of Louis-Phillipe, the last king of the cadet branch of the Bourbons! Surely that's enough history outlines for your next lesson!"

"Well, you may have lost your titles, but certainly not your haughtiness!" At this remark, she turned, with intent to abandon him, and he, with emotion and obvious sincerity, said plaintively, "Wait, please wait! This is getting off on the wrong foot! I think you are…smashing. And all I fervently wish in this world, right now, is to get to know you, so please let's start over again! May we?"

There was a brief interlude as she "mellowed" her annoyance, dropping her voice to a complaisant alto, and then said "Absolutely! I think it's going to be worth it." And she said that in a most congenial tone of voice, which gave him the pause to quiet his beating heart before he began the conversation over again—and most carefully.

Then she said something unfeminine and…and…marvelous. "A favor: don't examine me like a corpse in my morgue—or was it more like a side of beef in a *boucher fenetre* (butcher window)?—ever again. But to be fair, while you did that, so did I. Perhaps though, I'm a bit more subtle than you. Guess what? It so happens, at the moment, that I also wish to get to know you, as well."

"Giselle, are you in private practice?"

"No, I'm on staff at St. Anthony's, continuing my training as a heart specialist. Perhaps I'll be certified in another year."

"May I think of myself as an incipient patient of yours?"

"Come now! I just saw you make two running goals from halfway down the field, and you don't seem 'in extremis' to me!"

9

"By St. Valentine's Day, I'm very certain that I shall be! I shall need frequent appointments, perhaps on a daily basis, until then and even after, perhaps for our whole futures!"

"If your first clinical incident won't occur until February fourteenth, aren't your concerns slightly previous to the event?"

"Not at all! When you meet a physician who causes your disease, she is the only one who would have the capacity to cure you. Place yourself at her immediate disposal! Early treatment is most advisable, I'm told. To avoid an early crisis, I need an appointment—now! Do you have an opening in your office hours tomorrow at seven o'clock? I'll pick you up for dinner, and then you may give me my first examination."

"All right. But as my first advocate as a patient, I must ask a pertinent question."

"Yes?"

"Do lawyers have their hearts in the right place? If I could look into your heart, would I find honor and respect there?"

"Yes, and more."

"What more of importance is there, lawyer?"

"Yearning, giving, and incipient love."

"Ah, then, my 'oath' and my own heart dictate that I take you on for immediate care!"

As they started to step away from each other, in response to the whistle sounding for the teams to assemble, he caught her right hand in both of his, stepped toward her, and placed his two hands, holding hers, against his heart, as he pressed his body forward, pressing against hers. Only their hands, pressed against her right breast and the left side of his chest separated their bodies.

"Please don't break it," he said.

Then they mutually remembered in a burst of reality that they had failed to exchange contact information, and both spontaneously spoke of making the exchange.

Forever more, Giles would have his own name for her. It was the obvious abbreviation, E-l-l-e, the French word for "she" or "her," the quintessential pronoun for "the woman."

"We need phones and addresses right after the game. Meet me at this reception table, please," he said, and then he resumed his jocular turn of mind, which she had already begun to enjoy. "When I pick you up tomorrow night, bring your stethoscope and a negligee, if you might be so inclined! We really could play the old childhood game of Doctor-Patient. Oh well, just a frivolous idea you might entertain. In any case, I'll wear clean shorts, as my mother always insists I do, in the event one might be involved in an accident. And what a lovely accident this is turning out to be!"

IV

THEIR FIRST MEETING was the following day at 5:00 p.m., as dusk began to fall over Paris. The lights on the balcony of the Palais de Chaillot were visible from Giselle's chosen booth on the second level of the Eiffel Tower in the Le Jules Vern, where they had prearranged to meet. The restaurant was a spectacular 380 feet in elevation and provided one of the most romantic views in all of Paris. As the lights came on gradually on the nearby monuments, they glittered like individual jewels in the summer dusk, particularly those directly across the Seine along the wings and the two central buildings of the Chaillot Palace to which they were attached. As the evening grew in its metered way, so did the pattern of lights spread over Paris, as a coverlet is let to fall gradually and loosely over a cherished, silken divan by its lady.

The booth was on a window facing the Seine River and its bridge, the Pont d'Iena, and the Palais de Chaillot. She was seated next to a booth occupied by four German tourists, all males of middle age, dressed in styleless suits, doubtless German made, and wearing white shirts and nondescript ties. At first glance, they were picking out sites that would be of tourist interest, but on more careful observation, they were speaking of them in a possessive manner, just as though they might choose to buy some of them, making her feel irate and offended. They were noisy and unconcerned about others in the restaurant.

They were either low-level government employees or mercantile salesmen, she concluded. Then, to her amazement, she heard them addressing each other as "Herr Major" and "Herr Colonel," two of each.

She found quickly that there was more to dislike than the cut of their suits. They had the air of picking out the body parts that would suit their desires the most. Their presence caused the pale of war to descend upon her elated mood of anticipation. Her mind was drawn to review the seemingly relentless moves the Germans had made in the last three years, always without opposition by England and France, as though pacific acceptance would mollify the bully in the neighborhood: that he would ever be satiated by cowardice, when there was more to be gotten! Any common citizen could anticipate the results of their government's fecklessness. Assassination was the answer when the animal Hitler wrote his book, ten or more years ago! Now he was no longer accessible. Would the "kind" of the world always be the weak and diffident, always differing to the evil ones, always attributing to them good intentions though their world experience dictated elimination on first notice? The "kind" covered their fear with hope and self-delusion; and vacillation followed until confrontation and perhaps defeat because of dilatory or inadequate preparation or an absence of the will to win! It appeared to be a matter of knowing history and recognizing its constant repetition. The Germans have wrecked this country twice before, she thought. Shall they have their way again?

When Giles walked up to her table, some ten minutes later, he found her staring intently at these four cloddish-looking men, with daggers in her eyes. Her looks alone could have killed them. He asked her if there was a problem, and she responded, "These four are German officers, and I find their existence here offensive; and so shall you if you watch them for a bit!"

"Well, there other tables with views, so let's move. We are here at just the right time for the lights to go on, so let's enjoy that! That and being together are what we came for," he said. His voice and presence made her mood change, for much the better. From where they sat, they could view the most important sites in the City of Light.

She had noted the palace and its wings and the bridge between these and the tower, and to the right was the Church of the Sacred Heart on the top of the hill known as the Mount of the Martyr. He asked her if she recollected the reason why it had been built, and she said it was built as a sort of penance by the people of Paris for the anti-Catholic commune that followed the disastrous defeat at the hands of the Germans. This followed the occupation of Paris—plus the humiliating use of Versailles, the palace of Louis XIV, to declare the birth of the united German Empire and to crown Wilhelm of the House of Hohenzollern as its emperor: all at French expense. And then the commune tore down the column built by Napoleon from the bronze cannon captured at the Battle of Austerlitz. The building of the church was a national Catholic movement that ended with state support. The basilica's Byzantine cupolas and stark white surface caused it to appear as an oriental potentate's palace, floating sublimely in paradise.

"Yes," he said, "I recall it was Gustave Courbet, the realist painter, who acted to cause the destruction, and later at a court-martial procedure, he was sentenced to prison and, later, a substantial fine. He fled to Switzerland after the fine was levied, to avoid it, and died there. Yes, our city is too full of sad memories, regardless of one's political shade, don't you agree?" She slowly nodded her assent.

"I'll call the waiter, and we will choose from the menu," he said as he beckoned to the one who seemed to be on their station and who responded with menus under his arm. After some interchange of ideas about choices, she chose *cote de veau*, sautéed, and he, *coeur de filet de boeuf*. Sides included artichokes and macaroni au gratin. The choices were easily made and were rather mediocre, as expected in this type of tourist venue. He selected a rather robust red wine from the Bordeaux area, which was probably too heavy for her choice of veal, but the *de haut brion* seemed the only choice suitable for both, as a compromise. There didn't seem to be a wine steward on the floor, so he made his selection from the proffered wine menu that he received from the waiter.

The French Lieutenant and the King of Rome

They mutually admired the dome of the Hotel des Invalides to the south and the Ecole Militaire directly to the rear of them at the end of the formal gardens of the Champ de Mars. Then, of course, there was the incomparable Notre Dame to be seen, basically to the right, or south, of the Eiffel Tower.

After finishing their food, they held hands across the table and sipped their wine, and the conversation became more intimate and concerned their mutual attraction for one another. He then found that they had a red *mousseux* champagne from Bouzy, in the Marne Champagne area. He knew it to be light and spirited, with a nice bouquet. He ordered a half bottle, and they toasted, "To us," each doing so from the other's glass, as the toast was made by him and seconded by her. He candidly repeated his awe concerning her physical attributes. She in turn allowed him to know of her fascination with him. However, they both agreed that these things were not the things alone upon which a permanent life together could be built. She staunchly avowed that she could not concede her morality on a mere uncontrollable, physical, passionate urge. This seemed to place a wall between them, which he did not consider prudent to assault. Therefore, he importuned no further and suggested, upon their completion of their wine, that they walk in the gardens below and then go to the bridge for taxis. She needed to return to the hospital to relieve the "duty" doctor for late evening. He also needed a taxi to go to his apartment in the opposite direction. But first, their "walk" in the gardens.

V

THEY DESCENDED TO the ground in the special elevator reserved for the restaurant landing and strolled out to the Champ de Mars, which was bordered by low hedges done in the formal eighteenth-century manner. It featured formal flowerbeds on either side of the hedges, which were of various shapes and sizes, with arbors, grottoes, and even a cascade. It was beginning to be near seven o'clock, and both had pressing obligations. (He had some preparation needed for a court appearance tomorrow morning.) So they reversed their direction, with the intention of crossing the bridge and thereafter visiting the Chaillot rectangular pool and its stone and bronze gilt statues, its marvelous water jets, and its romantic lighting.

As they strolled, they did the things new lovers do, fondling, arms and hands intertwined, waist hugs, occasional stops involving full-body envelopments, more kisses, and then deep soulful kisses and intimate chortles and laughter—all of which carried the time-honored entitlement of "courting" or "the walking out" or similar tags that had arisen from late-medieval codes of conduct for ladies and their lovers.

While they were so enraptured, he related his previously existing plans to go to London to visit his English grandfather for a few days and then to pick up a new auto in Abingdon, near Oxford; then on to visit his old school for a day, in Rugby, Warwickshire; and then back to Folkstone for the ferry to Boulogne. He would be driving back to Paris from there, via the Pas de Calais country. He planned to leave tomorrow afternoon, after the court hearing, and return in a fortnight. He told her that he planned to call her from London and shared his phone numbers in London and the phone in Abingdon, at a B and B, where he expected to be while arranging for the car. He asked for and received all of her numbers he hadn't received in the Bois, those of her hospital and her mother in Lyon.

Then it occurred to him that if he had to call her mother in Lyon, he would have to introduce himself as "a young man who picked her daughter up in the Bois de Bologne one afternoon." She laughed and said to reserve that call until after he had met her more formally, which she felt they should arrange immediately. She used the opportunity to urge that she meet his parents, before they retired to the South, as he mentioned they intended to do also almost immediately.

He was elated at her suggestion as he felt his mother would recognize her as the "Artemis of top quality" who had the primary ticket to Olympus and whom she was expecting as his permanent alliance: and for whom, no less would do! As for his father, a ladies' man, but of good repute, she was a *shoo-in*, as the Americans say.

She had not chosen to delve into his maternal ancestry, but she was interested in his remark that his grandfather was a boyhood emigrant to England in the mid-1860s. He proceeded to tell her that he had come from Lithuania on the Baltic Sea when he was twelve years old, and all alone. Her curiosity was aroused, but he squelched it by suggesting that it was lengthy and for a future time.

VI

AND SO IT began: lovely romantic evenings in Paris and quaint weekends in the nearby countryside were to follow. Still, their next meeting had to await his return from England, after the expected fortnight. The aforesaid lovely romantic evenings and et cetera would have to await a solution to the important unresolved business, finally at hand—the business of religious differences, the unconfronted behemoth in the lovers' lives!

It would obviously be also necessary to placate the social amenities required by Elle. These would doubtless be expected and appreciated by her mother, as well as by his parents. These amenities were the meeting of the parents and then, essentially, dealing with unpredictable fallout from it. The ghastly contemplation of this scenario made Giles literally feverish and focusing on possible elopement. He did not consider that his parents would verbally assault Elle or her mother, *but* they might rather feel bitter disappointment at a belief that he was to be the apostate in their family—the last male in all their generations: he, who would end the long struggle, the thousands of years of retaining the belief in Judaism against all the organized opposition of the environment and Christianity itself: the hate, the torturing episodes, the murders, and even its vicious new kind of anti-Semitism, after the revolution for liberty, equality, and fraternity.

This newest nightmare created a book of evil phantasmagoria entitled *The Protocols of Zion*, which developed the insidious belief that Jews wished to control the universe. This book of malicious fiction was generously created and provided by the czar's secret service. The Russians were particularly alarmed by the explosive increase in the Jewish population in the "Stadl," the limited area of land where Jews were permitted to live in Russia, a strip of land running from north to south and bordering the central European powers. The book provided that all Jews, supposedly, were secretly in league; the capitalists, the socialists, the communists, the religionists, the secularists—all linked in an enormous plot, in which each had an assigned, nefarious place in a series of cells controlled by ever larger cells made to undermine the whole larger society in every country. Let's not forget: it accused them of draining the blood of Christian babies to make unleavened bread—making them Draculian. The peasants in the backwoods must have used that one to get instant discipline from their little children: "If you do that again, I'll call Isaac's father over to cut your throat and cook you into matzo!"

Thus, the loyal French captain Dreyfus could be tried twice and finally be fully exonerated, reinstated, and promoted and still be a traitorous Jew, forever. Forget the fact that one of the "club" was known to be guilty: a man of nobility from Austria-Hungary named Esterhazy, who held a French commission in France's army and sold secrets to Germany to support his life as a "rotter," never to be punished because he was a member of the continental "old boy" nobility system. Remember, if there is a Jew in the cast, he is always the "heavy."

No matter what benefits Jews provided the world (and they far exceeded any provided by other peoples exponentially greater in number), they were never to be truly trusted. First, they didn't accept their coreligionist Jesus as the son of God and, next, may have been instrumental in killing him and, thereafter, stubbornly continued to deny him—all to the discomfiture of his organized believers. Then, supposedly satanically bringing the Black Death to the Christian world and on countless occasions accused of poisoning the wells everywhere, they were also the perceived arm of kings and nobles, forced as tax farmers to collect their taxes and punished by riotous mobs for doing so, regarded as the hated arm of said feudal society.

Centuries later, after a new charge—that of their refusal to accept their fellow Jew as the Son of God—they lost their former status as God's chosen people, to become the cursed of the earth. The Christians of the world, under this replacement theology, were now the literal children of Abraham, Isaac, and Jacob! And the Jews were no longer simply deniers of the true God but were reduced to a lower form of human. Now they had become the *"dhimmis"* of their world to both the Christians and the Muslims. (Of course the Christians had no better status to the Muslims; however, this was of little comfort to the Jews.)

Giles knew it all by rote. Thus the Nazi Germans could rob and steal from a bourgeoisie who did so much to make of Germany a successful world power in seventy years and torture them to death, if they objected, and finally exterminate them ruthlessly—because no one cared! Scientific genius, art, music, business acumen to build the state, creation of law, to the benefit of humankind—and all that the Christians said was, "But what have you done for us lately?" The Ten Commandments, the Old Testament, God the Father, Jesus the Jew, Saul (Paul) of Tarsus, ethics, morals: "But what have you done for us lately?" Just because you accuse us Christians of matricide in killing our "Mother Religion," that is our right because of what you have been guilty of in *our* eyes! If God cares about you, why has he allowed all of us to treat you so hideously? And to this, Saul (Paul) repeated to his Jewish believers, in his new gospels, which his believers appended to the Jewish Pentateuch, the so-called Old Testament, "Love thy neighbor and do unto others as you would have others do unto you; that you cannot be forgiven until you have forgiven others!"

And the Christians have answered him through the ages with resounding silence. And the Jews remember their silence—and their acts against the words of Jesus of Nazareth: for example, the slaughter of so many of their helpless brethren in the Rhineland when the Crusaders came through and sharpened and blooded their swords and knives on the Jewish infidels who lived and worked and loved and died in their beloved Rhenish homeland. Why? "Because one infidel is like another, and besides, everyone knows there aren't enough Jews anywhere to put up a defense!" And all those relentlessly evil daily acts for nineteen hundred years by those pure Christian lambs who prayed to sweet Jewish Jesus every night after their most vile acts against their older brother Judah and their mother, Judaism: "Now I lay me down to sleep, and pray the Lord my soul to keep, and if I die before I wake, I pray the Lord my soul to take."

What should even a pious Jew think or say about his younger brother, Christian? He can only turn his head and ironically think of the Sermon on the Mount, and in his exhausted, driven, and weakened condition, think, "Turn the other cheek." The Jew even has a prayer to Jehovah to this effect: "Forgive me, O Lord, for all oaths and promises and acts that deny you and your goodness, which I was forced to take against my free will!" Just as an example, forced conversion to Christianity, on pain of death for refusing the generous Franciscan or Dominican who came to one's little ghetto synagogue on Saturday, by force, to convert all: refuse, and he avoided blood on his own hands by having the waiting mob outside kill you!

Giles would not, could never, abandon his faith! It was not even a matter of belief. It was his honor and his duty! His genetic duty that he owed before he was born! Somehow he would cling to it even though he was not even a willing initiate into its essential, fundamental, intellectual essence. He knew enough to see its purity, its perfection in thought, its logical beauty! Even if he faltered in the belief of omniscience and omnipotence, he would follow the ethics and the morality of its voice, even if it led him to nothing, because "a good doctrine had been given unto him, a Jew, and he would forsake it not." For Jews, it was not the promise of a reward after one's life, but life's wonderful journey that mattered. Living God's ethics is reward enough! If, in beneficence, God grants more, so be it! Merit badges earn nothing! Meritorious living may, but who knows! We must face the blackness of the unknown and trust God will do as he can or as he must. His will be done!

Now he prayed that Elle would somehow acquiesce in this. He thought, as he remembered a biblical tale and smiled to himself, "Was there not Sarah? Was there not Rebecca?" And he remembered Jehovah's admonition on every Yom Kippur for all Jews and all of his people, Christians and Jews alike, "For your sins to be forgiven, you must first forgive those who have sinned against you."

For him to take her as his, neither of them could reserve or harbor ills or resentments against the other because of the miniscule, trite, metaphysical divisions man has exacted or imposed on Jehovah! Giles believed that these religious distinctions were creations of man, not God.

He found his own religious diatribe to be overwrought and fanatical, but he was reminded of his fury against those who would harbor anger against the largely lawful, purposeful French people of Jewish faith: how they fought and died for France, or as its victims! They died quietly and without recognition, except where held somehow guilty.

These were not the thoughts he needed to occupy his mind when a review of his preparation for court was primary for tomorrow morning, and a good night's rest was needed both for that and his trip to England in the afternoon.

VII

ELLE'S TAXI DULY delivered her to the hospital. His, to his apartment in the fifteenth arrondissement, where he cautiously pondered the impact of his planned summation to the court, in the case to be delivered into the court's hands for deliberation at his conclusion. He felt the need, out of an abundance of caution, to review the proceedings in his mind as they had been presented to the court to date. This, the lawyer's obsession, he first observed in his father, also an attorney, who was considered by the Paris bar to be of worthy note. Apparently, the legal mind-set of meticulously evaluating one's position by constant repetition led to the correction of oversights and errors: pure drudgery, but a necessary function of the lawyer-advocate. His court, this morning, was a division of the Tribunal de Commerce, across from the principal Palace of Justice on Boulevard de Palais, Île de la Cité. The client had been notified by Giles to meet him there at 10:00 a.m., the time when the matter would be taken up by the court.

Monsieur Antoine Jaubert was his father's client for many years and relegated to his care because of his father's impending retirement. He exuded an "odor" of restrained hysteria on first contact. He seemed to be more comfortable in his hands after the "audience de fixation," at which he had been present to arrange a schedule for further written evidence and briefs to be exchanged between the adverse attorneys. Their little chat at the conclusion of that hearing, some four months before, relieved Giles, as Monsieur Jaubert seemed satisfied as to his advocate's competence.

This morning, before the court convened, Giles led his client into a side room furnished with chairs and table for the convenience of counsel and clients, to review what was to be expected at today's proceeding.

"May I finally be permitted to testify concerning the defendant's refusal to deliver the ordered and paid-for yard goods?" Monsieur Jaubert's asked again.

"Sir, I hate to continue to disappoint you about this, but my carefully prepared 'Dossier de Plaidoirie' contains your allegations as you would testify to them, and we have a few minutes to examine them. If they are not as you and I previously agreed, then I shall have to request the court to extend the 'Ordonnance de Cloture' again."

Then Giles spread the documents from the first summons served on the Defendant Corporation and the other written documents upon which they were relying, including canceled checks and correspondence sent and received, costs of replacement merchandise that greatly exceeded the original cost to the client, and corresponding loss of profits to him as a consequence. He also provided him with the "Cote de Plaidoirie," which was a summary of Giles's oral argument to the court, as he intended to present it when the court convened that day.

"It seems to me that the court would wish to evaluate the persons who were making claims and defending, in order to have an opinion of their honesty and competency!" said Jaubert.

"As I tried to explain, the court depends upon opposing counsels in most litigation for the veracity of their individual position and for the counterbalance of their opposing positions, thus to provide the court with the insight to ferret out misrepresentation by either side," Giles responded, taking care to avoid a professorial tone in doing so.

Then Giles explained that he had not and was not required to provide opposing counsel with the "Cote de Plaidoirie" summary of the oral argument that he would be presenting today. "Nor is he required to provide me his."

"And, Monsieur Le Maitre, what advantage does that provide us?" said the client, with some contentiousness.

"Only this!" said Giles. "His position throughout, as his filings have shown, is that you could have replaced his product when not produced by him, with other like-kind merchandise readily available: but he has totally failed to produce any hard evidence of that in any of his documents, and we shall volunteer your testimony to the court today!

"We have covered his point, which ignores defendant's failure to return your funds on demand and attempts to intimate that you could have satisfied your needs with such returned funds, and promptly, if you were reasonable, and thus could have ameliorated your damages. He argues only for amelioration in the amount of the difference in cost and ignores his breach of duty and your subsequent exponential loss by the delay. He completely failed to inform you of the availability of such merchandise and thus supports our demand for multiplication of damages, in the amount of probable loss. In short he claims he knew of substitute merchandise that you could have obtained if he would have apprised you of their existence and returned your funds as you demanded. Neither of which he did!"

"Yes, Giles, he delayed me long enough that I was too late to find a substitute, and I shall testify that he held me at bay and refused to return my funds though I made the repeated demands—that you show among your documents, which you have laid on the table! Will his advocate have an opportunity to question me?"

"Such oral testimony as is taken under the civil code is done by the judge and is direct and not constrained by rules of form or limitation as in the common law courts of England, which I know you have encountered in litigation there. Remember that our judges make determinations of both law and fact, based upon the advocates and the process they provide. If they wish oral evidence of parties or witnesses, they decide the worthiness of what they can or do obtain from a witness themselves. The judge pronounces the judgment based upon their own determination, and one may appeal for a new trial, which shall be received unless it is based on a minor figure, not worthy of retrial."

As Giles projected, after forty minutes of oral arguments by both parties' advocates, the court refused the offer of monsieur's testimony, concluded the hearing, and set a day for reconvening at which time he would render such judgment as was "dispositive" of all issues. He also gave notice that the reasoning of it would be provided the legal representatives individually and thereafter. Giles parted from his client with the reassurance that he believed he would be well satisfied with the outcome and that he had good reason to believe that a good portion of his legal expenses and a worthy monetary judgment would be awarded in his favor. Then, being in fine fettle and high spirits, he reached Giselle by phone at her hospital and told her which train he was taking to Boulogne, for England.

VIII

UPON RETURNING TO his apartment from his trip, Giles called Elle to tell of his joy at being back and his impatience for this evening together. There were mutual expressions of yearning during each other's absence and the unfilled vacuum keenly felt, in respect to their absence from one another. She was also pleased to tell him that her mother was coming up from Lyon in short order and knew of their spectacular interest in one another. He was pleased to meet the situation as soon as possible and had resolved to impose an atmosphere of affability and "pax vobiscum" upon the encounter, regardless of any unforeseen eruption that might occur.

It was a lovely evening, with just enough wind to make his *pare-brise* (windshield) welcome. His MG TC was his new acquisition from Abingdon, Oxfordshire. There, as previously stated to Giselle, he had picked it up and ferried it across the channel, driving it from Boulogne, through the Pas de Calais countryside, to Paris—a delightful trip, taking approximately two weeks.

He was proud of this new toy, which asserted his budding financial success as an advocate, capitalized upon by his choice of "racing green" as its color. He adored the spoke wire wheels, and he could almost reach out and down and touch the street with his right hand while behind the wheel of the car because of the oblique cut of the doors. The, factory, Morris Garage, would not compromise the placement of the wheel and its shaft to a left-hand drive, but he couldn't bring himself to purchase a Citroen Traction Avant 11B, the very new and open, two-seat, cab top, which he had considered. It was a bit clumsy and stodgy looking: certainly not as dashing as his two-seater MG.

He ruminated as he drove that in a year or two he might be able to afford Saville Row tailors and Cork Street "bespoke" shoes in London. Such egocentric thinking allowed him to momentarily escape the permeating thoughts of the deteriorating conditions in Europe, which confronted everyone. But at the moment he could shield his mind with his love-struck state, his male egotism, and the beginning of, hopefully, the most ecstatic experience of his life!

He departed his apartment, which was located in the fifteenth arrondissement round the corner from Grenelle Boulevard, driving of course his new MG. He took Grenelle Boulevard to the Seine River bank, turned right past the Eiffel Tower and then the National Assembly; the Quai D'Orsay and the Quai Voltaire followed: then, turning left at the Quai de Conti, just at le Pont Neuf, and crossing over to the right bank, had made another right turn on the far side of the bridge onto le Hotel de Ville Quai. Henri Quatre Quai followed; then, past Ile St. Louis, to the Bastille, and finally up Rue de Fauborg, he arrived at Giselle's parents' apartment: an invigorating drive at thirty miles per hour and stimulated by the scenery he passed!

He arrived below her parent's apartment at 7:00 p.m., promptly, as planned. The Rue de Fauborg was not bustling; street traffic tended to be light anyway because autos were frightfully expensive, and parking was "ad hoc" because of it. Police vehicles were not dispatched for ticketing parking violations, permitting him time to comfortably enter their building and escort her to his auto, which he did.

Her building was one of the old and stately Baron Haussman structures from the later part of the nineteenth century. Five stories, of cut limestone blocks; balconies on the third and fifth floors and dormer windows on the sixth floor for servant quarters: the entrance was double-doored and made of the usual brass (highly polished) with glass flutes at the top, to allow light to pass through in both directions. The uniformed porter was posted as doorman, giving an air of sophistication. They exchanged impersonal greetings, and he entered to find an elegant black-and-white checkerboard, polished-marble floor and two birdcage elevators fitted in before the spiral, carpeted stair case ascended to the various floors above.

The doorman also acted as the elevator operator for the one being used this time of night. A side office was enclosed in a far corner, probably for a superintendent of premises. The stair runner seemed quite new and Chinese, of bright oriental pattern, and gave the only accent to the large, sterile, white entry and staircase area, other than the classic, black-and-white marble or stone-cut flooring laid in a diamond or square pattern (which was one geometric or the other, depending upon your position or point of view).

IX

HAVING FIRST TRAILED Giles to the wrought-iron entry gate of the elevator, the doorman entered the elevator, closed the metal, birdcage entry door, and lifted Giles to the second floor entrance of the d'Hozier apartment. Giles rapped the knocker of the door lightly, twice, and expected to be greeted by a servant or perhaps a parent but, instead, was greeted by an absolutely radiant Giselle, with a warm, "Good evening."

"I wish you the same. I've been wishing you the same all day long!" He stepped into the entry hall of the apartment, by her invitation, and made a quick summary of its appearance and that of the drawing room beyond.

"Please do come in to the apartment and sit down, and I'll get you an aperitif if you like," she said.

"No, thank you. My car is standing in front of your building, and I think it best if we move along as I made a reservation at La Tour D'Argent for seven thirty to dine. We could have an aperitif in the first-floor bar if you like."

"Well, if we start at the best restaurant in Paris our first special night, we will have no place to go but down after that!"

"But I think this evening together should be memorable in every way!" he replied. "I had expected perhaps to meet your parents, as you said it was your mother's Paris apartment."

He had prepared himself and hoped to pass a peremptory parental inspection on arrival, and actually welcomed it because he believed he would never appear better than at the moment. His expectation prompted her to explain that her mother chose to spend most of her time in Lyon, their native area, where she maintained their family house. "As I told you earlier today, she will be coming here very quickly, from Lyon, because of you and me. Actually," she continued, "Father is deceased and has been for many years; he was regular military, a lieutenant colonel in the Foreign Legion. I was twelve when he was killed in the Rif war in Morroco. Perhaps you remember some of that war happening? The Berber leader Abd-el-krim?"

"I'm so sorry for you! So tragic for you and your mother. And, I believe, you have no siblings?"

"No," she replied, pensively, "just the two of us, and we had lost others of the family in the 1914–1918 war—uncles, so hard for my mother and grandparents. A sad topic to commence a gay evening." She paused as she took his hand and stepped toward the entry hall for their departure.

"Giselle, you look so splendid and so beautiful, and, yes, I love your black garden hat: the brim frames your face. Only Greuze could capture that ecstatic passionate face, framed as it is!"

Now it struck him that the "wind-torrent-swept" MG wasn't stylish-friendly for formally dressed beauties, apropos of Giselle! Good Lord! Could it ever come to her or his MG? He thought, "We shall defer to her future demands, without question, and hope for her charity and tolerance!"

"To change the subject: what magnificent taste your apartment has. All done in Louis Seize and Directoire! And what a beautiful Aubusson rug in the sitting room. I am particularly aware of décor and deeply appreciate outstanding combines of fabrics, furnishings, and accents in paintings and crystal. I still believe, however, that I make a better lawyer than an interior decorator. Don't be deceived by my expression of taste in this way. In other words, give me the opportunity, and you will quickly find my sexual orientation to be masculine and normal!"

He continued to the door, where she switched her purse to the opposite hand in order to take his arm, and he turned toward her and asked if she had forgotten her little black bag that all MDs carry (with her stethoscope and negligee included). She pulled his arm forward and moved the two of them toward the elevator, to press the button for service, and said, "Office hours are over, and I have a date with a 'dream' tonight; we will talk about business later, my love! Remember, please, the porter is not in on my private life! To him, I'm the grave, severe, 'bitchy' MD who lives on the second floor and is an impossibly demanding occupant. Shall we go?"

As the porter closed the elevator door and it descended, Giles could only say cautiously and in her ear, in a whisper, "I love your style."

X

WHEN THEY ARRIVED at 15 Quai de la Tournelle, the uniformed doorman greeted them with a slight bow as he swung Giselle's door open. Being tall, it required him to bend forward, causing his *fourragere*, hanging from his epaulette, to catch her brim, as he assisted her in rising from the passenger seat with his other hand. She managed to secure the crown of her hat with pressure from her other hand as she was placing her feet on the drive, all without twisting or wobbling as she completed the balancing act. Giles thought to himself, "No repeat of her unfortunate spill at the alumni game. What composure and aplomb! And not even a look or movement of distress."

His practiced, assessing "eye" reviewed her ensemble. Her total attire was black and included a flared skirt and fitted jacket; wrist-length, black silk gloves; black patent-leather, slender heels, strapped sandal-style; a single-strand pearl necklace; and black silk hose. He had never been more flattered by a woman's tribute to him, paid by her "turnout" for their rendezvous. He prayed for the opportunity to view the remainder of her ensemble, her lingerie, at the end of the evening!

They entered the restaurant and diverted to the first-floor bar for an aperitif. There he gave the barman their order and directed him to tell the restaurant maître d'hotel, at the restaurant's top level (sixth or seventh floor, he could never remember how many), that they were delayed in the bar. Her Chartreuse *jaune* and his Lillet red, served on ice, were delivered promptly to their table in a corner, placed near to the elevator they would use ten or fifteen minutes later.

Some preliminary discussion of their individual day's experiences were exchanged, with due regard by each of them to their ethical restraints as to the particulars concerning patients and clients, which might risk revelation of their specific identities. This utterly mundane "chatting" helped to move them in the direction of familiarity.

They were two magnetized people, searching for common chords upon which to play their independent spiritual yearnings and essence, on a sole instrument. But then, is it not a wonder that two human beings should ever find the ability to render their independently programmed music in harmony?

They were both mature and open enough to expose themselves to that chance, and so they pursued life's dance with quickening fervor, each beginning to believe that the mutually exchanged smiles, lifted eyebrows, timely frowns, and traded innuendoes signified a preordained joint pathway. These so sincerely rendered insignia of the ego, or so-called id, of each shored up their growing, but still wary, beliefs that they could truly find safe harbor together.

In short, they sought inseparable friendship, spiritual bonding, and mutual values, all out of the spur of enormous animal attraction to one another. He remembered from out of his English reading, the great eighteenth-century poet, Alexander Pope, with his words of irony, "Hope never dies in the human breast, man lives only to be blessed." It seemed they both were nearly convinced they could buy the winning ticket for total love, life's rarest lottery!

XI

THEY HAD FINISHED their aperitifs and mounted the elevator for the roof restaurant, where Giles had, earlier in the day, specified that they were to have one of the few tables for two that was on the window with a full view of Notre Dame Cathedral. It stood directly across the Seine, on its island and at their eye level.

They were attended by the head waiter, who seated Giselle and placed a ladies' menu before her on the table. After Giles was seated, he welcomed them both, by their titles ("Doctor" and "Master") and names, and gave Giles the principal menu. Then followed the prompt attention of busboys, the table waiter, and his assistant, and soon the violinist, seeking personal requests. The couple pondered that momentarily and responded with "Zigeuner" and such other Bohemian or Liszt pieces as he knew, or the new American composer, Cole Porter, if he was familiar with any of his works.

They were still discussing their choices of aperitifs and why made; his Lillet red was a Bordeaux drink that he had learned from his father, made of local red wine and tropical and citrus fruit steeped in alcohol, then barreled and aged. Now he questioned his own choice because of the challenge it might present to the wines they would choose with the evening menu. She puzzled about this with him because she felt limited in knowledge concerning the acidic effect it would have on full-bodied reds or sweet whites, in particular Sauternes from the Bordeaux area of Grave.

The yellow Chartreuse variety she chose was cloyingly sweet, and neither she nor the monks who made it in the Rhone-Alps region could recommend such cross drinking. She, however, jested with him that she drank the monks' recipe as often as possible because "it stood her in good stead with God and her religion, and it was a great deal better than what the stingy priests bought for communion."

Now the awesome subject of religion had reared its divisive head, and it would have to be addressed. He had been hoping to defer it until they were in each other's arms and had at least consummated their union, potentially minimizing their differences. He therefore avoided the subject of religion, being convinced that it was the one subject upon which even reasonable people could not agree, even to disagree. Later would be soon enough!

The view was stunning, the sky still offering streaks of the sun, low and behind the two towers and the spire of the cathedral; and above the streaks of the residual sun, a slightly light blue sky was being gradually swallowed by a descending midnight blue bowl above it, which was slowly revealing, as it descended, its white, bright, clarion stars.

Their vocal appreciation of the view was interrupted by the appearance of the sommelier, in red mess jacket, massive gold chain with suspended cup and wine list, bearing a most serious facial expression, which was intended to encourage their attention to the subject he intended to address—that is, wines. With courtesy, they indicated the need to address the menu before wines could be considered and instructed him to return after that, at his first opportunity.

Their perusal of their menus led through its contents and after much palavering between themselves and the waiter led to a single decision of choices, which Giles presented to him. There were amendments, however, based on the advice of the waiter because, in his opinion, certain of them "were not up to the standards of the house today." The restaurant's famous *Canard a la presse* was not a choice for either of them, since, to him, it seemed a ghoulish rite and she had witnessed a surgery earlier that day, which was replete with blood. So after fifteen or more minutes, the menu was as follows: foie gras, followed by lobster *a l'American*; thereafter roast partridge; and lastly, the requisite three cheeses: Brie, Cheshire, and a mild Dutch round.

They, thus had the hors d'oeuvre, the entrée, and *le plat*, with a small lettuce *salade* with the chef's choice of a simple dressing, without any vinegar (which would foul the taste of any dry wine being drunk with dinner), and finally the cheeses, to be eaten with a chosen wine. Perhaps as a final course, *le digestif* might follow, a *pousse-café* or a liqueur.

Giles asked the waiter to send the sommelier around to complete the order with their choice of wines, and, while awaiting his return, they discussed Gothic architecture in general and Notre Dame in particular. They both liked it but not the earlier Romanesque style, which was so much less ethereal and so much more massive, such as the church architecture at Cluny and Orcival.

The sommelier again hovered, so they discussed the possibilities, carefully considering the fact that three wines would be in order, a Sauterne for the first course and also the second, but the third, le plat, required a light, robust red, but refined. For the foie and lobster, it was agreed that they must resort to a Puilly-Fuisse, from lower Burgundy: a white, of course, that was not too dry and yet robust, with savor at the same time. This would meld well with a red Burgundy from the Cote de Beaune, which should be distinguished and delicate for the partridge. The thought was to avoid an acidic result from the strong food flavors of foie and lobster, which, when combined with something as robust, having enormous bouquet and "sap," as the grand cru, Chateau d' yquem, from the Grave region of Bordeaux could so result. The sommelier and the couple thought this would destroy the partridge (le plat) and the wine choice of the Cote de Beaune from Burgundy. Perhaps, a grand cru sauterne would sip well with a piece of ripe fruit, after the repast was complete.

XII

AFTER A QUARTER hour more of waiting, the foie gras was served along with the white wine of their choice, which was first tasted and approved by Giles. The presentation of every course was beautiful and memorable, indeed as Giles had hoped it would be. However there were some reservations about the total pleasure in the taste of the food, but not the wine, which both agreed were superb choices. Giselle loved the foie; he did not. Giles enjoyed the lobster fully; she did not. Both found the pheasant delectable. The finish of fresh fruit and the two pousse-café were pleasant as expected. And so the repast ended.

Two very happy people emerged from "the Tower" and departed in his MG for her mother's apartment, at her request. His left hand was free for most of the short journey and, except for turning, rested on the floor gearshift, where she found it and casually placed her own right hand on his when it was there and not occupied with the steering wheel.

They returned along the same streets by which they had come to the restaurant. She directed him through a side entrance, down an alley not noticeable from Rue de la Fauborg, which led to an inner courtyard that must have been originally intended for delivery by coaches and buggies and the parking of the same. They left the MG there and entered the lobby through a set of rear doors, which were somewhat obscured by the winding stairway in the lobby. They obviously had been more apparent and frequented before the elevators made their appearance in the last decade or two of the nineteenth century. Baron Haussman's buildings had to adapt to changing times, as did the rest of nineteenth-century Paris.

The same porter scurried toward the front of the elevators as he heard and saw them circling the rear of the elevators, in order to reach the front of the lobby and the entrances to them. He bid them "good night," instead of "good evening" as he should have, when he bowed slightly in their direction. The former would be more intimate and in this situation could intimate bed and sex. The French well know the difference, and in this instance, his snide inference was palpable. He disguised a slight, cloying smile as he pulled back the elevator door to permit their entry, and she visibly stiffened and glared at his presumption. His act was a time-honored exhibition of a lower-class attempt to intimidate a superior, in a minor way, which would not result in retribution but was adversely critical by intimation.

His intended, unstated jibe meant, "Here you are again, bringing a man into your apartment, and are you then so much better than I, Mademoiselle Haut-Bourgeoisie?" Giles was curtly aware of the abusive inference by the man and already "madly" possessive of her, and the unspoken "again" alerted his attention, causing his cheeks to heat and color with anger. But he inherently conceded that her life before his appearance was sacrosanct to her and not open to his delving. However, since he saw his devotion to be a joint venture, including all its parts, he knew, eventually, that their mutual pasts must be revealed or his hoped-for union with her would never stand.

She retrieved her key from her purse as they stepped off onto the Chinese oriental runner, which climbed the spiral staircase and threaded down the hallway, past the elevator doors and the entrance to her mother's apartment.

As they stepped into the entry hall of the apartment, he placed an arm around her and drew her to him, and as they looked into each other's eyes, he knew she was open to being kissed; he lightly brushed her lips with his, and she closed her eyes, and he kissed them and then her cheeks; she had embraced him with both her arms, as he took each of her lips separately between his and so lightly nibbled them one after the other.

The mutual searching began; gradually their tongues sought, each for the passion of the other. He held her face between his hands as they more stridently invaded each other's mouths, each tongue, each set of lips seeking, first a gentle begging of spiritual acceptance, followed by spiritual recognition and then the passionate, instant demand for unification through bodily union; but her feminine prerogative intervened, warning her of the need for more assurance, more than their simple sidling of these few days. They must know more than the romantic side of each other; slow steps and gradual revelation was demanded for what she had in mind. And that was for permanent mating. At this point she thought he was spectacular; he had not only her soul in his hands, but her every organ and thus her very essence!

For his part, he found that she was the very sublimation and exaltation of all he expected and was ready to drop to his knee and yield his troth (and everything else he might have now and in the future).

She asked him to respect her feelings, that though she wanted him as much as he obviously wanted her, she was not willing to throw her feminine caution to the winds; she wished them to spend more time together to learn more of each other before she could throw herself to him. She, in short, was more Victorian than he might suspect, and she must be convinced that she was going to be loved and cherished "as long as they both shall live."

Further, she could not believe that they were "at this stage already," and if they both felt "in time" that this was as right as it seemed, that he would find her to be, in spite of her twenty-four years, "in tact."

"Further than that," she said garrulously, "why is an 'A type,' absolutely gorgeous male like you unattached and roaming the streets of Paris—I'd just like to know!" And then she added belligerently, "Most likely chasing every pretty female whose skirt looks easily removable, no doubt!" And then, in an irate tone, manifesting jealousy, she went on: "Furthermore, how many love affairs have you had? You probably left some girl or girls at the church door or 'wherever'; and by the by, I don't think you're a Catholic like your friend, the bishop's nephew, because you don't know high mass from a 'Geneva shirt collar band.'" Rambling on in a kind of emotional explosion, she burst forth, "And I don't think you are one of them either, I mean a Calvinist, or any kind of a protestant. I think…I think you are Jewish, and furthermore—I don't care. I mean, it doesn't matter because I already want you and love you, and God is God, is he not? And he will mean as much to me in a synagogue as any kind of church if we find that we and our children should be there together!"

Now their position had changed in that she was holding his face in her hands, and he had her wrapped in his arms. Their faces were noses touching, their lips intermittently corners against corners, and she felt him shudder a bit and suddenly felt a welling tear falling so, so silently from his cheek onto hers. Alarmed, she exclaimed, "Oh God, please forgive! I didn't mean to hurt you with what I said."

He was struggling to gain control, to speak to her, but she made it ever so much more difficult because she now held his face with one hand and stroked his hair with her other hand, alternately, and then one of his cheeks and then the other, all the while making soothing motherly sounds. He was unable to control the falling of his tears because he knew, from their turbid and highly charged scene in her entry hall, that she was—she was indeed—everything that a woman could be, and he was so deeply touched by the things that she said, and did, that he didn't think he could walk out the door and leave her behind, not ever!

XIII

MARGUERITE D'HOZIER, MOTHER of Giselle, arrived in Paris at the Gare de Lyon, with Beatrice, her maid of twenty-six years, two days after her daughter's epic evening with Giles. She had had a long-distance phone conversation with her daughter a matter of hours after Giles had spoken with Elle, the day of his return to Paris from Boulogne.

She knew her daughter so well that when Giselle spoke to her about this new young man in her life, she recognized the quaver and hesitation in her voice to be of monumental importance. Her mother was always apprehensive about her eventual choice in a man because of her uncompromising, perfectionist disposition about people whom she chose as friends and companions. It, of course, was true that she had her father's relentless sense of discipline, which was made obvious by her fulfilled determination from childhood to be a physician.

Marguerite was convinced that her husband's untimely soldier's death had cheated Elle of his rare and cherished presence. Children assumed guilt sometimes where they were not conceivably involved. His sudden absence from her life was a trauma that caused her to construe his departure as somehow connected to her. She continuously pined to have him with them: Elle, as a child, chose to believe that his death could have been avoided by timely medical attention: a baseless conclusion that her childish heart would not abandon until her middle teen years, but one that laid the foundation for her fervent desire, over time, to follow her professional path.

Giselle asked her mother to come to Paris momentarily to render her advice, comfort, and counsel. Giselle would truly not depend upon those contributions by her mother, but rather sought to make her feel a part of her daughter's plan and decision, giving her the belief that she contributed to it meaningfully, thus to perhaps avoid her having injured sensibilities and consequently irate reactions. Her mother carefully nurtured her with sincere love and enormous attention, always guiding her but not leading her. By breeding and by birth, she was every inch a lady, and in her earlier ancestors' times, she could easily have been a castellan while her spouse was absent on a long military campaign.

Marguerite was worried and concerned and, at the same time, prayerful that the outcome would be the best for the person she loved most in the world, the person for whom she continued to exist. There had been only the two of them for so long, and now she hoped that this could be the beginning of a new, wonderful family for Giselle, and of course for herself as well. Beatrice, both her servant and friend, was part and parcel of them because she had been in the family when Giselle was born, and abiding love held the three of them together, as it had for all these years.

Marguerite eschewed the interest of other men, even the few whom she considered acceptable in position, not because of an arbitrary reason. Other men seemed to be hollow, and unsatisfying sensually, compared to her deceased husband, a man of virtue, nobility, and all-consuming passion in his love for her, Giselle, his command, and his country. He would palpably have given his life for any one of these and proved it by doing so for his command, his battalion in the Foreign Legion.

The three women planned a small reception for Giles, his parents, and themselves as well, for the following Sunday, early evening. A French-style buffet was planned, to include aperitifs or American-style cocktails, as desired. All three realized that little would be eaten that evening, but a great deal of gall was likely to be regurgitated in the throats of most of those present, along with "prayerfully unspoken" angry words.

Beatrice, in black uniform, white waist apron, and linen crest-lace cap, met Giles and his parents at the entry hall doors when the chime was rung. Marguerite, Giselle's mother, stood just inside the salon, where she awaited Beatrice, who preceded the guests in order to formally present them to her and then, of course, to fade to the dining room (there to await Marguerite's instruction concerning aperitifs and wine, to be brought by tray, as specifically needed by each guest). *Les amuse-gueule* were already on a large sterling tray, placed on a low table in front of a set of French double doors, opening to the balcony that overlooked the avenue two floors below. These *amuse-gueule* consisted of a variety of small crackers and nuts, appropriate in France to accompany preliminary wines and aperitifs.

XIV

MARGUERITE, ACTING AS hostess in her Paris apartment, was treating the whole matter as a late-afternoon reception for a much larger company of people. The introductions were made, and Elle stood as stiff as a marble statue, perhaps like Galatea, as previously imagined by Giles, but considerably more stiff then she. Her thoughts, though unspoken, were announced by her facial expressions of embarrassments, which were a condemnation of her mother's pompous attempt to make an inappropriate statement of her aristocratic importance. Giselle's mother could be supercilious and tasteless about herself and at the wrong times. It was her way of reminding those without a noble family history of the fact that material success was no elevator of class. She felt threatened by successful, educated bourgeoisie with material wealth. That could include of course lawyers and physicians, such as Giles, his father, and those of her daughter's profession.

Her family was no longer "landed" or monetarily wealthy but had regained much during Louie XVIII's and the later Louie-Phillip's reigns. Being of noble status, they knew how to live extravagantly but little about "counting the change." A gentleman (chevalier) never looked in his hand to see whether the merchant, lawyer, tenant, doctor, or so forth had put the proper amount there after a transaction was concluded. (It was too petty and humbling to grovel at that demeaning level.) The lesser classes of people wouldn't have dared to cheat for the hundreds of years when the rules of "fealty" applied, or even during the ancien régime, when these classes could have expected to be punished for insufficient honesty toward their betters.

Thereafter the surviving nobles usually learned little or nothing about pragmatic things and would live to find out the truth of the old adage, that "a fool and his money are soon parted." Before the nineteenth century, for a noble to be involved in earning money from property, constituting a part of his titular grant, would lead to a loss of title, its privileges, and being stricken from the "College of Arms." Since the republic had been instituted, a series of laws had been passed that protected, curiously enough, only male titles and, with certain limitations, made the misapplications by others of such titles and names a crime. Inheritance of the title and name, however, carried no hereditary rights or benefits as were formerly connected to the title.

To others of ordinary status in her world, her conduct was governed by kindness and noblesse obliges. Her daughter had not introduced her to the fact that these guests, whom she hoped would be included in her future family, were of the Jewish faith, only saying that they pursued a different belief system.

Marguerite was a woman who, in her every public act, feigned a formality that conveyed her breeding. Her attire was in compliance with her status, and her still magnificent physique easily justified her daughter's mesmerizing beauty. For this occasion, she dressed in a two-piece costume suit, Cambridge gray in color and wool flannel in texture, a diamond engagement ring and wedding ring on the same third finger of her left hand, and a diamond necklace. A black ribbon hung loosely about her neck, from which her silver-framed pince-nez eyeglasses were suspended. Her large, oval-shaped eyes were gray and intense, closely shaded to the color of her costume suit, acquired doubtlessly with that in mind. Her black calf pumps and gray silk hose accentuated her delicate ankles and shapely calves, and when she moved, her firmly rounded thighs, encompassed by her narrow skirt, demanded the attention of any male, regardless of the fact that she was, as the French would say, "a woman of a certain age." However, that age referred to a woman of fifty or sixty, not Marguerite, who could pass most easily for forty, or even less when animated.

One could describe Giles's mother as a handsome woman, tall, composed, and quite comfortable within herself. Clara was exceedingly fair of skin, the color of parchment, with blue eyes, the blue of northern skies, both of which could be attributed to her Baltic inheritance. Her father, at the age of twelve, escaped Lithuania (then a part of Russia) through a swamp area having to breathe through a straw while submerged, at one point, to sneak past the German border guards and into Germany. Finally reaching Hamburg, he begged, borrowed, or stole passage to London, where he worked in a shoe factory sixty hours a week, was bar mitzvahed at thirteen, and thus by Biblical law, became a man. One might argue that he became a man somewhat earlier, considering his astounding courage, fortitude, maturity, and cunning, all exhibited at the age of twelve. In a matter of years, he became an established merchant of some status and means—means sufficient to educate his daughter in a private girls academy in London and then on to St. Hilda's College, Oxford University, one of the oldest of all the women's colleges at the university.

Clara didn't quite complete her bachelor's degree, meeting and marrying Gilbert, the father of Giles, before the last term of her third year at Oxford. She met Gilbert the summer of her second year at Oxford while in Paris, visiting there with a friend.

They had a full-regalia, traditional Jewish ceremony, with all parents present and all most pleased. It took place in London at the old Marks-Bevis Synagogue with a reception at the Savoy Hotel with 417 of both families' "closest relatives and friends." The London *Times* took due note of it in its society section, establishing, for all and sundry, that Clara's father had "arrived" in worthy Jewish social circles in London. It also notified the stodgy, upper-middle-class English gentiles who knew them by personal encounter or reputation that English Jews could move up *their* ranks in one generation, compared to three generations needed by them to do so, and with comparable assets. Fortunately the Anglo-Saxons had a unique culture that believed "all should if they could" and "admired them for it," but "hang it all, our greedy peers marry their daughters for dowries" and with "Disraeli a Prime Minister of England, become an Earl of the Realm and the Rothschilds now Barons and the Montefiories Knights, "what the bloody hell is wrong with us and where will it all end." Obviously nowhere different than usual, except for a difference in religion and a generation younger of new blood seeking to emulate their established social betters would become like the ideals they sought to emulate; but Jews in an unrestricted, free-market society didn't apparently need a John Galsworthy to write a three-generation "Forsythe Saga" about them to succeed in a truly free society.

Their wedding took place ten days before the start of World War I, and Gilbert left Clara in their new apartment in Paris, two months later, for the front. He had been allowed two months to close his law practice and get personal matters in order. He ended the war unscathed and as a lieutenant colonel, having fought through the Verdun campaign, where he was mentioned in dispatches and decorated for valor, as well. The Croix de Guerre was awarded for being "mentioned," and a "palm" on the ribbon for a second "occasion," after which he finally received the Legion d'Honneur, Classe Chevalier. He had frequently received direct orders from General Petain, being an active member of his battle staff in the defense of Verdun. Oddly enough, he was thought by many officers in Petain's command to strongly favor him in facial resemblance, but a generation younger.

XV

AFTER VARIOUS WHITE wines were drunk a second time, the atmosphere began to lighten, and the true purpose of the gathering was laid by Marguerite, who broached the subject by asking how it was that Giselle and Giles met, and they each presented their encounter at the class reunion from their separate recollections with a humorous series of interruptions by one and then the other, neither agreeing wholly with the other's presentations.

Each of course subjected their view of the incident to their personal evaluations and conclusions made as the encounter moved through its rapid phases. As later developments were recounted, Marguerite made the point that very little time had been invested by either "and therefore wasn't the step (marriage) they were considering a little previous including the arranging of banns with the Mairie 's office"? Clara then asked where the religious ceremony would be held after the civil ceremony.

Now the sparring began in earnest. Gilbert made it clear that this was clearly not to be settled this evening, and all persons were to consider the matter further. Even the most liberal rabbi in France would not wed them if the non-Jewish party had not gone through a conversion to the religion, an onerous thing to undertake, involving dedication and time.

Marguerite said very forthrightly that they had been Catholic since Henry of Navarre declared "that Paris was worth a mass," and he and his followers abandoned John Calvin and the Huguenot way for his installation as Henry IV of France.

Further, Marguerite said they could be married in church and within the altar rail, providing Giles would sign an agreement that their progeny would be raised Catholic, and he would never seek to interfere with that. Of course, he said, he could not agree to that because it violated his and his family's serious values as previously set forth.

Being at an impasse, all agreed that the burden in this was upon the two most affected, Giselle and Giles. All three parents were naturally, ardently absolute and hoped the "children" would come to realize the too-difficult road that lay ahead in life for them and their offspring. Both the bride to be and the groom were essentially secular about their religions, and as Giselle previously stated, her position was that God was everywhere, and the Jewish faith would do for them if it seemed right.

This was a concession but not one to plan upon totally. The real decision would be made with the first male child and the immediate need of a Jewish ceremony called a "bris," if Judaism was to be selected—that is, if the no doubt enraged pleas of Marguerite for the "Baptismal font" on the birth of the first child could be withstood by Elle, who might in turn, relieve herself by passing the pressure on to Giles, in one of the many subtle, or unsubtle, ways that a wife might have of emphasizing the dangers of purgatory facing their unbaptized child. On the other hand, she could very well follow her original impulse and tell all and sundry that their children would follow the religion of their father and eventually so might she, thinking, that in her small way, she could repay a few lives that Christians had wrongly taken. If, simplistically, God the Father was everywhere, she would have to traduce the Trinity, the Eucharist, and transubstantiation and not be fearful of damnation.

She thought of that intimate moment in the entry hall with Giles and knew that her frankness to Giles about religion had rendered him defenseless against her and rendered him her willing subject. Her very first feminine instincts made her understand that they belonged to one another. She knew that, in this enormous world, the chance was nil that two pairs of eyes, each with searching minds and spirits, could instantly discern each other, as meant to join their destinies; they were fused together by a jolting strike of their eyes, like nature's lightning, that day in the Bois de Boulogne. It was the most manifest of destinies. Their eyes were fixed, but her mind was swirling and inexpressibly joyous.

And she instinctively knew he was in this same numbed, sublime state. Sensuality was there as a manifold layer, encompassing the ethereal joy of finding their oneness. Among the deep revelations they openly shared was this unique experience. She could never betray their spiritual unity and her nearly spoken vow that God was everywhere. She, without hesitation and without even discussing it with Giles, committed their future offspring to being the descendants of Abraham, Isaac, and Jacob. Wherever Giles would go, she would follow, only limited as the laws of man would allow and their unknown future would dictate.

XVI

THE PUBLICATION OF the banns were proclaimed as required by the mayor's office, but the marriage would be delayed a few days beyond the ten required because of the increased flurry of requests, due to the impending war scare. This was a welcomed delay for Elle because she needed to have a white wedding dress made to her exacting taste. Unfortunately, her mother's wedding dress was terribly "Edwardian"—that is, too massively embellished with overlaces and buttons and too covering and emphasized the prewar appearance and taste that had disappeared with the first war's conservatism and the ensuing move toward the emancipation of women. Her mother understood completely. She believed that, like all women, her daughter desired a white wedding dress because a virgin should choose a white wedding dress and because they believe their first wedding will be their last, or they would not be getting married. Marguerite was correct about her otherwise naïve belief that her daughter was a virgin, only because she was a Victorian and could not have imagined anything else. Elle, however, had the universal justification for the wearing of white ceremonially, more so than many others of her sex. Only Giles was privy to her secret, and no man could have worn it with more pride than he, who cherished it in wonder, amazement, and awe and with a conviction of his unworthiness. Each day he realized more how much he had underestimated the intangible worth of the "pirates' treasure" and the "inventories" he had found. In something of a return for all of that, he chose for her engagement ring, a two-carat, ultra clear diamond ring, with its diamond emerald cut and set in platinum, bordered by two slender diamonds. Her wedding band was separated from the other ring but conformed to it as its outer rim. He presented them both for her approval, which she thrillingly gave and professed her surprise at the size and was ecstatic over the beauty of them.

Elle didn't speak of her disappointment in not having a religious ceremony following the civil ceremony, but she felt somehow that God needed to be the third party in this thing. It was in order to feel total peace in her breast for the foundation that she and her chosen were entitled to have. She cringed at the feeling of being an outcast, of being a pariah because no religion would say grace over them. Educated, and a physician or not, she couldn't think of one Cartesian, Catholic, Jansenist, Calvinist, or biblical reason why some benighted or humanistic priest or rabbi couldn't turn his head a little or bend or yield a small bit for a tiny, easing, Shakespearean-like gesture of kindness "that fell from heaven like gentle rain."

The bride and groom had humbled themselves before as many as they could find, who would even give them audience, but of course, to no avail. To the rabbis', "One shouldn't change one's religion to accommodate matrimonial vows" but for clairvoyant spiritual reasons. Once you were in, well, you couldn't get out, apparently for thousands of years, no matter whether you performed ethically in life or not. With all the others, the male had to perform some act of contrition or sign papers removing religious paternal rights. One would have to wonder that, if such contracts were executed and if God sat in judgment, wouldn't summons and petitions have to be drawn and served by some supernatural *huissier* or bailiff? What earthly other avocat, barrister, or lawyer would be qualified by the court to appear on anyone's behalf?

In the end she told her mother that they had done their best. To his parents, it had been a forgone conclusion. There was little to say, except the couple hoped all would put a good face on it and help them make it a joyous occasion for all to remember happily.

XVII

EVERYONE WAS IN something of a dither on the morning of the wedding. It had been agreed that it would be a formal affair in spite of the lack of a religious wedding to follow. Gilbert had the required cut-away, swallow-tailed coat, pearl-gray waistcoat and gray-striped trousers, winged, collared white dress shirt and gray, patterned cravat. Clara, totally in accordance with the ambience desired, was ensembled in a turquoise blue, two-piece cocktail suit, matching hose and black pumps, and a smashing matching fedora hat with a small angled brim slightly tilted over the right eye and hugging her hair in the rear. They both were to meet the rest of the party, Elle and Marguerite and Bridget at Le Hotel DeVille, the city hall at 10:00 a.m. on the first floor, where the maid of honor, Magdalene Gautier, a classmate of Elle's living in Paris was also to appear.

Neither the groom nor his best man, Etienne, at this stage of their lives, possessed the formal day attire that Gilbert had. Giles escaped the need because court attire required black gowns and, in certain circumstances, perukes, not formal day wear. His best man didn't believe his lifestyle justified it. What to do? Simple—wear their officer parade uniforms, which they were sure to be wearing shortly anyway! They were in *vereuse* jackets in khaki color, flat shirt collars, and khaki-colored silk ties, plus Sam Browne belts. His and Etienne's jackets had two bellow pockets on their chest and two bellow pockets below and seven brass buttons down the center. To complete the uniforms, they were each wearing tan cavalry twill riding breeches and highly polished brown riding boots that were appropriate for officers in all branches of the army at this time. Of course, they were wearing their kepis, which were uniquely the cap for the French commissioned officer in the army. They tore out of Giles apartment and literally leaped into his MG and raced off to avoid being late.

The Hotel de Ville was across the Seine from Notre Dame, and it was almost ten, and their appointment with the mayor's assistant to perform the service was at 10:30. They reached the side parking for the building and ran for the doors, where just inside was his gorgeous, worried-looking bride and the rest of the party. Elle was in an off-the-shoulder, long, sweeping white wedding dress with an elegant group of folds falling from the one strapped shoulder to her waist and falling in loose folds from there along her left hip to puddle slightly at the floor. Her veil was held in place by a silver coronet crowning her hair. She looked to him like a queen in the entrance to her palace, awaiting her coach and four. He paid her the compliment of telling her in the presence of their little group that very thing and that he would remember her just that way, forever. She was enormously happy at the compliment but had taken precautions by engaging one of Paris's best photographers to take full photos of the party, during and after the wedding.

Poor Elle had no one to "give her away," as was customary. There were no uncles or brothers, but Gilbert approached Marguerite and quietly asked if he might stand in the stead of her husband, saying, "I've always wanted a daughter but never thought I'd have one as beautiful as she, and since she will shortly be so, might I have the honor of giving her away for the colonel, in his sad absence? It would be such a great added honor and make me feel almost as though he were my dearest friend!"

Marguerite was deeply touched and particularly felt the presence of her dearest lover and husband, even more so! The sensitivity and civility of her new in-laws were beginning to astound her and to build a true bond, though still somewhat imperceptible. She gladly agreed to his offer and found herself accepting the hand of

Clara as they stood, side-by-side, awaiting the call from the mayor's assistant to ascend the stairs for the ceremony. She had chosen a suit of pink and a pillbox hat. She had carefully selected it because the color was oddly her choice for her traveling suit for her "Lune de Miel," her honeymoon. She hoped that wearing the color might bring the happiness she had with her soul mate to her daughter as well.

The wedding went swimmingly. Etienne seemed most taken with Elle's maid of honor, Margot, who seemed to reciprocate.

After the reception, the couple were off to the Pas de Calais for a country honeymoon—the means of transport, of course, being the MG. The focal point or destination would be Arras, its town center, WWI caves, and the countryside and perhaps as far as Bruges. Both of them had clear calendars, and after this, fate dictated that they would have little time together.

XVIII

THESE SEEPING "THOUGHTS" of the romantic past must not, he knew, lull his vital attention from his perilous moments at hand. Though he was ruminating, somewhat abstractly, his attention was not even slightly deferred from the bridge, the street, or the still brightly clad, sparingly placed chestnut trees, framing this lovely Parisian autumn day.

His plight, which had down spiraled into the present nightmare, commenced upon his serendipitous escape from the combat area around Arras. He finally struggled back among an endless host of civilian displaced persons who were wandering toward Paris, in an attempt to evade the Germans and the war. His single frantic purpose was to evade capture and, as a French officer of Jewish extraction, being murdered in one of their stalags.

He had departed on May 20 from the military fiasco in Arras, where he had been attached to British Expeditionary Force headquarters as a French liaison officer of intelligence communications. This return occurred only as the result of amazing good fortune and the aid of his new friend and fellow officer, Clive Dunsby. Captain Dunsby was assigned to General H. R. Pownall, Lord John Gort's chief of staff, and therefore detached from the company he commanded in the Durham Light Infantry. Thus, he became part of the headquarters Support Company.

Giles had been ordered to Arras from French headquarters at Vincennes on April 25 in his specialty as an intelligence-communications officer. He had been commissioned a reserve second lieutenant in that specialty some two years before because of his "native" competency in English, learned from birth from his English mother.

This "competency" was further perfected as a student for a year at Rugby, at age fourteen. The school was his choice, but his mother dictated that it happen, and his father amusedly acceded to her wish. Consequently, he spoke English with the upper "U," Ox-Bridge accent, including the "thistle" sound, so impossible for the native French speaker. Obviously, Vincennes thought he would be, even if only a subaltern officer, an impressive icon of French suavity and sophistication. And so it did give him immediate purchase with General Pownall's officers when he arrived there.

Arras lay approximately 110 miles to the northeast of Paris "as the crow flies" (in English parlance). To be exact, British army headquarters was located in Habarcq, a village eight miles west and slightly north of Arras. Unexpectedly, he served there quite briefly. He arrived their very unceremoniously, by military transport, which dropped him off with his kit near an officers dining facility, where a subaltern not unlike himself greeted him in fairly good French, to which Giles responded in English, "Good of you to greet me! I'm sure I shall feel like one of your flock most quickly. Just share a few dos and don'ts about the officers mess with me, and I'll be right in step." The English subaltern amiably replied with details about times and type of uniform required, relative to duty: "Function governs propriety, so long as one does one's ablutions and changes 'stable encrusted' boots first."

Small talk buzzed through the group as they waited for luncheon to be called for the twenty-five or thirty officers. A long table and benches were set at the end of the tent. This tent, Giles noticed, was one of a community of tents set up for the command headquarters and obviously intended to be temporary until buildings could be arranged, through French headquarters, by fall or early winter. A mess sergeant announced, after he struck a gong, "Gentlemen, luncheon is served."

The French Lieutenant and the King of Rome

Some of the officers present looked startled at his "odd-lot" addition to their staff while others unabashedly stared. One major, hooking his left hand around his Sam Browne belt, threw his right hand in Giles direction, tossed his name toward Giles with a smile, and asked, obviously amused, if he were the "new man" from French HQ. Giles smilingly agreed. He was conveniently fitted into a bench between the major and the subaltern, to lunch in the mess; it was suggested that he report into HQ with his orders thereafter.

The British officers at Arras quipped, for some time, that he was actually an English spy "plant," slipped into Vincennes as a "mole" to masquerade as a French staff officer and then posted to Arras headquarters to surreptitiously betray French military secrets, menus, and proper wine lists to their English HQ. Very dry and subtle and very English, the jibes were very much appreciated by him, who was attuned to "Anglo-Saxon wit." Some of them referred to him as "Tommy" or "Atkins," a reference to Kipling's personified image of the British infantry "lifer": the stout-hearted, stubborn cockney, stoic and admirable, uneducated but replete with common sense and "bloody resolve." Not very apt, but very droll, what!

His new friend, Clive Dunsby, was made such over "pink gins" that evening. Clive invited him to "bunk" with him in the same temporary quarters. He was an "old Harrovian" at the same class level as his at Rugby. Harrow and Rugby were English public school competitors, and so, with this in common and "jelling well," as the English say, they seemed to "get along famously." Their friendship may well have (and shortly) saved his life.

Giles was assigned an empty desk and shared a telephone with another officer. Curiously, he found that his connection with his superior in Vincennes was spotty at best. The lines were cut or congested frequently. It was importantly noted by him that the British used radio frequently for communication. All forces in WWI had used telephones, as radio practicality was just a dream. There was, of course, the teletype, which was available at headquarters. But the code made use of it slow and restricted. He fell into a self-imposed routine of providing status information about English movements as they were provided him. Vincennes was strangely uninquisitive about developments in Arras if it didn't involve the Belgium campaign. He realized later that it was ignorant of the significantly crucial breakthrough between the French Ninth and Second Armies at the Ardennes-Sedan area.

XIX

GEN. GAMLIN HAD, in the interim, split intelligence by sending half of it to the war ministry under Prime Minster Daladier and the other half with his chief of staff, Gen. Doumenc, to Montry, fifteen miles away. Gen. George, commanding the northern armies, was in La Fierte, thirty-five miles east of Paris, where he received the elements that dealt with the enemy army. Motorcycle dispatch riders were carrying all sorts of important dispatches and documents for signature and return in satchels as they moved about the countryside in a manner that ignored the progress achieved in the modern world of war. Only one officer in Montry was available now to coordinate and pass on his evaluations to these various superior offices, but he handled so much material that he could not truly separate the "wheat" from the "chaff." Final decisions remained at Vincennes after this incredible bureaucratic process was completed. It became clear to Giles before he departed that his posting to Arras was pointless. He felt irrelevant, and so was his post. Both he and the BEF were not significant to the French command, as best he could conclude.

He became daily more acutely aware that all modern armies had radios and depended on them even in battle. How could an army depend on phone lines in a mechanized, lightning, new-type war? Moving units must have moving communications. When he returned to Paris in June, after the battle for France was lost, he heard that General Gamelin and HQ Vincennes were not simply hours but days behind news of the German breakthrough at Sedan and the Ardennes Forest and did not understand its significance. These important areas were north of the Maginot Line, which in principle is much like the ancient Great Wall of China and proved to be just as useless. His country was a fat Buddha, hugging itself in defense, while its enemy thought only of attacking this clumsy, effete, quaking, antiquated victim.

Within a day's time of his arrival on April 25, he discovered that seven of the nine divisions of the BEF were on the Belgium border with the most professional of the French armies, awaiting the invitation of King Leopold to enter and defend his country. On the tenth of May, while Giles was still attached to BEF HQ, the Germans entered Belgium, without the king's permission, and Holland, without the queen's permission. The talk around the mess was that the French and British believed the Germans were going to fight WWI all over again. But the 1914 Von Schlieffen Plan was not their intent. It proved to be that it was the Sichelschnitt (sickle swath) Plan of 1940. The primary attack was to be in the Ardennes to Sedan area, at the French armies' weakest point. On the tenth, the panzer corps of the southern armies, Group A, broke through into southern Belgium and Luxembourg, and on the thirteenth and fourteenth, they took Sedan, routed the French Second Army, and pushed through the Ninth Army (the mostly reservist forces at the most crucial points); they then went through the Ardennes Forest (which the General Staff had assured for twenty years was impenetrable). Shortly, the panzers would arrive at the Peronne-Cambrai gap, perhaps a mere twenty-five or thirty miles from Arras and BEF HQ.

On the morning of the seventeenth, an anguished-looking and intense corporal hopped up to the floor of the tent, brushed through the half-open flaps of the entry, and brusquely saluted Colonel Andrist, the ranking grade, who was standing near Giles's desk, and said, "Returning from assigned patrol, sir! Permission to report!" The colonel quickly nodded assent. "Sir, clear evidence of German presence between Peronne and Cambrai; saw three half-tracks in the countryside and a quarter mile on, to the east, three heavy tanks assembled, taking a break—smoking, eating, that sort of thing. Perhaps there were as many as twenty-five or thirty infantry, route step, one hundred yards to their rear. Can't say they didn't see our (four-by-four) Austin (scout) as we made it over an escarpment. We turned back to report, sir!" He stomped his foot and continued at attention and saluted again, all in the time-honored British Guard Division way, to indicate that he awaited the colonel's further orders.

"Right! Take your companion, and alert the duty officer of the Welsh Guard, and convey my order that he immediately meet me at General Pownalls's command tent. You and your private report to me at the command tent, with your vehicle, immediately after."

XX

FROM THE BREAKTHROUGH area, the German panzer units could strike west and north, heading for Abbeville and the channel ports, maintaining a scythe-like, cutting swing. This would, in all likelihood, smash into Arras and the nerve center of the BEF—the very heart, mind, and soul of the British military forces engaged in France. Thus, they found out the German panzers were within striking distance, entering the Peronne -Cambrai Gap just southwest of Bapaume and then, doubtless, on to Arras, to strike British headquarters.

Sudden and frantic countermeasures had already been planned and were nearly underway. A strike force of two battalions of the Durham Light Infantry and seventy-four tanks of the Fourth and Seventh Royal Tank Regiments were put together as "Frankforce" to cut through the spearhead of General Erwin Rommel's tanks and SS Totenkopf infantry. If General Franklyn couldn't cut through the German advance with a simultaneous French attack from the south, to meet his drive from the north, severing German forces from the infantry following them as support from the east, then they would have an unstoppable disaster, the Germans going on to Abbeville and north to the channel.

Clive Dunsby gave Giles the above information and such other specifics as he was permitted to in the privacy of their quarters. The tall and spare blond Englishman leaned deeply over an area map, which he spread on to the small writing table between there

The French Lieutenant and the King of Rome

bed cots. It was "Director of Engineer" numbered and presented the area covering the Perron-Cambrai Gap region to the immediate southeast and St. Pol, Doullens, Amiens, and Abbeville to the direct west and Beauvais to the southeast and north of Paris.

He explained that more reports had come in regarding enemy movements today and that their panzer corps were moving into the opening of the gap, which would give them good open country to the channel. It would then allow them to turn north and then back east along the channel, occupying all the ports and surrounding all of the French and English forces from the Belgium front to the area in Arras. So, after a meeting, just north at Lens, to take place on the twentieth, between Sir Edmund Ironside, CIGS, Lt. General H. R. Pownall, and French General Billotte, it would be agreed that the gap itself and the gap between the British and French forces must be closed. Two French divisions would attack toward Cambrai. The last two available British divisions, the Fifth and the Fiftieth, already committed to defend Arras to the south, would, by legerdemain, become that creation. That newly created force, codenamed for its commander, Major General Harold Franklyn, "Frankforce," would act as detailed above.

"The French won't have the force to be there, and I predict that we won't be able to spare the force from the Scarf River banks, where we are now committed. That then leaves us with the Sixth and Eighth Battalions of my lot, the Durham Light Infantry, the tanks from the First Army Tank Brigade, and whatever tanks General Billotte can put together against unknown numbers of panzers, who are moving fast, just as our military analyst, Capt. Liddell Hart warned that they could over ten years ago!"

Clive then moved his right forefinger from the map to Giles's chest and, in the half-light above the green lamp shade, narrowed his eyes eerily into a warning glare and quietly said, "It's time for you to go if you're going."

Giles responded in a shocked and agitated voice, "Go…go where? What the devil do you mean?"

"Giles, you haven't had any connection or orders from Vincennes for two days. Has it occurred to you that French Army Headquarters may be having serious problems?

"Your army is in retreat in the north along with ours, and your front in the Ardennes south was breached, just north of your Maginot Line, and the enemy is pouring through. There is no way we can make a difference with the few troops we have and the disjointed forces wandering around the Pas de Calais countryside. Remember, the BEF is only eleven divisions and support branches. We are outclassed and outgunned. We Brits shouldn't be here at all! I'm no tactician, but if this little move in three days doesn't work a miracle, our troops everywhere are going for the channel, for embarkation. We will have to try to beat the Germans to the ports in the northeast. You're not a real warrior and don't need to face this retreat! You are not trained for it!"

Giles was on his feet, furious at him and feeling totally betrayed. "How dare you accuse me of cowardice! What right have you to assail me in this way?"

"Listen, Giles, these are hard facts, and if you will listen to me, I have a solution for you that I think will do." He had modified his strident tone and was about to present what he thought was a viable plan. "Chum," he said, "just hear me out, and after this rotten thing is over, we'll meet in Paris or London—your choice—and toast in whiskey or wine (again your choice) and laugh over our survival!"

Clive's solution involved an extraordinary escape by motorcycle, cross-country, and, thank heavens, due to his shrewd calculations, it kept Giles one step ahead of the Germans.

XXI

AS HIS GOOD fortune would have it, Giles departed his post, using Clive's solution. Clive's colonel cut an order, on the seventeenth, returning him to Vincennes as "excess" to BEF's table of organization, giving him necessary cover with Vincennes if he successfully made it back to Paris. All of this telescoped in time, just before General Franklyn gathered and "stepped off" his two battalions of infantry, on the twentieth, with the support of the seventy-four available tanks of the Royal Tank Regiment, to counterattack the Seventh panzers. It, as foretold him by Clive, would fail in its attempt to fend off the German panzers, who started arriving at the Canal Du Nord at Perronne on May 20 (and the Frankforces fight followed, May 21–23): with the help of Gen. Billote's French armor, of sixty tanks, this caused the German panzers to divert, around to the west of Arras, as it headed for Abbeville, then Boulogne and the rest of the channel ports. It succeeded, however, in giving Hitler and the Germans serious worries, causing them to pause in their final assault against the Dunkirk area until June 1, giving the British four more days. This allowed the British time to evacuate most of the French and British troops from the beaches, but without their equipment.

General Ironsides, CGIS, in London had previously agreed with Lord Gort to take the BEF to the channel for evacuation without consulting with the French. General Gamelin had, before he was replaced with General Weygand, told Churchill, when asked where was "la masse de reserve," responded, "aucune." Where are your reserves? "There are none." They had been committed to support the northern armies on the north Belgian front. Gamelin was that certain of the choice he'd made. Weygand suspended Gamelin's orders to an attack in the Perrone-Cambrai Gap and then reinvoked Gamelin's orders—too late. Two days too late—Frankforce was over!

But the truth was that the French didn't have the available force to strike from the south across the panzers to separate them from their following support and infantry. The British had no direct contact with French headquarters at Vincennes for eight days—through Giles or otherwise. Also, French General Billotte was killed in a vehicle accident and not replaced, and, anyway, the French plan to complete Frankforce was known only to him!

These four precious days, which the enemy gratuitously granted, allowed British Admiral Ramsey to execute the plan "Dynamo" and evacuate 338,226 men with 861 ships, shuttling them to England. His losses were enormous: 243 boats and of those over half the destroyer fleet. Most of his fleet were civilian shallow draft boats with their owners on board as volunteers and in command, who made several trips back and forth across the channel under heavy air attack. They included, among the hundreds of thousands of British and French personnel, the headquarters and troops from Arras, who made it to Dunkirk and were included in the "collapsing sack" that emptied onto the beaches, jetties, and wharfs, and thence onto the boats and ships that carried them to England, respite, and sanctuary.

For all of these days, they remained under heavy artillery fire, tank and infantry attack, and air strafing from Messerschmitt and dive-bombers, madly screeching as they dove to bomb them—an indescribable maelstrom, pandemonium and hell. And who were among these evacuating small boats? Civilians, piloting their own little craft from their own little docks in southern England, doing their "duty" in the magnificent sense they were intended to do so by Lord Nelson over a century ago simply because "England expected every man to do his duty." And they did.

A great many French and some fifty thousand British stayed behind and kept the sack open and the German panzers and infantry out of it until June 1. British General Alexander personally swept the shallows of the beaches and the quays in a small launch to search for the last French and British stragglers, even as the enemy was charging on to those beaches on June 1.

French losses were more than double the German losses of approximately sixty thousand during this first phase of the war, and British losses were over eleven thousand dead and fourteen thousand wounded during this Battle of France (May 10–June 23).

XXII

SINCE HIS RETURN to Paris in the latter part of May, Giles had heard so very many stories, but by gleaning and considering all of the endless rumors and sources he had come by, the above essential information, screened and weighed by him, seemed to be the core facts. The paranoid cry of enraged French patriots—"Nous etion ruiner par trahison!"—was, as usual, not the case. He knew, as a soldier, that France hadn't been betrayed except by the fierce self-hatred so rampant among his people since the last war. In his final analysis, he knew his army was an army of poorly trained reservists with the last wars' equipment and poorly designed new equipment, pre modern tactics, and a paralyzed strategy—all cheaply bought to satisfy uncaring citizens, living in a dream world and foolish, selfish politicians. Consequentially there was the following litany and the ultimate military curses: incompetent and poorly trained noncommissioned officers, disloyal to their officers; upper-class, fascist-leaning officers and some noncoms of the same ilk; malaise and hostility everywhere in the forces; many officers and noncoms fearful of their own troops, if forced into combat with them.

That was the proof of "no support" for the survival of France. There was the treachery. It was the people and the politicians of France. The enemy—it was themselves!

All of this stood against an aggressive, prepared, contemporary army filled with loathing for the Allies and their values! Their Gallic individualism and personal freedom were detested, not to mention the humiliation of their adversary's defeat in 1918. The desperate French cry in the Russian retreat of Napolean sounded and resounded, once again: "Sauve-qui peut!" Those who are able, save yourself!

XXIII

AND NOW GILES knew all he needed to, and since June began, he knew he was a potential victim, eventually to be swept up into the maw of the relentless Nazi carnivore: unless, yes, unless, he could find a safe haven, a way to fall back, "to regroup" and strike back, regardless of the price he had to pay, even if it was the only thing in this world that was indispensable to him, besides Elle—his life! He would pay the price if the price were right. He would have to determine, and quickly, that right price.

In any case, he had, of necessity, become acutely aware of the wildly dangerous conditions under which he was surviving each succeeding day, in "his" Paris. He had learned to scan the look of the pedestrians' faces, attire, and the potential "risk" as he moved along, and on both sides of the street, as well. If they were close enough to be a threat, this would require an evasive move into a side street or building, providing an escape route. The fear of choosing a "dead end" was always with him when he was meandering through the streets, as he felt relentlessly compelled to do.

Now he checked the time on his Bulova exhibition wristwatch, an American gift that exhibited the date as well as the year. It was from his parents, in earlier, better days. It confirmed his tardiness. Elle would be beside herself with worry. He would need almost twenty minutes to reach her. The question he had to ask himself always was, why did he do this cruel thing to her when it could only drive them apart? The answer seemed to him to be his anger and frustration, a sort of striking back at his sense of being victimized by the life situation in which he was trapped.

He had just now reached the Bastille column, and he knew that he must stay with the speed of the crowd. The date on the watch, as a matter of fact, stated that it was December 1, 1940. Dates meant little or nothing to him in his reclusive state. The Germans had created a time warp, twisting reality so much that his previous Parisian world was now a foggy memory, encapsulated in an enigma, and his present—an intangible nightmare!

He put aside thoughts of her anxiety and anger and attempted to relax with thoughts of the pleasure he was anticipating with her, his ideal woman, this creature of perfection, with whom he was now blessed—this glorious, nude flawlessness that shocked him each time her splendor was revealed! Only David or Ingres could capture her essence, this female prototype who needed no embellishment that couturiers could devise.

For one to know Giles Lambert, one must reiterate that he loved women, including their characteristic shortcomings: not all were shoppers; not all were "bitchy," but most of them could be, and all of them were cunning, regardless of intellect: not all were devious, but many were because their basic ethics did not conform exactly to that of the male "race." Most were opinionated: some silently, others manifestly. Not many were forthright; few understood male candidness and so always at least questioned it. None understood man's ability to remain in love and loyal, though lustful and desirous of other sexual adventures (with the exception of French women, who did).

All believed the world would be a better place if their gender controlled destiny. Manipulative men recognized this last element of the female psyche and accordingly feigned being headstrong and "male-child-like." Sometimes, the natural courtesy and courtliness of a refined male, through simple generosity of spirit, would, in the case of women underexposed to it, lead to the primitive belief of a vacillating weakness of will and a gross failure of masculinity. But he believed that woman's inherent ability to love and to heal as both mother and mate, as Demeter and Aphrodite, overcame these shortcomings and rendered life ecstatic and enrapturing.

Giles, obviously an opinionated, educated man and, above all, a Frenchman, had other fixations and firm views, among them, not only the above rendered nature of a woman, but how and why men cherished them. Actually, he had never had a woman as a friend, except his mother. (Therefore, thought Giles, one must, according to one's experience and values, treat his feminine conclusions as either naïve, chauvinistic, idealistic, or precisely correct depending upon one's feministic and "politically correct approach to contemporary life.") Women seemed to him to be more easily swayed by social herd mentality and compunctions levied, for example, by glib stylists—that is, couturiers. To present accurately, we provide the following stream of his thinking: "The pathetic 'coat-rack' females that walk the fashion runways looked a third gender, without defining shape, flesh, or muscles. Couturiers need 'coat-racks,' but males prefer 'Venuses' and 'Dianas.' These feminine prototypes know whom they are and their physiology. Their femininity sickens their worst enemies, the couturiers, who have no chance to neuter them as women. Ah! to create a hipless, bottomless, thighless, breastless fashion that 'coat-racks' wear to please their couturiers and other women! Little does the feminine sex recognize its natural enemies and competitors, the couturiers—they who themselves wish to be the pleasure and playthings of other men! Somehow, thus to be the Venuses and Dianas of their favorite 'real' male."

Helen of Troy was obviously not, he believed, a "coat-rack." Men didn't go to war over "coat-racks." Men went to war for hate, land, religion, arrogance, power, pride, vengeance, subjection of enemies, racism, paranoia, and rigid meanness—but not for female "coat-racks." On this subject, Giselle thought him bizarre and readily changed the subject on the rare occasions it arose.

Just now, Paris fashions featured broad-shouldered, fitted, high-waisted jackets and form-fitting skirts; high heels and frivolous platform "wedgies"; and elevated hair and exorbitant hats—all most flattering to Giselle.

XXIV

BUT THEN, OBJECTIVELY speaking, Giles was right about Dr. Giselle d'Hozier; she looked breathtaking in anything or, in his considered opinion, nothing! We must remember that these were the thoughts and words of a very young, unseasoned, idealizing man who was thunderstruck by love and was destined to live in a state of narcosis, to spite all the horrors of his present travail. He was mesmerized, while teetering on the lip of an inferno—struggling to maintain his balance and to escape the unjustified terror enveloping him. He was incredibly in love, in a state of infatuation, while in reality, free-falling into a chasm of violent hate and death.

"Time" and "motion" were now shrinking the distance between them to so many meters, and the drama was accelerating within their apartment, apace.

On the inside of the apartment, behind the double entry doors, was Giselle, awaiting the return of her husband, Giles. She paced back and forth across the parquet floor between the French doors and the second-floor balcony of her mother's apartment, now their own dwelling.

As he dare not apply for a food rationing card, because he was technically an escaped prisoner of war and, of course, a Jew, she was relegated to shopping in black markets and bringing some small rations of food from the hospital rations, which were quite slim and of compromised quality. The merchants were already making their illicit deals with the neighborhood German occupiers, who were frequently dishonest and building their own little nest eggs.

It was frequently a matter of having something to trade—anything from household goods to, eventually, a piece of one's body. It didn't take long for hunger to corrupt morals, and only the affluent could stave off the corruption and compromise.

By November there were only seven thousand cars functioning in Paris, under careful German permits, with Paris police cooperating as their lackeys. The flics were always a class by themselves, even historically marrying into each other's families. They were well known for placing lead bars in the bottoms of their cape linings to use as weapons by swinging them at rioters and opponents. They didn't propagandize by holding infants in their arms. It was never wise to seek their counsel unless one knew them well. As the lowest form of governmental authority, they sought for their own security and henceforth worked willingly as toadies for the German authority and rounded up Jewish men and children and women even before they were asked. The poor Jewish emigrants from the Germans' Eastern European campaigns were quick to enroll and submit to the yellow star and, thus, early deportation and death. The well-off segments of established or historic French standing, by and large, escaped the German meat grinder of death until later. The French police weren't sure whether or not they would suffer from other influences if they turned over such people. However the "Abwer," or German intelligence branch, was not on a "Jewish mission" and delighted in annoying the SS and SD by ignoring their Jewish fanaticism, but for that reason alone, not for Jewish sympathy.

Approximately seventy-five thousand Jews were murdered by the Germans, mostly sent from Drancy, a hellhole in Paris, by transport to Auschwitz, to the furnaces. Another four thousand died in other camps, run by the French themselves, all over France. They were rounded up and starved or neglected while awaiting transport to Germany and death. The best hideouts were hilltop areas where the Germans hated to go. By all means it was best to be absent from the fashionable parts of Paris or to call attention to oneself. The story is told that many Jews, having influence with the Vichy government and, of course, a lot of nerve, continued the gay life through the occupation.

One only had to have the right papers, forged or otherwise. An example was Baron Guy de Rothschild, who made it to New York City and who, after the war, got his estates, houses, horses, and paintings back. Before leaving, a friend met his valet or butler on the street in Paris, during the German occupation, and asked whom the German ambassador was entertaining in the baron's house. The reply was, "Why, the same people the baron did, sir." Many of his relatives were not so lucky and died at the hands of the Germans. Another good anecdote is the tale of the Italian officer and his detail of men at the Nice railroad station. Italy took Nice as theirs when it entered the war. In 1942, the French Malice (the French militia) and some French police had an unhappy group of Jewish people in tow to be shipped north to the Germans. The Italian officer forced the French to stand down and return these people to their homes immediately. Italy ignored German and French Jew hatred until it surrendered in 1943, and then German troops occupied Italy and began to sweep up the Jews, formerly in Italy's control.

XXV

BACK IN THE apartment, Elle maintained her increasingly distraught vigil. The pendulum clock, standing its post in the entry hall, struck off another quarter of an hour of her developing agony. Now she was falling into her abyss of terror, which was becoming almost habitual on these repeated tardy returns of his. Now she knew her compulsive, painfully established ritual must begin. Now her only course was prayer, and the one she always fell upon was vespers. That is what she recalled from her recollection of Evensong, inspired by her drill as a Catholic child. "Dear God, I can call on nothing else in this vacuum. If you are there—I am so desperately worried and afraid for him. Please let him come back; let him come back to me unharmed—please, quickly. I know it's selfish, of course, but I think of him suffering torture in the hands of the Germans—I can't live without him."

She intertwined these personal exhortations with the formality of the chants and prayers as she recalled them. She had lived a life surrounded by death and knew so well its sackcloth and doom. As a child she reluctantly accepted the resoluteness and irreversibility of death and learned to accept the fact that, though God was omniscient and omnipotent, he chose not to respond to the earthly prayers of his supplicants, as proposed. She knew the adage well: "Man proposes, but God disposes."

She intermittently wrung her hands and importunately folded her arms, grasping each of her forearms with the opposite hand, as she paced the twenty-five- or thirty-foot width of the room; it was almost the instinctive repetition of her mother's arms as they had enfolded her when she was inconsolable.

She felt a coldness, a wall of formality in the religion she knew. She couldn't abide the distance that seemed to block the warmth she knew must—must—be there! Why was there not the presence of the Jesus that his original followers heard and felt when they were in his presence? What had all the marble, bronze, gold, and other embellishments of Europe's churches to do with the hot sun and warm feelings of Judea? She had no answers to satisfy her yearnings and emptiness. Only the memory of her mother's arms enfolding her hovered in the recesses of her mind, as she frantically considered him in the merciless hands of the Germans.

When she thought of him in such frantic moments as these, her thoughts came tumbling from her mind in a sort of catechismal rote or format of English "remarks," which seemed to please him the most in ordinary moments because, above all, he found her attempts at English to make her most innocently feminine and consequently most endearing to him. Her Gallic attempts at English phrasing and pronunciation caused him to playfully joke and tease with her as she intentionally played ever more tauntingly her role as an English ingénue, both inept and beguiling in her supposedly native English language—inept and cherishable at one and the same time! It could end only as she planned it, with him holding and caressing her, to the unspeakable delight of both.

She reached the hallway entrance again as she paced and fixed her eyes on the door handle, praying the one on the right would turn under the pressure of his hand. He always promised her that he would return to the apartment no later than twenty minutes ago, which was 6:00 p.m. But he failed her in that so many times. So many times she was forced to curse him, pray for him, touch the outmost reaches of despair, cry, suffer in the depth of her bowels with pangs of pain. This life with him was hell, but the thought of life without him was mortification and death. Ah, the English again—Hobson's choice! It was the horse nearest the door and the one the Creator's livery man intended for her and, of course, the only one delectably chosen for its perfection—the "magic white stallion." So she was blessed or cursed with him and knew she would ride to hell or heaven on his back, as the Creator intended. She knew she would fear, hate, and thrill at the ride but clutch on to his mane, her knees digging into his flanks, shedding her tears in the driving wind, as he tore relentlessly into their future.

They both knew there was nowhere to turn. The police force was now completely treacherous—mere German tools to be exploited as they saw fit, who would lick the hands of their masters for any scrap they could beg. They were probably loyal to one another because the betrayal of treachery by one would lead to like revelations of others. To complain to them about the disappearance of a French officer, loose in Paris instead of in a German stalag, was invitation for them to get a special bone for he might be organizing a plot against the SS, the SD, or the Abwehr. And if they found out that he was a Jew, well there was "a communist leader, for certain!" And, of course, his wife, a physician: "What a risk to her patients and the hospital this Jew-lover could be." To report anything to them would be an invitation to hunt Giles down and to list her as an enemy of their new masters.

Before doing that, she thought she would seek revenge herself on such Germans who were unlucky enough to come by her as patients in the hospital. The very thought of professional betrayal shocked her into understanding what her love for him could do— even the betrayal of her Hippocratic oath.

Ten minutes later, more chimes sounded, more of her pacing, no more vespers, more thoughts of Giles. In her thoughts, he was much more important than the preserved description of him in her mind, of his physical beauty. His intense, incisive brown eyes penetrated her mind, her soul, her sensitivities. His expressive brows conveyed without words what his full lips need not say. "How long must I continue in this suspended state of hell?" she groaned.

Whose knock would she hear first? His tormentors—police, German soldiers, SS? Or just his key turning the lock and the interior handle, as he entered, his eyes looking for hers, with his damned "little boy" tardy look? But now, the apartment building was only a matter of a few feet away from Giles's forward-thrusting body. One of the double doors was being held open for him by the new porter, an older man; the hand-me-down uniform he was wearing was that of his insolent predecessor. It was excessively loose, the trousers too long and turned up, and the cuffs of the sleeves almost covered his hands. Somehow the kepi was too round to set correctly on the poor man's head. He and Giles smiled at one another and bid one another good evening.

XXVI

NOW! NOW! GILES could start a rush for the stairs as he cleared the door. He bounded across the black-and-white checkerboard marble entry hall, past the birdcage elevators, and up the curving, carpeted staircase, where he found the stairs were too long for him to mount them two at a time. At last he reached the double doors to the apartment, turned the unlocked handle of the right one, and stepped into the entry hall so charged with tension it nearly sizzled. And he felt fully deserving to be chastised for creating the anguish that Elle had suffered for almost forty minutes.

She was standing two feet away from him in the entry hall, her feet firmly separated and planted, her arms akimbo, her shoulders staunchly erect, and her face furious. Her eyes could only have duplicated those of the Medusa, and all of this animosity was centered on him alone. His only thought was that of awe and gratitude that her hair had not changed into the Medusa's head full of serpents, wriggling in anger, with spitting tongues of poison, reaching for his paralyzed and stricken person. He awaited the imagined and the deserved viper's strike and Elle's blows of rage. He felt so deserving of it and so guilty of wrong that he felt unworthy of taking a defensive posture. He was the proverbial medieval flagellant, ready to chastise himself before she could act!

He stepped forward intending to take her into his outreaching arms, as he began to plead his obeisant creed of forgiveness. At that precise second, she slapped him soundly across his right cheek.

He froze in motion, shock having instantly possessed his being, overwhelming his previous intent to encompass her in his arms. He began again to voice his desire for her forgiveness, trying to explain his need to stay with the walking speed of the crowds as they wended their way toward their homeward destinations, as well as the need to await the departure of the crowds from the Left Bank to provide him with the most cover available from drawing the attention of the police or the Germans. He had explained all of this to her before, but from her view, it made little difference, since he should not be on the "streets" because of the danger to them both.

He tried once again to reach for her, and she stepped back again, spewing her accumulated verbal spleen, growing in store ever since the Germans marched into Paris on June 11. Ever since, he commenced testing his luck each day. He even joked with her about how used to his presence his enemies were, that without his presence out there the flics and the Germans would be suspicious and think he was a victim of the French underground. Well, today she was finally "fed up," or as the French say, "en avoir assez de marre."

"I can't stand the emotional beating you subject me to week after week. I can't live with the fear every night that you have been picked up and are being tortured or shot—or that you might just disappear, never to be heard of again. Surely love is not to mean only fear and torture! When I leave you in the morning, am I to think every day that it means I may never see you alive again? You make me live in constant fear of every day being your last! Must I buy widows weeds to hang in the closet for use some evening when I come home to your death?" She sounded so melodramatic even to herself, and yet, it was only the truth, the horrifying truth of what their lives had become.

"Giles, darling, I can't live this way anymore! You must stop leaving the apartment alone! You must complete your plan and leave. I will follow you as soon as I am able, with or without leave from the hospital. I never ask you for your plan, nor do I now. It's safer for both of us if I don't know."

His plan rested all on one man. And he didn't know where that man was—or even if he still was! He'd been looking in all his old haunts as stealthily as he could, and that accounted for much of his wanderings, hoping to encounter an old acquaintance or mutual friend, but to no avail! He had one last place to go, but he was afraid to risk everything by doing so. But he must finally do so and very soon! With the quarantine that Elle insisted on, he had little choice.

She stood before him, more subdued, helpless and wistful now that she had expunged some of her anger, though not all. The residue shown in her now shaking hands, which he took in his. Her eyes were glistening with moisture as she bit her lower lip to avoid her now welling tears. Her negligee had fallen open below her navel, which was deep and sensual. The sash of her sheer, gold-colored silk dressing gown held the garment closed, but only just below the nipples of her breasts. She seemed unaware that a perfect V-shaped opening fell from her navel to her thighs, revealing her pronounced "mons de Venus," its blondish hirsute embellishment, and below that, the wondrously snug and perfect triangular meeting of her pudenda with her round, full, hard thighs. She was unencumbered by any lingerie beyond the dressing gown. She was now the very reality of his fervent, prurient thoughts, earlier conceived, as he struggled with the long tense walk to the apartment this evening.

His temples were pounding, and his desires were both craving and confusedly adoring; he desired to both possess her to her very depth and to simultaneously unite to the point of melding with her and, thus, to be immersed, lost and at oneness with her, in her eternal depth. He followed the round line of her thigh with his right hand, inside her gown, caressing her buttock, and reaching on to her anus, which he knew to be a highly erotic area for her.

She tried to push him away but was, by this time, fending away his other hand and fingers, which had sought and found her clitoris. She cried out that she was not prepared for this and wanted and needed her bath. He knew that she smelled of the sea, but this seemed only to drive him on, increasing his arousal, causing him to half whisper a summons to her, that "like Napoleon wanted Josephine," he wanted her as she was, "au natural." She fought him as best she could, but her most sensual treasures had been reached before she could defend them, and by an enemy she adored. She fervently wished to and would surrender her most precious things if he only permitted her to surrender them when properly perfumed to be gifted. She wished them to be presented as a sumptuous feast for her noble lover because to her he was and would always be so.

He pitched her half over his shoulder, roughly as in a fireman's carry, took her through the sitting room, the bathroom, and finally the bedroom, where he uncerimoniously tossed her onto the silk coverlet of the unopened bed. This effort was not easy for him because her size was nearly equal to his. All the while, she was denouncing him as a Cro-Magnon rapist, a vicious prehumanoid, and a repugnant monster, and she slapped and punched and kicked at him, just missing his engorged member, the possible striking of which could have elected her the victor, but would have crowned her with a Pyrrhic triumph, with herself as the sole celebrant, probably for most of the night.

He proceeded to uncross her legs and bury his tongue where he knew her clitoris to be. Her reactions to his tongue became instantly frenzied. She unconsciously, succumbing to passion, caressed her breasts with her hands, while her fingers instinctively stimulated her nipples, enhancing her feeling of ecstasy. She began to thrust her body upward, repeatedly begging him to more intensity, while her spasms of pleasure uncoiled each time with more ferocity. Her words became half curses and half prayers, until she fell back, exhausted. He then entered her vagina, gently but fully, only to see her rise again, kissing him deeply with her searching tongue, having forgotten completely the smell and taste of the sea, which she so ferociously sought to eradicate with soap and perfume.

He still sensed the smell of that thing from whence all of earth's life crawled to land, the ocean—that place from where the body fluids of man and animal match the proportions and the composition of it, the sea and its very elements, the sea, from which all of earth's creatures evolved. Should it then be bemusing that the smell of the sea still resided in the place where life began? The smell bespoke the humble, prehistoric beginnings of the occupants of our world.

    The couple reached mutual paroxysm, and he collapsed forward onto her as she wrapped her legs about him; and they both fell into a guileless sleep, a lovers' sleep of innocence. They woke sometime later that night, due to his still partially dressed discomfort, which he corrected by disrobing from the bed, throwing his remaining garments onto the floor at its foot. She now chose to reposition herself, with her buttocks astride his thighs, in the reverse position so that she did not face him as she fondled his organ until it was throbbing in her hands and he was urging entry into her vagina. She thrust it in and began to ride him with almost a wrathful pumping, without regard to his reactions or comfort. It began to seem to him to be an act of dominance rather than pleasure, of fury rather than affection. Of course it was that very thing; it was the expunging of her balance of wrath, in exchange for the repeated torment he had caused her. He stayed with the whirlwind as she pressed hard on his thighs to give her the purchase to make her upward thrust each time she ascended and then drove herself downward. Although he could only see her back and the tousled hair hanging on her shoulders, he could measure the exhaustion of her stored anger from her rising groans and their shrill replacement with ecstasy preceding her orgasm. His present, instantaneous purpose was to be an equal part, to share in that orgasm. Now he sensed her ready, as was he! The world and all of the galaxies vanished in their shrill climax. For that instant of mutual gratification, everything was a vacuum, filled only with them alone.

XXVII

THE MORNING STARTED with their awakening and her bathroom ritual before her departure for the hospital. In accordance with their understanding, he was apartment bound. He would eat his usual, insufficient breakfast and would plan his day with exercise and reading. He remained in bed, perhaps to sleep a little longer.

In his usual idle minutes alone, he sought to avoid thoughts of his rather recent escape from Arras and British headquarters. But often they entered his thoughts as uninvited nightmares, both while sleeping and awake. He lay in bed while the "tugging and trying" thoughts began. Recollections poured in, in disorderly ways.

He began to remember his cot in his quarters at Arras, the morning before he was to leave. He feared that he would not be able to use the roads because of possible fleeing civilians and traffic. At least the weather had been dry, and this was not a rainy season in this area, the Pas de Calais. He knew the main roads from his many trips to England from Paris. He reached to his nightstand for the lamp and then his compass, in an insecure reflex. He always wore it on his right wrist. (He wore his watch on his left, as he was right-handed.) Clive was aware that he had one and reminded him that he couldn't make the trip without it.

The land was rolling but essentially flat between Arras and Paris, but he wasn't sure he could manage the fields with the stubble from last years' crops. If he couldn't use the roads, (Arras-Doullens-Amiens or Arras-Bapaume-Amiens), Clive indicated another way to aid him: his need was to stay well ahead of any panzer scout cars and bikes out there, many of which carried sidecars with a well-armed companion.

There were rivers; though small, to manage the canals, a bridge for crossing would be required. Finally there was the Somme River at Amiens, which was a formidable barrier to clear; then, Beauvais, and finally Paris. It was more than obvious that his ability to "cross-country" would be limited. He lacked crack experience on a bike and knew he needed a road, or he faced an impossibility. He was suffering an extreme case of "nerves" the whole night before his departure on the nineteenth at dawn.

He kept reviewing the distances to Paris and safety: Arras to Doullens, about twenty-five; Doullens to the Somme River and Amiens (pray the German scout cars are still involved around Arras), about twenty-four; Amiens to Beauvais and on to Paris, seventy-six. It would be so much shorter if he dared to risk a direct route from Arras, but "sooner" could mean capture or death. Could he force his way through possible crowds of refugees with carts and perambulators full to the brim?

There was the old, "cart road," direct from Arras to Amiens, through Bucquoy, Mailly-Maillet, Puissieux, and the Serre road, T intersection, which led to the old "no man's land" of WWI. Then followed other nearly nonexistent villages, until the edges of Amiens. This was perhaps as little as thirty miles. It would be unlikely to have crowds of people thronging the roads because the villages were small, and refugees from the east were unlikely to seek or find it. This was the way Clive was sponsoring, and he said the surface was "macadam" and was made so because of the fifty-odd, nearby cemeteries, filled with British dead from the battle of the Somme River, July to November 1916. The road had been improved by France to accommodate British families who wished to visit the cemeteries, and of course, numerous other cemeteries lined neighboring roads as well.

Rudyard Kipling, author and once a BIA (British Indian Army) subaltern, referred to them as "vast silent cities; and that their names liveth forever more," a quotation that was taken by him from "Ecclesiasticus," of either the Catholic Old Testament canon or the Apocrypha of the Protestant version. His son Jack, an Irish Guard officer and a very young subaltern, died in an attack on the German lines in this Battle of the Somme. This battle, lasting from July 1 until November of 1916, along with the Ypres area in the "salient" of Belgium, became the graveyard of a complete male generation of Great Britain and Ireland.

XXVIII

THE WEATHER HAD been dry for a long period. In case he had to deviate onto nearby fields for unforeseen reasons, this could be the quickest way of all. All of this countryside would be crossed by the panzers if they broke through the Arras-to-Perrone line (running south to north), and, if so, he could be trapped or killed by their cycles or advance scout cars. His danger would increase the closer he came to Amiens. Clive's map showed this as a possible collision course with one or two of the panzer thrusts if they were successful in the next two or three days.

The afternoon of May 17, Capt. Clive Dunsby had a corporal from the vehicle section prepare a Norton 16H motorcycle for Giles's departure the next morning. The Norton takes about sixteen liters of gasoline (he was reliably informed) and knee pads, which he was told he absolutely needed because of the rough terrain he would be covering. There was also a leather scabbard attached to the handlebar and the forks for the front wheel, which contained a Lee-Enfield 4 mk1 (T), with attached telescopic sight and special cover for it, plus the standard dust cover. Naturally he would have to dismount to use a rifle, and he thought, with the ability he showed on the practice range used by the headquarters group and with the instructions on the sight he was given, he could manage it well enough. He had become a marksman as a boy, hunting wild boar in Remouillet, an hour south of Paris with his father. His father maintained proficiency after the last war and taught him, as well, with a shotgun for birds and a rifle for game.

The corporal saw to it that he had three mettle boxes (from British stores, containing ammunition for his rifle and a Webley 38

MKIV pistol) carefully secured and bolted to the frame, front and rear. There was no ammunition for his French 1935S pistol, other than two magazines he had on hand. His weapon was automatic, and theirs had a replaceable cylinder. He decided to carry his own in a holster under his left shoulder, inside his British coverall uniform, which he was wearing over his French officer's vareuse jacket and jodhpurs; his flat overseas cap with ranking was in his saddle bag, which also contained a bed role, personal kit, an inner-tube patch repair kit, orders to and from Arras, and his jodhpur leggings with side straps. He was wearing his jodhpur boots, and he only hoped that he wouldn't have any long-distance walking, which would have called for the stout infantryman's boots. He also had three days of can goods and a can opener, plus a bayonet on his coverall belt. For good measure he carried his Sam Browne belt (for ego comfort), in his saddle bag, which was slung over the rear fender and attached by leather thongs to it and underneath his seat as well. His coverall uniform included a pilot-type helmet and, of course, glasses on a band, which passed through snaps on his pilot's leather helmet.

He was encumbered and felt overstuffed and only hoped that, if any action came his way, it would somehow pass him by. Still he felt he needed two more liters of gas and a hand tire pump. Where to place them? "Corporal, try and use whatever space is left on the handlebar to connect them. Maybe I can pass for a traveling tin smith or junk dealer! Do you suppose, Clive?"

He arose the next morning and dressed in the manner planned. He grabbed some sustenance in the company of Clive in the breakfast mess. Clive warned him to stop bolting his food down as this was the last prepared meal he would get for an untold amount of time. He listened. He reminded himself of the relaxed familiarity he had grown to feel with Clive in such a short time. He felt the closeness of a brother, almost the closeness he felt with Etienne, with whom he was raised. There was that "trust" between them that an only child, such as he, clutched tightly. The feeling signified itself by the absence of "space" between them, a kind of "bonding," much like "sidekicks" in a stable. After all, he was trusting his life to Clive's plan, enabling him to escape from the coming battle and the war. That was proof of his trust. He was going to miss him!

He planned on taking the morning lorry with the guard relief from their part of the encampment. That would be about five forty-five. It would take about fifteen minutes to mount the guard or "fall the men in" from the relief guard and replace the others, individually. The Welsh guards had disposed of "technical speech" by the relief man at each post, that is to say, of his ritualistic rendition of standard "orders of the day" except "specials," which needed specific alerts or developments expected for that particular day. Each man knew he was accountable for all of them, spoken or not, unto court martial and death.

Giles said his farewells to those who were at the mess. The others good-byes, including formal departures to superiors, he had done the day before. He had felt an integral part of the organization; he owed them all so much for their camaraderie, and for that, he couldn't say enough. As they would say, so curtly and so sufficiently, "A bloody good lot of fellows, what?"

He was on his way to the motor pool area by 5:30 a.m., in the lorry seat next to the driver-private, where he promptly fell asleep. The lorry was full of the relieved guards, who were probably also asleep on the seats under the canvas top in the rear of the lorry. They were on the way to Izel-les-Hameaux, where the Welsh Guard First Battalion headquarters were located. It was also where the motor pool was and where his previously prepared Norton cycle was awaiting him, under the oversight of the responsible sergeant of the guard: responsible, with his minions, for vehicles such as light tanks, Bren gun carriers, cycles, and lorries: all were there, en masse. The village of Izel-les-Hameau was all of three miles away from Habarcq, toward Arras. From there he would start his journey to, and through, Arras and then southwest on d919, also known as Serre Road, Cemetery no. 2, to Amiens: then—God willing—Amiens, Beauvais, and Paris.

XXIX

HE REGRETTED THE insufficient sleep of the previous night. He had remained awake, tossing and turning with nightmarish interludes of the next few unpredictable days, days to be spent striving to avoid Germans and return to Paris. He simply couldn't help the surging feeling in his limbs and the vacuum in his stomach, all urging him to get going and face the fearsome unknown.

The lorry lurched to a stop, and his head and neck abruptly ricocheted, first backward, nearly glancing off the rear wall of the cab, and then forward in his seat. His first sight then became the guarded gate in front of the hood of the lorry. The sergeant of the guard was in front of the lorry, standing at parade rest, perilously close to being smashed by their lorry against the wooden-framed, barbed-wire gate. The gate provided access to the high barbed-wire enclosure, stretched across the lengthy distance of the enclosed area, barring entry to unauthorized personnel.

The sergeant duly noted the insolence of the guardsman at the wheel and moved, at measured step, to the window of the driver's door, behind which the offending guardsman now stiffened his body and rigidly sat, prepping for the onslaught to come. The sergeant ordered him out, called him to attention, "dressed him down," and asked him, "'ow would you like me to put you on report wif your officer of the gard?" Answer: "Not at all, Sergeant." The sergeant's swollen-necked response was, "This 'ere lorry belongs to headquarters, and don't you forget—bleedin' 'ouseold regiment or no—you're still a private in 'is Majesties army, and you show bloody respect to these stripes, or I'll see you pie the price! Now, after the gite's opened, you move your ars on out, and remember oo you ar and oo I bloody am!" Two privates swung the gates open, both looking cheerful about the fact that the sergeant's anger was directed at the Welsh guardsman and not themselves, for a change.

In the meantime, as the gate opened, Giles alighted from his side of the lorry and waited for the truck to pass by him. He approached the sergeant, who came to attention, saluted, accepted Giles's salute in return, and wished him a good morning, which was followed by the self-same salutation from the French lieutenant.

Giles requested the whereabouts of his motorcycle, and when the sergeant accompanied him to its location, Giles made a cursory check of it. He was also reassured by the sergeant that it had been "under 'is eye while on 'is post and, who 'imself had been assured by the duty sergeant that he had earlier relieved, of the same." The sergeant then imparted the following, and for his "ears and only them": "About four thirty, sir, a Bren gun carrier departed here, with crew, to reconnoiter your intended route d919 heading southwest toward Amiens, maybe for Jerry cycles or scout cars; if so, they are to take them out and report what they can about their units. They have been asked to keep an eye out for you and support you if they can. But, look you"—ah, a Cornishman or Welshman in his ancestry, thought Giles—"they cannot compromise their mission in your aide, as I'm sure I need not say such to an officer. Forgive me, sir, as I ain't intending to presume such a thing as you would not expect such. Sir!" This last was almost an expletive, spit out by the sergeant, as a conclusion to their conversation. They exchanged parting salutes.

"Oh, Sergeant, any advice about turning on the way to Arras, and then in Arras, for locating d919 south?"

"Oh, yes, sir, right turn out the gite, then left at the T intersection two hundred feet or so on and stay with it two mile or so, and you're there. Run east on your road past Place of 'eroes and the Grand Plice, then taiken d917 south, aside Grand Plice, past the railroad station, and in short order it runs into d919, and there

The French Lieutenant and the King of Rome

y'ar. And stay on er all the waiy til Amiens." He continued, "Road's also called 'Cemetery Road,' for the Somme dead, executed by the Jerries, by order of our own WWI Imperial General Staff. Thank the Lord, we got a new staff now!"

The road he traveled to Arras was rutted and filled with chat, obviously trucked in to fill great depressions due to wearing and weather. The word was that last winter was very severe and was only relieved by the cheery visit of the king to honor the guards, who entertained him rather lavishly, as only a household regiment could do. The king, of course, was the colonel in chief of the regiment, and Company One was designated "The Prince of Wales Company," to honor the king's heir apparent, and in every generation to follow.

XXX

UPON ARRIVING IN Arras, Giles found the streets deserted, but signage assisted him in quickly locating both of the famous squares between which ran d917. He needed to follow this south, by the railroad station, to reach d919. As he traversed the two squares, he found them jam-packed with every form of locomotion known and currently in use, from horses and antiquated buggies to farm carts, baby buggies, modern autos attended by befuddled bourgeois owners, and liveried drivers with upper-class occupants. Pandemonium reigned throughout! Crowds gathered to talk of the best routes to use to stay ahead of the Germans, whether to continue to the south and Paris or west to Abbeville and the coast. These people were of all varieties: peasants, middle-class townspeople, even leaders and mayors of towns and villages, who were running away because in the first war the Germans held them hostage for the good conduct of their citizens. They all came from Holland, Belgium, Artois, and Pas de Calais generally. None wished to be on the German "side" of an occupation line. Their recollection of death and destruction by the German war machine was too fresh a wound. Giles parked his bike under a corner of the arcade in Le Grand Place, which followed around the four sides of the square, and walked among these unfortunate people to better understand what he was about to confront. He both intermingled and spoke to diverse types.

 He noted that some persons made comments strong enough to move whole groups aimlessly in one direction or another.

Some statement by a person who looked and sounded authoritarian gained enough impact to move the crowd "to and fro" around the edges of the solidly parked square; the crowd moved not unlike a flock of pigeons, skittering in unison across the bricks of the squares' edges, after one or two of these "knowledgeable birds," chasing after their valueless grain of "sound" advice; then they were off in another direction when their last surge proved unrewarding.

None of them appeared to be prepared for extended journeys, and all were eventually to be dependent when their supplies evaporated. It was best to stay put and protect their property and try to survive whatever came. What would they do when they reached a town, hungry and bereft of everything, and the townspeople barred their doors?

He knew he had no more time to waste, mounted his cycle, and rolled out of the edge of the square and down d319 to the station. The site there was equally disturbing. There were two full trains, with one on a siding and no engine but full of people, who were spilling out and milling about the tracks. Apparently the engine crew had abandoned them in the rail yard, probably to make a faster getaway to the south and away from the Germans, whose Stuka dive bombers had been attacking and bombing trains in this direction of travel. They were getting a flow of such reports by radio, to this effect, at headquarters. Their obvious purpose was to create bedlam and terror in the population and thus interfere with French and British troop movements.

The other train had its engine and was attempting to take on coal, with passengers shoveling their share to speed the matter. Of course, German Messerschmidt 109 fighters had been strafing the roads as far as here, to create the same bedlam as the Stukas.

He rolled on until he found the hookup of d919 and d917, his road to Amiens. He only hoped that the refugees had not considered d917 a viable route of escape to Amiens and Paris. And by the by, where the hell were the Allied air forces when they were needed? The Stukas had little defense and needed fighter cover to operate against British hurricanes and spitfires, which could chew them up and spit them out.

Maybe, he mulled, the Brits had lost their French airbases to the invaders, and maybe French air was knocked completely out of action. Maybe the Brits thought the fight in France was almost over, and they couldn't risk any more planes on a losing country. He was thinking about why he was running out on this fight and what Clive said about the likelihood of success and how tactically they would be heading for the safest channel port, immediately after the likely failure of Frankforce.

Clive was right about his preparation for close combat. He hadn't any. He wasn't trained to lead a company of men or a platoon or even a section. Let's not even think about the effective placement of weapons or establishing strong points or tank strategy or—let's not continue in this vein of thought but concentrate on what he could do and what he had to do to stay alive on this trip!

So far so good! The road was flat, not too serpentine, two lanes wide and not full of refugees or people, for that matter. There were cemeteries bordering the roads, with occasional farmed fields interrupting them. He was dodging some farm animals and their owners, who were moving them farther afield, perhaps with a thought to possible theft or worse. There were some milk carts and plough horses pulling them. He was able to maintain an average speed of perhaps twenty-five miles per hour, with due care.

XXXI

WHEN SEARCHING THE peripheral horizon, as he constantly did, a cold chill ran through his body, followed abruptly by cold sweat and a feeling of clamminess between him and his under layer of clothes. His greatest fear appeared in the apparition of a German cycle with sidecar, and it was occupied! It was perhaps twelve or fifteen hundred feet to his left and heading for him. It was at right angles to his southerly direction, coming from the east across an open field, between cemeteries. He had just passed the village of Bucquoy and then, thereafter, Pussieux. So he was approaching Serre and its Cemetery Road, which T intersected with d919. There were still moving objects in his way ahead, to be avoided.

He had to believe that one of the two sidecar men had a machine pistol, and the driver would not have to stop for him to be shot. Once they reached half the distance, the sidecar man could use his Schmeisser submachine gun to kill him, whether to his rear on the road or beside him. After all he couldn't be mistaken for anything but an Allied messenger. Motorcycle scouts don't take prisoners! Giles knew he was going to live or die by the action he took right now. He must make that Serre cemetery turnoff and hope for at least a small culvert there, so he could stop, dismount, and pull his rifle out of its scabbard on the front fork. The rifle was ready, and the distance would be as close as a charging boar would be, so there was no need of the sight.

He made the Serre turnoff before the Germans got to the road, d919, which it was now clear they intended to take. Good! The driver wasn't going to run along beside him then. Without a still platform to fire from, the sidecar man couldn't get his machine gun properly aimed. Therefore it was the driver he had to kill or wound, so he would lose control of the cycle. At forty or so miles per hour, he would careen and crash. Well, he knew he had made a lot of possibly incorrect assumptions, but what else was there to do?

"Pray, God, they don't know about this Cemetery Road turn-off," he thought as he turned into the Serre road and careened to a halt, spinning the cycle around to face the direction the German bike was coming from. As he dismounted, he kicked loose the bike's stand, but the road wasn't level at that point, so he held it balanced against his legs, long enough to get the rifle out of the scabbard, and then dropped the bike against the cut of the hill. Then he got his left arm through the sling on the rifle to steady the shot, checked the bolt, dropped to his left knee, with the left thigh to support his left elbow, placed on it to support the rifle for the shot or shots he had to get off, just before the Germans reached the Serre intersection, and he was ready, as he heard their motor coming closer and closer.

They were about one hundred feet to his north when he commenced to squeeze the trigger. The driver's Eisen Krueze ribbon behind the third button on his *feldgrau* tunic was to be the chosen point of impact of his bullet when—to his great shock and paralysis—he heard the heavy chatter of a Bren gun above his head! There was an instant explosion, and the German driver and the sidecar men and their cycle seemed to flip in the air, and it landed on two of the three occupants. The Bren gun carrier was above Giles's head on a grassy point about fifteen feet above the Serre intersection on the north bank and close to a cemetery: it was just below some trees, which provided it cover.

"Sorry to spoil your hunting, Leftenant! We knew you didn't see us up here, but we couldn't take a chance that you mightn't have done the driver in, you see! Besides, seeing your reaction was worth the price of admission, don't you know! However, sir, you looked ruddy like the manual of arms—good and proper!"

The French Lieutenant and the King of Rome

"Is 'thanks' enough to say to all of you? It seems the guards just keep on giving—well, to say the least! My mother thanks you, my father thanks you, my wife thanks you, and my unborn children thank you! Most of all, Leftenant 'Tommy Atkins' thanks the lot of you, Sergeant."

"Wait, Leftenant! Don't run off! There's the 'mother' of those Jerries—a pretty nasty piece of work. Let me tell you about her. She runs on four rubber tire wheels and sports what looks like a twenty-millimeter gun, which we can't take a hit from cause we're a troop carrier mostly—all open, you see. But we're OK in front for rifle or a machine gun, but not a twenty millimeter on our top. Too open, don't you see; but their cycles work off of these scout cars. They need roads to get up to twenty-five or thirty miles per hour. Crossing fields they're not fast. So we spotted this mom about three miles east before we spotted the cycle running just east of here, headin' for you and this road. Now they're just three dead gents what 'ad a bad accident on the road below. Too bad there ain't a Bobby around to maik a report.

"Now, good sense told the three of us men in this 'ere carrier that mothers gonna come a-lookin' for her chick to see how she come out with you! Our Boys antitank rifle can penetrate her skin by five or six mm's. Her skin's not too thick for the Boys, from what we heard about her when Mr. Hitler did in Poland last year. From up here at a hundred fifty yards, we can put our five-shot magazine inside her hull a'fore she knows she's a target. Some of those will stay inside her, rollin' around and round till they bury themselves in soft targets, like Mom's crew. Of course, all this works unless she spies us first and gets off her cannon a'fore we get off our Boys.

"I think, Leftenant, you better get down where you were, down below us. You can't do nothing up here to help unless you think struttin' around like a captain, directing a helmsman at the wheel, will help."

Giles jumped down from the back of the carrier and went to the edge of the cut in the hill, which was about ten feet away from the carrier. He stepped and slid down the fifteen or so feet to the road, using the stock of his rifle and the heels of his jodhpur boots in balancing himself as he did.

He then decided to post himself just east of the right angle of the turn-in at the T intersection of the Serre Cemetery Road, with his rifle at the ready, in case some need or opportunity presented itself. He had to expose himself sufficiently to see north on d919 for twenty or thirty yards, so he could fire into the slots for vision in the front of the scout car. His sniper sight should give him the ability if he was fast enough with the moving target. At least it would make him feel he was contributing.

So he stood frozen in front of his cycle, where it rested against the cut of the hill and his right foot and partially lifted leg. He held his rifle at sort of a relaxed port arms, ready to assume the position he'd held before the two-seater got destroyed by the Bren gun carrier. And then he waited for the sound of the enemy's rear-end engine coming down the d919; he expected its motor, a rear-engine type would make a low growling sound, like a much larger vehicle. He later came to know it was a SDKFZ 222, with crew of three, possibly with a twenty-millimeter auto cannon.

XXXII

AS EXPLAINED EARLIER, the sergeant commanding the Bren gun carrier had been two or more miles east on the Serre road before the destruction of the German cycle. He stationed the carrier on a field of higher ground, between cemeteries. His purpose was to enhance his ability to scan the eastern horizon with his field glasses for German activities. He first noticed the large two- to three-man BMW 75 cycle while he was reconnoitering, and later, just before meeting Leftenant Giles Lambert, would have the pleasure of decimating the same. He had seen the silhouette shots of it passed around among the officers and noncom ranks, along with those of other German armament, including the light recon scout car, SDKFZ 221. It had a possible twenty-millimeter cannon or a MG34 machine gun. This was the same alternate weapon emplacement as the SDKFZ 222 commonly had, instead of the twenty-millimeter cannon.

The sergeant, at that time, decided to remove his vehicle back to the intersection with d919, where there was some elevated shelter, which provided some hope of camouflage from the north and the east. So he had returned to where he and his crew would later destroy the German cycle and two of its occupants. A third man of its group was thrown into a ditch area and not dead but broken. This was later determined, after the next episode involving the "mother hen," better referred to as the SDKFZ 222. He was more than confident that the Bren and Boys could handle whatever arose if he could commence the firefight. After all, he was a "twenty-fiver" and knew enough to have been an officer, if he had "come down" from Oxford or Cambridge and been from the "right class," of course. Well, at least "on parade" he was the "color sergeant," and he was proud to wear the red sash and tassels and frequently be "the officer on parade" for his company.

The sergeant was thinking that he had been so close to retirement and the garden in the rear of his little house in Belfast. He was most ready to settle with waking up every morning to have tea with his wife of twenty-six years. Barracks life, the boredom of peace time, interrupted by spasmodic tent life on the northwest frontier of India and—oh, sweet God in heaven! The treacherous Pathans of that area always reminded him of Kipling's veracity about them. "We always felt the need of armor on our back side. Mean and sneaky Moslems, they were!" Once again Kipling was right—the women were more evil than the men. "That's because, if you beat a dog enough and it has to take it, and its death to turn on its vicious master, and the low life turns you loose to kill another, oh you will!" That's why Kipling said to keep the last cartridge for yourself! Pathans turn their prisoners over to their women who would start by carving up the parts of their own men that they hate the most and then, after filleting that, gouge out the eyes and see that the victim dies very slowly over a barbecue pit! Yes, to bring out a killer animal in a person, start him off in life as a baby Muslim!

Well, the Germans ain't no better. They pick their vicious leaders and follow their orders and use that for the excuse of why they do it, to get off their petard when they're beaten! "Pickelhaube Willie" was the worst of Queen Victoria's family, for certain. Could have been because of his shriveled arm or maybe because of that cunning devil, Bismarck! Never give them a fair chance 'cause they don't understand no Marquis of Queensberry Rules. I started with them bastards when I joined the Welsh Guards in 1915 when "The Welsh" got started as the last household regiment. I wanted to get in ever so bad because it was brand new and all the officers and other ranks were from the other four infantry guard regiments to fill it out, you see. Good lord, I'll never forget the look of him, the first regimental sergeant major, handsome tall devil who transferred over to pass the "spit and polish" to the young buggers and make 'um into ruddy guardsman from their "toes to their shakos." And by the lord, he did it. He did it in a year, too! His name was, and I'll never forget him, RSM (Regimental Sergeant Major) William Stevenson, MBE, DCM, and MM. Every bloody clod of a "lifer" knows it's that kind of a man who makes a regiment, along with his cadre of noncoms. The officers can't do it! They're too busy with their balls and clubs and stables of horses and both fast and slow women, looking their best for each other. They're smart enough, but they never realize that we make the regiments. We just wear them like the flowers they wear in their buttonholes when they're in mufti, just strollin' down St. James with their furled umbrellas and bowler hats!

And so his ruminating thoughts continued in an erratic stream, reasoning and speaking in the same vein as the guardsman walking his post in Gilbert and Sullivan's *Iolanthe*, making several questionable postulations upon which he based his speculative conclusions.

Come to think of it, he mused further, it was a good thing that the family dropped them Saxe-Coburge and other German names, like Battenburg, for Windsor and Mountbatten. After two hundred years, we *expect* they are English. If my fifth form teacher was right, George I was half Stuart. Everybody knows that a Scott is an Irishman on the way to being an Englishman anyway!

All the while, this sergeant of the Welsh Guard followed developing eventualities with his field glasses.

XXXIII

"AT LAST, IT'S coming across the field as we thought it would!" shouted the carrier sergeant, loud enough for both his crew and Giles below them to hear. He estimated its speed to be thirty-five to forty miles an hour. Its profile carried the open white Balkenkreuz to the rear and below its turret. It had the upside-down *y* and three dots in yellow to show which panzer division it was and the platoon number, as well. The Heinies liked everything to be in order!

The turret was an open top with flip-open, wire-filled doors, which, when closed, would fend off hand grenades. There was the driver and, in this case, two other men. The turret slots revealed a fearsome-looking auto cannon, and a next slot showed an MG34 machine gun. It was a worse scenario then he'd detected earlier, with his field glasses. He needed to take out the two gunners before they spotted him, and so he fired first. Their heads were unprotected except for their *stahlhelm*, which couldn't stop direct shots to their heads. They operated those weapons standing up—wonderful! One more problem, stupidly overlooked! The wreckage of the BMW motorcycle lay spread in the road and directly in front of the recon vehicle, as it would travel south on d919. If the driver or crew saw it before it came into the carriers' range, then their cannon had a better reach than they had in the carrier.

"Men, we're getting off this bloody hill! We are going behind this cemetery and come in behind them on the d919 and catch them while they are ruddy smashed from looking at what we did to their BMW and its men. Then you follow the orders I'm going

The French Lieutenant and the King of Rome

to give you. Remember, their weapons are facing their front. All we must do is track from the rear. Maybe we can nail them from the rear before they even reach the road."

As the German recon car passed to the north of the first cemetery on the Serre road, headed west, at right angles to d919, the Bren gun carrier was off the high ground bordering the south side of the same cemetery, headed for the rear of it and knocking over headstones in its way as it headed north to swing in behind the German car. It was moving at top speed, about thirty miles per hour on its tank-like treads, but he remembered from the profile description that the German car couldn't move at top speed across open fields, as it could on roads.

"Get the Boys shots below the turret to avoid its armament, and get your full clip in when I say, 'Fire!' And keep on firing into the body. We need to take out those two gunners!" He ordered the third crewman to have the second belt of thirty cartridges ready to feed into the Bren gun and the substitute barrel ready, in case of overheating. He knew it was up to himself to kill or wound that driver, to make his recon vehicle careen out of control.

The Bren gun carrier got within two hundred yards of the rear of the scout car, which was about to start its left turn onto d919 to head south when the British sergeant gave his order to fire. The German crewmen were shot through their heads and chests from the rear, and Giles, from his post, probably never achieved his target of the driver's front shutters.

The Bren gun carrier rammed the rear left side of the scout recon car, which it continued to push, as the Boys rifle continued its fire into the car without interruption. Finally, the scout car was pushed over onto its right side. Petrol was pouring out of its underside. The entry hatch door was on the left side of the vehicle, between the rear of the front left fender and some fixed metal boxes attached to the upside body of the car, as it now lay on roadway, d919.

The hatch door was being pushed open, directly skyward. There emerged, half-oil-covered hands, followed by a scraped face with a bloody forehead, exhibiting a dazed and yet arrogant scowl. Smoke and fumes were rolling from the open top of the car, as it now lay with its right side flat against the road. This was the driver, who was attempting to escape from the now burning scout car. The other two occupants were obviously dead inside.

It required that the driver-commander get both of his elbows over the edge of the hatch and then lift himself by thrusting his body upward with all his strength and then crawling out the rest of the way. To accomplish this extrication, he had to be essentially uninjured. He wasn't expecting any assistance from the Bren carrier people, nor would he get any. All their weapons were on him, including the sergeant's sidearm, a pistol of previous issue and a reliable old friend of the sergeant's from "wars past." This was obvious to any observer, by the manner in which he casually trained it on the *Unteroffizier*, a lance sergeant. He also wore that peculiar thing the Germans called a "Portapee," or tassel, wrapped around and suspended from the handle of his bayonet, which signified that he was an officer aspirant. He could work his way "up" after a base number of years and, of course, success in the various levels in between. The German enlisted grades did not carry any side arms, except a bayonet. Oddly enough, he was not wearing the prescribed new black uniform for mobile units, perhaps because it was reserved for "tankers only" and not support people, like scouts and cyclists. He was, in addition, displaying a holstered pistol (which appeared to be a Mauser 1934 model). The German had dropped himself to the ground, from the trapdoor opening, being signaled to do so by the color sergeant, who waived the muzzle of his pistol in a decisive downward motion. The elemental signal could not be misunderstood by anyone subject to potential death at its unpredictable discharge.

The German's Mauser was promptly removed from its holster, handed upward, and surrendered, grip first, and then his bayonet, as he was ordered by the color sergeant to do. He received them in his free hand and ordered the German on board the carrier from the rear, where his wrists were bound in back of him and his boots were removed, for further security.

Giles was returning up the road on foot with the third German. He was acting as a crutch for him as he apparently could put no weight on his right leg and had his right arm over Giles's shoulder. His left arm was hanging loose at his side, and his tunic was shredded where he must have landed on the left shoulder and arm. As a consequence, Giles was holding him up, acting as the German's right leg, as thy hobbled up the road toward the carrier.

Giles called out that it was the third German who had been on the back of the cycle from which he was thrown clear and unhit by the Bren gunfire. "Oh, Christ and Joseph too, we're goin' to be the bloody constable's wagon!" hollered back the color sergeant.

"Sorry, Sergeant. I couldn't leave him or shoot him, so I brought him to you to worry with. Is it not that which sergeants are for? Nursemaids?"

"I didn't know you was a French comedian, Leftenant! A regular Charles what's-his-name, you are! 'Cavalier,' was it? Ah, to be sure ! Well, stack him in the back with the other Jerry. He's in for a terrible ride, I don't doubt. Damned, to be sure! These are the guard's first prisoners of this bloody war. I can just hear the warrant now."

"Well, you took them; now you can make full arrangements to guard them, Color Sergeant."

Giles and one of the carrier crew helped the German *Gefreiter* (private first class) up the rear of the carrier, with much pain and discomfort to him. The buffering by English knapsacks under his left shoulder and arm and right leg were all that could be done for him, as he lay on the floor. The color sergeant released the wrists of the *Unteroffizier* (mit portepee), or officer candidate, on nothing more than an oath of honor concocted upon his oath to Hitler and the Wehrmacht by the British sergeant for two reasons: the other German needed caring for all the time, and secondly he would assign the Boys rifleman to train his sidearm on the *Unteroffizier* all the time. He also knew that all German military were loyal and obedient, and the habit had to be strong in a twenty-five- or twenty-six-year-old who had a Reiter Kreuze second class and a wound badge, probably from the Polish campaign. What he couldn't understand was why a *Gefreiter* who was near thirty, by the looks, and had both the Reiter Kreuze first and second class, the assault badge, and the close combat badge was not the *Unteroffizier*, instead of the scout car driver.

XXXIV

HERE IS THE unbelievable story, as explained to him in a few English words and much sign language by the German *Unteroffizier*; he was assisted by such German as the sergeant learned while stationed on the Rhine for a period after the first war:

The *Gefreiter* was something in German called a *"Mischlinge"*—that is, a German who is unfortunate enough to have a Jewish forbearer. The percentage of Jewish blood determines not your degree of acceptability but survivability. That is, the better your Aryan ancestors were, the better the chance of keeping your closest Jewish ancestor and siblings out of a concentration camp and, finally, death ("Holocaust") camps. Forget about aunts and uncles and cousins: they wouldn't be included.

Hitler made the final determination of who made the "cut." He took the time to examine photos and body measurements. If Hitler thought you passed, he could order a Blood Certificate, which made you acceptable as an Aryan and sometimes a limited number of your family. The army and navy took about 150,000 *Mischlinges* between 1934 and 1945. Though Hitler stridently persecuted Jews from his inception, the records of ancestry were inconclusive unless the Mischlinge admitted his background. Many didn't know because the Jewish ancestor had converted to Christianity a generation or so before the birth of the Mischlinge. Hitler had the irrational conclusion that Jewish blood was an infectious disease that made a person corrupt beyond purification, and such a person with as little as 25 percent would destroy all Aryans around them.

The Unteroffizier also said that in their battalion they had two. Often their own army officers tried to help them avoid detection. A certain technical American company provided them with the hardware and know-how to master it until the United States got into the war. By 1940–41, Hitler had a punch-card system that enabled him to find men who had lied on racial statements required earlier. It also enabled the Nazis to find and organize listings for the Jews and dispersal of them to the death camps.

In his unit the other soldiers knew but kept it a secret, but the Mischlinges didn't know that they knew! Also he said his captain told him there were many, many experienced generals, a field marshal, an admiral, naval officers, and endless colonels, majors, captains, and lieutenants. Mischlinge and Jewish combat records were among the best. No Mischlinge enlisted man was supposed to be above Gefreiter. After a successful French campaign, the Mischlinges would be discharged, and what would happen to them and their families could only be guessed.

Why did they fight? And do it for the Nazis? Many had different reasons, but the usual reasons were to try to stay alive and keep their close family members of Jewish blood alive too.

When asked by the color sergeant why the men who knew a "soldaten vas ein Juden" would accept him, the answer of the Unteroffizier was "Du beist ein goodt soldaten. Unt du kampf mit mire! Unt du biest mein brutte!" There is no relationship closer than one combat soldier for another; if you are a good soldier and you fight with me, risk your life for me, and I mine for yours—you will always be my brother! The color sergeant was an old, old soldier, and he had many, many brothers; some living, many dead—different bands of brothers, but all with the same creed.

Giles was standing fecklessly in the rear of the gun carrier, where he had helped the German prisoner being placed on his back. He had also aided the German sergeant in placing the knapsacks as forms of pillows beneath him, to help ameliorate the pain of jostling he was bound to suffer as the carrier lumbered back to its base at Izel-les-Hameaux. Giles was unconsciously dallying, while his mind and body were leeching away the tension that had consumed him from the battle. His self-doubt about his courage and fear of "freezing" when immediate response was called for were "scotched." He felt himself an objective observer, overseeing his own performance during the vicious and quick violence of the dual encounter with the cycle and the scout car. He was immensely relieved to be freed of his fear of being incapable of his desired response. Every man must have this fear, he knew, but all did not have the opportunity to relieve themselves of it, as he had this day.

However, his encounter with death was another matter. He couldn't abide the shock of seeing those two dead Germans lying in the road. In a form of bizarre estrangement from reality, he metamorphosed them into mere dolls, left as broken playthings on the floor, abandoned by the child who owned them as he was rushed off to bed, later to be straightened out by his mother when she placed them on the shelf with the others of their kind.

The two left in the burning scout car were never seen by him but revoltingly smelled like roasting flesh. He avoided thinking of them at all, except that he found himself consciously breathing through his mouth to gainsay the wretched odor. The effect upon him of these violent deaths made him acutely aware of his fastidiousness. He knew delicacy could be no part of his foreseeable future, viewing his life as it now began to unfold. His life, as well, promised to be totally unpredictable: he, himself, a toy to be broken, destroyed, pulverized, unidentifiable, or consumed by relentless fate: perhaps not to be allowed to "wind down" and expire at the end of his natural life, as our God inexorably provided, but by a calculated fate beyond his control, dictated by some unknown Valhalla monster called "War."

Giles's contemplative meanderings were interrupted by the color sergeant's abrupt address: "Time for you to be on your way, Leftenant. The morning's almost gone, and you've a distance to cover, and an unpredictable day it is, sir."

"Yes, Sergeant, I'm going to trot down to my cycle and rev it up and strike out for Amiens, Beauvais, and home. What is between Paris and me—I hate to think after the morning we've had!"

He dismounted the carrier and started down the road, first by the wreck of the scout car, which was more smoldering then ablaze. It was likely still to explode from fuel, if not from ignition of the ammunition—perhaps both together. The color sergeant was pulling the carrier onto the road, headed in a northerly direction for his motor base. Giles was several feet north of the wreck but still close enough to be effected by the blast. The sergeant called out after Giles in an impatient voice, "Move along, Leftenant! I'd like to hear your cycle roll over before we take off. It's getting bloody dangerous where we're sitting. Please double-time, will you, lad." The last was said in a fatherly tone, rather typical of a senior noncommissioned officer to a fledgling subaltern, for whom he was felt to be responsible by field grade officers, and indeed, felt himself to be, as a guide and an initiator into combat.

Giles began to run as fast as he could, past the two dead Germans and their motorcycle and finally to the T intersection of the Serre road and his cycle. He pulled it away from the earth wall that was supporting it, shoved his rifle in place, buckled the strap of his leather helmet under his chin, and then hit the starter and jumped his pedals. The expected roar of his motor reassured him, and he pushed forward and swung left in an arc, onto d919, headed south to Paris.

XXXV

HE THOUGHT ABOUT how quiet the road had become. It would be obvious that anyone headed south would have fled back, and none would follow as they approached the carnage ahead of them. Ahead of him were the villages of Mailly, Contay, and Allonville, in that order, and then Amiens, according to Clive's map. At Amiens, he expected to encounter a large concentration of French troops massing to defend Paris by using the south bank of the Somme River as a line of defense. If an officer in authority told him to assume a command, he expected to stand and fight, as ordered. He hoped beyond all hope that Clive was wrong and that troops from the south of the Maginot Line had been transported there to make a vital stand for France. He no longer feared a loss of his life, but only French defeat!

He soon began to encounter large numbers of refugees of all descriptions and all varieties of vehicles. He now began to move at a snail's pace. He even turned off the motor and wheeled the bike but not successfully because of its weight and the assemblage of items he had attached to it. Autos were breaking down for all imaginable reasons. Some people's choices of things to carry as treasure were inconceivable. Some children had lost their parents. He had in mind a Dutch boy of eight or nine who tearfully was asking in Dutch for help in finding them. Close by Allonville, by the side of the road, sat a small French girl holding her doll to her breast while she waited for her family to somehow find her. It would have been so much better, he thought, for these people to have stayed where they were in the beginning and chance the worst, at least to know what would happen to one another, rather than to flee madly across different countries and end up lost to one another, possibly forever.

The road was uneven and bumpy, causing him continuing discomfort in the groin, buttocks, and back as he proceeded along, making constant jolting stops and starts. He estimated his average progression at perhaps five miles per hour. He realized that the road—now jammed with an indescribable hodge-podge of horses attached to wagons, filled with families and household goods; with cars of every description, model, and year, both on and off the roadway; walking refugees of all classes, sexes, and ages, in all sorts of physical condition, from northeastern France, Belgium, and of course, Holland—would continue its flow of humanity and its detritus to Paris and endlessly beyond. For this reason, he resolved to press on for as far as his physical reserves would allow.

He felt numb and exhausted from constantly avoiding collisions with those persons and objects surrounding him. The eyes of his fellow travelers were vacuous, and their faces, gaunt, seemingly without emotion (unless, of course, their hopeless state of reverie was interrupted by a spoken question, requiring attention, or the tug of one of their children at their arm or hand).

There were even servants along with employers in some of the more "posh" car models. Those of this class always seemed to have a second or winter home in the south; the others seemed without destination but were simply seeking succor from the Germans, from war and its unpredictable consequences. They, none of them, had any true lasting food supply for such a venture. Those without clear destination seemed to be just wandering aimlessly! This merely confirmed his conclusions made in Le Grand Place, in Arras. But that crowd of refugees was, of course, still to his rear. Therefore their thoughts and conditions were, more or less, endemic to all of them. How many displaced persons? Perhaps to be millions!

His wristwatch indicated the time to be 3:00 p.m. The weather was continuing to be fair, as fortunately it had been from the time

The French Lieutenant and the King of Rome

he had arisen at headquarters, this morning, outside of Arras. He passed through the village of Allonville under the continuing constraints of the road, which had existed and continued to exist with wearying continuity. In the last three or more hours, he had managed to adjust himself to the creeping, relentless, boring repetition of the inch-worm speed of travel with which all were moving. The incessant, manifested tension and physical discomfort of those he passed on the way and those that replaced them as he did required him to turn a deaf ear or, in the alternative, grind his teeth in anger at his stultifying helplessness: all this, as he sped up and slowed down in a relentless pattern of hop scotching around those blocking him directly.

His thoughts were turned to concern about his consumption of gas and whether he could make it to Paris if he continued at this rate of travel. He simply could not test his ability to drive off to the side of the road and in the fields bordering it until he crossed over the Somme River at Amiens. He knew this area well from crossing it frequently, in traveling to the channel ports and crossing to England for school at Rugby and to visit his grandfather. When young, he did so frequently with his parents, and thereafter, alone. Amiens was no more than a created series of islands in the marshland that is the Somme River area around it.

Now, a series of small viaducts or bridges, connecting irregular-sized areas of ground, formed the town over the marshes, which, as a result, created the crossing to the south and Beauvais and, thereafter, Paris. The "hard" ground was the heart of the town, containing an impressive, but approximately eleventh- to twelfth-century Gothic-style cathedral, somewhat superior to Notre Dame of Paris. Those of course were the spires he noted on the road, just before reaching Amiens.

And now that the cathedral of Amiens's spires had come into view, he thought that, once across to the other bank of the Somme, he would be free of his geographical hurdle. His present route of d919 converted quickly into what was then Boulevard Roubaix, and after a temporary thinning of the masses of refugees on the route, he came to national route d1001, which would take him on as the Paris road. However, the present, simple roundabout did not exist but instead a series of branch roads, leading in different directions, which were not marked in all cases, to Abbeville, Rouen, Dury, and other, lesser places, as well. Many of his companions of the road seemed to hesitate and cluster at various intersections of streets, not knowing which way to turn. This clearly establish for him that when they had left their homes, they had lacked a destination. Their state was much as it had been when they, or similar people, had been occupying the two major squares in Arras the night before. Some few shops were open here, doubtless out of the need to protect them from ruthless stealing from the unwelcome visitors or an inability to board the fronts to bar their entry. Some few probably stayed open out of consideration and kindness for their needs.

Giles hoped to reach Beauvais that evening of the eighteenth, to rest and eat. But now he realized that he had little chance of gaining a hotel room or a restaurant and would have to eat from his meager supplies and sleep along the fields at the side of the road, perhaps with one of his pistols at hand and sleeping with one eye open. He had his canister water but needed to find potable water from any likely source, such as a well or cistern, after bridging the Somme River.

At the rate he was traveling, he estimated that he was covering twenty miles a day at most. This meant almost two more days to Beauvais, which finally determined was about thirty-five miles south of Amiens. He sorely missed the Michelin map he left in the MG: it was superior to any other for completeness. If he could only find a farm road parallel to the main road he was on…but how? If he could, he could leave the traffic and refugees behind, divert to it cross-country and return to the main road before or after reaching Beauvais. The only solution would be to watch for a substantial-looking turning from the main road, looking like it was such a road and not simply a "way" leading to a farmhouse.

While mulling over these thoughts, he was crossing the Somme and almost on the south bank. He had managed to dodge the crowded conditions as he progressed southward, by weaving in and out and around people and obstacles at a persistent, low rate of speed over this last short span. He continued on as before, with the same interruptions to his progress.

They were caused by the same things but better managed by him. He gave these things as little concentrated thought as possible, trying to direct his thinking elsewhere: thus avoiding emotional involvement due to the pathos of their situation that he was forced to share with them.

He was yet wondering about the possibility of a secondary road that would get him to Paris, thus avoiding the continuation of this creeping, unendurable torment. By eight o'clock that evening, he was about halfway to Beauvais, much to his surprise. Instead of two days, it had taken approximately four hours to reach it when the road out of Amiens widened, probably because it was on the main road to and near Paris. However, the roadway was just as occupied as before. He believed they had been very fortunate in missing air attacks (probably because the Germans lacked an airfield near enough for Stukas to strike and return to base).

He had been riding along the edge of the road, or on what constituted the shoulder of the road, since leaving the bridge on this south side of the Somme River. This had surprisingly given him the ability to continue, slowly but consistently, at a low speed. Exhaustion was rapidly setting in, and he urgently needed a place to sleep along the road. He wasn't passing any houses at the road's edge. Therefore, he had little choice but to pick a field alongside it and cross the area to see if it looked safe.

With this in mind, he pushed into a field that was on the east side of the road. He uncomfortably followed a furrow, laid by a farmer in spring planting, which led upward to a small copse of bushes and trees. It was apparently surrounded by ploughed furrows on the three sides that he could see from his moving cycle.

Jay Macey Rosenblum

The ground under his wheels was soft but, thankfully, solid enough to allow him to keep the cycle upright, with frequent foot shifts from his peddles (or "pegs" if you prefer) to the tops of furrows when the wheels slid from side to side in an occasional, troublesome furrow. This Norton was not intended for rough country but obviously for roads or, at most, for pastures.

XXXVI

THE COPSE WAS about fifteen hundred feet from the motorway he had been on and might very well provide him with the night cover and safety he was seeking, for the few hours of rest he sought. Upon reaching it, he pushed himself on his cycle into the heavier brush that was the first buffer of it and a few feet more toward its perceivable center. This gave him the camouflage he felt he needed for security from the menace of unforeseen, unwelcome intruders. He dismounted and placed his bike against a tree so that it faced the road and walked through the copse. He gazed downhill to discover that a stone house, with fireplace smoke (no doubt rising from a cooking fire), was in a shielded little valley below.

He considered whether it could represent a risk of any kind, and he quickly concluded that it was the farmer's house whose land he was on, and in the morning he could properly explain his intrusion and seek water and food and pay for the same, as would be most appropriate to the farmer and his family.

Although he had showered the night before, he felt dirty and dusty from the day's travail and needed to create some form of latrine with the small shovel that was part of the cycle's kit. This he did some feet away, near the edge of the copse. He had to remember to fill it in before leaving. He had the requisite base issue paper, which would "make a man" of anyone unfortunate enough to have to submit to it.

He slipped out of the British coverall he was wearing and unbuttoned his vareuse (jacket) but left his holster and French pistol under his left arm. He rolled the coverall in to an unsatisfactory substitute for a pillow and laid it under his head as he stretched out on his back on top of a grassy area next to his bike, knowing full well that he wouldn't roll over because of the discomfort of the holster and pistol. He remembered to snap the top holster strap over the pistol to secure it inside the holster so that it didn't fall out of place and remained where he needed it at all times. That's the last thing he remembered until the bottom of his right foot was kicked by Roger, the farmer, at approximately sunup the following morning.

Giles first saw them when he had opened his eyes with a start, not being familiar previously with the "foot kick" method of awakening. However, his period at the Rugby school in England familiarized him with forms of awakening more hair-raising and exceptionally vile, reserved for "new boys" such as he. This new method gave him redolence of his school days, but not a yearning for them, based upon this single, jarring experience alone.

The first view of his unwelcoming hosts was while he was prone, with the sun behind their heads, giving them a somewhat otherworldly aspect, which was quickly amended as he rose to his feet. Once on an equal level, he first noted that the whole lot were uniformly dressed in blue de Nime cotton overalls with cotton shirts of different colors, probably home sewn. He thought, "Their faces are friendly, and so shall mine be," upon which observation, he beamed his most amicable smile, as they then did, in return!

Neither Roger nor his wife Marianne, nor his two sons (one, six or seven, and the other, a teenager) seemed hostile, though they all seemed to feign that the intrusion by him was something uncalled for and required substantial explanation. They were well armed for this, the occasion of his intrusion. Roger and wife were each with single-barrel shotguns. These were probably last presented in anger by his father to defend against Von Schlieffen and his frustrated plan of 1914–18 and in 1870–72 by his grandfather, when Pickelhaube Willie Hohenzollern "unt" Bismarck and his lot of Germans visited Versailles, as uninvited guests. Giles didn't feel intimidated, but the time for speaking English was over, and in his best form of native French, he advised them of his facts and that he had to reach French HQ in Vincennes (Paris) as quickly as possible, with orders to do so, that he was in need of a speedy route to evade the refugees that were "inundating" (no, "filling") the roads so that the military were blocked from speedy use of them. "Do you know of one without refugee traffic?" he asked. Roger answered, "Yes, just south of here is the intersection of Breteuil-Sur-Noye, which will take you south to the St. Denis entrance to Paris. I doubt there is much traffic on it because it's not a good road but full of ruts and holes."

In short order, he had received the hoped-for road information and an invitation for food and water and found his incipient hosts to be likeable and patriotic. He whiled away over two hours with them, while he washed up and used their outhouse, ate breakfast, and added to his gas tank from the supply he was carrying, which he had received from the corporal at the carpool center before departing.

It was about nine o'clock when he returned to the copse where he'd spent the previous night. He stowed the bread and water received from Marianne and took the advice of Roger with regard to the road he was about to take.

He repeated the trip he had previously made, to the motor road, and then, when he came to it, diverted to the road to Creil, a small village on Route 916, a back road that, after Creil, would lead to Chantilly, famous for its racetrack, and then through the valley of d'Oise to St. Denis, the industrial town that was the north suburb of Paris. The road was as rough as was promised by Roger.

XXXVII

THE REFUGEES HAD not found it in any sizeable number because it was a road that led nowhere. But it did—it went to Paris! By entering from its suburb, St. Denis, to the north of Paris, he would avoid the refugees coming in on the main road, Auto Route 1, entering more to the east. They would be intending to go south through the Orleans Gate to the south of France or the railroad stations, Gare d'Austerlitz or Gare de Lyon, which were on either side of the Seine and somewhat east of Notre Dame. And to do so, they would become lost in a bevy of streets, squares, and boulevards. Whereas he would take Rue de St. Denis by the Gare du Nord, to Boulevard de Magenta to the Place of the Republic and then to Boulevard Voltaire and along it to the Place de La Nation and finally, with a right turn, onto Rue de Fauborg to the apartment and Elle.

Among the few that were on the road that he noted as he passed were two soldiers, appearing to be infantrymen. They were in disheveled uniforms from travel or duty. It was hard for Giles to determine. They seemed to be having a disturbance with a family in a Citroen, which was standing idle in the middle of the roadway, several feet ahead of Giles's motorcycle.

The two soldiers had a young girl with them who appeared to be in no better condition than her companions. She stood apart from the soldiers and had a frightened demeanor both in body language and facial expression. Giles noted these things as he approached the edge of the place of confrontation. No blows had

The French Lieutenant and the King of Rome

been struck yet, but it appeared from the position of the soldiers, one between the driver's door and the back of middle-aged, male driver and the other facing the driver with his arm raised and hand clenched into a fist that it was about to happen. In the car was a woman, obviously his wife, and a young boy in the rear seat; both were crying and screaming fearfully. Giles pulled to a stop, identified himself as a French officer on a mission, and demanded to know why they were separated from their units and why they were in the company of this young woman. She immediately expressed her position as being their prisoner, being provided food in return for sexual bondage. From the regimental numbers on the collars of their vereuses, it was clear that both were deserting members of a regiment of the Second Army.

This was the reservist army that broke and ran on May10 and 11, allowing the Germans to breach the defenses and cross at Verdun and Luxembourg. The French Ninth Army to the north of the Second Army was no better. As a result the German panzer divisions broke through there and also came through the Ardennes Forest (which the French General Staff said they couldn't possibly do, and so they placed their poorest troops there since no defense would be necessary). The best French armies were behind Belgium and Holland, where their high command had been suckered in, believing the Germans were going to repeat their losing strategy of WWI. Actually the French high command had full notice of the old plans captured from a plane crash, which ended up at French HQ, where they thought it was planted to confuse them into rethinking their strategy. The French high command had ignored the secret information they had received probably because they preferred the inertia of avoiding the mammoth changes requiring enormous troop movements and battle plans. The French ignored the campaign in Poland, in which the Germans had used the panzers and the lightning war, and refused to conceive of Blitzkreig. In fact, the panzer tank corps in France were mostly composed of Czechoslovakian tanks given to the Germans when they were forced to surrender to Germany by France and Britain at Munich, to provide "peace in our time" in 1938, to use the infamous words of then British prime minister Neville Chamberlin.

The road being rough, the driver explained to Giles over the objections of the corporal, the two soldiers had jumped in front of his vehicle as it approached them, to stop the car, and when he did, the soldiers had attempted to steal the car from them by force. The corporal, having an apparently vicious disposition and still believing himself in control of the three, had attempted to grab the girl by her arm, as she blurted out her sad tale in a loud voice, so as to be heard above the cacophony of voices, while he was steadfastly denying the driver's rendition of the incident.

In the meanwhile Giles unbuttoned the top of his coveralls with his right hand and reached to his pistol in his shoulder holster, pulled it forth, pointed at the corporal, and explained that as an officer he had the judgmental right to execute the two of them as deserters and was about to do so unless they could show him their orders to be where they were at the moment. As Dr. Samuel Johnson, an English lexicographer and savant, had said approximately two centuries before, "Nothing clears a man's mind so much as the immediate threat of his execution." The two deserters bore clear aspects of terror. Their faces paled with shock.

They manifested soundless horror from their gaping mouths, which were unable to form sounds at the stark realization that the officer had the cool, composed look and precise, stony enunciation in his words that found them jointly guilty and ordered them executed, forthwith! The French term for the officers' diction was "au bout des levres," said "at the end of his lips," to people who were too low to be human, below the caste system—a proper style for dealing with deserters!

Both soldiers admitted as true everything the vehicle driver had said, admitted their guilt, plead extenuating circumstances—that is, that they were deserted by their section in the middle of the night and that the girl was a liar. Giles, of course, was not taken in by their story, but he also felt skittish about his own military status and squeamish about fulfilling his threat of invoking rough

French military justice. He thought it too much. Even the British ordered deserters "shot at dawn" after a court was held the night before (quite cursory and no appeal was allowed, even if the court authority was a battalion grade or lower). But then, he thought that the British were an unforgiving lot, for example, the "shot at dawn" group were buried in the same cemeteries as "the honored dead" but in a separate section and listed as "shot at dawn," so their relatives were certain to be embarrassed on visiting the gravesite. "Oh, yes, here is great-great uncle John Jones, Pvt. The bounder and lily-livered coward who was drafted and sent here as a soldier in November 1916 and refused to go over the top in the face of seeing that all the men who did were shot dead as soon as they stepped above the parapet of their trench, killed by relentless German machine-gun fire, machine-gun fire that was supposed to have been destroyed by ineffective French 75's shell fire."

One thing about the cannonading: it lifted the German wire well off the ground, causing it to drop back down in a jumbled mess that wire cutters couldn't solve in the few seconds granted the British who were fortunate enough to reach it before the machine guns hungrily mowed them down. Well, Giles thought, unless the lead in the bullet that kills you makes a difference, the end result was the same. Giles also thought that reflections upon the Cemetery Road he had traveled and the multiple others in the Somme region wouldn't solve his present problem.

But who would forget that the British commander of the Somme River front was none other than "pinch bottle Haig," one of the members of "The Imperial General Staff," which was referred to by the kaiser's General Staff as "the Donkeys."

Giles remembered his visit to the castle with his mother as a five-year-old. Remarkably, there is on display in Edinburgh castle, a mounted bronze rendition of him as a renowned hero and horseman. He was most renowned for the Somme River campaign in which he and his second in command, Gen. Rowlandson, were responsible for the loss of over 57,000 men on July 1, 1916, alone! And, incredibly, a total of 420,000 men before it was over on

November 6, 1916. Neither of the generals ever went over the top of a parapet, nor even stayed on the front line!

Giles quickly rendered his judgment. The vehicle would leave with its original owners and take the girl with them to Paris. The two soldiers would wait here where they were until Giles and the vehicle were out of their sight, and if he saw them again, he would simply execute them. Since they had no weapons, which he had earlier determined, they would most likely happily concur with his findings.

XXXVIII

HE WAS PLEASED with his military, marionette-like pose in the matter, but he hadn't forgotten his shock and his incapacity to mentally process the two dead "dolls" from Germany near the Serre road, on the d917, just the day before. Also, he was uncomfortably conscious of his own rather fragile and class-preferred separation from British HQ, to which however he felt entitled. It was the way of the world! Even the French commies and liberals had their privileged nobility, maintained at the expense of their people and privileged at the people's expense.

He continued down the road, alongside the Citroen, toward St. Denis and Paris. Occasional glances over his shoulder established that the two deserters were not closing the gap on them but were remaining carefully behind them. His present idea was to stop "riding shotgun" upon reaching the edge of St. Denis and then ride like the wind for Elle and home. He would attempt to reach headquarters at Vincennes by the intelligence phone number he'd received upon being dispatched to Arras and British HQ. Thus he could determine its status and discover if there was someone to whom he could actually report!

He looked inside the vehicle at his side and noted that all of the occupants seemed to be getting on well, so he assumed they were making a plan for parting from the girl on arrival. "Good," he concluded, "all's well that ends well."

He waved good-bye to the occupants of the car as he sped up, passing though the Porte de Clignancourt, following it in a convoluted manner by Le Gare du Nord. The streets were jam-packed with people, who were detraining from the overrun areas in the north of France, Belgium, and some from Holland. He felt fortunate to reach Boulevard Magenta and escape the turmoil. He finally got across the Right Bank, reached La Place de La Republique, and made his turn down Rue St. Antoine (which became Rue de Fauborg).

XXXIX

HE TURNED INTO the alley and then the inner courtyard of his building, left his cycle in between two autos, rushed through the rear doors, and careened up the stairs. Before he reached the doors to the apartment, he had a sinking feeling that she might still be at the hospital. He didn't wish to knock but to give her the surprise of her life and the pleasure of bringing it to her. He nearly had to strip, looking for his keys. He felt totally disheveled with his British coverall jumper down around his jodhpur boots, his leather helmet still strapped under his chin, and goggles pushed up on his forehead. He steadied his hand, having found the key, and, with a shaking hand, inserted it into the keyhole and turned it. He opened the door and hollered her name. As he did so, he stumbled into the entry hall, dragging his jumper through the door, just missing a collision with the long clock standing just inside the entry.

She was there, at the door, at his call, grabbing him, holding him, smothering him with kisses, and he doing the same to her. They were both crying with laughter—simultaneously, joyously, words not descriptive enough! The moment was both hallowed, festive, reverent: like the unexpected, innocent reunion of prepubescent friends and—oh yes!—most vibrant-like: the reuniting of sadly yearning, ecstatic, trembling lovers finally escaping forced separation.

Now they sidled into the sitting room, he still dragging his coverall, they maintaining their possessive clutch of each other. They had the mutually unspoken intent of sitting on a couch together, to simply and connubially express the peaceful pleasure of their oneness, so unexpectedly regained.

It took the better part of the remaining day for him to recount the happenings since he left her to be posted to British headquarters, near Arras, and then returning this day. He then listened quietly as she recounted the progress at the hospital and her mother's situation in Lyon. Her old friend and servant, Beatrice, was still looking after her in the old family residence. They exchanged such information as they each had of the war, as of today. She told of the mobs of people coming into Paris from the north, which he confirmed.

She had heard at the hospital, early this morning, that Amiens was bombed and later lost to the Germans yesterday, along with Abbeville. If this were true, he barely made it to his overnight stay in the copse before them—that is, if they were going straight to Paris.

But they were not. Giles was frantic to know whether there was a new line of defense. He called the number he had for his intelligence unit at Vincennes. It rang continuously but remained unanswered. He would need to report there tomorrow, by his British motorcycle. Perhaps tomorrow he could receive some valid information upon which he could rely and perform some duty assignment given him by an intelligence superior in charge.

In the meanwhile the couple found little in the icebox or cupboards to eat that afternoon but eggs, which they conveniently made into omelets with prosciutto and green peppers, plus bread and white wine. Actually the thrill of reunion and an intimate early night was all that was both required and desired. The next morning life would begin again with its complications and uncertainties. They both knew it, but neither said it, each pretending that only their silent little vortex, composed of them and the apartment they occupied, was "forever land." Nothing in the whirling world around them could change the nature and beauty of its feeling of peace, stability, and enchantment, even if it were for this single night alone.

The French Lieutenant and the King of Rome

The next morning inexorably followed the night, though each in their hearts prayed it would not. Elle was preparing for the hospital and out of the shower, robed in terry cloth, with her hair up and loosely bunned. She was about to apply lipstick (though it was "gilding the lily") when Giles walked into the bathroom and, standing behind, placed his arms around her and his cheek upon hers. She turned in his arms to face him and kissed him gently on the lips, and he responded with a playful nibble kiss of her lower one. They both smilingly looked into each other's eyes, and he said in a whisper, "You know, I don't know when I'll see you again." He smiled again and, in his low tenor voice, hummed and whispered the words in English of Noel Coward's sentimental musical, "Bittersweet": "I'll see you again, whenever spring breaks through again.

"I really don't know what to expect when I report in at Vincennes."

They held their embrace until "life" insisted that they conform to its beckoning.

XL

THAT MORNING, HE turned himself out as a "spic and span" officer, including his kepi he had stored in the apartment. The only part of his British cover he was wearing were the messenger's pilot glasses, which he was using to ward off the wind and cinders from the speed of the cycle churning its wheels. He followed Avenue Domes through the "gold entrance" port to the Vincennes preserve and then through the woods until he approached the walls surrounding the "caserne," the entrance to which had a mounted guard. The sergeant of the guard demanded his authority to enter, and he displayed his orders from the British colonel at Arras, which the sergeant couldn't read but finally accepted because there was no superior present that he could refer it too.

Elle told herself that Giles would be back for dinner. The pit of her stomach said otherwise. She didn't want to face the possibility that his strange return under British orders, without earlier French permission to leave his appointed post, could be considered desertion. That was just one of the scenarios fleeting through her mind. "What if he were immediately reassigned elsewhere, without even a short temporary leave," she thought. No, no, she refused to even consider it! She called into the hospital and reported, telling the duty doctor that she had a personal emergency. She then commenced the long walk to Les Halles to buy meat and fish for their sumptuous dinner she was concocting in her head.

Possibly she would buy her vegetables there also, or from a peddler in her neighborhood if she didn't find what she wanted at Les

Halles. She passed two *crainquebilles* within five street corners of her apartment, both with wide varieties of fruits and vegetables, who would be in the area all day. As she walked on, it seemed that every locale was having some form of festivities, balloon merchants, a sword swallower near the main entrance to Les Halles, and a juggler drawing a crowd on the street of the Pont Neuf nearby. All such distractions afforded her the ability to avoid returning home before she must, to make dinner. Thus, she avoided the phone that would not ring and her obsessive listening for it to do so. Being there with the hellish device was the anguishing thing for her. Out of reach ludicrously relieved her fear of missing his call. For thus, she could not miss his call, which probably wouldn't come. These neurotic fears she didn't share with Giles, for fear of imposing a further burden upon him. Like John Milton, the great, blind English poet of the sixteenth century, she painfully, "also serves, who stands and waits."

If only they had known, or had the slightest inkling then on that score alone, they could have relaxed. His obligation to the French army was nearly over. Neither of them realized that total French defeat was only days away, and it would be every man for himself possibly, through the whole German occupation, if a soldier wasn't in a captured or surrendering body of soldiers. Then, only in the German zone would there be a problem of a food card and conscription for German labor, and in the Vichy zone after late 1942, the same possibilities.

In other words, he need not have reported at all, and after the German defeat, he could have taken his uniform out of mothballs, and de Gaulle and his government would have welcomed him, probably before recognizing an officer from the Maquis who risked his life every day during the German occupation. Why? Because many of them were FFI or communists, and the others were not regular army and were not answerable to the regular chains of command and were always suspect by the new government of de Gaulle, who connived and stole France right out from under Eisenhower's and the British noses in 1945–46.

President Roosevelt hated de Gaulle, as did Churchill, but President Truman was too new at the game and was not an insider and had to learn the "game" mostly on his own and with a partially disassociated, if not hostile, cabinet.

XLI

GILES WOUND HIS cycle around the lake and past the small chapel to Hugo Street and right to the chateau and then on to the barbican leading into the fort, which was quite medieval, with its central tower, its walls, and its inner surrounding moat. Again, there were two guards asking for his business there. His orders gained him entrance. He left his cycle at the barbican. He then mounted two flights of the winding steps in the dungeon, which were not wide enough to draw a broad sword on the outer side and not safe enough to defend with a drawn one if you weren't on the wall side of the stairs.

Well, so much for concerns of the fourteenth century: now for those of May 23, 1940. He had careful thought about what his colonel might say, and his obvious position would be that since he couldn't get in touch with Vincennes, he was of no use to them, and since British headquarters was in immediate battle mode, he was more a liability without the combat training needed to be able to assign him a "table of organization" post.

He stepped off the top stair at intelligence level and didn't recognize the formerly orderly corridors of desks and filing cabinets. Everything seemed to be in turmoil. A captain, whom he recalled as "Bizier," was frantically searching through some of the division cabinets with two technical sergeants for "things." Others, to the approximate number of ten or twelve, were going through the same movements in different cabinets. He was totally unnoticed except to be pushed aside by a sergeant, who didn't so much as utter an excusatory sound.

Finally, he caught the right arm of the tall, red-faced Norman, Captain Gaspard Bizier, who registered a slow recognition of Giles and who abruptly said, as though Giles had overstayed his lunch period, "Where the hell have you been, Lambert?"

This prompted Giles to remind him of his assignment to British HQ and all that happened since he was assigned there by order of the general de brigade. "Whom shall I report to, now that I've returned?" said Giles.

"I don't know anymore!" said the captain, and then he began to rant. "Our present colonel left for our present front on the Somme River! Our commandant, the day before, and I don't know who is upstairs anymore—I'm afraid to go and look! They left me because I had the least combat experience. I have no idea what's even happened fifteen miles away at General George's headquarters. Everything started to fall apart ten or eleven days ago. Ever since Weygand whirled through here replacing General Gamelin, there were three days between, and I heard those three days allowed the Germans to cross whatever line Weygand thought he had time to throw up to stop them. On the Somme! We are looking for the Fourth Army, which was behind the Maginot and south of the breakthrough at the Ardennes and Sedan. We are looking for anything that's still big enough and fit enough to get north to Weygand. He may, with luck, have fifty or sixty divisions to stop twice that many plus armored panzer divisions. Can rifles and bayonets stop tanks? We don't now have any armored units but what may be remaining of the cobbled together Fourth Armored Division of about two hundred tanks. That is what de Gaulle failed to stop them with at Montcornet, north of Rheims, on May 17. Where is whatever remains of them?" he asked rhetorically. "On the eighteenth our troops at Cambrai just surrendered rather than face the tanks—even though their tanks were out of action for refueling and repairs! I'll tell you, Lambert: this is a nightmare—a nightmare!"

The French Lieutenant and the King of Rome

Giles placed himself at the disposal of the captain, who immediately assigned him to examine the files on the other side of the row of desks dividing the one group from the other. Giles enquired of the captain what he was to look for, and the response was both irascible and brief. "Well, of course, search for the Fourth Army and any other unit of battalion size that could still be immediately moved to the Somme River area."

Upon doing so, Giles found that the files were not organized for this purpose and could not be made to reveal these facts with any reasonable expectation. However, he noted that on the south wall, above a platform, accessible with a ladder at either end, was a situation map that had not been updated since the Germans broke through the Ardennes Forest and Luxembourg, and Sedan fell. The pins had not been changed, nor the magnetic army numbers changed or moved. The Second and the Ninth Armies were still in play on the map, though he knew that while he'd been at British HQ, the Ninth Army of reservists had surrendered en masse to the enemy, and the Second, badly mauled, had lost its general, now a German prisoner. He thought, what a quirk of fate that our two worst reserve armies were at the point of the German onslaught. Both in the Pas de Calais and again in Picardy, the lack of ability to communicate by radio could have caused headquarters to miss the opportunity to separate the overextended German panzers from their infantry. We were still using our armor as backup for our infantry instead of as panzers. Bad leadership!

Was this map neglected because of disbelief and an inability to accept reality or because there were so few personnel to follow developments and coordinate plans for planning countermeasures on a timetable basis? Or was it worse: was it defeatism in the very headquarters of the General Staff?

The day finally ended in a total waste. He knew he must return to perform this or other worthless services while this travesty continued. But his best thoughts told him it was all but over, and the pain in his stomach told him he had to quickly connive a way out. "Sauve-Qui-Peut," as Napoleon said, in burning and foodless

Moscow. "One must save oneself!" He must find a way out for Elle and himself.

He found the time to call Elle on the phone and found, to his dismay, that the Vincennes line was functioning. On enquiry, it was found not to be out of order, but the switchboard had been "somewhat neglected" recently, depending upon whether the clerks had some more frantic assignments to perform. "Catch as catch can" may explain why he didn't get through from Arras when he had called on his last attempt before leaving British headquarters.

Elle's reaction on hearing his voice was apprehension, followed by a sigh of relief, succeeded by, "Are you free to come home?"

"Yes and right away for diner."

"I love you, I love you!" she said with passion.

He cycled back as he had come and noticed a continuing flow of traffic heading away from Paris, as he had noticed on his way to Vincennes. He began to surmise that perhaps people were in fear of an imminent German occupation of Paris and perhaps even beyond. He and Elle must also think promptly of the same. In spite of all he had seen on his way back to Paris, he found it ungraspable to believe that France could fall to the Germans. Millions were killed defending France twenty odd years ago for four years, and in three or four weeks the country and its people could fall like a ripe piece of fruit, without even shaking the tree? And this Germany was a monstrosity compared to the kaiser's Germany!

While mulling over these thoughts, he arrived at the apartment, and as he entered, he smelled the delicious preparation of mixed seafood, to be the entrée; and sticking his inquisitive nose over the steaming pot, he discovered that boiling lobsters were to be the main course.

Elle had insisted on receiving meritorious attention for this feast. First he must sit down and snuggle with her on his lap while she recounted each experience of her day and all that was entailed in her elaborate and somewhat exaggerated adventures. Deciding the recipes and making the thought-provoking decisions involved required that he must render obeisance for such gifts. She, of course, was intentionally boring him and regaling him with little housewife tales. She thought he must believe all wives use these to demand attention from their husbands upon return from the workaday world, where important male decisions are made. After all, wasn't she entitled to spoof a bit, just to make her feel a dependent female, to boost her femininity. Truthfully she always felt the need to make him feel the strong male and she the dependent female, not the medical doctor she was, making medical decision affecting lives daily. Truthfully, he adored her, above all for being so admirable and every bit not only an equal, but a challenging human being he could never take for granted.

It was only fair to drop her to the kitchen floor when she began to nuzzle him behind the ear with her nose and tongue. He fell with her, and they were both like children, giggling as they frolicked and larked, tickling one another until amorousness succeeded jollity.

XLII

DURING DINNER THAT night, he revealed all he had discovered at Vincennes and his beliefs about the outcome of the war and what there was to do for their own safety, which included the abandonment of Paris. He even pointed out what the Germans were likely to do about him and possibly her, as well. They both spoke of concern about the fact that they and all their personal information was known by too many people, and such information as his army status and his being Jewish was too available and could destroy them.

They both thought about the MG and the British cycle he was using. Both would have to be shed in some way in the event the Germans ended by occupying Paris. The MG was registered in Paris, making it easy to identify as Giles's. There was little doubt about the reliability of the old French enemy, the Paris Police, and whose side they would be on. He knew for certain that the Germans were at least as close as Amiens, a day away if the so-called Weygand Line didn't hold them back. No one knew if Weygand would have reinforcements. The troops remaining in the Maginot Line might be available and possibly the Fourth Army, which was behind it, but no one knew what the Germans had been doing about either. They had moved so rapidly, and the French obviously had no communications.

"Should we try to get to Lyon and your mother, Elle?" he said. "We could easily be overtaken by a German motorized column that has broken through. Or, thinking that Weygand defense line

The French Lieutenant and the King of Rome

through, this supposed line runs all the way to Sedan and the Maginot Line. With the force the general has, he couldn't cover even thirty miles of that distance. On the other hand, it will take the Germans time to get Paris organized, even with the police and the civil government helping them.

"We must decide what to do as quickly as possible! That auto and the cycle must disappear, and so must I from headquarters at Vincennes—and quickly! But I must time it to determine the final outcome with the Somme River line of Weygand.

"Does your mother have a garage or barn to hide the car?"

"So many questions and no answers. Well, yes, she could do the auto," said Elle, with little enthusiasm. "Giles, as you know, I finish my specialty in September, and with all the male physicians called up, we are terribly understaffed!"

"Well, then, should we stay and be imprisoned or shot?" was his heated reply. They were about to have their first disagreement, and it was going to affect them crucially.

She responded, "Even the Germans wouldn't surely do that."

"You've read what they have done, and you know the details of the conduct of these maniacs—that's why they are called Huns! What more need be said. You know they are murdering Jews at the first opportunity. Why should my wife or I be treated differently?"

"Yes," she said, "I know you are right, but what shall we do? Mother's home and estate are bound to be commandeered by their officers if they occupy Lyon, and why should they not? They might allow her and her family retainer to remain in some part of it, but we would be unexplainable, and you would probably 'shoot it out with them' even before they found you out as a Jewish officer. And who knows what my haughty mother might say in anger! They would overlook the remarks of an elderly female aristocrat or her dotty old maid, but we would be another cup of tea entirely. All four of us would be dead or worse! I do not think that fleeing there is a good option."

Giles said it would work all right for her at some point, as her return would be explainable. "Your mother's age and widowhood and wartime conditions and to practice close by her and so forth. Fortunately you have retained your family name for professional purposes. That should offer you the cover you may need. I need not be in evidence at all!"

They seemed to get little further though there ensued a great deal of pacing by both of them. Finally, Giles stumbled upon the thought of his father's old adjutant in WWI, who served with him through most of the war. They started out together—his father, a lieutenant, and Eduard Bullard, a sergeant—in the infantry platoon he commanded. Eduard was a sheep farmer, originally with his own father. He was a young reserve sergeant called up for duty at the same time as Gilbert, and Bullard was assigned to his father's platoon. He followed Gilbert as he advanced, and finally he advanced to an acting regimental colonel. He was his "adjutant-chef," or as Americans would say, a "regimental sergeant major," the "top soldier" in the regiment. They spent almost three years being at risk of constant death. No, let us say rather, they were constantly immersed in a life of death! Killing, during those years, was their "trade."

After the war Eduard went back to his large farm and became the principal after his father's demise. His property was in Rambouillet, about twenty-seven miles south of Paris, where he lived in a very spacious and pleasant farmhouse built by his grandparents on his properties. Giles and his father always used to stay there when they went boar hunting in the forest nearby. They always left the "kill" with him and his family. He maintained a herd of more than five hundred sheep and had several border collies, which Giles wanted to play with when he was young but was denied it because they were "working dogs" and not to be interfered with, as "Uncle Eduard" and his father explained to him more than once.

It was in this forest that he learned to be a marksman, under the tutelage of these two men, on their frequent hunting visits over many years. Shooting a two- or three-hundred-pound raging boar two hundred or three hundred feet away, perhaps between low tree branches, was a quick and courageous act, calling for steadiness of hand. Boar tusks could kill if one were knocked off one's feet. His father and Uncle Eduard knew intimately of death and danger, and Gilbert insisted that Giles be ready for the European world in which he would have to live.

XLIII

"THAT'S WHERE THE car could go!" Eduard could hide it deep inside one of his sheds, hidden behind or beneath hay or straw. With the tarpaulin over it, it would never be noticed (and the cycle, too, if need be). "I'll cycle down tomorrow, from Vincennes, and talk the whole picture over with him," said Giles. "You know, dear, I have not received any money from the paymaster for almost a month. I hope you have some funds in the bank. I shall try to find out tomorrow if we still have a paymaster and if there are any funds to disperse at the donjon."

The next morning Giles continued up the staircase to the third level in search of the paymaster for personnel attached and assigned out of the donjon. The confusion he found elsewhere in the headquarters was endemic. The major acting in charge seemed vague and defensive, as though he had misplaced the money and wished to take personal responsibility for its absence. "Pay was not being 'regularly' issued since so many assigned personnel were not accounted for out of headquarters." He was now accounted for and could receive his back pay. Although it was only fair to say that the French banks were having runs, and cash ability was a possible problem for all of the military service. Of course, he must carry on with his assignment. Giles immediately wondered what that might be, as he had no existing assignment and no superior to say. In fact, he was beginning to feel the advantage of this; with a verge toward defeat staring them in the face, perhaps that freedom was most favorable.

The French Lieutenant and the King of Rome

He took a possibly worthless check from the major, planning on depositing it in his own bank account, realizing that it might in fact be a futility. French francs might shortly be worthless! "Then what?" he thought.

He stopped on the next floor down to see if his captain had pondered a solution to the problem of locating support troops for General Weygand. His answer was that, in fact, the general had asked the armies in the north, where the British divisions bordered them, to stay in place. "Why would he not have told them to disengage, leave part of their forces as a sacrifice rear-guard force, and the rest fight their way out of encirclement. They could then veer west toward the rear of the panzer forces to make a new advancing front, always fighting westward and smashing into the German infantry supporting the panzers with petrol and munitions, regardless of the cost (and the threat of the Belgium king to surrender). They are part of the reason that the French and British got into the trap! Those armies in the north were his best regular troops. The Belgian army was of little use and couldn't go on the offensive anyway. The British are managing to get their divisions out of there! Why couldn't the French have paid the price and done the same? It's still August 26, and it's not too late! Apparently the Maginot Line is still intact from Sedan south to Switzerland! Why not move those troops to the north, where the Germans are?"

Giles could add little to what the captain thought, and having nothing to contribute, he asked him for a requisition order for petrol for his cycle, took it to the pumps (which were running on nearly empty), and left for Rambouillet, some twenty-two or twenty-three miles southwest of Vincennes.

He was in emotional turmoil from the exasperating vacuum that he found permeating all of Vincennes. It was all so "lost"— the only word he could think of to describe the weak and worthless motions that were the daily operations that he witnessed there. The wind in his face, as he drove the cycle, gave him a feeling of vitality that had been bled from him in the surroundings of the Vincennes office. He continued to ruminate as he rode.

What was missing was Napoleon! How we French needed him at this instant, instead of Weygand or any other leader that was on the scene. Even one hundred fifty years after his time, he could see and do more than any leader we have, because of his genius. In one hundred days, with fifty thousand men, he created the image of France's rebirth as he dashed up and down the Rhine, fighting his enemies. And it took another genius, Wellington, to finish him off, and with larger forces.

As he drove through Rambouillet on the way to Eduard's farm, he passed the old fourteenth-century chateau and its grounds, which lay directly across from the town square. He remembered visiting it and the Palace of the King of Rome, built in 1812 by Napoleon on the grounds of the chateau used by him as a summer palace. He recalled that Napoleon had planned a much more ostentatious one for his successor, next to the Pont de Jena in Paris, but his need to start his Russian campaign seemed, unfortunately, more pressing. Somehow, at the time, this one was done instead. Now all that remained of it were two wings: one still belonged to the state, and the other wing had been purchased by the town, as a meeting hall for the town council and other municipal purposes.

How mundane a purpose after such an auspicious beginning—a wretched finale, so apropos to the godforsaken end of its namesake, torn asunder and forgotten except for its name, which was more than Napoleon II retained after a nominal reign of twenty-one or twenty-two days, following his father's abdication. The five-year-old was deprived of his imperial title and even his childhood baptismal title and identity as the King of Rome. He was whisked away to Vienna, by his father's enemy, his maternal grandfather, Francis, Emperor of Austria-Hungary, where he was kept, dispassionately, as a bird in a gilded cage. He was without a friend or the love of a parent or a social existence—a persona non grata. He became, at the pleasure of his grandfather, the Duc de Reichstadt, until dying there at twenty-one, from tuberculosis, as the Hapsburg whom he was forced to become. He was literally, "a Duke" of the Austro-Hungarian state—an empty title! No place was his, and he had no place where he was accepted unconditionally, with the exception of the small suite of rooms assigned to him in the Schonbrunn Palace. His only family contact was an occasional dinner with his chief jailer, his grandfather. France and all its connections were denied him except one marshal of France, trusted because he was a betrayer of his father. His mother "had forgotten where she had lain him down" and, as the new Duchesse of Parma, was captivated with new social interests and a new life in northern Italy.

He had the requisite servants, his tutor, a possible fencing master, and an acquaintance, whom he saw as a late teenager. He called his crested lark, also kept in a cage, "my only friend." His infant years, spent as the next emperor of France, were revealing of a sensitive, highly strung child, who was then deprived of father, mother, and a highly privileged status—in short, all of his personal security, at an age when it was most needed. He was probably the template for all the "poor little rich boys" of the future.

XLIV

GILES FINALLY REACHED the farm road that belonged to his friend, Eduard, and swung up it for the long distance to the house and farm buildings. Flore, his wife, greeted him at the front entrance door to their home, with obvious surprise both at seeing him and at how much he had changed in the last few years, and complimented him on his handsomeness, his uniform, and his rank. By this time, Eduard had heard the voices and had come into the hallway, shouted in dismay and pleasure on seeing him, and embraced him in his bear hug. He smothered him and smacked him on each cheek with a kiss. He actually lifted Giles's feet off the floor in the process, as he once had done when Giles was a child—only then he literally swept him up into his arms. Eduard was gruff, emotional, and had no "grays" with regard to people. In his outspokenness, he was brazenly candid and generous, but still had the peasant's cunning about evaluations of people and, of course, business matters, about which he had apparently been most successful.

In a lengthy tête-à-tête, family matters were covered on both sides, and Giles learned that they had doubled their land holdings, including business buildings in town, and in the process he had become a chosen member of the town council of Rambouillet. Flore had poured them all some glasses of light red wine, accompanied by some plain cakes and flakey biscuits from one of her crockery jars kept in her spotlessly maintained pantry.

Giles thought it important to reveal to his friend what he knew about the real probability of France's fall to the Germans, for both his own purpose and to provide Eduard with time to cover himself in whatever way he could. After all, he was under no orders in this regard and in fact only had technical superiors who were not even present in command of their posts at Vincennes.

He then told Eduard and Flore about his need to find a place to sequester his English MG. He explained the excessive danger, from the police and the Germans, of having it on their premises in Paris. Eduard did not disappoint him. He took him to one of the smaller barns, immediately, where a canvas-covered, small MG could be completely blocked off from view by equipment and haystacks for his milk cows and few horses. The building was one of two similar ones, outside the railed-in farmyard. Eduard only asked that he leave him a key in case of need to move it. He also assured Giles that if he came down on a Sunday afternoon, his helper wouldn't be there, and he and Giles could secure it in place, just the two of them. He also said that the sheep-shearing crew wouldn't come through until next spring. That was another one of his problems, whether there were any of them still in operation because of the war.

Giles agreed to follow Eduard's suggestion as to the day and would plan on returning by the metro from Rambouillet into the Gare Montparnasse in Paris after leaving the car with him. He didn't mention the Norton cycle because he felt he could ditch it somewhere at the last minute. He turned to leave and said his adieus to his two hosts, until a near Sunday when he promised to return with Elle. Her presence would be necessary for Eduard and Flore in the event she would be the one to retrieve the car if he should not be able to do so. Life was forseeably unpredictable, and he was not optimistic. As he retraced his route on his cycle, he decided to stop at headquarters in Vincennes, just to justify his queasy feelings of being a deserter by being available to perform a service if a proper directive were rendered him.

He found it closed, with a duty sergeant posted at the staircase inside the donjon, who informed him that all had left the premises and would return tomorrow morning. He himself would be relieved at midnight. Of this, he seemed skeptical, by the expression on his face. Giles used the phone on the sergeant's desk to call Elle. He spoke to her briefly, in low tones, to tell her not to prepare anything for dinner as they would eat out on his arrival there, in short order. He asked her to have the doorman move the car in the courtyard, next to the rear door, with her assistance, for their use tonight. He presumed there was petrol in the tank as he had taken the precaution of filling it two days ago, though she had driven it since. They could make a choice of restaurants on his arrival home.

His feeling was that they should enjoy each moment together while they could and before Paris fell, as he fearfully believed it would. If he could only figure it out. North Africa? How could they beat the Germans to the Mediterranean? That was only possible if their armies could hold the Germans by making a stand at the Loire and Sommes Rivers, for a week at least. Would they be able to find a ship? Would they need papers? What about the Italians? Had they sent occupation forces to Nice and Marseilles already? Could he reach his parents in Nice? If headquarters didn't know, then the only one that knew for certain was the prime minister of France, Paul Reynaud. The north was obviously closed. If the German mechanized forces moved south, east, and west of Weygand's limited defenses, they would be caught by possible scouts or even an armored column. He could think of no plan of escape for the two of them together! What should they do—just wait for the Germans? Go down fighting with the weapons they had? Was a quick dash for Spain before the Germans covered the southwest a consideration? Why should she die because he would be a wanted person? Could they make it over the Pyrenees? Would Franco's people let them stay in Spain?

His mind was a whirling, centrifugal sinkhole of questions that he couldn't answer. He turned into the alleyway of the apartment, parked between two cars, and made for the second floor and the door. After a kiss and a hug, he changed out of uniform into mufti. His reason for doing so was that he felt his presence in uniform would raise too many questions as to his absence from what had

The French Lieutenant and the King of Rome

been termed in the last war "the front," in the civilian, frivolous ambience they were about to enter. They then entered into plans for the evening, both trying their best to show to one another an upbeat insouciance that fell rather flat because of their well-founded worries, which were mutual and truly irrepressible.

XLV

SHE HAD USED the time between the phone call and his arrival to consider some possible restaurant alternatives. Elle settled on Le Vaudeville, which was opposite the Bourse (the stock exchange) on the Right Bank of the river, close between it and the Bibliotheque National (the main library), with parking adjacently located. It was a brasserie with much atmosphere but much different than the typical Alsatian atmosphere. It sponsored the stagy presence of the comic theater, with dancing and gaiety—definitely for the young of heart and not for a restful meal. Wonderful for them, however! Giles spoke little of their immediate problem, though there were only a few days to solve it. They thought a relaxing drive to the area might be just the thing, along with dancing and wine. The best evening places were in that general area, as they had been since shortly after the war. Most of "their crowd," so to speak, should be there—that is, most bourgeoisies men and companions, not in service.

Most people who could were abandoning Paris. The flood of people from the north was beginning to influence Parisians, who caught fear and began to flee to the south in droves.

"Elle, there must be millions of people on the road. I passed the Gare du Nord, and there are such crowds of people detraining in Paris and then wandering through the city. I actually saw shops being boarded up!"

Elle ignored his remark, determined to set a carefree tone for the evening. She said in a blasé tone, "Let's go to Le Dome, to the

American Bar, there is always a vivacious crowd, and we could also end the evening there. We might be able to leave the MG under the linden trees on de Lambre Street not far from Le Dome."

This is what they did, being fortunate in finding a place. The scarcity of cars was also a sign of the *exode* (the evacuation) taking place in Paris.

Le Dome was nearly empty, and so was its annex, the American Bar. One of the few bartenders, leaning on the counter of the bar, looked glum and spoke accordingly when asked about it: "With the Germans so close and people leaving too, it's this way everywhere now."

They departed the morbid atmosphere and stood outside under the awning, pondering a plan in order to avoid a "too-early" evening. Simultaneously they thought of La Coupole, just some yards away on Vavin, just between the triangle that made the three streets abut one another, thus creating the peculiar Parisian intersection, which in this case implicated Vavin with Boulevard Raspail and Boulevard Montparnasse. It all amounted to a really short walk in a light summer rain. Fortunately the canvas top was up on the MG, and they would avoid sitting on wet seats if the rain continued.

When they arrived there, at La Coupole, Elle remembered that she had left her parasol behind the driver's seat, in the narrow space available, the last time she drove the car. It would have been sufficiently thick to ward off the light rain for both of them. She smiled to think of how he would have disliked the swags between each hinged rib, radiating out from the central pole handle—not to mention the large multicolored fabric from which it was made. She used it in summer because she thought she was olive complexioned enough without any additional help from the summer sun. Ah well, good enough! Not having it saved her from a discussion on the subject.

La Coupole was elegant and large with a great restaurant, a bar, which was separate, and a dance floor, with a bar as well. It was situated on three floors, with a terrace on the sidewalk level, which also managed to use part of the public sidewalk. It had booths and tables in the dining room, a bar above, and dancing in the lower croft. All ceilings were high, and the décor was art nouveau—if anything. Ceiling paintings were prevalent, with framed paintings and pictures hanging everywhere below on the side walls on all floors. The atmosphere could be formal, if in holiday season, or not so at other times. It was reputed to hold over two thousand people—but not on this night. It was deserted except for the bottom floor, where they danced to a reduced-sized band. Their favorite was the tango, and they were usually good enough at any dance to gain a lot of space and many admirers, among the other dancers and ringside tables. They ordered cocktails, which were, more or less, the new "American thing"—and which had stayed longer than they had. Since the American depression began over ten years ago, their money had gone, and now the war had come again, and the amusement had gone, and so, finally, had they all.

They returned to the car to find it quite dewy inside because of the rather loose connections between the window panels, the canvas top, and the doors themselves: a snap-button arrangement of a sort of plastic glass inset in canvas placards that gave little protection from either wind or weather and distorted vision out the side windows, besides.

The horrific problem of blackouts for air raids was always present. This turned the streetlights out and all of the splendid memorial lighting as well. This made Paris the "City of Light," known as such throughout the world, no longer such. The boulevards were not so dangerous because one still had one's hooded or slit-covered headlights, but all connecting narrow streets were particularly dangerous for pedestrians and cars turning at corners and, of course, rear-end collisions. A speed of over fifteen miles per hour was an invitation to disaster. Of course, instead of there being more police about, there were fewer. They disliked the darkened streets as much as the other Parisians.

Only the rats from the Seine seem to have benefited. One saw them crossing the boulevards, scurrying from curb to sidewalk, their furtive little eyes caught in the slit beams of auto headlights as they searched for garbage, which shrunk daily as human discrimination shriveled and their increasingly boney pets fought to survive on what human refuse remained. All Parisians railed at the constant tails of the "old timers" of the commune, who remembered the obscene stories of how rats were a regular part of the siege diet. This nightmare had gone on ever since the "phony war" had started on September 1, 1939. So far, neither Elle nor Giles had heard of a Paris air raid to date.

XLVI

AS THEY REACHED the alleyway and proceeded to park in the interior courtyard, the doorman came out with an umbrella to assist them in through the rear entrance and to tell them there was a message at the main desk for Lt. Giles. It had come by military courier much earlier in the evening. Giles picked up the envelope, which was stamped "urgent-restricted." Giles preferred to take it with them to their apartment before opening it but asked if he was instructed to reply by message or telephone this evening; he then realized the message itself would contain instructions. They both quickly suffered with reignited fears of separation and helplessness, coupled with frustration, the feeling of being sensitized puppets, mere minutiae in a desensitized world of mad puppet masters.

Elle unlocked the doors and, upon a first whiff, flung them both open to expel the stifling, oppressive air in the apartment, which seemed to have gathered in their rather short absence, perhaps as an ill omen.

She was eerily and briefly put upon by her old "haunting," which ran by her like a film reel, reversing at triple speed and then completely gone. It first made its presence known in her early puberty and seemed to appear as a precursor of troubled times in her life, but not necessarily as a measure of the trouble's significance. She was grateful that the feeling, or passing of it, first came after childish fears had vanished. However, she always wondered if it connected somehow with her deceased father, or another ancestor. A woman of science, she rejected all superstitions as simple ignorance, but this persistent shadow made her doubt that all her pagan ancestors had, even past the grave, been tamed by the deceased men of the Age of Reason—assuming, of course, it had been allowed to share their presence. Amusedly, she always felt it to be a recalcitrant "holdout."

She was always aware that her Celtic derivation bore a genetic disposition for mysticism, but she scoffed at the Catholic concept of "bell, book, and candle." Thus, she suffered this "inherent," unriddable feeling, which was intangibly threatening to her intellect. It subsisted as a sort of shading, perhaps of a Gallic past soul or spirit. It seemingly brushed by her physical being, like an inexplicable, vapid ancestor or shade. Nondescript, it flickered and passed but was substantial enough, in passing, to momentarily disturb her composure. Of this intangible, evanescent presence she had never spoken, it being other worldly, zany, and inexplicable. Her grasp of it was emotional; of it she was clearly skeptical, and the apparition itself, indescribable. Therefore, it must perforce remain solely her own perversity.

She crossed the room in order to throw open the French doors on the far wall, expediting the evacuation of the air in the room and, hopefully, its bedeviling content.

Meanwhile, Giles walked through the room, reaching the kitchen, where he switched the light and prepared to open the heavy brown paper envelope. The return was typed, but the address to him was all in cursive. "Well," he mused, "it couldn't have been an afterthought." He slowly tore the glued flap loose, thus giving himself time to brace for the unforeseeable shock these orders might present. He had purposefully moved out of Elle's range of vision so that he could prepare for the agony the contents might cause her if related to her in too harsh a way. This would buy him a moment to present it in as mild a way as possible.

It read:

Order of immediate detachment and reassignment of following officer

Time: 1900

May 24, 1940

2nd Lt. Giles Lambert, active duty, army reserve officer number—security retained.

Date of reserve commission—security retained.

This intelligence officer specialist, presently attached to Intelligence Section, Headquarters Division, Vincennes, herewith detached and reassigned, the date of this order, effective 0800 May 25, 1940, as follows:

Assigned for duty to Lt. Colonel Paul Villelume, cabinet member and director of National Defense and War, for Prime Minister Paul Reynaud, to serve, at his pleasure, as an assistant on his staff.

Report to his aide-de-camp, Captain Rolande Margine, Palais de L'Elysee, Ministry Building, Place Beauvais and St. Honore, Paris.

Signed,

Capt Gaspard Bizier

Acting Head of Intelligence Section, Headquarters Division, Vincennes, Department of the Army, General Maxime Weygand, Commander

There was a very important enclosure. It was a draft on the Bank of France for his stipend covering the total amount owed him through the month of December 1940. It was so notated on its face and executed by Captain Gaspard Bizier. There was a brief handwritten note attached by pin. It read, "Bon chance!" (or, in English, "Good luck!").

"What could this mean?" a shocked Giles asked himself. Is this tantamount to a discharge? It certainly seemed to be, but there was no mention of a termination or further orders to follow after this assignment. Or was it a way of paying him while there was "still money in the till" and an army account to pay him?

Elle stuck her head around the doorframe of the open kitchen door and asked how long she would have to wait to hear the newest encroachment upon their lives. He answered, somewhat facetiously, "We are coming up in the world socially, after a fashion. I have been assigned to Prime Minister Reynaud's staff. I am now an assistant to his war advisor, Col. Paul Villelume, who also advises him on foreign relations.

"Actually I am to assist his secretary, a Capt. Margine. I surmise that there must be some English translation work involved. I go to the ministry's building, just behind the palace of the president, the L'Elysees, on the Right Bank of the Seine River. The Quai Dorsey terraces are on the Left Bank. You know the area. I'll have to call you about dinner together, perhaps about noon. Why they need me I can't imagine! If they need me, they are as seriously in trouble as one can imagine. Or is it simply that Capt. Bizier wants 'shorn' of me at intelligence section? Well, my sweet, you will be among the first to know!" He then showed her the draft, and she was likewise astounded and as confounded and perturbed as he. He decided it was best not to mention it at his next posting and to exchange it for funds at the Bank of France in Paris at his first opportunity, and not deposit it in their account at Bank Lyonnaise. The draft prophesied that the end was, in fact, as near as he feared.

XLVII

NEXT MORNING, THERE was a tussle for bathroom space between them, at 6:00 a.m., since both had to be on duty at the same time. Cafe au lait and croissants were the minimal things available for breakfasting. For her, she could "boost" something from the hospital kitchen! For him, who knew what he could expect from the Palace Beauvau, now the "Ministry of Home Affairs," separated and behind the president's palace, in the Place Beauvau. Surely the "meetings" provided meals for the attendees between sessions, as an accommodation, concluded Giles, as he turned right onto Boulevard de Marigny from the Champs Elysees to the Place Beauvau, where the ministry building stood.

He brought his bike to a rolling stop in front of the large, wrought-iron gate, separating the ministry from the president's palace and having two Republican Guard sergeants in walking-out uniforms attending it. He reached for his kepi, in a bag suspended from the handlebars, with his right hand. He removed his goggles from his eyes and swept them off his head with his left. As he did so, his kepi was smoothly placed on his head, smartly tilted above his right eyebrow. This he followed with a curt salute, which acknowledged and returned the salute of the two sergeants.

He asked for escort to the colonel's offices. One of the sergeants did so and asked, as they walked along, to see his orders, which he produced. It seemed that both the colonel and the captain were already in the main ground-floor room, called "the Louis XV Room" by the sergeant. It was apparently called so because it was exquisitely of the period, filled with paintings and drawings, including a Chardin, several Watteaus, a Greuze, a Rembrandt, a Canaletto, and a bewildering number of other painters and some sculptures and even a Beauvais tapestry. The room was being arranged for the meeting. It now contained a large conference table and multiple chairs, which necessitated the rearrangement of some sculptures, it would appear. There also was a side table and chair, apparently for a reporter for the meeting.

The meeting was scheduled for 1400 hours and would be formally chaired by President Le Brune, of the *republique*. Of course, Prime Minster Reynaud would control it as the French form of government provided. A general pandemonium surged through the room as each new minister arrived and was greeted by the others informally, or formally, depending on the newness and closeness of their individual relationships.

Upon his entry into the room, he was first introduced to Captain Margine, whom he found to be both cordial and affable. Giles spoke of his assigning orders, in sotto voce, to the captain, who chose to step aside with Giles to examine them. He was perplexed at Giles's orders, which were in excess of the colonel's request for some support assistance for Captain Margine, for two days at the most. Col. Villelume, in uniform, was chatting with a short gentleman, quite dapper, dressed in a swallow-tail coat, gray waistcoat, striped trousers, and all the other accoutrements of formal day wear. The captain beckoned to the colonel upon catching his eye.

Giles found, on first impression, that the colonel was a man who was direct, scrutinizing, and given to expecting and receiving rapt attention and quick, accurate responses from subordinates. He was a tall, rangy (or lanky) man, who would prove to be short of word and temper. His immediate questions to Giles began. "Are you able to speak English without a French accent and quick enough to translate argot to me? And, of course, such innuendos as may pass between our English visitors, tête-à-tête? We are expecting Monsieur Churchill; Gen. Spears, military attaché in France; Monsieur Campbell, English minister to France; and possibly Lord Gort of the Imperial General Military Staff, commanding British forces in France." Giles responded affirmatively to what seemed to be two questions, and he responded accordingly. "General Weygand, our new commander-in-chief will be here to present his latest plan for defending that part of France still under French control." The vitriol in his voice and the ironic curve of his lips glowered into a bitter smile, which was wedded to the last part of his statement, "still under French control." This clearly summed up his wry opinion of the generalissimo and was a signal to Giles of his expectation that he should be specifically on guard where conduct or communications regarding the general should arise.

The second table in the room was large enough to accommodate a second chair, and one was brought over to accommodate Giles for the meeting when it eventually commenced.

It being nearly noon, a buffet table was rather substantially laid in a side room, for those present at the occasion. In the meantime, Giles met with Captain Margine in his office, on the same floor, just beyond the Italian rooms, containing quattrocento paintings and some Tuscan primitives, in glass display cases.

Giles primary intent was to gain some familiar warmth, without presumption upon a superior, so as to find what common purpose there was to accomplish. He asked himself, "What is the purpose of these meetings, and what will be the result if this purpose doesn't materialize?" Captain Margine was, as he had first concluded, affable and candid and more than happy to have another junior officer to share in the perplexity of his situation.

The captain welcomed the attitude and questions of Lt. Lambert and his open revelation of his ignorance about the immediate French war status. Therefore, he commenced by reviewing the fact that, within the period of Giles's departure from Arras and this day, the Germans were past Amiens and Abbeville and in control of all of the north of France, with the exception of the channel ports, Brest in Brittany, Bologne, and to the east, past Dunkirk and perhaps Ostende, which were still in British and French hands. Further, it appeared that the British intended to attempt an evacuation of their army from France, regardless of how it affected the French defenses. He was unable to say whether the French had attempted to counterattack north to join the British, cutting off the German panzers from their supplies and infantry. The only information, presently, was what he was telling Giles. Further, they expected the new defense posture to be presented by Gen. Weygand, perhaps at this very cabinet meeting today. Gen. Gamelin had been replaced by Prime Minister Paul Reynaud on the seventeenth of May, and Weygand had been in place on the nineteenth and apparently had let the next three days "evaporate" while the German panzer armies were moving at a speed of one hundred miles per day.

Suddenly, the colonel's head jutted around one side of the framed edge of the door opening, and he blurted out, "Come immediately. The meeting begins." The captain and Giles reacted in tandem and bolted after the colonel through the door and headed for the main meeting room.

The three of them stepped into the meeting room, which was now literally turbid with movement, created by some thirty odd individuals, composed of cabinet members, the president of the state of France, and the British representatives of its wartime government. All were gathered there to unravel the facts of how and why France was now a collapsing nation and to create a plan to revive the disappearing future of the stricken, deteriorating wreck of a perplexed state: a state that, within fifteen days of May 25, 1940, had lost over half its army, had six million displaced persons roaming its roads aimlessly, and was 35 or 40 percent occupied by its mortal enemy, Germany.

XLVIII

GILES ALMOST INSTANTANEOUSLY recognized the near hysterical ingratiation by a number of the members of this unwieldy, bloated cabinet before others of their group. They had seldom met as a cabinet group, and only a few had any significance to either the president of the republic or the prime minister. They were manifesting a need for the development of creature comfort in a group that came to exist under the auspices of the prime minister last March and were composed of civilian specialists, supposedly crack experts in the field for which they were chosen. Reynaud patterned them after the English prime minister's own cabinet (which was filled with men who were much more adroit in their respective fields and held practical posts). And, it had been part of the British government since King William and Queen Anne reigned at the very commencement of the eighteenth century.

Giles's experience as an advocate and the short, remarkable experience as an intelligence officer added to his natural perspicuity. He believed himself qualified to interpret the body language of all those now around him.

Giles had been introduced to the ideas of whom these men were and what their posts were when the two officers had been in the meeting room earlier. He had even been provided a list, which he read again, so as to avoid any embarrassment. He attempted to deftly manipulate it between his hands as he regarded it surreptitiously. In all, in his mind's eye, it was simply a ludicrous list of "musical chair" changes, which should have been written with a burlesque musical format, perhaps a syncopated form of the "Marseillaise," the national anthem, and rendered by an amateurish Sicilian village wedding band.

His imagined cacophony of erratic sound seemed to him to permeate this atmosphere filled with words of defiance and victory. The switching of chairs began with Prime Minister Reynaud, who replaced Deladier as both the prime minister and minister of National Defense and War on May 18, George Mandel as Minister of Colonies was replaced by Louis Rollins. Then he was replaced by Leon Barety. Petain was recalled, as ambassador to Spain, to become assistant to Reynaud. These were just a partial list of changes from the list! It seemed to be the one thing over which the government had control. Apparently doing such changing provided nervous relief, concluded Giles. Changes continued through early June, and by the eighteenth, Reynaud had been replaced by Petain, who made the infamous armistice; but Giles would have parted from his assigned post of watching the British in advance of that.

It is necessary at this point, to interject commentary regarding the purpose of these desperate, befuddled men, who had gathered here to find a way to avoid rendering last rites for France, if any were even still timely. They had, at this point, grasped the fact that the country was in extremis. After all, the nation had been riven politically between left and right movements for over eighty years, more or less. The population was also asunder morally and spiritually: partially anticlerical, antimilitary, and socialist; increasingly pro-Russian and Communist, and on the other side, pro-Catholic, pro-army, and fascist, anti-German, and monarchist. The conservatives hated the labor movements more than the Nazis, who threatened their country with war and inundation. A government so parsimonious and asleep as to believe that this next war could be won with twenty-year-old methods, while being aware of the tank, the radio, and automatic weaponry, relied on a wall in the wrong place to defend itself, instead of modernizing. The inefficacy of the ancient Chinese wall was a two-thousand-year-old proof. Castle walls had been abandoned because of modern weaponry for three hundred years. But France devised a new, improved wall, and the Germans simply ignored it. France replayed WWI, planning on a large attack through Holland and Belgium, thinking all along that the Germans would adhere to the "Von Schliefen plan," thus placing their best forces opposing them. There they were surrounded and cut off by the fast-moving German panzer forces. Weygand probably spent the first three days of his command trying to plan an extrication and couldn't. These were the three days in which he was said to do nothing while the Germans continued to swallow France in huge gulps.

By the date of this meeting, the worst had come to pass, and Germany was past the gate and had France by the throat. It was achieved within fifteen days, quickly and decisively.

What dream could now be materialized to reverse the inevitable? But, of course, the miraculous Gen. Weygand, who claimed to have the secrets of his WWI commander, the brilliant Marshal Foch, claimed the answer. He would speak to the saving of France at this meeting!

How had this happened to the most vaunted army in the world? As follows: it had a reserve army that had been reduced to a one-year training program by annual classes since the late 1920s. It had a four-year vacuum of recruits because of its WWI losses. It was outstripped by population resources in Germany. It was without a regular army sizeable enough to oppose the Germans when they chose to take back the Rhineland forcibly in 1936. The British had stopped backing the Versailles Treaty since the Ruhr confrontation in 1923 and left the French to manage by their own devices (which were insufficient to even successfully enforce the terms of that treaty).

In short, the Germans felt that they didn't lose the war but were simply bullied into a peace. Their army performed victory parades when they returned home and even commonly received flowers in their gun barrels from the admiring crowds who greeted them as they marched. Hitler coming to power in 1932–34 simply confirmed their beliefs. Preparations for the next phase of WWI were about to begin. Only the French anticipated it, but they then hid from reality by creating the Maginot Line—incomplete, ending just to the south of the Ardennes Forest. Thus, they were in the wrong place, all because of money. Germany started from scratch and devised a contemporary war, with contemporary equipment. Interestingly enough, the ideas were basically British but ignored by them, as they were for an aggressive war and not the defensive war on which the Allies depended. The WWI generals, still in command, had decided the Ardennes Forest was impenetrable—a charade the assessment of which the German army didn't share.

XLIX

MEANWHILE, GILES INTENSIFIED his visual examination of the room in order to follow his orders from the colonel to locate the English delegation, whom he found to have glommed together, almost cheek by jowl, behind General Spears, their native French speaker.

The small man in the formal day attire—referred to by others in the room, in sotto voce of course, as "Mickey Mouse"—was the prime minister, Paul Reynaud. The meeting was called to order by President Lebrune, dressed as was the PM, but "largish" and timorous in his voice and manner.

His opening remarks included the introduction of the PM, who was taking over the meeting. Just as he commenced to speak, he nodded and noted to those present the new addition of General Weygand and Admiral Darlan, head of the navy and, in addition, the chief of air. He continued by saying he was now pleased to call this a "war cabinet" meeting, as well as a civil cabinet meeting of its twenty-two members. He stated his disappointment at not being able to host PM Churchill, whom had been expected, but introduced the four delegates from Britain to the group as a whole. He called for the sergeants of the Republican Guard to accommodate the additional numbers with added chairs to be placed as near as possible to the other attendees now at the table. Capt. Margine and Giles were at the supplemental table, with notepads and pencils.

Amid the confusion of a crowd melee and reverberating sound, the formerly adequate-sized room had become a suddenly small room. An unexplainable addition was an intense and aggressive little female, a "women of a certain age," wearing a dowdy bluish-mauve dress, who scythed her way through the crowd. She acted without rendering the slightest courtesy to those whom she unceremoniously displaced in her drive toward (to Giles's surprise) the speaker, Prime Minister Reynaud. Upon her arrival at his side, she attempted to distract him by whispering in his ear while he was speaking his opening remarks. He willingly accepted the distraction as though it were a commonplace occurrence and made no attempt to reconcile her conduct with these men of state. At that moment, Col. de Villelume came to the podium and, with great deference, suggested that she take the minister's chair until he had concluded his opening commentary. She gave the colonel a look of disdain but reluctantly took the chair and twisted her face into a look of anger, frustration, and childish pouting. This person, Giles was to learn from Capt. Margine, was the disagreeable mistress of the minister, and she held sway enough to replace cabinet ministers. In fact she placed their colonel as military advisor against the preference of Reynaud for de Gaulle. She had insisted that the latter was needed in combat and the minister "must respect that." Their colonel was reputedly a right-wing conservative, and she had fascist leanings, particularly with the Italians. Reynaud supposedly allowed her to control whom he would meet with and whom he would not.

Her name was Helene, Countess de Porte. She, like many other aristocratic and affluent women of Paris, during this "phony war" period, were busily creating their individual "Madame Recamier" courts to snare politicians with ascending stars, thus to affect French politics, solely for the purpose of benefiting their superficial social position and thus placing their brand on events of the day, without regard to the consequences of their acts. Unlike the eighteenth-century society wit of great intellectual endowment, these were simply women frittering their charms and money elsewhere than home. In passing, gossip had it that Charles de Gaulle referred to her and those of her ilk as "dinde," the French word for a turkey.

The captain and Giles being still seated and preparing to perform their disparate assignments at their small table awaited the PM's continuation. He proceeded to comment on the presence of Gen. Weygand and his sacerdotal duty to preserve "our" nation at war and that he was the new Foche, our savior in the last war against the ruthless German invader. Weygand was recalled by the PM from Syria to perform his sacred military duty as the brilliant successor to Marshal Foche, of WWI fame.

With this introduction Giles saw a small uniformed general rise and move toward the two-step podium occupied by the PM, who shook hands (for English benefit) and rendered the double-cheek kiss for the benefit of the French cabinet and president. In the few steps he took from his former seat next to Admiral Darlan, he moved with both speed and agility, startling Giles into the recognition that he was not the typical stodgy ectoplasm of a WWI French general, but a man still of vigor and dynamism.

His opening remarks were only a greeting to all present, and then he commenced to speak of his plans to arrest the relentless forward movements of the enemy. He inferred that the previous command had not moved quickly enough to retreat from the Dutch-Belgian border to save the cream of the army from being entrapped by panzers. When he had arrived on the eighteenth of May, he had sought a way out of that dilemma but could not do so.

He was required to consider other alternatives, which included the formation of new armies (the Seventh and the Tenth) now placed in the west and the formation of a new front along the western waterways, including the Somme, and a line of defense, easterly all the way to Montmedy, close upon the Maginot Line, which was intact. Further, he had devised something that he referred to as "hedgehogs" to counter the fast-moving panzers north of Paris and south of Amiens and easterly, to counter the panzer attacks. These were constituted of tree groves containing a 360-degree parameter each and containing a seventy-millimeter piece of artillery and machine guns and men, set to pick off enemy tanks as they moved forward without their infantry. When asked by Col.

de Villelume if he had replacements for artillery and men as combat progressed, he responded with a fiery stare, remarking, "Every senior officer in the French army would be of enormous use in view of the shortage of personal."

Then he added that this situation today was exactly as he had warned the government in 1934. The inference was that a perverse left-wing government had caused the current crisis—that the honor of the army was stainless in the matter of the current crisis. When he was then asked by the colonel about a second line of defense, if his plan failed, he spoke of perhaps an armistice and refused to consider the possibility of fighting from the central Massif or a slow retreat to the southern ports, to continue the fight from Algeria or other French areas in North Africa. He denied the ability to replace or deliver arms and ammunition there and said that there were no factories for these things there. He asserted that the civil leaders should not consider abandoning the people as had Queen Wilhelmina and the Dutch government, which had fled to England.

Then why had he and other commanders of the French army not done more to alter this situation by going to the Estates General and the people? He vehemently responded, "The honor of the army did not include a duty to instruct a remiss government to do its duty or require it to tarnish its own honor by begging the government to perform the obvious!"

Weygand's principle thoughts were that the English should not hold back their air force for its own home defense but should be fighting in France. England should be desperately making a call on all its empire for troops and equipment for fighting in France as it had done in the last war. Giles already had firsthand knowledge that the British were fighting to get out of France and, if successful, would not return to where the French army was in desperate straits.

Giles couldn't understand why there was no talk of bleeding the Germans dry with the French army and civilians so that by the time they got to the ports to face our intact fleet they would only wish to be back in Germany. "Why should not the same French people be willing to give their all as they had in the last generation," he impetuously and spontaneously whispered to Capt. Margine, seated next to him. The captain looked at him and closed his eyelids in affirmation.

L

TWO THINGS SEEMED obvious to Giles as he listened to the questions put to the general: first, he didn't have any faith in the French will to fight as a people, and secondly, he harbored a great concern of the rebirth of the 1870 commune and the succumbing of the French people to communism, as had been the strong direction of the recent leftist civil government.

An undercurrent of murmurs were buzzing throughout the room along with the outcries of some cabinet ministers. The outcries were from those who easily detected in the general's plans the lack of a backup plan in the event his line of defense didn't hold the German onslaught, which was continuing as it began—relentlessly!

Giles felt the blood in his temples surge as he realized that this "bastard-born aristocrat" intended to wreak havoc and punishment on France for its acceptance of socialism as a government choice. Truthfully, Giles did believe that the socialist government had divided the country further, and further had undermined its preparation for war.

Unknown to Giles, and unforeseeable, was that so long as Germany had an alliance with communist Russia, as it did in September of 1939 through the Polish campaign, sabotage continued in French armament factories. Only after Germany successfully enslaved France and attacked Russia in 1941 did the French underground (which in the beginning was mostly communist and socialist) start to become a threat to the German occupation of France.

Giles himself, as a member of the upper bourgeoisie, preferred the English sense of individualism and nongovernmental interference, not properly comprehended in France. The nation had not developed in stages from feudalism to freedom, but from one form of absolutism to another, always seeking a government to depend upon as a people, a government that would deliver both security and nurturing, thus forever guaranteeing strife between those who sought the teat and those who were weaned. Socialist democracies could never resolve the fact that government suckling required the draining of the same private resources that were, in fact, the breast milk with which they nurtured their encouraged dependents. Eventually, when the bourgeoisie's resources were to run out, the flying circus would end. It could no longer be done with mirrors, and the curtain would fall on the fairytale: only to end in another riot or revolution. Giles suspected that there would be many more French republics after this, the third, if it survived another German occupation (which he felt sure would shortly occur).

Capt. Margine informed him, after the final comments of the meeting, that the prime minister would be spending tomorrow in London with Churchill and his advisors, travelling by secret flight and returning tomorrow night. Consequently, their next meeting at the L'Elysees would be held at noon, followed by a meeting at 10:00 p.m. on the twenty-seventh of May, across the Seine at the Ministry of (War) Defense Building, behind the Quai D'Orsay embankment on St. Gemain. He directed him, "Take the Point de La Concorde Bridge from the Right Bank and left onto the boulevard. The entrance to the building is along the front of it, on your right. Park wherever you are able. You will be directed after that."

The captain seemed to believe that Giles either didn't know Paris or was just obtuse, for a Parisian. He had told the captain that he was a local advocate, but the captain kept his belief that Giles was deprived of a sense of location, which may have been common to his belief about junior officers being naïve as a group. Probably, Giles was being impatient and a bit ungenerous because, probably, the captain was just looking after him as his assumed responsibility.

Giles was about to leave the room and then the building when he noted that Marechal Petain was making his way toward the same exit from the room. The impulse struck Giles that this was doubtless his only opportunity to meet this revered man. He had heard so much from the common sources open to all and the personal tales by his father, as well, who was one of his staff officers, for a time, at the Sedan in 1916.

He warily set an angular course for the marshal, hoping that none of the cabinet members would intercede between them before he could reach and speak to him. He managed to sidle up to his right rear and addressed him, "Permission to speak to you, sir." The marshal politely stopped and looked to his right and, seeing the uniform, turned to face Giles with an inquisitive stare. He was clearly not accustomed to being addressed by second lieutenants. Without showing any impatience, he gave Giles just enough time to speak, and Giles quickly identified himself as the son of his father, giving his father's rank, a major and then colonel, while they were both at Verdun. A smile broke on the marshal's face as he enthusiastically asked after his father and what had become of him. Giles briefly related the high points and said that, before Giles's being called up, they had been together in the practice and that his parents were retired in Nice. The marshal then related that he had thought of him "many" times since his life was saved by him. Col. Gilbert Lambert had, according to the marshal, guided and pulled him out of a hollow, about to be filled with phosgene gas, and then through some blinding smoke during a bombardment, in the direction away from the Germans' descending shells. He had also shielded him from some ground fire on another occasion. "One can never forget such a man, nor such occurrences, so long as one lives. Lieutenant, if I may ever be of service to your father or you, call upon me." The conversation was clearly concluded, as the marshal advanced, with a somewhat broken gait, toward the door.

Giles survived the next day by leaving the apartment at 9:30 a.m. and reaching the Ministry of War Defense Building just in time for the shortened meeting, which he was not invited to enter. His stated purpose of English translation was not involved. There was no purpose in his being there at all. He was excess and relatively unnoticed while there. In fact except for some irritated, raised voices, there was mostly silence where he was stationed in the hallway.

However, being on duty, he was still expected to be there that night when the prime minister would return from his English meeting with Churchill. The meeting was set for 10:00 p.m. with some of the cabinet, to hear the French proposals. These were to keep Italy out of the war by possibly giving it part of Africa, such as French Somaliland-Djibouti and the Addis Ababa Railway, and perhaps the internationalization of Malta and Gibraltar: thus, as a part thereof, making Italy "the honest broker." Only France wished these gifts given, and these were opposed by Britain. It signified its position, by telegraph, to Paris that evening, after the French ministers had left London.

It was obvious to Giles that there was nothing more to do until the planned night meeting was called to order at ten that night, and as no one was exercising any authority, he could leave and return just before the meeting was scheduled to commence. He departed after the last of the ministers had left, most of them in solemn moods: some wearing faces both dejected and morose, others with faces of anger, perplexity, fury, or bewilderment.

Only the police sergeant at the door reflected a calm expression, which graduated into sublimation as he saw the last person through the door, who was Giles. Now he could return to more mobile and less stultifying duties than securing the door of a building for aged men, whose presence there was not explained to him. Nor was it explained that it concerned his immediate future and that of his country's survival.

XLVI

GILES MOUNTED HIS bike and reversed the direction of it to recross the bridge with the purpose of traveling the edge road of the Place de La Concorde toward the Boulevard Madeleine, following it into the Avenue de L'Opera and then turning onto Rue Marcel. His final goal was the Bank of France on the Rue Marcel. He planned to cash his draft on the bank, which he received in the envelope containing his last orders.

He held his breath as he approached the teller at the commercial window, for fear of some defect in the instrument. It was so exorbitant an amount for a second lieutenant to receive in one payment. In spite of that, he was paid upon presentation of his army identity card and endorsement of the draft, in cash, as he requested. Obviously, Capt. Bizier had paid him for six months, thinking that no paymaster might ever be available to Giles in the future!

He then headed for his apartment, hoping that Elle would be able to join him when he phoned her at the hospital. She was thrilled when he called, arranged an early relief, and arrived at the apartment thirty minutes later. A light luncheon in bed and a lustful afternoon ensued!

Dawn sunlight gradually increased the intensity of its flow through the crescent tops of the two windows on the bedroom wall. The drapes on these windows above the boulevard had been left open through oversight, as they had both fallen quickly into slumber. Restlessness surfaced shortly as their subconscious minds were far from untroubled. The flow of light became a flood, and their sleep floundered into wakefulness.

After morning ablutions and over coffee and croissants, they planned a day together. This was an opportunity both rare and anxiously grasped by these two, who were full of foreboding, but who managed to constantly avoid mention, to one another, of their abject fear for their future.

Some walking trips were mentioned, and finally Giles proposed, with a raised right hand and forefinger and in a mock-stentorian voice, "I have it. We shall buy a cold lunch and a bottle of white wine, walk over to the Luxembourg Gardens, sit by the fountain and pool, soak up the sun, and pretend we are the guests of Marie de Medici! We shall lunch under the shade of those grand old plane trees. We shall visit the palace and view the paintings (if the Senate is out of session). A truly capital day!"

Elle responded cheerfully, "I'll buy the lunch if you buy the wine!"

Giles countered, "Yes, providing I pick both."

Elle had a sufficient-sized basket, red-and-white checkered napkins, and substitutes for wine glasses. Giles suggested that he carry the basket unloaded to the shops for loading. Then she could carry the load to the gardens. Elle assumed his same affected speech and "declaimed" her pompous acceptance of the proposal. Then they both lightheartedly laughed, each thus covering the ongoing voids in the pits of their stomachs. But the overwhelming feelings of fulfillment, in having each other, trumped the nagging agonies of their situation.

They reconsidered their impulsive plan as to the walking aspect of venturing to the gardens and quickly amended that decision, driving over in the MG. The reasons were twofold: the wonderful weather and, secondly, because they were going to take the MG for storage in Rambouillet on Sunday the second of June. Driving the MG had become one of Elle's passions.

Giles felt the defeat of France was very close, and thus the time for securing the MG was at hand. They intended to follow the plan Giles had made with Eduard and Flore Bullard, storing it in one of Eduard's sheds on his sheep farm outside of Rambouillet. Thereafter they would return to Paris, to the Montparnasse station, and make their way home from there. They were just hoping that the metro service from Rambouillet would continue for another five or six days.

But on this glorious day, near the end of May, they would revel in its pulchritude and pretend there was no tomorrow. They would definitely not take the time to shop for food and wine on the way to the gardens but instead drive over to St. Germain de Pres, as Elle now suggested, and eat melted goat cheese on toast with a bottle of "small Loire wine," or some other "regional" available. As they reached Pont Neuf and turned left to cross to the Left Bank of the Seine, Giles said, "Don't forget that the Café de Flore is just across the street from Les Deux Magots, and we can get a wider selection there."

Elle asked where to park since the Boulevard St. Germain would be unparkable.

He said, "Since both are on St. Benoit, let's go to that far corner and hope to find a place on Rue Jacob or, even better, the street that borders the church across the street, on Rue L'Abbaye. Turn right on the boulevard when we get there, and we can decide at which one to eat after we find a place to park."

They chose the Café de Flore, where they agreed on a bottle of rather "small wine" from the Loire (red); she ordered a bowl of onion soup (a house specialty) and quiche, and he, an omelet with Welsh rarebit. They sat at a table on the walkway under the café awning and indulged in the age-old custom of watching the traffic and pedestrians move past them. They tore themselves away from gawking at the world as it moved by. He paid the bill as she corked the half bottle of wine, taking it with her as they crossed the street to the car. They then drove toward the gardens on the Rue de Rennes and parked on the Rue de Medicis, very close to the fountain and pool of the gardens. They intended to find a stone bench by the pool, shaded by the plane trees' leaves. The leaves nearly blocked the sun from lighting the pool and fountain. There was no dearth of benches but only one free of bird droppings. That made for a simple choice. Elle produced the cups, which she had taken from the basket in the MG, for their use when they would drink the wine, which she had also carried from the car.

The quiet, the almost gloomy atmosphere, the nearly inaudible sound of trickling, tinkling water from the fountain at the far end of the long pool—all lent an air of moroseness to this scene. From its conception by Giles, the day was intended to be light and frivolous. Instead, they had both settled into individual silence, mulling over their own dark thoughts, which were much the same and thus pointless burdens to repetitiously foist one upon the other. Best, then, would be the reigning silence! Their bench, at the far end of the pool, seemed an island of aloneness to each of them. Unfortunately it could not isolate them from the Paris in which they were existing.

Elle broke the heavy silence first. "Shall we give the palace a try?"

A startled Giles responded with an enthusiastic yes.

They rose as one and started on the path to the palace entrance, she with the cups and he with the wine.

"Let's hope," said Giles, "the guard will allow us to leave these thing at his post."

The palace seemed nearly abandoned. It was except for one attendant at the door, who carelessly allowed them entrance. With a shrug of his shoulders, as he turned to walk away, the attendant gave them the freedom to gain the second floor.

They didn't find the two Delacroix works or the Jordaens zodiac ceiling paintings stimulating. They decided to fall back on their original plan of walking in the gardens, which they proceeded to do, spending much of their time playing guessing games as to the identity of the numerous statues. Many of these were the various and sundry queens of France. Finally tiring of this, they made for the MG and then, with the windshield down, made a pleasant drive to the apartment.

XLVII

AS HE RODE toward the War Ministry Building, Giles wondered if anything at all was being gained by these war cabinet meetings. He ruminated: "Here it is, May 31, and no news has been released that indicates that the Germans have been stopped anywhere. The radio news and brief additions mentioned in the newspapers seem to avoid the subject, but the mobs coming here are larger each day. As the mobs increase, Parisians fearfully leave, as well. Thank heaven the public service people remain here. Why? No one dares to ask! The police remain also. No riots. No disturbances; just moving mobs. When will the stores begin to shut down as they did in Arras?" He parked his cycle in the same place as before and entered the building. A policeman on door duty directed him to Captain Margine's present location on the floor above and, having been alerted, cautioned him that "a meeting of importance" was already in session.

It was almost ten o'clock in the evening. This was the second meeting of the day, and Giles, as had been usual since the first day of his assignment, had been carelessly ignored as to the requirement of his presence. This night, however, he was apparently missed and rushed with pad and pencil into a meeting room. The room was filled with cigar smoke. A large counsel table and another makeshift table were placed at right angles, to accommodate the additional number of men in the room. It was a large Supreme Council of War meeting, attended by four or five Englishmen, as well as PM Reynaud, Marechel Petain, and Gen. Weygand.

Giles was thought to be useful, of course, to take notes on the Englishmen's comments and translate them into French. He sat obscurely at the back of the room, in an ordinary folding chair. There was a rather short, rotund Englishman standing in front of his chair next to Reynaud at the main counsel table who was expelling most of the aforementioned smoke, while alternating these expulsions with florid eruptions of rhetoric. He was grandiloquent in verbiage and resonant in voice, beyond any contemporary English speaker ever imagined by Giles. He was stunning and clearly mesmerizing to all those in the room, English speakers or not.

This enthralling personality was none other than Winston S. Churchill, prime minister of Great Britain, who was attending the meeting of the Supreme War Council as the principal head of the British delegation. The purpose of his presence was to confront the devastating developments that threatened to end in the defeat and occupation of Britain's only ally, France. His hope was to engender fighting spirit into the flagging courage of the French government. It had taken a defeatist attitude since May 15, when Reynaud had telephoned him in London to tell him France had lost the war—that the Germans had broken through its lines on May 10. The best of the French armies seemed ponderous, confused, and accepting of their inability to break out of confinement in the north Belgium area and hysterically inept in the Second and Ninth Armies area in the Sedan, Luxembourg, and the Ardennes region, where the Germans had broken through.

Accompanying Churchill were Clement Attlee, Generals John Dill and Hastings Ismay, and Churchill's personal representative to PM Reynaud, Sir Edward Louis Spears, of native-born French background, but an Englishman. After speaking of French valor and resolve—that is, "the taxi campaign" in 1915, saving Paris and France—he fervently urged their sons to remember and display this innate part of their inherent character. At this point the small meeting was thrown open to questions and discussion.

The small French portion of the delegation present were Premier Reynaud, Marshal Petain, and Maxime Weygand. Both the

French premier and General Weygand decried the lack of effort at evacuating French troops along with the British at Dunkirk in Operation Dynamo, the British naval operation to save the British army in France. Churchill promised to amend that situation if indeed it was going on. Weygand was furious about the British "desertion" when they had been still under French command. At this point, the British had, according to the present British delegation, taken their personal command back because the French in the North were in total confusion. The accidental auto death of their delegate, General Belotte, without immediate replacement, and the French failure to strike north as agreed and meet the British in their attempt to separate the German panzers from their supplies and supporting infantry had left them no choice. The French had moved as though entranced or paralyzed, as the Germans swept with lightning speed across France. So spoke the members of the British military who were present.

Weygand also found the British air force totally at fault. He blamed the lack of bombing, but the use of bomber command was futile against tanks. (The British were limited in the use of its fighter command because of "home defense"), and the loss of French bases to the German ground forces capturing them. There was also a discussion that Italy was about to invade France in the South. British unwillingness to concede any territories, British or French, had already been established in London at the war council meeting on May 26.

The British were mingling and preparing to say good-bye when the subject was breeched about a separate surrender by the French to the Germans. Then Churchill mentioned the prior agreement between them of no separate peace being allowable. At that time, British general Spears addressed Marechel Petain, stating that if the French did that, "then the British would block your ports and bomb German occupied ports in return." Later Petain told Reynaud, The British got us into this (war), and now they threaten to bomb us." Giles stood separated from the cabinet, but no effort was made to clear the room of support staff as this heavy-handed repartee occurred. Giles, at this point, knew that his worst fears were coming true.

Giles made for the door to the corridor, first leaving with Capt. Margine the notes he had taken by dropping them on the seat of the captain's chair. Giles's anger was all consuming. He realized that the three French buffoons had never in twenty years had any thoughts for France but only for their own egoistic interests. The tones of their voices and the interplay with the British made their ineptness apparent. Blinded by his anger, he hurried down the corridor toward the outer door. Upon reaching it, he thrust it open, ignoring the police officer on duty there.

His anger transferred to his handle grips, as he revved his cycle beyond need. He sped rashly toward home and felt his hot tears of rage slipping out from beneath the rubber rims of his goggles and the dusty, sooty wind sting his cheeks, like needle penetrations.

XLVIII

ELLE AND GILES decided to have a last night out while they still had the MG. They had decided to take it to storage on June 2, to Rambouillet and Eduard's sheep farm, where the German occupiers would not find it and trace it to Giles. Now, not joyously, but soberly and selectively, they chose a place to dine and for entertainment thereafter.

The next evening they drove the MG to the Place Vendome with the intention of dining without a reservation, at the Ritz Hotel restaurant, called L'Espadon. Most of their class of customer had left Paris or were making preparations to depart because they had information of the German proximity to the capital.

The waiter brought them martinis, one with olives and the other with cocktail onions, but only after a battle over the style of the martinis. The waiter could not comprehend the difference in content between an "American" style and the usual French or British one, even after an excruciatingly clear explanation as to the amount of gin and dry vermouth to be included. Apparently the barman understood when the waiter emphasized the word enough for them to overhear him say "American," in an exasperated manner, bringing a knowing response from the barman—all of which made the couple sorry the cocktail had been requested at all. What was wanted by them was a quiet, memorable evening, not turmoil! They soon forgot the experience with the receipt of their satisfying dinner orders. Even with their future hanging in the balance, the French would never gainsay the importance of food.

Neither were tempted by dessert, and so they decided on continuing the evening "on the town." They had parked the MG just north of the Place Vendome on the Rue de la Paix. Elle had suggested that they visit one of the night bar scenes in the area, such as Harry's New York Bar or The Dingo Bar on Rue Delambre. Both were jazz scenes and close by. Harry's was just a corner away at the intersection of Rue de Daunou and Rue de la Paix, plus one block, and this was the one chosen. It was a piano bar, and any friendly patron could join in, providing the individual was good enough at the instrument not to be thrown out for a lack of ability. The patrons would decide after a very few moments of playing! The American jockey Tod Sloan sold it to Harry McElhone who made it the first cocktail bar in Europe, in the twenties. When Gershwin composed part of *An American in Paris* on its piano, fame and future reputation were guaranteed.

Giles and Elle decided to continue with "American martinis" in this most American of all bars in Paris. English gin was the principal ingredient, with dry vermouth and olives (or, for a Gibson, with onions), along with vigorous shaking in a container filled with ice, which made up the balance. However, the lack of any of these canceled the "American" expatriate label. As said before, American expatriates were gone with the war, along with their "mystique," but there remained a redolence for them, among the French, who rejoiced in their camaraderie in this aspect of Paris nightlife.

Giles said, "It's a pleasure to stand and be jostled for a change."

Elle responded, "Yes, the first crowded place in weeks. Let's change places."

"Why?" he asked.

"Because one of these vile old men at the bar behind me likes the bump in my torso too much!"

"Which one?" he angrily asked.

She replied, "I don't know, and you don't need to care. Just change places with me—now!"

They exchanged places, stayed another hour or so, enjoyed the scene, and decided to move on.

Dancing seemed to both of them to be last on their agenda, but doable. Their choice was new to them and desirable. It was the Villa D'Este, which offered the atmosphere of an Italian garden, quite colorful, with artfully created architectural qualities, both ornate, tasteful, and convincingly done; all but a fountain of the actual villa were similarly present. The dancing arrangements were commodious and provided a worthy orchestra. A bottle of "good" white Burgundy was the price paid to enjoy the ambience and the pleasure of holding each other romantically, absenting themselves from the world, as they danced for an hour or so.

XLIX

THE NEXT MORNING, Sunday, June 2, after breakfast, Giles and Elle departed in the MG for Rambouillet to store the car as planned. The drive was most pleasant, with Elle at the wheel, which was on the wrong side of the vehicle, being of English manufacture. She had not had any problem adjusting to it, however.

The true problem was the amount of traffic of every kind and description on the road. The volume of mass movement had not slackened but been added to by people from north of Paris joining the mobs from the north and east of them. This made the twenty-seven to thirty miles take approximately three hours and several minutes.

When they finally arrived at Eduard and Flore's farmhouse, they were warmly greeted by both of them, and Elle was made to feel as comfortable and at home as Giles had always felt. After trading family information and Giles's catastrophic news and views about the likelihood of immediate French defeat, they began to arrange for the placement of the MG in one of the small barns, behind a wall of bales. This took hours of hard lifting and moving by all four of them. Before the bales were moved into place, a tarpaulin was placed over the MG, and two levels of bales were placed on top of it. Then a wall of bales was built dividing the small building in half, with tractors and bale equipment placed beside the wall, inside the door. However, space was left to get to the bales, to remove them for use, as might be needed for the animals. Otherwise, prying eyes might believe it to be a wall hiding something. From this time forward, Eduard said he would keep the three outlying barns locked to the workers, to avoid the suspicion that a single locked barn might contain something of unusual value. Theft in oncoming hard times would be another reason. Giles gave one set of keys to the auto to Eduard and one to Elle for use in the unpredictable future.

They spent the night with their hosts because of the lateness of the hour when the job was completed. Tomorrow, early morning, Eduard would drive them to the station, to take a train to Montparnasse in Paris. Giles was increasingly indifferent about his presence at the cabinet meetings. It was obvious by the indifferent attitude of the colonel and his captain about Giles's being there that he was totally excess. He told Elle that he was going over on the fifty as he would thus continue to have immediate news of what was going to happen to France and to the two of them.

L

ON JUNE 5 Prime Minister Reynaud held a cabinet meeting specifically to encourage its members by naming three changes. When Giles made entry to the same chamber where they had most recently met, General Weygand was there along with Marechel Petain and several other members. Petain was named as assistant prime minister instead of his position as secretary of state. Weygand became secretary of war, and Charles de Gaulle, the other new member of the cabinet, was also understood to be the new personal advisor to Reynaud. This seemed to eliminate Colonel Villelume. Giles realized his vulnerability were the colonel to disappear and thought to approach him as soon as the meeting concluded. Giles asked the colonel if he were leaving his position, and the answer was yes. This prompted Giles to ask what disposition was to be made of himself, and the colonel made it clear that General Weygand would likely transfer him to some humiliating post because of his dislike for him, personally. He asked Giles if he would like to be assigned to Chateau du Muguet in Breteau near Briare, the new army headquarters, under General Weygand. No was his emphatic answer. The earth had been moving under his feet ever since he left the British headquarters at Arras, and he didn't have any plan made to respond to the colonel's question. Therefore he threw the die and asked whether the colonel still had the authority to assign him further, and the colonel responded, "At this time, yes."

Giles, with his heart in his mouth, asked to be ordered returned to inactive service, until further notice from proper army authority.

The colonel's response was, "Good thinking. It will be one of the last things I will do in this post! Captain Margine will execute it at our earliest convenience. Try us on the seventh for the executed order. This order shall carry at least as much weight as the one assigning you here from Vincennes, the old army headquarters. At least you will have a new order, like the last one, which fobbed you off onto me. Tell me, just for my amusement, how long have you been floating around on these kinds of orders? No, don't! In the 'World's Best Army,' which became the 'World's Worst Army' inside of two weeks, there must be tens of thousands just like you. I was a much decorated officer in the first war, where we got the title of 'the best'! I am so ashamed of my country and my army—of the French people. I am descended from the ancient 'Nobility of the Sword.' You couldn't know how humiliated I feel. If I had my cadet saber from St. Cyr, I'd fall on it!"

Giles simply saluted, as the colonel petulantly continued, "At least this order should enable conviction for desertion to be avoided. Thus, Lambert, you will suffer no firing squad." The colonel then mumbled to himself after Giles had walked toward the entrance, "I only wish I could do the same for myself."

When Giles reappeared for his separation papers, he was told to return instead on the morning of the ninth for some necessary duty to be performed before his separation was granted. This, of course, caused him to speculate on the true likelihood that he was being hoodwinked in some unrealizable fashion, and he wondered whether he should return at all. However, not to do so would leave him in a status of desertion if the French army survived the German onslaught. Therefore, return he must!

When he did as ordered, he was given the separation papers under the colonel's signature, just as requested. The captain then told him that the trucks—of which there were many, many parked along Rue Constantine, beginning at its intersection with the Quai D'Orsay and continuing along the Boulevard des Invalides, to reach past the side of the Hotel des Invalides—were being filled with sensitive records, records from the Ministry of Defense and the other ministries. They then were to be driven from where they were presently parked to Tours: yes, dispatched to Tours, along with cabinet members in private cars! The government was abandoning Paris, which was being declared an "open city," and the Germans would doubtless move to occupy it in the next few days. The route would be along back roads to avoid causing the population of Paris to riot or rampage in hysteria. He had been instructed to ask Giles if he wished to volunteer, as a civilian driver, of a sedan or limousine carrying cabinet members. "Giles, you must however consider it as a civic duty and without pay and without remuneration or reimbursement for expenditures. This, of course, would provide you an escape from being subject to German control here and an opportunity to (possibly) move with the government if it decides to abandon continental France, to carry on in North Africa. However, it's only fair to state that that possibility, sponsored by Minister Reynaud, is appearing to be dimmer all the time. Weygand and Petain are gaining strength in the cabinet and are in favor of an armistice if they find the German terms acceptable—a totally uncertain enigma. The choice is yours."

Giles, without much forethought, blurted out that in case he had not noticed, the population was almost half departed, which of course was a clear form of hysteria. They had obviously lost all faith in the army and the government already. The streets were empty, except to convey people toward the exits to the south. Most of the shops were closing and, in many cases, boarding up.

Furthermore, he had a wife here, as the captain was aware, and he would not be interested, as a consequence. After thanking him and sending his thanks to the colonel for his thoughtfulness and kindness, he wished them the best of good luck. As he took his leave, he heard the captain's parting remark: "Giles, keep your head down!"

LI

ON JUNE 14, early in the morning, German troops began to march into St. Denis and the other northern suburbs: first scouts, then armor, and finally infantry in long columns of threes, all with specific targets in mind, such as railroad stations and other key points, all seemingly known and carefully selected in advance, along with the heart of the city. Now, at last, the French had one single thing upon which they all had to agree: they were a conquered people!

Giles and Elle had, as indicated earlier in this story, been corseted by contemporaneous circumstances to remain in Paris until fate would perhaps grant them release. They had survived more than four months of German occupation, which had become a gradual strangulating of the French as the Germans brought in the SS and the SD for that purpose.

The unnamed man that Giles had been looking for with such risky perseverance was Etienne Picard, his closest friend, who had been called to active duty in the same "reserve call" to duty as Giles had been. Giles knew that Etienne had inherited property, including a large unoccupied house, in the black Perigord region, near the town of Sarlat-la-Canéda. This was a hilly, gorged area of back roads, medieval castles, and caves, once utilized by Cro-Magnon and possibly Neanderthal man. The Dordogne River and its small derivatives flowing through it all created an unrealistic ambience. It would be difficult for the Germans to supervise and control it. This was the haven that Giles had been frantic to use and needed permission and directions from his friend to locate. The Germans had just begun to try to enforce the border between Vichy France and the occupied zone, which was about 50 or more percent of France. Toward the last part of November, they were beginning to post signs of warning and arrest for violation by those going into, but not properly residing in, the Vichy French independent region.

Giles knew he must flee to the unoccupied zone immediately. He had no connections in the South except his parents in Nice, and their circumstances were unknown to him at this time. Thus, he continued his search for his best friend, Etienne. He knew Etienne would happily lend him the house as a perfect shelter for both him and Elle.

In desperation at not finding Etienne, or news of his whereabouts, he decided to risk his complete safety by visiting the archbishop, Etienne's uncle, by whom his closest friend and schoolmate was raised after both his parents' deaths. Giles, as a child, had known the archbishop and his home well, and he always found him welcoming and cordial over those many years. However, the revival of open anti-Semitism in France left Giles worried that the archbishop might be on the wrong side of German hatemongering and, possibly, intensely propagandized by the Germans. Over the centuries, the church had been vicious or indifferent in turn and worse in some locations than others. He might report him to the Germans if he were an opportunist, or he might connect him with Etienne if he were still favorable to him. One thing was certain, he had been avuncular in his treatment all those years, and he need not have been if he were a Catholic doctrinaire. Children sense an adult's feelings toward them, and he, in turn, felt warmth toward Etienne's "Uncle Emmanuel."

But his thoughts inevitably returned to "home" and what was to be done to preserve the safety of his beloved Elle if he abandoned her in his quest for his personal safety. There was Lyon and her mother. They appeared to be her safest harbor, but how to manage her crossing the new "demarcation line"—that was the inevitable quandary. Obtaining the German *Ausweis*, or white pass,

The French Lieutenant and the King of Rome

to cross the line was a mystery, the explanation of which was about to be dictated to the French people by their German masters.

Both he and Elle were without any form of private transportation. They were on foot for everything. He had disposed of his motorcycle by pushing it into the St. Martin Canal, which was not nearby. He had accomplished this at night in early July. He had done so shortly before the Germans had organized patrols throughout Paris. He had also mothballed his uniforms (but not his weapons and ammunition) the night before the Germans marched into Paris. He did not fear police patrols, at the time, because they didn't have the means to make motorized ones. He mused further that the police were immediately submissive to the Germans. The Parisians were passive during the first weeks of the occupation, seeming both stunned and befuddled, as if to say, "Wait a minute: there are no rules in the playbook that say you can come over the edge of the chessboard and walk in and claim 'checkmate' like this!"

In thinking of Elle and their relationship, he pondered her response to their most personal and most difficult moments. He could not repeat the escapades that had led to her fear and fury of a few nights before. Those arose from his peregrinations and ended in a confusion of combative violence followed by intense sex, the latter arising from the torment of the violence. The whole of it was a disaster and destructive to their unity of spirit. Such scintillation from violence to sex was evil and easily habit-forming. They both realized that sex should never be used as a purgative for anger. When he could make his departure successfully, he would not agitate her further with his furtive searches. But then, what would be her future if he failed to plan an extrication for her from "German Paris"?

On a more routine level, each day their lives had become more narrow. There was no ration card for him because his existence must be hidden. Their monetary resources became slimmer; he could not assist her and became little more than a dependent invalid. Even the building manager and the doorman, her friends at the hospital, others in passing could by accident expose them to unforeseen danger. He must make his final move! He must go to the archbishop's residence and expose his situation by seeking Etienne there. He must simultaneously make a dependable plan with her for her departure. They had held to their pledge to one another not to discuss their independent plans for safety reasons, in the event of German or police detention of one or the other of them. But now, it became impossible to keep, as their mutual cooperation to escape German Paris was necessary.

XLII

AFTER GILES HAD been called to active duty, Giselle began asking the medical director of her hospital to make enquiries of the Hotel Dieu de Lyon, a significant and major French hospital in her mother's home city, Lyon. Would he aide her in obtaining a transfer to their staff, as soon as possible? He eventually agreed as she was, by then, qualified.

She had completed her specialty in cardiology in September of 1939 and thought the best place to be was with her mother, for the many reasons imaginable, during the duration of hostilities. With the whirlwind defeat of France and the creation of the demarcation line for the "new France" of Vichy and Marechal Petain, new stringent German regulations would apply for movement into it. Giselle knew she needed to cross to Lyon before the German *Ausweis* became the only means of legal exit from the occupied zone.

She was familiar, for most of her youth, with this ancient hospital and its almost timeless history, as she had spent many of her early years in Lyon. The Lyon hospital had been founded in the twelfth century. It commenced as a clerical meeting hospice for both auxiliary and regular members of the church and had particular pontifical recognition. It became a fully functioning hospital in mid-sixteenth century and grew ever larger in size and importance thereafter.

After the armistice and the establishment of the Vichy government, the unoccupied area of France included Lyon. The German army withdrew behind the demarcation line, leaving these areas, including Lyon, to the Vichy administration, to be "independent." This line began to be enforced after the end of November 1940. The line was subject to arbitrary change, at the whim of the Germans, and was difficult to enforce because of its meandering through villages and farms, separating fields and houses and streets. The fact that the Germans maintained a force of perhaps as few as twenty-five hundred soldiers to police a line of some twelve hundred kilometers (two men per kilometer) made penetration relatively simple for a multitude of *passeurs*, who made a commercial enterprise out of crossing it. Few arrests were made for violations before February 1941 when German customs people replaced the German army. The first flood of people after the armistice were going north, to return to their abandoned homes: thereafter, the traffic reversed to escape the German occupation. The Vichy French established a force composed of police, the *milice* (their militia), and their armistice army on the other side of this line, but they did not overactively aid their German counterparts in staunching the movement into Vichy territory.

Giles and Elle awoke at 6:00 a.m., according to the small windup clock on the lamp table beside the headboard of their bed. Upon rising, Elle pattered barefoot to the bathroom, and Giles moved to one of the windows, to speculate on the likely aspects of the day they were about to face. It was, on measure, a gray, stark, barren, and dry boulevard below. "Nothing new there: just the usual melancholy aspect," he abysmally noted to himself. It had been bitterly cold for November, and his limited view of Paris, through the frosted panes of the window, looked grimly foreboding. Only she, having her hospital duties, would venture out this morning, and he…Well, he wasn't certain what he would do! Much would depend upon the crucial decision they could make, hopefully this morning. Was there time to talk about the critical subject they had mutually decided not to breach but must now address? He had repeatedly mulled the forbidden issue over in his mind, and her agreement was all that was necessary. Their time to escape Paris was rapidly evaporating! It may as well be over coffee this morning. They knew that telephone conversations were out of the question now because of the possibility of tapping by the police or their masters, as their stranglehold grew tighter.

He decided to prepare their croissants and coffee while awaiting her dressing, which she customarily accomplished between her closet, the bathroom, and their bedroom. Awaiting her preparations, he donned his robe and proceeded out the bedroom door, toward the kitchen-breakfast room, to first make the coffee. Their morning coffees were different, and that difference was inviolably maintained! She insisted on un café au lait, a composite of steamed milk and a little coffee, whereas he took only un grand crème, an espresso with steamed milk, served in a standard-sized cup.

She entered the kitchen area as he had completed the two coffees and was placing them on the kitchen table. She approached him to place a good-morning kiss on his forehead and then stepped back as she pursed her lips into a sort of grimace and stared for a moment before postulating a question regarding his plans of the day. "I must ask you what you have heard about the German plans for an immediate blocking of exits to the new Vichy zone."

He responded, "That it could happen—even today!"

"Then, Giles, we must disregard our previous understanding and reveal what we each have done and immediately do it!" She then turned to leave the room, saying, "I'll return in a moment."

When she did, it was with an envelope, which she handed to him and which contained a letter from the director of her hospital, directing her to leave at her earliest convenience for the Hotel Dieu de Lyon, to take up her new assignment as a cardiologist on its staff. He would assist her in any way possible to facilitate her departure. The letter was dated five days ago, and no, he said, he couldn't help her clear the occupied zone, other than to vouch for her need to go to Lyon to fill the post provided her there.

Giles was startled at the welcome news and then concentrated on the immediate problem at hand—how to get her out of Paris. But she, anxiously, first wanted to know what, if anything, he planned in order to solve his own dilemma. She had no intention of leaving him without an acceptable identification to "get by" in Paris and without a personal ration card. His response was that he had only one plan, other than fleeing south to the Cher and Loire Rivers area and sneaking across the demarcation line. That plan was to find Etienne and move to his house in the Perigord region, leaving Paris before the demarcation line became impassable because it was too well established and guarded. Since the Germans had established the *zone libre*, which included Lyon, it might even be possible for him to go to her mother's small estate and vanish there, while he made other plans for them both or for him alone, as she might wish. Now it became clear that he must go to the archbishop's house today to search for Etienne. If, upon going there, he found it to have been a mistake, he would take the metro to Rambouille and ask Eduard and Flore to help him get to and over the line; then, he should be able to get to her mother's in Lyon. If Etienne were at his uncle's, then he would try to arrive at a solution for one or both of them.

After an hour of frantic discussion, a carefully calculated plan was to be executed as follows: She would pack this morning, carrying two sizeable suitcases, commensurate with a person who was changing her place of residence. She would sew her wedding rings into the seam of a heavy woolen garment, for security and unobtrusiveness. She would carry no written evidence of marriage. She would carry all of her personal documentation, such as birth certificate, ration card, driving license, passport, and so forth. She would then go to the hospital and give a key to her medical associate so that he and his wife could occupy the apartment for such time as she might be gone. This had been arranged some time ago because they were living with his wife's parents, an uncomfortable situation for them all. There was to be no rent charged, and she already had a letter signed by both that they had no right of possession and would relinquish possession to Elle, Giles, Elle's mother (who had ownership of record), or an estate in the stead of any of the three of them on forty-eight hours' notice, oral or written. Giles saw the letter and commended Elle on her practical legal sense, thinking that it was a binding layperson's agreement. If she were examined by the police at the Gare de Lyon tomorrow, about this letter, she was to say that he had been her mother's attorney on some matter two or three years ago. Occupancy was to commence on the date filled in on the blank line provided in the letter. That date was to be dependent on his risky telephone call that night or no later than the next morning, at eight, to Elle.

In that phone call, if the archbishop would aid her in her departure to the free zone in some way, then, instead of her going to the railway station tomorrow, he would convey the archbishop's instructions. He would give Elle a date and time certain to be at the archbishopric's office to discuss her position regarding a pontifical honorarium and letter of personal commendation and support from the cardinal, available to her as the archbishop's delegate-physician on the staff of the Hotel Dieu de Lyon. She was to understand from that message that all was well and that he had been successful in arranging an escape from Paris and would contact her at either the hospital or her mother's in Lyon. Further, Giles would rely on his memory for her mother's phone and address in Lyon. In the event of falling afoul of the Germans or the French police, he would rely on both sets of his military separation papers, giving his old residence address, the one before their marriage, with no reference to theirs or her or their marriage.

"Giles, I shall repeat the details now," she said, which she proceeded to do. "Darling, I have one other question. If I don't hear from you by eight in the morning, what should I think and do?"

"Think the worst, go immediately to the train station, buy your ticket to Lyon, and leave on the first train out. And if the authorities won't let you go, act the adamant female, ignorant of any restraints preventing you, a physician, from leaving; act in a huff, and return here to the apartment. Apply as quickly as you can to the Germans or the police for a pass, simply because you have a legitimate and timely reason to leave. Surely, it will eventually work!"

"Darling, I must ask you something else for my peace of mind. Are you going armed?"

"Yes, I am! My overcoat will disguise that. You know that I shall do everything to avoid being taken alive, and if I have to go, I'll take as many of the swine with me as I can!"

Elle seemed to stare into space, looking away from the set expression on his face. "I—" she paused and then said, as if to herself alone, "shall just hang in the balance, like my mother did for my father, waiting for you to call or walk through the door, to answer my prayers!" Another long pause followed, heavily pressing on the silence between them, while they both stood motionless, both silently realizing this to be their sundering—the sundering of their one into two! "Until that awful, final news!" she said.

He reached for her, across the vast emptiness of their depression. They embraced each other with a binding ardor, which could no longer melt them back into one. They both departed the apartment, sharing what might be their last kiss in their entry hall: she, for the hospital; he, for the metro and the archbishop's residence.

LIII

WITH EACH DOWNWARD step, he felt more exposed and trapped by the narrowness of the passageway to the track. How long would he have to wait for the train to reach the exit station for the Place des Invalides and its nearby Rue Barbet de Jouy? He put the question to himself out of inner tension, requiring no answer nor even conjecture. Only the materialization of the proper train would resolve it. So far, so good! There was no foot traffic in the passageway in either direction as he arrived at the platform for departure. Ah, this was the right one! As the cars began to blur past him, the last three or four were slowing to a stop, and he, with furtive glances across the cars, tried to determine which, if any, contained potential threats. Two of the three seemed clear. He chose the middle of the three and entered through the automatic doors to find it sparsely occupied. A good choice! The name of this game was alertness: not to play it could be fatal.

Two young German soldiers were seated together on a bench at the near end of the car. They were enlisted men, pink cheeked, guileless in facial expressions, and utterly befuddled by the ambience: more fearing than to be feared!

He tripped on the edge of the top step as he reached the sidewalk on exiting at his destination but felt a steadying hand under his left forearm, thus regaining his balance as he strode forward. It was the hand of one of the German youths from his car on the train! He looked over his shoulder and said, "*Danke*," in his limited German, and increased his pace to avoid the possibility of an encounter.

In less than fifteen minutes, he had found the street he sought, Rue Barbet de Jouy. He sighted the house in short order but was several hundred feet away from it when he did.

His Eminence had taken residence some time before taking up his manifold duties, first as cardinal and then additionally as archbishop. His position in the church was significant, to the extent that he was a member of the conclave of cardinals who had selected Pope Pius XII in 1939—a man to be reckoned with! But Giles was banking on him being, still, "Uncle Emmanuelle"!

Giles passed himself through the pedestrian entry in the wrought-iron gates, which closed the driveway to vehicles. Now he stood below the two entry steps with the bell pull hanging in front of him, waiting to be pulled. "In for a penny, in for a pound." He gave thought to that English expression as he sucked in his breath and pulled the bell with assertiveness, having squelched his negative thoughts about adverse possibilities.

The door burst open from within to reveal Lucien, the remarkable, capable, memorable Lucien—valet, butler, personal servant, consigliere, and majordomo to the archbishop. Lucien: stood in the doorway—just as he always remembered him!—tall, emaciated, and dignified, but now with a paunch, obviously straining the waistcoat of his dark gray serge suit (somewhat shiny with age). His slow smile of recognition began with raised, startled eyebrows, progressing to enlarged sparkling eyes and descending to his broadly smiling lips, which inaudibly formed, "Giles," as if his brain had mechanically thrust the name to his facial muscles, which then burst forth with the jubilant, spontaneous, delightful grin and the whispered name, "Giles!" This was instantly followed by his arms thrown about Giles as his more-than-welcome visitor stepped up and into the entry hall to receive the exuberant French double-cheek kiss. Class distinctions were forgotten by such two old friends with such familiar memories, finding each other alive amid this misbegotten war!

The French Lieutenant and the King of Rome

The archbishop, having heard the noisy ebullience reverberating from the entry hall and into his study, which lay beyond the salon, abandoned his desk project and hurried to join the ruckus, be it joyful or troublesome. An enthusiastic and positive man, not only in spirit but in devotion to his God and humankind, his only wonder in life was how humans could ever be fearful of anything, since humanity had the compassion and promise of an ever-forgiving Eternal Father.

When he reached the foyer and Giles materialized before him, the vacuum of the many years of his absence was filled. His right hand seized that of Giles's, as they each closed the gap between them with enthusiasm and a giant, joint hug. His Eminence fairly spewed the words, "My boy, my boy!" They smiled into each other's happy faces, and Giles experienced that rare, unique human relief—homecoming! The archbishop's stout legs and thick corpulent person coached Giles through the salon toward his study as he punctured the air around them with happy inquisitions about Giles's history since his marriage to Giselle, interrupting the possibilities of Giles's responses with his own laughter and nonspecific, rambling phrases about Etienne's remarkable good fortune in evading death or capture by the "German steamroller."

"Giles, dear boy, sit down!" He indicated one of the two side chairs in front of his desk, he taking the other one, thus emphasizing the familiar relationship that was formerly youth and close adult friend and now, fully, close friends and equals. On sweeping the book-filled room with his eyes, Giles noted one section that seemed to be non ecclesiastical.

"Giles, I see that you have found the soft, underbelly of my spirit—my George Simenon detective stories about Detective Maigret. I have been consumed with him from his early beginnings! Such lay interests are not admired within the church, as, say, etymology might be, but we all have our peculiarities, do we not?" He rose from his chair as he continued to speak, approaching the open door between the salon and the study, reviewing the salon, which was empty of people. He promptly reseated himself but had left the door between the rooms open, and the room, thus, to his continuing observation.

"But enough of small talk. Let us speak in confidence of what concerns us most: your status and that of Etienne's."

Giles blurted out, "Good! Where is Etienne? You have indicated that he was fine. At least, I concluded as much from your remarks—from which I gathered nothing of substance!"

"First, tell me if you are free to talk of your own predicaments of which I am certain some serious ones must exist."

"Yes, sir, they certainly do! It has taken me since mid-July to get the courage to come to you, and I add that I have done so with fear for my safety still in my heart."

The archbishop, somewhat taken aback, said, "Do you fear me then?"

"Only in that the church has not always been a supporter of Jews, and I do not know what constraint you may be suffering now. Perhaps your personal regard for me is now impeded by German control and that of their Jewish enemies among our own people. I must rely for my safety on your honorable answer for I am in your hands, as of this moment and regardless of what that answer might be."

"Giles, never fear me! I trust you as you must trust me. I care for you as I love your best friend, my nephew Etienne, and will strive to do for you both what I can, silently and with the same dedication. I well realize that your situation is much different than his and therefore calls for different solutions. And now I will reveal his situation. My boisterous guidance into this study was to mislead the servants other than Lucien. But remember that the other servants in this house are not in any way to be relied upon. Of course, you may emphatically depend upon Lucien, as I do and must! More of that a little later. Now, details about Etienne, but after our understanding that I am about to propose."

LIII

"FIRST AND FOREMOST is that information related between us is confidential and therefore secret and not to be revealed under any circumstances. Minor generalities are just as significant as specifics. Only our basis for knowing one another and our close friendship is ordinary and revealable, and that is because it is known at large. You must agree to this now before we endeavor to proceed. Nothing regarding our arrangements may be in writing; all must be oral."

"Yes, sir, most emphatically!" Giles immediately felt a release of his bodily tension and the fight-or-flight syndrome that had been coursing through his muscles. He felt so incredibly fortunate to have put himself at the archbishop's discretion. (Though he knew he had, at this desperate stage, no choice.)

"Now, with regard to Etienne, he is now in the vicinity of Vichy, where he has become a junior officer in the new armistice army in the free zone controlled by Petain's Vichy government. I was able to arrange that through people in that government. Of course, I know the marshal personally. As you no doubt realize, Hitler dictated that it would be the same size as the army allowed Germany after the last war and was intended to be used in the event of civil strife within its borders. It moves on bicycles and is without heavy weapons and maintains itself by exuberant physical exercise. Its purpose actually is to emphasize the new attitude of 'family values and French tradition,' rather than liberty, which was abolished in violation of our law, as also was the Estates General.

The government is a petty dictatorship within the total authority of its puppet master, the large dictatorship of Hitler's Germany. Our church is considered a part of the Vichy government because of its anti liberal attitude and anti-Dreyfus history and xenophobic past.

"Before you ask, let me state that he was subject to internment in Germany as a prisoner of war for an indeterminate time and under horrifying circumstances. Or, at some stage, he could become forced labor in Germany, which is likely to happen as the war goes forward, as it doubtless shall because it is against the will of God that evil shall prevail in his world. Meanwhile, I deem that I have made him as safe as possible!

"In the meantime, we must all bide our time. Petain has proven himself to be, through his most recent conduct, a full partner of Satan. On October 9 he created a law depriving Frenchmen of Isrealite blood or belief of their rights, including being removed from all occupations and professions in France and those naturalized after 1936 to be revoked as citizens—even before the Germans had asked for it. Soon they shall deprive them of their funds and property. Eventually they shall be turned over to the Germans for deportation to concentration camps. After that, who knows? Which brings us to you! Where is your non-Isrealite wife now?"

Giles proceeded to relate all important details of his recent military history and the whereabouts of Elle and her immediate plans of tomorrow morning. He still did so with trepidation, realizing that they were now both in the archbishop's thrall. She would now be, without her even knowing it, a potential victim without her even approving his decision, to lay them both prostrate and open to German viciousness, if he were wrong about the archbishop!

The archbishop began to move about the room as in a state of agitation, stopping by his desk, but not with the intention of being seated, seemingly wandering but mentally cogitating a point with his eyes half lidded in concentration. "What time will she leave in the morning for the Gare de Lyon for the train?"

Giles answered, "Not until she hears from me before eight tomorrow. Either way, she leaves at eight."

"Somehow we must collect her tonight or in the morning. You must have a code you are using to tell her you are all right before eight! What is it?"

"Why do you need that?"

"Because, dear boy, we mean to bring her here to stay until I can obtain an *Ausweis* through the German diplomatic representative Otto Abetz, who is referred to as 'Ambassador.' Perhaps, within a week or less. His wife is a French woman named Suzanne. I know them both, through church and diplomatic affairs. Again no connection must be known between you. We have a few bedrooms here, and you and she will be disparate, coincidental guests. All here shall believe it!"

Giles thought to himself that the archbishop was beginning to assume the person of Detective Maigret and enjoying it greatly! He fervently hoped that he didn't run out of the plot he was enacting before they were both safely out of Paris.

Giles decided to call Elle from the library in the presence of the archbishop as the arrangements were to be made between them, before he called her, to avoid any confusion as to the arrangement for her pickup with luggage. It was also necessary to remind her to give notice to the building manager. If the manager must communicate with her, she must do so by writing to her, care of, the Archeveque de Paris at 7 Rue St. Vincent, Paris, France. No personal names or addresses were to be provided of her in or around Lyon.

Lucien, at this point, was called in to prepare to perform in his ancillary duty as chauffer. It would be necessary to explain, in exact detail, what must occur and where and how he was to retrieve her tomorrow morning. He would be attired in his chauffeur's uniform and drive the Archeveque's limousine, which Giles was informed was one of only seven thousand vehicles allowed to continue on gasoline performance in German Paris. The limousine bore the two front fender pennants bearing the cardinal's coat of arms on each one, containing a cardinal's red galero (the wide red-brimmed hat) with fifteen red tassels descending from each side of the hat and a motto underneath an escutcheon, proper to the cardinal, resting between—a most impressive display, all in all, but too memorable to every observer who would see it as it drove along the nearly vacant streets of Paris, which now were dominated by bicycles and the bicycle- rickshaws that were now replacing taxis. This was a tensely discussed consequence but passionately approved by the perhaps overconfident clergyman, who had, in Giles's increasingly troubled view, a problematical buoyancy about the likely outcome of risky, critical decisions. Giles mulled the matter over in his mind but had little choice, as he remembered his own internalized comment just before he pulled the bell to the front door and thought, "In for a penny, in for a pound."

But then who could have foreseen that their redeemer would be a devotee of George Simenon and might, in his mind, be matching wits with Detective Maigret or, even worse, playing at contesting wits with the French police or the German SD.

LIV

NOW ONLY THE where and when had to be agreed upon between the three of them present. Giles resolved that the instructions must be simple, precise, and brief, to avoid the interest of the possible phone monitors of the police and the Germans. The message took some serious planning. It must convey to Elle the instruction, without the need of refining it for her understanding. It would be best to write her name in care of the archbishopric's business address on a simple piece of paper and send her to the business office when Lucien arrived with it tomorrow, rather than discuss it over the phone.

Giles dialed the apartment number, and Elle answered after two rings with "Hello," and he responded with the carefully scripted words, "Everything OK?"

"Yes, and you?"

"Fine." Then Giles added, "Meet me at the rear entrance at eight. Bring everything you might need, as we shall not return until late. Sorry I have been so busy, but we have all day together tomorrow." After pause he concluded, "Well, then, good night."

"Good night, love!"

This ended the conference for Lucien, who would, of course, return with Elle and her valises tomorrow morning, using the rear garage entrance into this house. If stopped by any authority, Lucien was to state that she was under the archbishop's charge, to be dispatched to Lyon as the church and the cardinal's emissary to the assigned hospital in Lyon, with an Ausweis to be provided as required.

Giles gave his coconspirators the details about the address and the back entry to the apartment building for the 8:00 a.m. pickup. Giles was not to accompany Lucien in the morning, as Lucien could more easily and without danger explain his errand, if stopped and required to do so by the police or Germans, were he with Elle alone.

The other servants were to be occupied in other parts of the house and not be permitted to be on the second floor when she was taken to her room. All bedrooms had keys possessed by each guest. Giles would be present in Elle's room to greet her when she arrived, but thereafter, the master of the house insisted that each guest keep an independent, impersonal relationship so as to provide a hotel-like atmosphere.

The archbishop planned on calling Ambassador Abetz to have luncheon with him and his wife as soon as possible. Of course, the incidental subject would be an Ausweis for Dr. d'Hozier, for use to Lyon, "one way." Meanwhile, he needed to make other plans for Giles and found them to be much more difficult to make. He rummaged through a number of possibilities, but they all ended in the necessity of moving him into the free zone across the demarcation line.

He knew he couldn't keep him there forever. What to do? Could he disguise him as his missing monsignor, who went "missing in action" in June? But what if he were here merely temporarily? How to account for him in the administration even then? "Priests are assigned administratively and don't materialize out of thin air." When Pierre left for his army posting, he stored his civic attire and church vestments.

As recalled by Lucien, he and Giles were the same slight build and approximate height; therefore, the archbishop began to think in his unconventional way, which evoked, as a result of his "challenging" thoughts, many self-protective Hail Marys. What wily plot would George Simenon have created to project Giles over the German 'demarcation line" with safety to all? What outlandish but workable storyline in one of his novels would suit this circumstance? This was a death-defying game of chance for everyone involved. The consequences were unforeseeable for poor Giles and Elle, Lucien, the archbishopric, and himself, in every way. Therefore, he must plan by foreseeing the reactions of Ambassador Abetz, perhaps his wife, the French police, and the SS.

LV

HE CAME TO a clear resolution after much consideration and a careful review of his vows (with a favorable view to his desired resolution), and complying with his metaphysical, secular, and world views, which were, insofar as the immediate problems confronting him, as follows:

It was his firm belief that the God of Jacob is God the Father and that the first five books of the Old Testament, or the Pentateuch (also called by the Hebrews, "the Torah"), were the Bible. The New Testament followed. Somewhat thereafter, thus the religion of the Jews, or ancient Hebrews, was necessarily the mother of Christianity, and the Messiah, or savior, or fulfillment, was Jesus of Nazareth, and therefore, the pagans were the "to-be" Christians and were the New Jews whom Jesus came to redeem; further, perhaps the Jews (or Hebrews) were not necessarily to adopt the Messiah because they were already clearly "the chosen," but in any case, they were not to lose their place in God's firmament but remain "a light unto the peoples." But they suffered for ages at the hands of the New Jews, who refused to recognize them *except* as deniers of *their* Holy Messiah.

He felt personally saddened that the Jewish people, as a whole, failed to recognized that the promised Messiah had arrived: further, that they suffered wrongfully at the hand of the New Jews because of their refusal; instead of maintaining a privileged position as the first to know God the Father, they were those who pointed the way to God. Among them were the Apostles and Paul, the messenger (all being Jews), and Mary, his very mother, so chosen by God. To exterminate the Jews and Judaism was pure and simple matricide—no believer in Christ could murder his mother!

They were forced into controlled areas (called "ghettoes" after the first of such places) wherever they lived and frequently forced to convert, only to then be executed by the secular power that be when found by the church to be guilty of heresy if they reverted to Judaism, thereafter. Dominicans and Franciscans were often charged with this obligation in the twelfth, thirteenth, and fourteenth centuries. Worse was to come to them in the sixteenth and seventeenth centuries, primarily through the new Protestant sects, as well as the Greek Orthodox religion with the new "Replacement theology." This created the doctrine that because of their evil refusal to accept the new religion, they were "evil" and may have been responsible for the crucifixion of the Messiah, Jesus, and were thereafter replaced by the Christians. Of course, the doctrine was selective as to the Christians who replaced them, always being of one's own particular sect of Christianity.

Poisoning the water wells and causing the Plague were common charges made everywhere Jews were unfortunate enough to be through the Dark and Middle Ages. All of this laid the groundwork for the Holocaust, which the Germans were bringing to occupied France at this very time, in Paris and in France. And in unoccupied France—by discriminatory statutes made under the auspices of Marshal Petain in Vichy, all before the very eyes of the archbishop—robbery, deportation, and murder were to follow, and the archbishop was well aware of German activities in the rest of German-occupied Europe and Germany itself under the Nazis' boot.

Because of his personal attachment to Giles, and his personal vows and beliefs, he felt deeply obliged and spiritually and emotionally committed to saving this closest child of the maltreated people. It was, to him, both his privilege and duty.

LVI

NOW THEN, IT was time to examine the things that Pierre had left behind. Lucien took the storage cases to the archbishop's bedroom so that the two of them could make a private inspection of the same. No one had claimed them in Pierre's family, who lived in Alsace. The Germans had reclaimed Alsace as a part of Greater Germany. Personal family heirlooms would have to be dealt with separately, if included in his belongings, now that they were sifting through them.

There were two black civilian suits, two rabat black shirts with two detachable white Roman collars, along with a black clerical waistcoat. There were also a pair of black "monk front" shoes, with buckle closures, which might or might not fit Giles; black cross onyx cufflinks; black stockings; a few family photos; and not much else other than vestments, which were hardly used. That was perhaps because Pierre was involved, most of the time, as an aide to the archbishop.

There were also his ordination confirmation certificate, signed by the bishop ordaining him, and his "Papal Diploma" creating him a monsignor in the third order, "A chaplain to his Holiness," so marking him as a potential for further advancement, no doubt achieved because of his recognized scholarly endeavors.

Pierre and/or his family had purchased only the minimum in priestly garb before he was elevated to monsignor and nothing after, or he would have been better prepared for possible ceremonial functioning at Notre Dame Cathedral. However, he was a pleasant, quiet young man, though inexpressive and incapable of creativity in sermonizing or affability in social church events. Still, his very analysis of Pierre, objectively, made the archbishop feel ungenerous, irreligious, and unchristian and perhaps, and consequentially, in his own opinion of himself, unworthy of his high offices.

He knew right well that when he was called to answer for all of his shortcomings, by the ultimate authority, he would be at great risk but hoped and trusted that, at death's door, his honesty and courage would enable him to face the eternity that the Almighty, having duly weighed his performance, meted out to him. In short, he trusted in the Lord's willingness to accept the peccadilloes of his creations, if not beyond the boundaries of the confessional. But he was not at all certain that such parameters would include what he was about to propose and do with Giles, further that his own confessor would fear to forgive him what could be the largest sin ever perpetrated by a cardinal/archbishop!

Thus perplexed, having allowed himself this condition of bewilderment, only the voice of Lucien, saying, "What of the vestments, Your Eminence? Are they sufficient?" shook him to awareness.

His response was to examine each item, as a kind of inventory, spoken, not ironically, but eerily, with the intonations of an auctioneer. The final phrase, following each item, "What am I bid?" was only unconsciously implied, never stated!

"We have one black biretta hat with silk trim and a tuft plus three ridges, or horns (for the trinity), supporting the tuft, the ridges having purple trim, appropriate for monsignors; no size being shown inside, we must hope, as with the shoes, for the best.

"We have one cassock, ordinary (not choir). Of course it is black and, as expected, of full length. Upon perusal, the cassock is correct for a monsignor, having the red-cloth-covered buttons, all thirty-three, one for each year of Christ's life, in place, down its front. One fuchsia-colored sash, to be worn around the waist of the cassock, symbolizing sexual self-constraint and chastity."

He followed the same procedure with the maniple, an ornamental damask cloth to carry on the left arm in Mass, to illustrate the labor and hardship of the priest; "the stole, a long scarf worn around the neck for Mass or for administering sacraments, similar to the gown of a Roman justice worn while performing official duties; then a surplice, worn over the cassock and absolutely essential in order to perform Mass (unless the priest possessed an alb, which took priority over it), knee-length and white, with full long sleeves and, in this instance, quite fancy.

As the two of them repacked the boxes, for temporary storage, in the closet area of Giles's room, and descended to the first-floor entryway, His Eminence sighed and in a murmur to himself said, "May God forgive me, for that I knowest what I am about to do." As the two separated, the prelate directed Lucien to locate Giles and instruct him to meet him in the library before dinner. "Say, at five thirty. Tell him that I deem it most important."

LVII

WHEN GILES ENTERED the library, he discovered the archbishop pacing slowly back and forth in front of his desk, as if on ceremonial guard duty. A short greeting between them was followed by both being seated and a visual sweep of the salon by the prelate, outside the door, to insure their privacy. A short conversation ensued, reiterating the perils of Giles's position in Paris and in the household, how extremely important it was to both of them to continue to disguise his presence and to move him over the demarcation line, which had now become a formidable hurdle.

His Eminence, as a matter of courtesy, asked Giles for his suggestions regarding a solution or a plan. Giles understood that the limousine would not be an answer because it was some 125 miles away from the line and no gas was available, nor could its presence on the road be overlooked by the Germans. Finally, it was agreed that only some plan of the archbishop's could solve this enigma. The archbishop allowed as how he did have a plan in mind—a daring, breathtaking plan, which rendered him at great risk, perhaps more so than even Giles: one that would provide Giles the necessary paperwork to travel over the demarcation line; one that would require Giles to assume a bogus identity and perform most convincingly as that bogus person and, if caught, to assume all the responsibility himself; a role that Giles must prepare for so thoroughly that his life might depend upon its authenticity; a role for which training needed to commence immediately so that he would be prepared to depart Paris in perhaps two weeks, probably before plans for Giselle would be completed for her entirely separate and unrelated departure.

Giles was about to begin to question when His Eminence leaned forward abruptly and interjected, "Wait until I propose my basic plan for you to accept or reject!"

Thus, he began to reveal the plan for Giles's escape, or the detailed "plot"—that is, the "storyline"—which were, all three, tantamount to the same thing. The presentation was well expressed, as each detail built itself solidly on the last. As they were constituted, they doubtless seemed flawless to His Eminence but, nevertheless, caused Giles to seethe, internally, with apprehension.

The very last step was the obvious hole in the whole scheme. That entailed passing the German Ausweis inspection point at the Gare de Lyon before boarding the train for Lyon. There would likely be an inspection again en route and, very soon thereafter, at the demarcation line, by both the Vichy police and possibly a German army, once again, at that time.

How could he possibly carry his pistol under a priest's cassock, or over it, with his English-style shoulder holster? Even his double-breasted, black overcoat would have to be unbuttoned to impress them with the cassock and sash. He didn't believe that the biretta covering his head was enough to warn them off. "What if the German officer is, let us say, a Bavarian Catholic or an Austrian? They know your religion! Supposing they ask me some obscure question in French, such as what saint day it is that day, or some friendly question that involves some religious matter or fact. Then what do I answer?" He wasn't going without his pistol! "Uncle Emanuelle, how is this going to happen? I won't risk being a prisoner. I intend to die fighting first! I'm one Frenchman who will not surrender!"

The archbishop replied, "I anticipated this problem and am scheming a solution for it. You shall not leave, by this plan, until I have done so, and you shall understand it and agree to it before we step off." With some fervor, he further declared, "We cannot have 'a cowboy shoot-'em-up' involving this archbishopric—remember that!"

The French Lieutenant and the King of Rome

Abrupt silence ensued, then seconds of a soundless void succeeded by calming words being exchanged between them, followed by tangible dollops of the archbishop's plan, proffered to Giles, who was to masticate and swallow the Catholic doctrinaire being served him, thus to enable him to perform, for a few vital moments, as a sham Catholic monsignor, traveling by train to the Lyon Cathedral (where the archbishop was known to be sympathetic to the Jewish cause). The trick was to make him a more-than-plausible presbyter of the Catholic Church, able to flawlessly pass a Gestapo inspection.

The trinity doctrine was digested within minutes. The Eucharist was quite another thing for him to receive. Transubstantiation was inconceivable: though quite familiar through his knowledge of history, accepting it as an accomplishable fact was another matter for him. Fortunately he only had to comprehend, not believe, it. As for ecclesiastical Latin as distinguished from classical Latin, Giles had been a Latin scholar, and thus, having been so, this would be easily achieved and practicable through prayer book reading and perusing the Vulgate Bible in the prelate's library.

He was given texts prepared for converts: primers on all of the sacraments and on the doctrine of grace, an outline of a seminary program for priests (an eight-year program, in approximation), a document entitled "Proof of Catholic Doctrine from Holy Scriptures," and a tract on the purpose and use of holy vestments by priests, monsignors, bishops, archbishops, cardinals, and the Holy Father, the pope. The individual holder of these offices needed to have a convincing demeanor and body language to match. Lessons in all areas would be conducted by his "teacher" (the archbishop) and absorbed by the student over the next several days.

Most of the evening was consumed in the library, but the all-important clothes fitting was absolutely obligatory, so the two of them adjourned to Giles's room along with Lucien, in the event measuring for alterations was necessary. The extra length in the trousers of the suits were amendable by adjustment in the suspenders, without "strangling" the groin area. The jackets, to them, were fine in the shoulders, but the cuff lengths of both arms were a bit short. However, they were within the measure of the "indifference" of the average man, who wears factory-made suits (which both of these suits were) to sartorial splendor. The cassock was itself loose fitting enough through the chest and shoulders so that, if the right inside pockets of it were loaded with objects, the right side would hide, and balance out, the shoulder holster and pistol. Giles would appear somewhat puffy between the neck and the fuchsia waist sash, but ecclesiastics did not often physically conform to the warrior mold. This, at least, would no doubt align with the psychotic Gestapo view of how the French and their priests should appear: both malformed and inferior to the Germans, regardless of whether priests or soldiers!

Grueling work was accomplished by Giles under the strict eye of the archbishop during the next ten days; the next handful of days thereafter Giles lived the part within the confines of the house. He was explained to the servants simply as "visiting clergy," awaiting an assignment to a parish in the archbishop's jurisdiction or as a possible replacement for Pierre in the archbishopric.

Meanwhile, the archbishop had his luncheon with the German ambassador and his wife, and he achieved his goal for Elle. The prelate had used her passport photo, which had been removed and appended to her Ausweis permit. She spent one more night with Giles in his bedroom, and thereafter she was gone by train, uneventfully. Lucien, in proper garb, drove her to the Gare de Lyon in the limousine and, carrying her luggage, walked her to the security point, for permission to board the train, given by a German intelligence (Abwehr) sergeant, detailed with an assistant private. He looked at her, totally agog, obviously so overwhelmed by her beauty that the doctor had to ask him to stamp "permission" on her Ausweis. Fortunately, the SD (Gestapo) units had not been delegated or in supervision of Ausweis departures this early in the Parisian occupation.

LVIII

THE ARCHBISHOP DID not believe it advisable to burden his growing "state" familiarity with the German ambassador by calling upon him to gain another exit arrangement for his "monsignor" to depart for the free zone so soon after the Giselle arrangement. It might incite him to suspicion or at least concentrate his thoughts on the archbishop's neediness. It was important to attempt to appear impartial to the invaders, to seem neutral. Otherwise, he could lose any appearance of neutrality, and he was building that to appeal to the Germans as French transgressions developed, which he felt was a certainty.

Therefore, he had to fall back upon his majordomo, Lucien, to utilize his astounding collection of legerdemain. Lucien had to determine whether he could maneuver this through his rather important brother, Geoffroi, whom he knew to have a significant position in the local police. No delay could be accepted, but the alternative of using Otto Abetz was too risky, and the archbishop revolted at the idea.

Geoffroi was much like his brother in appearance but most dissimilar in disposition. He was sour and sullen and laconic and resentful of predictable human failings. He had spent most of his life in a struggle. In conforming to the stringent, superficial robotics of the technical aspects of police officialdom, it was not unlike his old reserve duty in the army, where close-order drilling was the facile manner, instead of battlefield maneuvers and tactics of war, which were avoided, avoided because of the expense and planning, which would have been duplicative for the "Best Army in the World," as all but Germany had agreed. Both organizations failed in the performance of the anticipated service expected and required of them!

He was somewhat older than Lucien and had chosen public service over the private service in the church chosen by Lucien. They were bred of a close-knit family and remained so even to the present, so much so that Geoffroi spoke of violations of conduct that were of the most privileged, from a lawyer's point of ethics, and to which only a priest in a confession box could give absolution. He obviously felt no compunction in revealing these over a privately drunk glass of wine with his brother, but more significant was his slyly put suggestion that he could be "of service" to worthy souls of his brother's private circle if true need arose. Naturally, there would be a price, based upon the person and purpose involved. "We speak, of course, of 'forgery,' 'fraud,' and 'black marketeering' as well. But we shall speak of them with only the utmost discretion, my little brother."

The huskier Geoffroi was a more bumptious male than Lucien in every way. But Lucien, though morally uncorrupted, had mentally catalogued each detail and applied his brother's vaunted capabilities to smooth his way in life: and both "little" and "big" brother glided along smoothly together in their own Parisian aquarium. This *inspecteur* of the gendarmerie had full arrest authority and was one of those police considered most trustworthy by the "*boche*." He frequently shared profits with the Germans but felt most elated when he could exercise underhanded revenge against them. He cherished and enshrined every instance of such underhanded vengeance invoked and happily forced the criminal specialists subject to his unscrupulous control to provide birth certificates and stamps, ration cards, and now the new, but forgeable, German Ausweis.

Giles's necessary ration card and birth certificate, his ordination and confirmation certificate as a priest, and his papal diploma as a monsignor were forgeries and were provided to him. A photograph from a Kodak, Brownie-type French camera was taken against a blank wall in his room. The originals of Pierre's papers were nervously surrendered by the archbishop to Lucien for copying and to mimic the quality of the paper in each instance. Great care was taken to eliminate the Jewish ancestry of Giles, altering the maiden name of his mother and her place of birth (to Provence) and his father's occupation and place of birth as well. Giles was shown to have been born in Lyon. All of this dissembling served its purpose. All records were just out of reach and inconvenient for the occupiers to obtain.

All papers were received from the forgers, both old and new, and the new found to be much better than expected, exceedingly better than the price allowed the "creators" by Inspecteur Geoffroi for performing "a patriotic duty." But the Ausweis was uncertain because it was copied from that received by the archbishop from the German ambassador for Elle's use, for her move to Lyon several days before. However, it was a new form of document and probably not frequently seen by the Germans' intelligence service (the Abwehr) in early December.

Giles had now to be "vetted" in public. He could not be allowed to render or participate in any church function in the guise of a priest but could be visible within the vestibule, the vestry, and the nave, but not at the altar rail or beyond the rood, if there was one, or in the chancel beyond it during Mass or communion. By creating Giles, the pseudopriest, His Eminence had laid a trap for himself, as he constantly reflected, involving his own right of "redemption."

This vetting was accomplished, even at Notre Dame, but judicious care was taken that he be inside the safe places at the correct times and outside the forbidden ones at all the times that were wrong. Prodigious practice and fear of the German abyss made for quick perfection of performance. He made limousine visits to priests in their outlying locations in the parish, sometimes with instructions about how to cope with ecumenical problems that concerned the German occupation. It should be noted that His Eminence saw to it that Giles never touched a consecrated wafer or container of wine; nor would the meticulously ethical Giles have ever sought either.

Sunday, December 15, in the afternoon was chosen for his train departure from the Gare de Lyon railroad station. His appearance, including his pistol placement, was scrutinized, and the processing procedure was practiced, including what questions might be asked and how they should be answered. Even body language was practiced and anticipated. Lastly, His Eminence instructed him on how he believed he could reach Ettienne, with the army of the unoccupied zone (dangerously, possibly, for the three of them) in Vichy.

If exposed in any way, His Eminence would be criminalized and could suffer deportation to a concentration camp, and Giles and Lucien also. To prevent that, he would have to convince the Germans that he carried the weapon, if it were uncovered, for self-protection against robbery or mayhem because of the present perilous circumstances in the free zone, which of course was his destination. After all, he was a helpless monsignor, and he had heard of ruthless "Jewish gangs" that were after vengeance against the church for allowing the armistice with the German authorities. This hallucinatory idea was just the kind of conspiracy theory the lower-rank Germans would likely buy at the railroad station inspection before he would be permitted to enter the train if his weapon were discovered.

LIX

THE AGING, HUMBLE Capuchin friar breathlessly ran to the front door of the Kapuziner Crypt Church in Vienna, which was kept locked overnight, as no visitors to the Hapsburg vaults were received before 10:00 a.m. It was necessary to have a reasonable period for the eight to ten resident monks to perform prayers and have churchly duties completed before receiving visitors. But the incessant pounding with some massive implement was not the diffident ringer-knock of a Catholic tourist from Bavaria wanting to gain entry to the vaults. The tumultuous shaking of the doors from the impact was imminently threatening to the orderly, devout, and timeless aspect of this most mendicant order of St. Francis of Assisi.

This single gabled church, built in the early seventeenth century by order of the then empress of the Holy Roman Empire, was to exist only because of the subterranean crypts built to hold the coffins, tombs, and elaborate mausoleums of the royal Hapsburg clan—all branches, even the remote, non reigning relatives thereof—for eternity. The most humble mendicant order of the church, the brown-robed, long-pointed-cowled, or hooded-and-tonsured brothers with full beards, had the single duty here of tending the little church and the defunct princelings and their rulers against disturbance in their eternal slumber.

The friar opened the heavy wooden door hesitantly, panting and gasping for breath, as the door was violently pushed aside by the momentum of a private soldier in campaign dress, shoving the stock of his rifle against the door—and the friar behind it. A sergeant stood on the street level below him, and to his rear were thirty or more soldiers with a fuming officer whose state of mind could clearly be understood: understood even by this startled friar, who was barely able to maintain his footing as he made way for the soldier and his sergeant, who were in full assault on the church entrance. The officer was in hot approach to the door when he called a halt to his two point men in the church assault.

The young, lean, swaggering, yet gawky, officer bore a sword by an obviously inappropriate order of his commander, thinking that a call on the burial vaults of the ancient Holy Roman emperors was a full "A-class-uniform" occasion. But this officer was a northerner, thus, a Nordic, probably a Prussian with a "von" in front of his name and, of course, a Junker militarist and a *Lutheran*.

The older friar, an Austrian by birth, had knowledge of the Prussian attitude toward the Austrians, whom they had relegated to a second-class position among German peoples, along with the other Alpines, principally the Bavarians. They had oppressed and humiliated the Austrians in one war, saved them in another, and simply absorbed them in the current one. They now regarded them as jocular "airheads," like their own Bavarians, fit only to follow!

Hauptman von Whomever's first words were, "Why have you closed and locked this church? The Third Reich Army has business here, and you were so advised of that by a dispatch rider yesterday."

This army captain had the face of a hawk—narrow and elongated, with an aquiline nose, narrow lips, piercing, frigid gray eyes, and chalk-white skin—and he glared menacingly down upon the timid, bald, and bearded mouse-like friar. The monk, in near hysteria, interpreted that glare as a desire to virtually dive upon his throat for the kill.

At this point, the friar peremptorily excused himself, as he literally fled, hysterically, to search out the friar in charge of the church and vaults. If there had been a dispatch, he would have received it.

The officer was sublimely arrogant. As he restlessly waited, he continuously struck his black leather gloves, gathered together in

The French Lieutenant and the King of Rome

his right hand, against his right thigh, which made a resounding thwacking sound. It was simply his impatient fury, but his troops, hearing this signal to stand at attention, so reacted, as the automatons they were.

The officers fury was actually directed originally toward his major, a bumpkin, not a war academy graduate of Prussia, but a reserve officer from somewhere in Rhine-wine country, with a very limited sense of who he was or the rank he held. He was born to lead from behind and would never visit the land where Iron Crosses grow! Even more than that, he had humiliated Hauptman von Whomever by ordering him to wear a sword inappropriately to visit some insignificant monks in a small church, which wafted a smell of garlic, boiled pig, and perspiration and which guarded a great gaggle of mixed-blood cadavers!

LX

THE STATIONMASTER IMMEDIATELY phoned the railroad yard master to relay the news and his orders. He was to defer all trains headed west on the twelfth of December until this military train left the yard for the Gare de L'Est in Paris. It was to be composed of a hearse car and a baggage car or two containing troops and equipment, driven by a military engineer and crew. He was informed of nothing except to give it top priority. The order was from Berlin. "See to it!"

Meanwhile, the friar in charge of the church and Hapsburg crypt had reached the church door, surreptitiously followed at a safe distance by the original door opener. This churchman was quite in control of his domain, and his confident, quiet manner and smile somewhat calmed the officer, who began again by asking about the notice by dispatch rider of the day before. The monk hastened to agree to its receipt and presented it to the officer, saying that it offered no reason or justification for the release of the bronze coffin of the Duke of Reichstadt, who was an interred Hapsburg, placed here for eternity. He continued, "The Capuchin brothers would be derelict in our duties if we complied with this, an unsubstantiated order and not from the primary existing head of the Hapsburg family, who owned the crypt and built the church for this purpose more than five hundred years ago. Oh, we should also need an order in writing from the head of the Capuchin church, based at the Capuchin church in Rome. He is referred to as

'The Minister General.' I would be happy to provide you with his address and telephone."

In a caustic conversational tone, the captain's first response was, "This general of yours: how many troops does he command?" While the monk, somewhat taken aback, floundered for an answer, he, the captain, continued in a distinct and very curt command voice, "You will immediately take steps to obey the following orders!

"Order number one: you shall retrieve the coffin of this duke, also known as the son of Napoleon Bonaparte, the King of Rome, and place the same in front of the church steps by 6:00 p.m. this evening!

"Order number two: it shall be dusted and cleaned, as we have heard of the jumble and mess in the crypt among the non ruling relatives. You can read the Latin script, so be certain you make no mistake in its identity!

"Order number three: be certain to have the key to the coffin in your possession, and retrieve the second one from the Hofberg Palace to surrender both to my sergeant at 6:00 a.m. tomorrow!

"Order number four: you shall ignore and forget any idea of approval from the Hapsburg head as he is no longer anything but a citizen of the Third Reich and has no longer any previous privileges; as for your commanding general, he is now nothing but a stately, toothless old dog who needs to borrow one of your commodious begging cups, and perhaps Mussolini will give him his first donation!

"Order number five: if you fail to execute each of these orders, my men will arrest all of you tomorrow at 6:10 a.m. and take you to Gestapo headquarters, where *you* will be taught what it means to be an enemy of the state.

"Order number six: none of you have heard what I am about to say, and if this information is about before the sixteenth of this month, you will have violated a direct order from your führer, through this officer!

"Oh yes, I may tell you that the coffin is going by '*chapelle ardente*' car to Paris, where a great ceremony in the Invalides will unite him with his father, Napoleon.

"Carry on!"

LXI

AN ENGINE AND three railroad cars had steamed into place, next to the first passenger platform at the Gare de l'Est in Paris. It was approximately six o'clock in the evening, Paris time, on December 14. It was a train engine and cars that bore the *croix gammée*, the swastika of Nazi Germany, on the sides of each car, except the hearse car, which was the next in line after the steam engine. After the hearse car was a car containing German military personnel intended to provide for the needs of the mission. Thereafter, there was a flatbed car upon which was secured a half-track artillery tractor with winch, which provided benches for twelve men and under seat storage, plus a seat for the driver. As soon as the train had been guided to its place by railroad yard personnel and stopped, German soldiers debarked the train and opened the doors of the hearse, and a sergeant mounted a two-man rifle guard on either side of the open doors. The others prepared the half-track to be unloaded by the winch and separate gears. The arrival was not a moment too soon.

A battalion of infantry from the Grosse Deutsch Division had already been dispatched in trucks and was at the Gare de l'Est, trying to locate the train. Then it was to escort the detail of men, the casket, and the half-track that had been sent on the train to the Place des Invalides. All of the officers in the battalion understood that the exchange purpose was to be preceded by a night torch parade of great pomp, followed by a formal High Mass sometime thereafter—all planned in detail by the (so-called) German ambassador to the French, for permanent transfer of the casket to the French, to be placed in the Church of the Dome in the Hotel des Invalides, now containing the tomb of Napoleon, the casket's occupant's father.

The officers also knew the time constraints required the presence of their full entourage on the south embankment of the Seine River, on the esplanade in front of the Place des Invalides, and the casket in place on the half-track, behind the first company, which was to be formed up, as were the other two companies, in a column-of-three formation. The First Platoon of the First Company would carry rifles in order to present arms in a formal salute upon the ambassador's words of presentation of the casket to the French. There had been an officers call by the Germans on the thirteenth, at the Hotel des Invalides, to insure familiarity.

They were not to step off until the ambassador's limousine passed by them and ordered them to do so, as timed by him. Perfection of execution and timing was the order of the day. They needed all the time they could muster to arrive, as the weather was turning hellishly bad.

LXII

THE ARCHBISHOP RECEIVED an early call on December 12 from Ambassador Abetz, excitedly expressing his pleasure at receiving the approval from Berlin for the return of the coffin of the King of Rome, also in German circles referred to as the Duc de Reichstadt, to be reinstated with his father, Napoleon I, in the Place des Invalides. The more important reason for the call was to inform the archbishop that he was to be there when the coffin was formally returned and later to officiate at a celebratory High Mass honoring his return. There was a much-anticipated exuberance from the French, foreseen and fervently hoped for by Germany's chancellor, Adolph Hitler, who imagined himself an historian and an evaluator of French sensibilities.

By making this gesture to a stunned French people, depressed and morose in a flagrant defeat, he foolishly anticipated them to be duped by this bitter and false amicability, this surreptitious return of the ashes of a long-forgotten prince. The temerity of Hitler infuriated the people even more so because the Germans had by this month of the occupation stolen all of the coal that heated France, all of the gas and oil that provided its transportation, and most of the horses and moveable farm animals and food stuffs, to reduce the French diet to one thousand or so calories per day—and in the most severe winter in memory! The French had no need of the prince's casket nor of the *cendres* therein but of the stolen coal to warm them and, thereafter, to be rendered into meaningful "cinders."

The French imperialists had lost a prince of Napoleon's house who was nearer and dearer to them, by far, and who had died a hero's death in combat. That was the son of Louis Napoleon, the abdicated Napoleon III, who died as a British army officer in the Zulu wars in 1879. Thus, we confront Hitler's astounding folly, indelibly imprinted on the humiliated, stripped French, by his ludicrous, agitating act of adding insult to injury.

Abetz's telephone call caused a flurried reassessment of the plan for the departure of Giles on the afternoon of the fifteenth from the Gare de Lyon. Lucien made contact with his brother Geoffroi, the police inspector, apprising him of the highly secret information of the event. No information of a special event had reached the usual nerve centers of the occupation, and so Geoffroi was careful not to intimate any aspect of the incredible transfer coming to Paris.

It was thought that the event was going to be high drama and might cause some welcome confusion because of increased visitation to Paris, since the weekend's activities would be newsworthy and stimulating of public attention, thus diverting of routine. In short, it might draw public interest and crowds to the stations from the environs of the city on the fifteenth. Once the situation jelled, Geoffroi would know what police involvement would be expected and what the Germans intended to do about security at the Lyon station. The same plan of departure would remain in effect! There was nothing now to do except wait for the call from Ambassador Abetz to the archbishop giving the place and time.

The call came for the archbishop in the late afternoon of the fourteenth, with instructions to locate his car in the Place des Invalides, which of course bordered the gardens in front of the main gate entry to the Court of Honor, which had to be crossed before arriving at the inner entry to the Hotel des Invalides. "You may expect to rendezvous with Marshal Petain, arriving from Vichy earlier by train. You are to be in place there by 11:30 p.m. tonight. The Republican Guard shall also be crucial—an important part of this ceremony—and have been alerted by your General Laure to be there with six hundred torches, in parade dress uniforms, to light the way in the Court of Honor. They shall outline the paths of the four pavilions bordering the interior of the Court of Honor, commencing from the gardens lying to the south of the Place des Invalides, which are just to the north of the gateway into this courtyard. I intend to arrive simultaneously with the casket and its sizeable escort of German troops. At that time, the ceremony shall proceed as it has been planned with our troops and the guard."

LXIII

IT WAS AGREED by Giles and the archbishop that Giles would accompany the archbishop in the limousine for the preliminary transfer of the casket and the military proceedings that were to follow. He was to be a very silent acolyte and always to the rear of the archbishop to serve him in any manner that should, from moment to moment, be decided by the archbishop to justify his presence. Giles's two bags for his departure the afternoon of the fifteenth were loaded in the rear trunk. The location of the archbishopric's residence on Rue Barbet de Jouy was less than ten minutes away from the Place des Invalides.

The three of them entered the garage for the limousine and quickly discovered that they were about to enter a blizzard. Not only was it a frigid night, but they were entering a snowstorm that truly forbade driving, entirely. Having no choice, they proceeded on. The wipers could barely free themselves from the incessant blast of snowfall, and the auto blanket was inadequate for the two passengers. Poor Lucien had the car heater in front, but its output was tantamount to a "whisper" in the face of an oncoming "shout." Their auto crept the short distance to the Boulevard des Invalides and then north to the nearby gardens bordering the Place des Invalides and parked, Lucien having run into curbing on the way, and more than once, due to his blindness in the "whiteout." The massive fall of snow turbulently swept in every direction by the near-cyclone force wind, blocked the light and the natural horizon and prevented visibility as one became trapped in a total fog.

Everything was white around them, and there was a loss of the sense of up or down. Only the blackness of the car was visible. Finally, the headlights of the auto coming toward them from the north had no distance or perspective.

After a few moments, the other car placed itself nearby. It proved to contain Admiral Darlan, determined after Lucien exited the car and spoke to the admiral's driver. He had come in place of Petain, in his stead, being second in command of the unoccupied zone. Why Marshal Petain had not come, as expected by the German command, was unknown. Presently, a third vehicle's headlights shown, coming from the north, toward them down the esplanade. It seemed to be actually floating above the nonexistent horizon. It *seemed* suspended above the Seine and the Alexander III Bridge, which they knew were somewhere to its rear.

Before these headlights approached or were seen, an apparition at some immeasurable distance burst into view, proceeding south on the central walk of the esplanade, the broad park area between the river and the Place des Invalides, some two thousand feet in length. There appeared the specters of robotic manlike creatures in hazy uniforms, helmets, and boots, slightly darker than the misty white fog from which they were emerging—the first of the column of threes with featureless faces, followed by increasingly vague silhouettes of reproduced, endless duplications of themselves, in unidentifiable, bloodless repetition, and in like formation. Their tightly maintained formation and uniform movements were silent and fluid as they marched, barely disturbing the snow above which they appeared to glide. Everything about this phantom night spoke easily of these German soldiers being the chosen ones of the Valkyries of the Nordic god Woden. These heroes gave the appearance of being marched directly from Woden's glacial hell! They were the images of the heroes chosen by Woden to die in battle and be carried forth to their Valhalla, to relive their heroes' deaths each day and then to be reborn each night to carouse with their leader, in great joy, ad infinitum. To Giles, this is what they were, a rebirth of the darkest of the "Dark Ages."

The third vehicle brought Ambassador Abetz to the rendezvous. He stepped from the vehicle just after it parked. Admiral Darlan had been staunchly standing in the storm to greet the ambassador, who shook his hand and declared, "On the part of the führer, I give you the remains of the Duc de Reichstadt." In accordance with orders, the officer commanding the First Platoon had formed his men lateral to the admiral and Ambassador Abetz, and then the officer spit out the order, "Present arms!" in salute of the exchange and the two representatives. He held the platoon in the salute for an inordinately long time, per instruction. And then he commanded, "Order arms!" thus completing the salute.

As he made this gift, his other troops gave way to the right and to the left to allow the half-track vehicle towing the gun carriage, bearing the bronze casket of the remains of the Duc de Reichstadt, to come to the fore. Four or five other high officers of both countries had gathered at the site, concurrent with the two exchanging the perfunctory words, transferring ownership of the casket and contents. Thereafter, the twelve men of the half- track, plus twelve of the ranks just ahead, removed their helmets, stowing them under the seats of the vehicle. All twenty-four hoisted the casket to their shoulders and walked it through the garden area, under the flourishing light of the torches held in the hands of the French Republican Guard, unto the gates of the Court of Honor. There, as prearranged, they set it down upon a trestle, where the duty of completion passed seamlessly to the French guard.

From that moment forward, the remains became for all time the only, both past and future, King of Rome since the Tarquin in the fifth century BC!

LXIV

THE MAGNIFICENT DOORWAY in the center of the two-storied baroque facade, which itself was several hundred feet in width, opened ostentatiously into the Cour d'honneur, the Court of Honor. It was fully open to the sky and enveloped in white foggy haze, but much less intense than the whiteout beyond the four walls enclosing the court. Within these four walls, there was much less of the gusting, swirling, and blinding snow that had erupted upon central Paris this viciously cold night.

The glow of the several hundred torches in the hands of the Republican Guard, stationed intermittently along the internal bordering walls of the four pavilions, gave an eerie effect to the arcades and the classical pediments, built above the arcades, on each of the interior four sides of the walls of the courtyard.

The glow of the torches fitfully flickered in the high wind, which dipped into, and then swooped upward and out of, the courtyard. The tips of their flames shot skyward, angrily dancing and glinting off the dormer windows of the second level in the walls. The reflective bouncing of the tips of the torch lights in these windows and the ever-changing shadows around the architecturally balanced walls gave a weird series of visual reverberations inside the Court of Honor. The steep, sloping slate roofs butting off the arcades and overhanging the perimeter of each interior side magnified the occult, supernatural aspect of the total scene.

Guards displaying torches intersected from the four right angles of the courtyard through to its center, making a St. Andrew's cross but leaving the intersecting center just open enough for a "column of twos," carrying the bronze casket, to cross it and reach and enter the doors to the Chursh of St. Louis Church entrance of the Hotel des Invalides.

Twenty-four Republican Guards, evenly divided on either side of the bronze casket and in unison, hoisted the casket to waist height and then, in one heave, lifted it to their shoulders and marched forward to the intersecting center of the St. Andrew's cross. There, they lowered the casket onto a trestle, put in place to assist them in finally bearing it through the ornate door of the Church of St. Louis des Invalides, also known as the "Soldiers' Church."

Once in, the guards circumvented the grill gate into the Soldiers' Church and proceeded by a lateral corridor to the entry area of the masterpiece, the Church of the Dome. The baroque architect, Francois Mansart, created it for Louis XIV, at his order, to aggrandize the structure for the use of the royal family. The interior of the Dome Church was in marble and built in the shape of a Greek cross, from an aerial view, with three chambers, or chapels, on each side of the cross and a high altar with a baldachin over it. It had a highly decorative cupola over the baldachin, which was erected at the north end of the Greek cross. The Soldiers' Church lay just north of that, with a clear glass wall separating it from the baldachin and its own cupola.

There, in the center of the cross, was the crypt, it being an immense circular aperture surrounded by a low marble parapet above the lower floor, or cella crypt, later adapted and completed for Napoleon's tomb in 1861.

Rising three hundred fifty above the circular aperture was the enormous dome of the church. All of the Dome Church was built and planned much in the style of Bernini and Michelangelo in the Vatican.

In the southwest corner of the Greek cross that constituted the floor plan of the Dome Church was the St. Jerome Chapel (one of the six side rooms), wherein lay Napoleon's brother Jerome. It was the expedient, penultimate resting place for the casket of the King of Rome, on a *treteau*, or trestle. The guard lowered it there, for the period of time it took for the descendants of the imperial family, nobles, and high functionaries to reach their observation area, reserved for them to the far side of the aperture for the crypt.

The complete interior involved had only natural light, which didn't exist for the midnight and early morning hours of this macabre proceeding, only the fringe light created by the guard's many torches, now being transferred by them from the Court of Honor to the Church of the Dome. The torches created a bare and somber penumbra from their placement around the edge of the vast cavernous mausoleum. The melancholy highlights of this redundant funeral were soon to commence.

The high altar was draped in a flowing, tri colored silk cloth, which rippled in undulating folds down the high altar stairs and then flowed on, downward and to the side of the catafalque, and past it, to end just over the ledge that elevated the altar area above the level of the major floor area. The military catafalque was to the fore of the altar, on the top of which would ultimately rest the bronze casket. Then it was to be swathed in a silk tricolor of its own, after being moved into place, and so capped by guards. On either side of the high altar were a twin set of descending stairs that led to Napoleon's tomb below. These staircases acted as a framework for the altar.

LXV

THE SOUND OF fifes could be faintly heard from the Place Vauban, bordering the outside, south end of the Dome Church, where German forces were gathered to render a formal good-bye from the Third Reich to Franz, the Duc de Reichstadt. Their trilling sound was lightly heard between the fullness of the rolling chords of "The Grand Mass for the Dead," or "Requiem," by the composer Hector Berlioz. It was first rendered by him in this very place, on the very organ playing it now, from its enclosed loft in the Soldiers' Church, but now without a vocal chorus. It was written and first played in 1837, to commemorate the soldiers' lives who were lost in Algeria, defending a besieged French post.

After more than an hour had passed, two of the Dome priests, in full High Mass regalia, began to slowly move through the church with censers suspended on chains, burning incense. The pungent odor rose and spread as they swung the chains from side to side, forward and backward. Soon, blue-shaded volutes of smoke rose upward, caught in the wavering flames of the assemblage of Republican Guard torches, as the priests moved in the direction of the altar. Suddenly the organ ceased playing the requiem, well before its completion. The distant echoes of bugles sounded and then rose dramatically in a call to arms accompanied by the resounding music of snare drums tapping relentlessly the French drumbeat, "to the field"; this was the unique French martial drum beat of "To the colors and form for battle!" Giles thought, as he stood in the shadows of the St. Jerome Chapel, that even he, an administrative

The French Lieutenant and the King of Rome

officer, knew much of the ancient and famous French military drum music—perhaps from his reserve duty or perhaps from his childhood! "Les Nantis," the upper levels of "old France" that he knew, and of which he felt a part, knew such oddities from nursery age. "Ah, yes," he inwardly and reflectively scoffed, "such things would come with one's mother's milk!"

The archbishop and his mock monsignor had been waiting to the rear of this somber chapel for the ceremonial call for the removal of the casket to the catafalque, which, as stated, stood below and to the fore of the high altar. The archbishop planned to follow the casket and, when it was in place, to bless it and its content as the two priests moved around it, swinging their censers along and over it.

The guard-porters of the casket, being aware of the near conclusion of the bugle and drum calls, reacted to that. It was their signal to move the casket onto a stretcher and proceed forward into the main corridor to parade it around the floor, avoiding the circular wall around the emperor's tomb, and finally place the casket onto the catafalque. They were then to cover it with a large, tricolor flag. The archbishop and his acolyte followed along with the censer-bearing priests. Then a multitude of officers in the full dress uniforms of their two countries joined and followed as a part of the parade. The gold and silver embroidery and embellishments of their uniforms glinted when reflected by the swaying light of the guards' torches.

A moving spotlight had been activated to pass over the catafalque bearing the casket, the flag, and the high altar. Such touches were, no doubt, part of the German "Wagnerian" lack of subtlety, which permeated the whole garishly elaborate proceeding.

Ten of the Republican Guard, five on each side of the catafalque, rigidly stood post. Polished and perfect they were in black, shining jackboots; white buckskin breeches; blue seventeenth-century military frock coats; white cross-chest and waist belts, with saber sheaths hanging beside their left leg; white gauntlets; holding drawn sabers in their right hands, the rear of the blades resting against their shoulders; classical silver helmets, with red plumes ending down the rear of the neck. Only their cuirasses were missing—that is, their metal chest plates. Otherwise they were dressed to make the final charge against the British Highlanders' squares at Waterloo! But was it not December 15, 1940? Waterloo was June 22, 1815! There the French lost but gained "la gloire." Here, on November 18, they lost, without "glory." In place of glory, they received, in recompense, the return of the King of Rome. Even a loving father would not, were he still among the quick, have considered it a fair exchange!

The status of "lying in state" had now commenced after the guards were posted. Regular relief intervals were provided until the early-morning High Mass, which was the last scheduled event in the German rites ritual. One may safely conclude that no French person was there without some form of personal or general German intimidation, from Marshal Petain (who refused to come from Vichy) and Admiral Darlan (who came in his stead) to the Princess Marie Bonaparte, who was concurrently striving to save Dr. Sigmund Freud from the Nazi murderers (and was a participant in the audience and a senior survivor in the Napoleonic family) to the last Republican Guard. All were unpaid puppets on the Teutonic stage.

The archbishop was intently planning his ceremony, which had been set for 10:00 a.m. the morning of the fifteenth. He made two decisions. First he needed some sleep before undertaking the Mass. An immediate return to his bed was necessary, and so the three of them, Lucien, Giles, and the prelate, were going to make a return to the archbishopric, for a few hours of rest and then a hasty return to the Church of the Dome for the finale. The storm had passed, and Lucien was deftly able to return them, both ways, by 9:00 a.m.

The second decision concerned the subject for this second eulogy, given some 108 years after the first one. It had been given in Vienna and in the German language, for (Francois) Franz, the Duc de Reichstadt. Catering to the German occupiers was the obvious thrust if he wished to stay "on board" with them. Not to do so was

The French Lieutenant and the King of Rome

to disable himself from being of practical service to the French people, from day to day, for however long the Germans remained victorious. He saw his purpose during this period to be one of subtly frustrating the occupiers, concerning each thing the church was involved in on a daily basis in Paris.

Therefore, his eulogy would address "the magnificent foresight of Napoleon I in choosing the Hapsburg princess Marie Louise, daughter of the Austrian emperor, as his bride." This house was the largest symbol of all Germanic royal houses and thus the most significant German connection that could be made. Napoleon thereby foresaw the future as a fulfillment of the past: that of the ninth-century Frankish empire of the Emperor Charlemagne, in which the peoples of France and Germany were united for a brief period without the national division of the centuries thereafter. Now their origins would be their future.

This was the first indication of the unity of the leading peoples of continental Europe. The union of Napoleon and Marie Louise was intended to provide the leadership of a united German-French empire under the guidance of the offspring of their own union. The King of Rome, later known as the Duc de Reichstatd, would be the first emperor of the most powerful Europe of all time. The peace accord of 1815 politically defeated the emperor's foresight, preventing it from being fulfilled until the present day, which now was seeing its fulfillment! The dream of Charlemagne and Napoleon was about to be fulfilled, and the rejoining of the King of Rome with his father in Paris was the first symbol of this rebirth!

This was the essence of the eulogy (though not, of record), which was given over the catafalque, in the Mass for German consumption. The misgivings of the French who were present would be gradually allayed by his future conduct. But Charles "Le Grand" de Gaulle would not interpret his conduct favorably, and at the victory Te Deum celebrated in 1944, in Notre Dame Cathedral, he forbade the presence of the archbishop, no doubt, partially in consequence.

The archbishop, from the high altar, administered the formula of the High Mass to the assembly at large, who were as previously described. Many had stayed in attendance for the morning ceremony to take place at 10:00 a.m. The eulogy succeeded as a part of the Mass. The imperial family and nobles remained or regathered for this high point of the occasion, and the Republican Guards, as relieved at interval, were in place. Even comfort points were provided and in place as might be required for the attendees, through the hours of waiting for the final ceremony.

At the conclusion of the service, Admiral Darlan, Ambassador Abetz, and the German military governor, General Otto Von Stulpnagel, joined together in an oxymoronic gesture, the three, in unison, as allies and friends, placing an oversized floral crown with a tricolored ribbon attached, on which was written, "Marechel Petain," onto the casket of the King of Rome.

Thereafter, a crowd of the French public were allowed to file by the catafalque to view the bronze casket. This continued until evening fell.

"Sic transit Gloria mundi." So passes the glory of the world!

LXV

GILES'S TRAIN WAS scheduled to depart from the Gare de Lyon at 2:00 p.m. The archbishop had arranged to meet Lucien and Giles at the rear of the high altar immediately after the Mass, in order to slip away to the limousine and return to the residence to prepare for the trip to the station and Giles's departure. They had little time to allow the archbishop to change into the street regalia of the cardinal in which he had planned to appear at the station while he accompanied Giles to and through the security check by the Germans. Geoffroi had told Lucien to expect it to take place on the first "quay" (in English), the first platform bordering the first tracks; however, it would be covered with the snow from the storm. Therefore, it was likely to be held in the station building immediately bordering this quay. Soldiers would be stationed by the train going to Lyon, to check that a stamp accompanied the Ausweis as the guard waived the passenger onto the train. Obviously, no stamp, no train! Followed by ugly involvements with the security and SD Gestapo horrors thereafter!

The archbishop decided, almost in the beginning of this escapade, that, as its creator and perpetrator, its consequences would be laid at his feet, whether he saw it to completion at the train station with Giles or not. It would be a matter of one day or two, whether he didn't or did, if Giles were discovered as a fraud.

Author Simenon's character, Detective Maigret, now "His Eminence," would act with bravado and intimidate a German, with his official manner as a highest churchman. Pomposity, arrogance, saintly suffering mixed with piety—all would be used in the event of a too incisive question put to Giles or regarding a question concerning his pistol: "I insisted that he take that weapon because of antigovernment groups and antichurch gangs now forming in the lawless unoccupied area that is not benefiting from German control. Eventually your army must exercise full control there, as well! If you confiscate this weapon, I shall look to your military governor, General Otto Von Stulpnagel, with whom I am personally acquainted, to hold you and your immediate superior responsible for any consequences that might occur!"

He stomped his feet on the top step leading into the stationhouse from the snowy quay, and both Giles and Lucien did the same, in successive order. The main hall was being partially used by German security to process applicants wishing to depart for the South—that is to say, the unoccupied one-third of France permitted by the Germans to be under French control. As stated before, only those with an Ausweis pass could now be permitted to do so. Having such a pass was quite unique in fallen France. Even Marshal Petain did not possess one and needed special German orders to move across the line into the occupied zone.

Inspector Geoffroi was there, as scheduled by his brother Lucien, with two chosen underlings filling inspection posts at the long, worn, pitted, and unvarnished wooden table, along with a German team of three. Two were enlisted and familiar to Geoffroi, plus an SS officer who was not. Fortunately, he was an under lieutenant and not regularly assigned for railroad inspection, as determined earlier by Geoffroi, in casual conversation over coffee. Geoffroi assured him that he understood the new desired process under the Ausweis system and was, of course, at his beck and call. The lieutenant was obviously relieved, being from a combat Waffen SS regiment. His shoulder straps were the SS black, and his collar patches were bordered in white cord, with his rank enclosed on his left collar patch. His left cuff had his infantry regiment name inscrolled: "Fourth Regiment, First Battalion of Panzer Grenadiers," plus panzer black shield and enclosed symbol. The ubiquitous skull-and-crossbones

The French Lieutenant and the King of Rome

collar patch with black background was on the right lapel. Geoffroi also noted his officer's field cap with a frontal eagle of aluminum thread. All was in order and "spit and polish." He carried a sidearm, as well as the usual dirk on his belt. As was said in America: he was the "real McCoy" and freshly trained to murder.

The gendarme felt the need to be very careful in handling him. Great cordiality and superficial respect was called for, and Geoffroi intended to exercise obeisance in his conduct, by subtle guidance, to relieve him of the burden of trite decision making, by suggestions, but in a whisper!

There were many potential travelers in the Lyon station that day, many with one-way passes to the unoccupied zone, who were therefore important to the Germans as people trying to evade them because of some threat to Germany. It would be something of a specific nature and not the general antipathy to be expected from a conquered people.

A subtle negative nod of the head in the direction of Lucien was sufficient to retard the three from pressing their place into line. Geoffroi intently watched the German lieutenant for the development of impatience and then finally shear boredom from the unfamiliar routine. There were no unusual occurrences to suspend his growing lackluster attitude. This then was the time—some three hours later—for the yes nod to take place.

The German officer was impressed to meet his first archbishop, and no less than the one for Paris, one who had already endeared himself to the occupiers because his good works had already reached the ears of those most interested, the SS and the Gestapo at large. He also met the departing monsignor, Giles, and wished him well at his new post in Lyon. As for his papers, which not only included the Ausweis, the ordination papers, and his certificate from the Vatican as a monsignor, Geoffroi stepped between the three and the lieutenant and said, "May I check their authenticity for you, sir? Catholic documentation may be trying with church Latin, you see! With your permission, sir." A brief pause by the German lieutenant, and then, he said appreciatively, "By all means,

Inspector." A brief examination followed, and then the inspector concluded, "Ah, yes," as he placed the Ausweis on the table for the SS enlisted man to stamp. Geoffroi handed the German's very own stamp to him, to place the approval on the back of the Ausweis. All documents were returned by the inspector to Giles. All thought of a frisk was simply overlooked as the inspector and the lieutenant saw the three of them to the door to exit. Giles courteously nodded his biretta-covered head and proceeded to the coach car, walking beside the soldier, who passed him on to the train with a click of his heels and a salute!

LXVI

GILES PLACED HIS bags in the overhead, sat down on his seat, and sank for a few moments into a stupefied lethargy, giving him time to think further of his preliminary moves when he arrived in Lyon.

Meanwhile, and unknown to the three of them, Laval, prime minister of Petain's government in Vichy, had been arrested by Petain. The German ambassador Abetz did know presumably and departed from the Church of the Dome, gathered three cars of SDs with machine pistols, went to Vichy, and freed Laval, ordering him reinstated immediately (which did not occur, for some months) as prime minister of the Petain government. Obviously, some pandemonium was in process in the inner circles of the German SD in Paris at the very time that Giles was scheduled to take the train to Lyon. Thus, a happenstance may have contributed by creating some disarray in the routine of the German Gestapo, which caused the relative ease of Giles's passing though their security at the railroad station.

LXVII

GILES WAS MORE than elated to be arriving into the comparatively free air of the Vichy zone. Living twenty-four hours per day under the German threat of occupied Paris, commencing on July 11, had been an excruciating experience. The weight of his fear began to noticeably dissipate as the train moved southward.

From the train window, he noticed the sky, especially after heading in a more southerly direction from Dijon, turning quite azure blue, with a wind from the north pressing the trees southwardly. The larger ones were tilted permanently southward, as a consequence. Giles then recalled that the mistral winds always blew strongly in a west-to-south direction, from the Bay of Biscayne, commencing this time of year. The wind would then be cold in Lyon but without the snow now in Paris.

He carried his two bags down the coach stairs himself as the conductor was assisting an elderly couple who had come on board at Dijon, also in the free zone. The French police had also come on board at Dijon and walked through the train but, obviously having no orders from their German masters, left immediately without checking anyone, saluting Giles as they left.

He was at a loss as to where to go as it was probable that Elle was off duty at this hour. So the hospital didn't seem a likely destination from the train station this evening. He could not explain himself to her mother or her maid, Beatrice, over a telephone line at her residence, which couldn't be secure enough to risk explaining this whole scenario in a lengthy conversation. He didn't even know

The French Lieutenant and the King of Rome

exactly where her residence was, and even if he did, he couldn't risk just dropping in, knowing nothing of her circumstances.

The whole tale of escape from Paris was unbelievable except for what limited events were told her mother by Elle after Elle's arrival in Lyon. But Elle and Giles were sworn to secrecy by the archbishop regarding everything wherein he was involved. Giles found himself repeating the puzzle of his immediate destination in his mind as he adjourned to the men's room, with the thought of packing the biretta, cassock, and the rabat and its white neck band and donning a civilian shirt and tie. After that he would just be a conservative man, dressed in black. After all, he thought, even Jesuits did this frequently, probably a "habit" from their sixteenth- and seventeenth-century history as espionage agents for the church. (Giles being Giles, he was very amused by his own double entendre.)

To him, there was always the neutral observer or listener present, just over his shoulder, or so he felt. Or perhaps it was his own, ever-present personal audience whom, he coyly thought, evaluated his acts and thoughts. He was quite annoyed if his own internal ear had to fairly evaluate his performance or comments with less than "distinction" (as a grade.)

In order to do this costume switch without anyone's residual memory of the change, he needed to find the toilette, without an attendant, and, hopefully, with a stall. French public toilettes were usually "a la turque."

He hadn't even been able to imagine how to approach Elle in the hospital without the risk of her reaction when she first saw him and perhaps "rushed him" with hugs and kisses—with him now dressed as a monsignor. What a scene that would be! He had been struggling with these thoughts since he left Paris. He realized that he had to change to avoid some unforeseen incident. He could not, of course, have done it on the train. He would have to put off going to the cathedral until after seeing Elle.

He realized that putting off seeing her until tomorrow would not solve the problem of a first encounter becoming a collision of unpredictable, embarrassing circumstances. He decided, therefore, to go to the hospital and enquire, as a relative from elsewhere, and have them reach her, saying that "Cousin" Giles was here for a very short time and needed and wanted to see her this evening, if at all possible. If this failed, then he would get a hotel room and try again in the morning.

Giles found and visited both the men's and women's rooms and found that there was barely a distinction between the two sexes except for an open door of half height between them. This enabled a single, ancient female to see both sides and collect her coins from users of each side of the facilities. There was a door leading into a supply closet on the men's side, which, when ajar, gave him just enough cover to change the items, place them into his larger case, and button his substituted civilian shirt. He walked out, dropping three pennies into the plate on the counter, by the men's room wash bowl. He received an approving nod and a smile from the toothless old lady as he left. He was now seeking a window or mirror from which to receive a reflection, to aide him in tying his tie.

Completing that task, he exited the station, looking for a form of taxi to take him to the Hotel Dieu de Lyon, where Elle was now staffed as a heart specialist. (He had tritely told her many times that this was her natural calling, and she had begun to roll her eyes rather balefully by the time of their separation in Paris, suggesting glibly his need for some new "material.")

He found a "charcoal burner" taxi at the curb, awaiting a fare. The driver was disappointed when he discovered the destination to be on this west side of the Rhone and only a few blocks in distance, but he was then in turn pleased when Giles told him to wait for him in front of the hospital.

Giles left the taxi and entered the hospital by the main entrance. It was a typically enormous building of the mid-eighteenth century, although he believed some small parts might emanate from the fifteenth and sixteenth centuries. Some décor also showed both the first and second periods of Louis XV window and ceiling embellishments. It should be remembered, from much earlier in this book,

The French Lieutenant and the King of Rome

that his avocational interest was art and decor. It wasn't "frou-frou," as the French say, but genuinely and solidly a part of the gentleman of breeding and taste in France. He quickly noted these things as he entered the main vaulted corridor and approached the reception desk to make his enquiry about the presence of his "dear cousin, Dr. d'Hozier" being still in the building. The attendant agreed to determine so immediately and buzzed the second-floor desk. After some time waiting, the doctor herself answered and shakily said that "she would be right down."

And she was! Her white, cotton medical smock, the shallow light from the high vaulting, the encompassing reflection from the sheen of the waxed, dark marble floor—all seemed to frame her, causing him to remember her as he did on that glorious spring afternoon when he first saw her in the Bois de Bologne. She was, yet, the model used by Greuze for his seventeenth-century etchings!

They moved together in one grand, irrepressible enthralling clasp that, to any observer, frantically denied the existence of their encumbering clothes. It lasted for an eternity, to any such embarrassed observer. Finally she parted from this sensual embrace, "to check out and grab her coat and scarf," leaving Giles standing like a jilted lover, torn from the climactic or "third act."

While he gawkishly awaited her momentary return, his wit got the better of him, and he sheepishly looked at the attendant and remarked, "Well, we are kissing cousins, don't you see?"

They ran, hand in hand, for the taxi and its "fireplace," charcoal burner. Elle gave an address, which, by his smile, pleased the driver, even more than the amount he registered while waiting idle at the hospital.

Elle directed the driver to go north, then cross over the Soane River and go to the west of it, and then after that to make a switchback, followed by a northward climb for about five minutes to a heavy double wrought-iron-gated drive. On arrival, she stepped out of the taxi and released the gates and opened them for the taxi to drive through. After a further winding drive, there stood before them a small eighteenth-century *manoir*, prerevolutionary of course. The driver was paid and tipped, and he departed, leaving his fares and their baggage at the foot of the steps.

Later she would explain to Giles that the house was preceded by her paternal ancestor's Gothic semimilitary chateau-fortress. This had had thirteenth-century arrow apertures, lastly modernized to windows, as serfdom vanished along with their own status as a fiefdom with obligations to their liege lords, who were either the d'Albon family or the Comte de Lyon. Loyalty must have switched occasionally, with local strife and rustling. Both of these activities and the liege lords essentially disappeared, leaving her ancestors to deal with the standardizing, nationalizing Bourbon kings of France. And of course, the construction of the eighteenth-century manor house, from the razed materials of the Gothic chateau, was at the expense of her ancestors.

LXVIII

BEATRICE WAS STILL on duty, as Elle expected, and still in her black shirtwaist dress and white apron uniform, though it was most doubtful that any visitors would be coming for a visit. She had answered the door and was shocked and delighted to see Giles come in with Elle, who had of course been living there since her recent return to Lyon.

Beatrice had been born into the serving class, a particular group of people who had always provided servants to the *nanti*, or privileged, of France. Placement was expected and obtained by services in every locale. The families were known to the local providers, and processing included school activities and church records, so that succeeding interviews were based on nearly a handpicked basis by the family to be the employer.

The serving class, trained in youth, were often more conscious of duty, self-control, and propriety than their "betters" and showed their employers, either subtly or in undisguised ways, when they had failed themselves. For, what was the point if a butler, ladies maid, valet, housekeeper, chauffer, and footman knew proper and polite manners and conduct and their employers didn't? Well, there would go all the ducks in a row, and what sort of a world would it be?

Beatrice had always been a forthright servant and respectfully nurturing friend to her mistress, and an instinctively protective shield, where it was proper and warranted. She had helped Elle to grow from infancy to womanhood and seen both daughter and mistress through the pain of Marguerite's husband's death. Truth be told, Beatrice and Marguerite had grown to be sisters, yet neither had presumed on the other's position in life. Neither of them would have spared herself in protecting the other. Beatrice was within two years of her mistress's age and had shared in every joy and pain the three of them had ever experienced. She was already devoted to Giles, once he married into and thus became an integral part of the family.

Marguerite, Elle's mother, had made up her mind to accept her son-in-law Giles regardless of the immense differences in family background. The chasm of difference, in her eyes, only began with religion. Perhaps an even more expansive gap was in class. To explain her concern then, it was not a matter of middle-class status. If that were all it was, then that concern would have disappeared since he and her daughter were both professionals, and thus equal and at the best level of the middle class.

This class distinction was uniquely Marguerite's and never Elle's. Elle had told her mother before the wedding how fallacious and outworn her values and thinking were—"for at least a century." Being a "gentleman," in the French sense, never had any veracity. For according to ancient tradition in France, one was born a gentleman because his ancestors were so, for an unknown amount of time, and the fact that this was perpetuated by generations of hearsay, to that effect, was pure nonsense! Because you had a few ancestors who were known for their courage was no indication that you were as well, any more than an accomplished horseman would have a so gifted offspring.

Elle explained to her mother, "At least the English system made practical sense. If one received a title, he most always received land. He was expected to act as a gentleman or, if offensive enough to the sovereign, forfeit his title and land. This would be true also of a knight, though without a gift of land. Their offspring would be considered gentry, if not titled, but only because they emanated from a title or knighthood. If untitled, they were commoners but remained gentry (so long as their personal reputation remained without serious blemish). Title, then reputation and conduct, counted. Whereas in France, title and real estate were entirely separated the one from the other as a result of the French Revolution. Real estate, connected with title, was a happenstance, not a certainty." Therefore, monsieur was not a *gentilhomme* according to custom. A gentleman was born in a mysterious continuum; those who belonged could recognize one another and could duel with one another, but not with another who was not—landed or impoverished, tattered or embellished. A gauntlet thrown at your feet or one across the face could end with a coffin, but only if you were a gentilhomme.

Elle continued, "Mother, at least before the present German humiliation, we were a republic. You do remember 'equality and fraternity,' don't you, Mother? I told you before the wedding that I believed myself good enough to be his wife, and I knew that he was not only good enough to be my husband but that he was the only one I've really wanted. We were made for each other, and I know, more now than ever, the truth of this."

Margurite, head drooping and mind pensive, finally said, "I know your father would agree with you and not me, and since it's his ancestry that is more at stake than mine—his being ancient nobles of the sword and mine of the Valois and then administrative Bourbon nobles—I wish to drop this matter once and for all time! I only harbored it because of the lack of a religious ceremony. He is and shall be my son and the father of my grandchildren. Furthermore, he is a good-looking devil and finely built, and his parents warrant him as an offspring. I am most impressed with their manner and looks and proud to call them family!" She paused and, with an urchin smile, said, "They would make glorious Catholics!"

On this note, Elle laughed good-naturedly with Marguerite. They left Marguerite's bedroom, and both descended the staircase together, to join with Beatrice and Giles where Elle had left them when she had slipped past them and sidled up the stairs to have that necessary conversation with her mother to which we were privy.

LXIX

ALL THREE SAT down to a light repast, prepared by Beatrice with slight assistance from Marguerite. Giles's plans were discussed quite guardedly, and finally the subject of finding Etienne was broached by Giles, who mentioned that he was in the new French armistice army permitted to be raised by the French ostensibly to protect the Vichy government against left-wing rebellion in the unoccupied territory. The size was, of course, allowed in retaliation for what the French had allowed the Germans after the last war. It was to be composed of volunteers of the new age, would-be call-ups and officers who were thought to be the most reliable among the new class graduating from the St. Cyr academy in the spring. The army and its officers from the war were being held as prisoners in German camps, perhaps some two and a half million of them. There were also officer exceptions, chosen for favored reasons, of whom Etienne was one. How he was to be located was the quandary.

An amazing resolution was hit upon by Giles. Marguerite, being a noblewoman with a deceased officer-husband, was a primary element, plus the fact that several of the present generals were the deceased husband's classmates and therefore knew of his death in the Foreign Legion in the Moroccan war in 1925. In fact, General Charles Huntziger was now in Petain's cabinet, the rather newly appointed secretary of state for war, as well as the commander-in-chief of all land forces. He had to have been a product of St. Cyr within the four years that her husband had been a cadet at the

The French Lieutenant and the King of Rome

academy. Giles was thinking that, in some way, Marguerite could discover the location of Etienne or even gain contact with him.

Interestingly, General Huntziger was Petain's "voice" at the forced armistice, where he had been indeed given no voice but just a pen, and the same was true with the Italians on June 24. He volunteered a very favorable statement after the signing of the armistice terms allowed by the Germans. It should be noted that he had spent almost all of his time in the colonies during WWI and was the disastrous leader of the Second Army, which let the Germans cross the Meuse and capture Sedan in a matter of hours, having replaced the experienced Third Division under Gen. Chapouilly (an African division proven under fire) with a category B, which was comprised of old, undertrained men. In fact at the north end of the Maginot Line, next to Sedan and just where the panzers were going to break into France, Huntzigers Second Army was considered the worst, ill-prepared part of the army, yet it ended up in the most crucial spot in the war. He supposedly sent misleading dispatches to Gamelan, blaming all of his subordinate generals for his failures. It was rumored that he even caused the failure and disarray in the Ninth Army to his north. Between them the whole battle for France collapsed. His antipathy for the left-wing Third Republic may have caused him to become a traitor. He was a great support to Petain in his new position as head of state in Vichy.

Marguerite asked an obvious question of Giles. "Why do you believe that finding him at this time can make a great difference in your life?"

"Because I cannot continue in the guise of a monsignor attached to this cathedral," replied Giles. "Archbishop Gerlier does not even know of my existence at this time, let alone that he has to deal with my many problems. I am hopeful that Etienne can aide me in solving them." Then he stared intently at Elle and in a low voice said, "I expect that none of the names or details concerning our surfacing from Paris have been revealed to anyone in Lyon. I am correct, am I not?" She nodded with equal emphasis that he was. And then to Marguerite he asked, "Have you had occasion to ever meet or know Lt. Picard?"

She gave the expected reply. "Why, of course—through you and at your wedding."

"For us to execute this plan, you must forget that, including the wedding and that you have ever heard of me, no matter who asks you or when. Forget that your daughter is married. She remains under her maiden name and must do so for all of the foreseeable future. You may be required to know me as Monsignor Lambert, but not until I say so. Until then, if at all, I am unknown to you!"

He called for Beatrice to come in and then repeated some limited details, as stated, and received a befuddled, confused, and very unhappy look from her in response. Marguerite quickly intervened and explained to her that the life and safety of all of them were clearly at stake and she must not reveal anything to anyone regarding any of these facts. Further, she would explain what she could to her, privately.

Giles was alarmed at the situation. He realized that at least one person too many knew more than she should. Beatrice was a simple person without any understanding of necessary dissembling or the strength of character to do so if called upon—or even to recognize when confronted with the need to do so. He had realized that she could not be excluded. She dealt with an untold number of trades people daily and could prattle on about family circumstances.

Giles asked Marguerite discretely to meet with him in the privacy of her study the next morning. The purpose was to enlist her in his scheme to meet again with Etienne. He wished her to take the train to Vichy, a seventy-mile journey, and meet with General Huntziger, now minister of defense and war and commander-in-chief of all land forces. He explained to her that his office would, he believed, have all records of where the members of this small army were located in the small area now known as the "unoccupied zone." He had no knowledge of how the troops were dispersed in the limited region, but he suspected that they were, in order to suppress any unforeseen uprisings from the left political wing, which were such a powerful part of the Third Republic's government. There were in the Vichy jurisdiction only eight regions of the original eighteen created in the 1870s for all of France.

She could use as a purpose her knowledge of Etienne's family and acquaintance with his deceased mother and his uncle, the cardinal and archbishop of Paris, who had told her in early August of Etienne's desire to switch to the armistice army and that he had then left for Vichy.

Further, perhaps he knew her deceased husband, a lieutenant colonel killed in 1925 in the Moroccan campaign. It was more than likely because they were of approximately the same ages and were cadets at St. Cyr near the same time. Her superficial purpose was to offer Lt. Picard an invitation to visit with herself and her family at her manor house in Lyon when he had leave. Of course she would casually mention that her daughter, of approximately his age, was single, as well. Thus she had two reasonable enticements to cause her to take the trouble to make the train trip: herself for him and her daughter for Etienne.

The archbishop's influence must have infected him. He felt this plot was at George Simenon's level, and it would take the cunning of his Detective Maigret to see something suspicious behind the skein of this web.

At first, her reaction was shock: imagine that he thought Elle's mother could do anything so brazen! But Giles saw her as a woman in total control of herself. He remembered her at that small reception where she and his parents had met each other. She was the picture of a woman trying to maneuver herself out of what was a totally unacceptable situation for her aristocratic self and daughter. She handled it perfectly, without creating a scene or hostility. His parents made comment to him later how she had made her class and religious points with ardor and without offense, so much so that they were totally unsympathetic to a solution favoring the marriage. Of course, his father could not help being in favor of Elle because of her beauty and accomplishments. Their kindness and spoken feeling of hopelessness about a religious solution made

Marguerite's position actually supportable. Marguerite's "class and Catholic point of view" made marriage without religion a certainty.

The class matter between persons of similar education and breeding made the survival of nobility in France simply a matter of gossip, unless great fortunes were involved, which frequently made for "commercial marriages." However, by French law a female carried no titles and could pass none. Titles for men had no land attached, so a titled husband was that alone, unless he had unattached wealth. It all had become simple snobbism and nothing else since the 1790s.

Marguerite had talked it over with Elle, who fully understood the need of Giles to meet Etienne and attempt to make a plan before Britain should be defeated. After their review of those things Marguerite needed to do with Huntziger, she agreed and even suggested that she leave a cordial note with the marshal's aide, since she knew him from the period of her husband's service. She also knew that men whom she had met seldom forgot her, because of her persona. Now she had a justifiable and worthwhile purpose to use it! She planned to do so on Tuesday next and on the earliest morning train, without calling ahead, to avoid any evasiveness by some member of his staff. She would use her desire to offer her pleasure at the marshal's new leadership as an excuse for "dropping in."

LXX

MARGUERITE MADE HERSELF as alluring as she felt she could and left for the station in her car, which Elle now used as her physician's car, thus obtaining a gas allotment of a minimum amount. Of course this benefited the household, if used with propriety. The permit was perhaps harder to get than one in the occupied area because the Germans siphoned almost all petrol away for their own uses, except for the needs of Petain's army. She departed on the train with adequate time to spare and arrived on schedule at Vichy, where she actually departed for the Hotel Du Parc, now Petain's government headquarters, by "rickshaw" bicycle, driven by a sturdy female teenager. She hadn't seen one of those since her husband was stationed in Peiping (Beijing) on embassy duty in 1920 (or perhaps it was '21).

Vichy was not at all impressive, considering that it was now the single capital of all that was left of France except for the colonies. Petain's government had been able to save them too. Well, like most of the French, she thought of him as the "Father of France" and thought nothing of importance about that upstart de Gaulle, who had apparently deserted the marshal and gone to England, which always was a thorn in the side of France. But still she thought that the marshal had no right to reverse privileges her people had gained so painfully in the Revolution: even as an aristocrat, she liked the idea of all Frenchmen being equal in the eyes of the law. An aristocrat she was, but that didn't mean serfdom or abuse of human beings was right or that those below her should be trodden upon or treated unequally in the eyes of the law or that a privileged person's lies should outweigh the honesty of a poor person, no matter how low. That however did not make them their social equals—to party with, socialize with, or to interbreed with. Exceptions! Exceptions! She had made peace with the most irreconcilable ones, the closest possible of all—her son-in-law and his parents! She suddenly was happy to be cheek-by-jowl with them, and sincerely so! "There are no steadfast rules in relationships, nor in life, for that matter," she thought to herself. "Only fools could go through life never moving and fixed like a fireplace on a wall!" She finally admitted to herself that changing made for understanding and growth. She had been so "closed"—closed and lonely. She was still alive and changing!

She stepped down from the rickshaw after paying the stalwart driver and thanking her with a tip. There were armed military guards in front of the "one-size-fits-all" government building, formerly the best hotel in this second-rate, rather seedy French watering hole, left over from the fin de siècle.

The hotel's voluptuous secret affairs must have become hauntings, making life stiflingly close for officers virtually tripping over ghosts with fabulous bustles and ostrich-feathered hats; gentlemen in black dancing pumps, top hats, and valets; and lighthearted couples or triples occupying the bedrooms, in states of cupidity—all such bedroom suites now refitted with chairs and desks filled with weighty matters, the construing of mock war plans for the miniscule French army, made by cuckoo-clock toy makers in Germany.

But this was a serious errand she was on, and she would commence by addressing the sergeant of the guard, stating that she had business with the marshal's adjutant. She allayed his concerns by assuring him, "I am an old acquaintance of the marshal's and the widow of Lt. Col. Hercule d'Hozier, member of the Legion of Honor."

"Do you carry a card, Madame?"

"Certainly not! Simply give the adjutant my name—that shall be sufficient!"

And it was! She was escorted by the sergeant to the suite of the marshal, where the adjutant intercepted her to discuss the reason for her visit without a previous appointment. She then presented her heavily scented, well-phrased note of congratulations, which also expressed her and her families' loyal support and made reference to her husband's death and decorations as a result of the Rif War in Morocco in 1925. The marshal was not available now but would cherish her note and her husband's glorious memory. She now allowed as how she would need directions to the office of General Charles Huntziger on some personal business. The adjutant offered her little assistance in that regard, but she looked him in the eye and coldly replied again, "This is a personal matter!" The adjutant, being French, immediately thought it to be a "coup du coeur" a matter of the heart, and described the general's location without further ado.

After seeking some added directions, she located what had been elevators for servants, now designated for occupants' use. She asked of two junior officers waiting with her on what level the commander-in-chief's office was located, and they readily showed her to it. She paused to gather her emotional forces before entering the door denominated "Secretary for Defense and War," so as to glide in rather than tactically charging in like "a young Turk," only to lose the battle before it was joined!

She proceeded to sweep by the desk of a female secretary and then a startled lieutenant, whom she blithely informed that she had just come from "the marshal's suite," where she was encouraged to discover if General Huntziger could not be of some assistance to her—by the way, the general was probably her husband's classmate at the academy, a most surprising coincidence if so! All of this she presented in a glib, posh-styled, comfortably self-assertive, insistent manner—in a word, formidably.

The disturbance in the general's outer office gained his irritated attention and brought him to both his feet and his door, which he pulled open, agitatedly, to find his befuddled lieutenant seemingly overtaken by a remarkably attractive—no, a "smashing looking"—woman of a "certain age." This young puppy of a lieutenant was to the general's practiced eye overmatched and in need of an experienced relief column to assume the primary command of the situation. His first words were directed to his aide, but his unctuous smile accompanying them was directed to the unexpected, but welcome, intruder.

"Lieutenant, could you offer Madame an introduction if she is intending to visit this office, or perhaps even a chair."

"Madame, this is General Huntziger. He is the secretary of defense and war, and I have the honor of being one of his aides. And you, Madame, are?"

"I am Marguerite d'Hozier, the widow of Lt. Col. Hercule d'Hozier, late of the Foreign Legion. You may recall him from the academy as a cadet?"

"It certainly is a familiar name. Was he one of the heroes of the Great War?"

"No, *mon* General, he died with his Legionnaire battalion in the Rif War in 1925. He was greatly commended for his heroism by the state."

"Oh yes! It all comes back to me now!" He paused then before continuing, "Our recent, heroic defeat still dominates my mind. And then, of course, I have had the burden of reorganizing our new army that is rising out of the armistice we gained with the Germans." After another pause he added, "But, you see, I have been selected by the marshal to carry the added responsibility of being his secretary of defense and war in his cabinet."

"But this must leave you with little time for your wife and children, and such grandchildren as there maybe. And how many children have the two of you?"

"Madame, we must adjourn to this inner office for a continuation of our visit."

"But, of course, we speak in public of personal things—most thoughtless of me to go on like this!"

The French Lieutenant and the King of Rome

As they entered his inner office, she commented, "Somehow I feel a certain, as the Spanish say, *sympatico* with you. My manor house is close by—just outside of Lyon—and we simply adore visitors! But I must address a matter of urgent importance. A young son of old friends is a lieutenant in your forces, and I desperately wish to contact him. His deceased parents and his uncle, the archbishop of Paris, would expect at least that much of me. My lovely daughter of almost his age is anxious to see him again, and it would make for a delightful weekend for him on some short leave time, which I am sure your officers enjoy on occasion. Could your office locate him while I'm here today?"

"Well, I'll call my lieutenant now and have him check the roll of junior officers to determine his location.

"Lieutenant, please come in.

"Please locate the assignment and duty post of—Madame, his name if you please?"

"Lt. Etienne Pickard. I believe he was a cavalryman when serving in the old army."

During several minutes of the lieutenant's absence, the general pursued the hunt avidly while his game cunningly dodged and averted, enticed and evaded, the deft but too-eager hunter. Then—alas!—the secretary and the lieutenant burst through the door, one with an officers roll book and one with the good news that Etienne was in fact on post as an aide to the secretary for the colonies, which startled the general, who seemed miffed at the waste of a perfectly good cavalryman, and which gave Madame an opportunity to ask the lieutenant to call Etienne and have him meet her directly at the officers' cocktail bar. "Oh, where is that now? In the Algeria Hotel, you say, Lieutenant?"

While the aide completed the arrangement with Etienne over the phone, Madame continued to divert the general further by having him write down her phone number and address and assuring him how sincerely she would look forward to his call. "And have your wife call Madame so that she can arrange a weekend that they would all enjoy!" The tumult, like the sudden heavy summer storm it resembled, was passing.

The bespectacled secretary, still standing in the middle of the general's office and still holding the officers roll book, was pleased at the rare opportunity to satisfy the general so easily, while he, for his part, sat sprawled in his overly copious armchair, semi collapsed behind his desk, in a mortified state.

LXXI

SHE ARRIVED AT the Algeria Hotel by going partly through the park and partly along the narrow street on which it stood. It lacked the antique elegance of the Parc Hotel, but it was likewise filled with Vichy agency offices, such as the Commissariat General for Jewish Questions. In October of 1940 an anti-Semitic statute was passed, much in the same vein as that of the Germans. This finally led to the deaths of some seventy thousand Jews in German death camps. The original such statute was signed by General Charles Huntziger. French resistance didn't truly begin until the French realized the Americans, British, and their allies were going to win. The French, as a people, prefer to side with final winners, with as little early-construction damage as possible because of fighting with the eventual losers. They can be said to be a very pragmatic people. Ideology is therefore principled and not motivational.

Some five thousand of those Frenchmen who happened to be of the Jewish faith, by German and French definition, died in French concentration camps because of starvation and neglect before they were shipped off to the German death camps. This was an important part of Petain's presidency, hunting down French Jews—even those who were veterans of 1914–18! The French didn't notice that this didn't compute with the "Liberty, Equality, and Fraternity" of the Revolution of 1793 or of the philosophers Rousseau and Voltaire. Only 80 of the 649 members of the National Assembly voted against the dissolution of the constitution and liberty, fraternity, and equality; thus was created Petain's puppet dictatorship and unlawful constitution, which aped that of Germany, pure and simple. Furthermore, every important division of its government was replete with Frenchmen who were German spies, to prevent a revival of France surreptitiously.

Madame d'Hozier entered a barroom just off the lobby, marked, "Officers Bar and Guests Only," where she sat at an unoccupied table facing the entrance, in order to attract the attention of Etienne as he entered. There were no other ladies of the day in the bar, as it was shortly after lunch. It was too early in the day for the lobby to have ladies of the night plying their trade. The bar was nearly empty of officers. Therefore, the two of them would be subjects of study either casually or as "reportage." To be consistent with her story with the general, she must act "the long-lost family friend with an eligible daughter," waiting to make him feel comfortable, as if at home.

He finally appeared in the doorway of the bar. The well-lit lobby clearly outlined him though he wasn't wearing the kepi. Instead he was wearing a British-style beret, a part of the new-style uniform. She rose and quickly strode to him at the door, called out his name, and gave him a kiss on both cheeks and held him in an embrace with her lips against his right ear as she whispered to walk outside of the hotel with her, and then in a clearly audible voice, "How wonderful to see you again after all this time. Let's delay the drink and walk and chat in the park."

She modulated her voice to say for him to react as though she were an old aunt, as they reached the walk, where she quietly explained that Elle was with her in her Lyon house and practicing in the Hotel de Dieu on the Presqu'ile of Lyon every day. But she had told General Huntziger that Elle was single and would be interested in seeing Etienne, who needed to visit with them at the d'Hozier manor house in Lyon as soon as he had a short leave. Of course she let the general know how close she was with Etienne's deceased parents and uncle, the archbishop of Paris, who had told her of his whereabouts. She had also invited the general and his wife for a weekend, as well. Then she proceeded to the main point.

The French Lieutenant and the King of Rome

"One other thing, Giles is there too—in disguise—and needs to see you, secretly and as soon as possible. And that is the true reason I'm here! I'm leaving by train this afternoon, returning home."

Etienne started to ask obvious questions, and Marguerite immediately cut him off in midquestion. "I can tell you nothing further. Please do not ask—much is at risk! You are free to ask for leave time based on what I told the good general. Everything else is secret! Do you understand?"

The response was a resounding yes.

She gave him her phone number and address details and told him to call, and arrangements at the station in Lyon for pickup would be made.

LXXII

IT WAS FRIDAY. Etienne stood on the curb outside the Presqu'ile railway station, having just arrived in Lyon at 5:30 p.m. on the Vichy-Lyon train. He had set his two valises down on the sidewalk while awaiting someone to arrive in a four-door, black Citroen. The driver was not revealed to him in the brief telephone conversation of yesterday. He was only told where to wait on his arrival. In times such as these, such precautions were reasonable. The delay in arrival was tolerably short, and he was grateful for that. The reason was that he was worried about whether he was going to find Giles in one piece. He had been worried for months about him, wondering whether he were now a Jewish prisoner of the Germans.

When Giles was not in the car, he was ready to believe the worst. Elle was driving, and she saw the look of despair on Etienne's face as he entered the car. Elle said the quickest reassuring thing she could, "Don't worry. He is truly fine and waiting breathlessly to see you, so you can push each other around like children again and do the buddy-buddy wine toasts. I think I and Marguerite just might join in!"

Etienne asked Elle whether she and Giles had been north of the demarcation line when the armistice was signed. And if so, how had they gotten here? She informed him that that was a guarded secret that probably would not be revealed until they were satisfactorily convinced of Etienne's political position. She said, "Let's leave this subject until all four of us are at the manor house together." They fell into an odd silence untypical of their casual

The French Lieutenant and the King of Rome

yet personal relationship since they first became friends after the wedding.

As she went through the open gates to the estate, she casually asked him if he personally could commit himself to the de Gaulle movement.

He responded, "Officially, I find it reprehensible, as a member of the new chicken coup army."

"What do you mean by that?" she asked.

"First, the Germans have spies everywhere in Petain's domain. That way we can't do to them what they did to us after the first war. Next, they gave us a toy army, like we gave them after the first war, and they developed theirs before our eyes until they totally subjected us with it. The Germans are both sleek and slick, unctuous and vicious, cunning and cruel; if he were an animal, he would be a red fox.

"But our toy one-hundred-thousand-man army is just a chicken coup army where we chickens pretend we are an army; the roosters are the field-grade officers, and there are bands and parades to impress the mice in the barns when we thunder around with our toy weapons and horses and wagons. Meanwhile, the big hungry foxes sit outside and sell tickets to more foxes to watch the show, and at intermission they come in quietly and select a few Jewish or communist chickens to cook and sell to the audience for snacks. One problem is that the foxes have stopped giving us feed, and we ordinary chickens are getting thinner and thinner. Soon the foxes will have to eat us all to keep satisfying their ravenous hunger. But they don't care because they think by then they will have British chickens to eat. But maybe the British chickens may bring their friends who are tigers and lions and bears, and then they might kill all the foxes. Their friends—these ferocious, powerful wild animals—are called 'Americans.' The foxes are very clever, but the wild enormous beasts will just keep coming until they corner every fox and its kits until this time the foxes won't even be alive to be sorry they started with the arrogant, stupid, birdbrained chickens in the French coups because there won't be any foxes left—except for one dead one that a taxidermist chicken stuffed and stood in a place called the 'Louvre,' which belonged to the foxes. Originally it belonged to the chickens, but they were so afraid of the foxes and so birdbrained that they let the foxes come in to their very large and beautiful coup and take what they wanted, including the rooster's best-looking chickens. But through it all, the chickens and roosters never noticed anything the foxes did because they were busy fighting against each other. I guess the French chickens were very lucky the British chickens and roosters had lots of innards and were stringy and tough and had mean wild animals who loved them dearly, who just couldn't be stopped once they got started to fight!"

Elle turned the motor off as the car came even with the front steps leading up to the walk to the manor house. "I adore parables—your Jean de La Fontaine–like fable cruelly hits the mark. Like his, I'm sure yours has two meanings: one for children and one for patriots, which is political. Nicely done! I didn't know you were a raconteur! Do be careful: I understand the present Louis XIII doesn't like witty people and takes his very boring, very old self very seriously. Further, his fascist aides hated the Third Republic and admire greatly slick, sleek, vicious, and cruel red foxes. Let's go in; there are some people who are awaiting us!"

LXXIII

GILES WAS WAITING for him at the door and threw his arms about him in one immense hug, which Etienne returned in kind. Elle and Marguerite seemed to hang about them as simple observers, more or less waiting to be noticed. They didn't exist for the moment. The "boys" were talking at each other, neither hearing the other until Marguerite thought to shout, "Time!" Then the two "boys" went completely silent, realizing how they had made themselves the "main event in the center ring." Elle said that they needed to move to the sitting room, where Beatrice was nervously awaiting the opportunity to be of service. Marguerite proffered wine to celebrate this rarest of reunions. Beatrice was ready with wine glasses for all, and she was, of course, to join as a participant, at Marguerite's invitation.

Marguerite said to Elle, "It is your place to commence the toasts, Giselle!"

"Then I shall," she replied, "but the first one is to be the best. I must think to make one that speaks to Giles and my recent, miraculous reunion. And of course to my mother's seamless acting—the step-by-step performance, which she has shared with me. Her stellar wit and brazen performance, which has led to the presence of Etienne being with us all. Which of course, also brought the rejoining together of two inseparable, lifelong friends, Giles and Etienne. How, in a few words, do I make a toast that encompasses all of that? I have it!

"To all of us, together again: may we never part!"

All heartily approved with "Well said!" and similar adulations. Then Marguerite proposed a humble form of grace: "We thank the Lord of us all for this sublime blessing he has rendered us this day!" And "Amen!" was heard around the room.

The time together was to be short, and there was much to be said. First must be the reestablishment of total confidence again between the two erstwhile friends. The wrongful acceptance of one by the other could ultimately lead to a death sentence. They had to find in each other's eyes and words and body language the same friends that were there from childhood, still unchanged by two years of separation and now different armies and thus perhaps different loyalties—the probing had to commence!

The three of them, Etienne, Giles, and Elle, were in the sitting room, around a small table with snacks and two bottles of red. Etienne began, just to break the silence. They all three knew there was an invisible, leaden obstruction in the room, and it was setting between the "boys," and only they could make it disappear, if they worked at it hard enough, together. Etienne began the probing.

Etienne asked the two of them to tell him as much as they were free to do regarding their presence in Lyon, since it was clear that they had made it across the demarcation line from Paris. The couple confided openly that they came quite legally and thus had no compunction about revealing their right to be in the free zone. He in turn said that his uncle's connections gained him a place in the armistice army at its formation, to save him from the threat of a German prison camp and other risks in the North, such as having to deal with labor conscription for Germany, which was beginning to be a fear all over France. He revealed a total lack of loyalty to Petain and his miniature German dictatorship. He felt special remorse for the "fraudulent manner in which the Third Republic was dissolved," and how it died without a whimper.

LXXIV

"I MUST TELL you," said Giles, "that I had an opportunity to speak with your marshal during my active service in the army. He was even animated in speaking to me about the last war and my father's service on his staff. He even said he would be eternally grateful to him for saving his life—that he thought of him often for saving his life by shielding him with his own body at Verdun, that one could never forget such a man nor the occurrence. He said, 'If I may ever be of service to your father or you, call upon me.'"

"How peculiar," said Etienne. "Did he not know that your father was an Israelite? You do know that he sponsored the anti-Semitic bill of the Vichy government passed last October, which precluded all Jews from all public service. And that was before the Germans asked him to do so. And he follows the Germans in a mimeographed fashion! Holding camps are being prepared for the Jews by his Vichy government. He even converts the tattered camps where left-wing Spanish soldiers took refuge after Franco's fascist government took over Spain!"

Both Giles and Elle were startled to hear of his revealed attitude. Then Etienne said, "The marshal says little, but his men are more than happy to speak and act in his place. General Huntziger went to Compiegne and signed the armistice in his name for France and made a submissive little speech after it was over. And General Huntziger signed the anti-Semitic act in October instead of Petain. So far, he hasn't stepped off his isolated pedestal!"

Both Elle and Giles now revealed their fondest hope that America would enter the war soon, even though it maintained Ambassador Leahy here. They believed the American government was using it as a listening post without a belief in the permanent fall of "old" France. They confirmed Etienne's belief that no real underground or Maquis had started yet. They were devotees of BBC radio and realized that the "Free France" movement was still weak, but eventually when America made warlike moves, France would organize a true rebellious spirit and begin to sabotage and undermine the German occupation. In the meantime, Charles de Gaulle was the best hope; with his earnest efforts in the colonies, maybe French forces would grow.

Etienne was very discouraging about their beliefs. When he said that the figures in the possession of the Vichy dictatorship showed that the French people throughout France looked at Petain as their savior and their father and followed willingly his passivity and obedience toward the Germans, it translated to simple collaboration—a mindless acceptance of inferiority, with a slave's hope only of survival.

"This armistice army that I, Etienne, belong to believes that it is in control of its own destiny for the first time since the fall of Emperor Louis Napoleon. For the first time, since then, it believes itself to be the true image of the real French character, of freedom and patriotism even, in the face of defeat, caused by the left political wing in the Estates General, and a living guide for the French, particularly the youth.

"In fact, it is a defeated, toothless miniarmy, ridiculously celebrating itself as a victor and relieving the Germans from having to protect their backs from the defeated enemy who might rise up in a rebellion. And the armistice army thinks its greatest enemies are not the Germans, but the left wing of the French people, who might rise up and bring in communism. In truth the army high command is more afraid of the Russians and their communism than their ancient enemy, the Germans. It isn't fascism but communism they fear! The Germans control this army like the preposterous marionettes they really are!

"There is more to tell, but first you must tell me how you really got here. And what then are your plans?" Etienne said, with an assertive and serious tone. "I've laid my circumstance before you! Now a truthful statement is due from you!"

"It's not really a matter of truth, but a story more like fiction, and it involves a person most dear to you. And if you reveal it, that person will die at the hands of the Germans.

"Your knowing this puts that person in just that much more danger, and if you insist, then you too assume our burden. You must now ask for the story or not. The decision is yours. We also break our oath in revealing it!" said Giles.

Etienne did not hesitate to assume the burden because he knew it must be his uncle, the only person left who was dear to him, and he knew that Giles was aware of that. "What a foolish game you are playing with me!" snickered Etienne

"Not so!" declared Giles, over the laughter of Elle. "We had no choice from the very beginning because without you in our plans we couldn't extricate ourselves from our dilemma."

Elle and Giles decided to each tell their stories separately but agreed to leave out the identification of the other participants involved and proceeded to do so. But of course they had to tell how Abetz was fooled with the Ausweis and also about the luck Giles had with the German lieutenant at the railroad station.

LXXIV

ETIENNE WAS STARTLED about Giles being trained as a monsignor and performing so authentically. He asked whether he had shown up at the Lyon Cathedral and shown his papers to Archbishop Gerlier. "Not yet. We have been waiting to clear this up with you."

"Are you really intending to act as a monsignor at St. Jean?"

"Perhaps just to cover the story, to protect your uncle in case any authority asks him about his new monsignor sent down from Paris. Your uncle can suffer enormous penalties from the Vatican, and a German death camp, as well. The others would also end up dead. Torture of your uncle would reveal them, as well. I know that we here all get cold chills every time we think of how exposed your uncle is. I am lucky that Gerlier is known for his protective attitude toward Jews, and he will be pleased to know what your uncle has done for us.

"I have a hidden message for Gerlier, which will succinctly tell my little tale."

Etienne then stared at Giles and asked sarcastically, "If you're not going to be a monsignor, then what are you going to be? Not a Jewish lieutenant: there is no casting available for that part anymore! Tell me what your next roll will be. I know you're not able to go back to being an advocate since the new Jewish statutes have been passed. So what are *we* going to do? And I mean it!"

"I've got one hope," Giles said beseechingly, "and that's why we have done so much to find you and get you here for this meeting."

"Very well. What scheme have you thought out?" asked Etienne.

"Don't laugh at me," replied Giles, "but if I could only get to the Perigord region and stay in your parents' country house and hide in the back country there, long enough to get my parents out of Nice, in the Italian occupied zone to join me. Then somehow to get all of us over the Pyrenees into Spain, where we would get to Gibraltar and then on to England and Charles de Gaulle. I really want in the fight for a true France again! Help me somehow, Etienne! You're the only hope I have. If your uncle Emmanuel put everything he has on the line for Elle and me, please try to match his Christian virtue! If not for that, then for the brothers we have always been!"

"For God's sake, stop the histrionics! You just tried out for the lead role of *Joan of Arc*, and you're good, but you're not Sarah Bernhardt—your voice is pitched too low. Of course, you wish the same for Elle and maybe her mother and her indispensable Beatrice, as well? It just so happens that I've been to Lourdes and perhaps the Mother of God might help me do at least a part of that and begin by getting you to the Perigord and helping you hide there. But first I've got much more to tell you, and it will shock you. And this also may never leave this room! And you may change your mind about the Perigord after you consider what I'm about to tell you.

"I am not simply a second lieutenant attached to the secretary of the colonies as an aide," continued Etienne. Giles, sensing Etienne to be at risk, asked if it were pertinent for him and Elle to know of this. "Absolutely!" Etienne replied. "And remember: none of this is to go beyond our three sets of ears."

Etienne then placed his empty wine glass on the small table and began again.

"I am a member of a secret inner group charged by certain leaders in the army to collect and conceal arms and vehicles for use by the army in some future unnamed event of national awakening.

"I am of course at the lowest level of this scheme but feel fortunate to have been included," he continued, "and was so, I believe, because I am not a St. Cyr graduate-automaton, devoted to the idea that the officers corps must not deviate from the oath given in the armistice agreement to the Germans.

"Further, no defeated army should pretend that they are anything but a humiliation to their nation and their people. Parading and giving new decorations and promotions when their battle flags are spit on and dragged through German excretions and given back to them to honor—the horrifying pretense of it!"

Elle, in a befuddled manner, asked, "Why?"

"Because I am fulminating inside at our betrayal by our leaders and our own stupidity. Because I have seen dress parades where officers and men have been decorated with a new green Croix de Guerre medal for absolutely nothing—in humiliation of its history, always having been given for combat valor to the living and dead! A centime copy of a glorious medal! This comic opera of buffoons could only exist in 'our' France but truly belongs in a child's Punchinello street performance or, if you prefer, a rowdy rendition of the Italian commedia dell'arte.

"This secret activity is not known by the armistice army command above a certain rank. I might add that these items are in very large quantities and not known to the Germans and in contradiction to the armistice terms. Revelation could mean executions." There was a dire tone of warning in his last statement.

"Lastly, certain vehicles are at my disposal, and we have available fuel trucks as well.

"Now you can understand why this can be of vital concern to you and others close to us."

Elle and Giles stared at one another blankly, obviously reaching for the plan or idea in Etienne's mind.

"Giles and Elle, I know certain things, certain facts, which must be discussed, and I shall mention them as I now know them. Please answer any questions I now pose as exactingly as is at all possible. Thereafter, we shall formulate a possible plan of escape from this predicament for us all!"

LXXV

"FIRST, DOES ANYONE know the present address and location of Giles's parents?"

Elle answered, "Yes, my mother corresponds with them in Nice, where they moved just before the war broke. It is the same address they first had there. That is as recent as one month ago. They rent an apartment there. Retirement was their goal in moving. Gilbert left his advocacy practice to Giles, who shortly after was called to the colors."

Etienne asked, "Have they been disturbed by the police, as being Jewish?"

"Marguerite has told me no," replied Giles. "And they reason because he is not only native born but a military officer of high rank and a hero from the last war. Furthermore, this is an Italian 'open zone,' and the Italians have refused German access to the Jews in their area."

Etienne asked, "Did they remove their full household of furnishings from Paris or not?

Giles said, "Not, but only about three or four roomfuls, plus cherished items and their clothing and auto."

"Did your Father take his dress uniform with him, including kepi, Sam Browne officers belt, sidearm, and ammunition and decorations?"

"Absolutely yes, and hunting rifles and some ammunition as well," responded Giles vigorously.

"How many people in this group have their Vichy identity cards?" Etienne asked but received an answer from only Elle. She affirmed that she knew her mother and Beatrice had not only them but French passports, as well, since they had both traveled out of France frequently before the war. Elle had gotten hers as a member of the hospital staff but no passport. Giles stated that he was without both.

Etienne directed them as follows: "Elle, have two photos, each two-by-two inches, made, and Giles have four made, the same size as hers. Then mail them to me. I will take the necessary statistics from you both based on Marguerite's passport. Please get it for me now while I and Giles speak about maps."

Etienne produced a Michelin map of France, spread it out on the nearby couch, and folded it down to the southwest quarter section of the map and began to speak about the road distance from Lyon to Nice. This led to a discussion that was puzzling to Giles and increasingly animated by Etienne. "I have an escape route and plan for the four of you surging through my mind, and everyone here needs to agree to every phase of it or it cannot be done!"

At this point, Elle reentered the room, with Marguerite tailing her closely, annoyed and in a state of consternation. Her look quickly graduated to foreboding, and she said, "She has my passport. Now whatever do you want it for?"

"It's just as well that you are here because you are to be an essential part of this plan.

Without you it can't take place!"

All four were now as close as possible to the end of the couch, where the map was folded to show the area from Lyon to the Mediterranean and Nice.

Etienne then said, "My general plan of escaping France for all who need to go is as follows:

"First: Marguerite drives with Beatrice to Nice in her four-door sedan for the purpose of getting Gilbert and his wife, the parents of Giles, and bringing them to this manor house.

The French Lieutenant and the King of Rome

"The Lamberts shall drive their own vehicle, caravan-style, on the return trip. Included in the caravan shall be a truck of modest size provided by me. I shall have one of the trucks that my group has been sequestering from the Germans, through private companies who may use them in their fleet until an occasion when we call upon them for its use. I plan to choose one from the company that has our vehicles in Nice. It will be a transport vehicle with a driver who will probably be an officer or noncommissioned officer on protracted leave from the armistice army. The truck is for the specific purpose of transporting all of the household goods in Nice belonging to Gilbert and wife. He will be asked to have an assistant to help with loading and unloading, assuming that there are some cumbersome pieces in the move. We shall provide you with a specific Michelin route and map, but you must find out the best way to reach their apartment from the entry into Nice, from the end of our route. You must write them a letter now advising them, in a harmless way, that you are taking a small vacation in the area to enjoy a climate change. Tell them you are not going to impose on them, just intending to share a meal, not more. Tell them you will have some time to run errands for them in the event they have auto or petrol problems now. Mention that you have noticed a change in the army uniform and wonder if he still has that beautiful parade one with his decorations. You would like to compare it to your husband's still in your closet because you still cherish it. Tell them you need instructions from them on how to reach their apartment from the point (I shall shortly give you the complete map from here to there) where you are arriving. Be certain to enquire about their health as you can wait a few days if either of them have any minor health issues.

"It is very important that he drive his car here. If there is anything wrong with it, I will have it fixed there before they leave with you. We absolutely need to have his full parade uniform and proper shoes with him, and pray that it still fits him adequately. Don't forget the medals—very important! And their passports and any IDs, too. A fuel truck will meet you just outside of Nice to fill your tanks and fill some canisters to place in the truck in case of need before you return here. I shall fill your vehicle before you leave Lyon, and in addition I shall place two canisters in your trunk, at that time, before you leave. It is 292 miles to Nice, by Michelin's map. You must stay overnight and pack in the morning and depart as quickly as possible. The truck and men will arrive early the next morning. It's a four-and-a-half-hour drive between these cities. I shall deliver army plates to you for each car."

"What is the plan you have conceived after their return?" asked Giles.

"Allow me to ask you a question before I answer yours?"

"Yes, of course," replied Giles.

"Can you say with absolute confidence that age has not altered your father's remarkable courage and steel nerves? And, of course, I am not impugning his character in any way! You do understand that I have a vital reason for asking your best opinion of that, don't you?" Giles intently looked at his friend and knew the question was well tempered and the answer obviously necessary for Etienne's still not understood intent.

This caused Giles to give careful consideration before answering the essential question, realizing that a yes answer might place his father at great risk and perhaps the rest of this small group, as well. "Remember that I haven't seen him in almost two years, but he was still quite a youthful man and is only fifty-five years old. I have no reason to think of him as less stalwart than he was at that time. Probably he is furious at all that has happened and regrets that he wasn't called back to be in the fight!" Giles continued, "How could he feel when he and Petain fought over the bodies of thousands of men at Verdun for years and our army lost it in a day or less?"

The occupants of the room seemed suspended from action: all awaited the response of Etienne to Giles's answer. The apparent question in everyone's mind was whether or not it would alter Etienne's plan.

LXXVI

"I MUST TELL you that my plan has been based upon sheer gall. But I assure you that it is the most realistic one that you have to consider. All other plans put those who go at the foot of the treacherous, snowbound Pyrenees. There are one or two escape lines, meaning groups of civilians who hide shot-down airmen and pass them along from one to another as best they can, to the Spanish Pyrenees mountain guides, which I am told are of varying reliability, which means there is the possibility of being turned over to Gestapo, who are allowed in Spain and favored by Franco. All that aside, the climb is hazardous beyond belief, with precipices, sharp rocks, narrow mountain paths, water to cross, and blizzards. Even the airmen who venture it sometimes die in the attempt.

"One must be prepared with climbing gear and stout climbing boots and carry one's own supplies. A great number of British airmen land in France, and a desperate fight between civilians (trying to get them to Spain and then Gibraltar from the low countries, Belgium and France) and the Nazis ensues, with torture and death to the civilians who are caught. They are betrayed by our fellow countrymen, who, as often as not, curry the favor of our enemies. You have already learned my attitude, and lucky for me, only the people here have notice of it.

"It would be impossible for the two women who would go to survive it. Possibly even Gilbert, properly equipped, wouldn't make it. The air crews who parachute out are between eighteen and twenty-four or twenty-five years old. If they make it to Gibraltar, then they fly home from there or Portugal (England's oldest ally) or get a neutral boat home, where they repeat it all over again, God bless them!

"My plan of sheer gall is that Gilbert, in full uniform and bemedaled, will face Petain and demand, as an officer, that he pay the debt he owes him for saving his life on two occasions by putting his own life at risk to save him, that he provide him a pass for himself and his family—his wife, his officer-son, and his Catholic medical doctor daughter-in-law. He will be facing his God, a Jew, soon enough; then what shall he say to the Almighty in his own defense if he refuses to pay this self-acknowledged debt?

"The mechanics of Gilbert getting this done are my burden, but could the old man, face-to-face with his self-admitted savior, turn down such a pass out of France? I count on the fact that he was the child of peasants and was a product of a Jesuit boarding school, then a Dominican one, before he was accepted at St. Cyr, the 403rd cadet out of a class of 412. You all can see that I've done my research.

"He is known to attend Mass regularly and the confession box very often, probably because he is both married and a great womanizer, in spite of his eighty-four years. Such a God-fearing peasant would be predictable, confronted with this dire threat of hellfire, I truly believe."

"Yes, but this a man who is turning over his fellow French warriors and their families of Jewish ancestry to the Germans, even by his own statute of October 9, of this very year!" said Giles, most stridently.

"Oh yes! But I wager he has not had to face one of his victims!" replied Etienne. "And don't forget: he hasn't moved off his bronze base to accept the blame for anything. He will blame General Huntziger for the armistice terms he agreed to in the absence of the marshal. And the murderous Jewish statute was written by Huntziger, at, no doubt, Petain's request, and signed by Huntziger, of course—all because of Petain's 'confusion.' Petain only wanted to retire nine Jewish generals to save them from the

The French Lieutenant and the King of Rome

Germans, not outlaw all the Jews and confiscate their property for France! Pardon my ironic wit!

"Oh yes, and he recommends 'patience' to his victims! One multi decorated Jew in a French prison camp in the liberated zone, a victim of Petain's October statute imprisoning naturalized Jews, even our war heroes, wrote him in outrage, and he recommended 'patience.' On receipt of the answer of 'patience,' the man hung himself with his shoelaces. The stories about him are beginning to be whispered about."

"I pray that you're not incorrect," Giles said. "I pray that my father is not misdirected by you into doing this. There are so many risks, so many that he is taking here! How is he able to undertake this thing, and successfully? Or if Petain is supposedly senile much of the time, then what will happen to him if he doesn't remember Gilbert at all, or signing the pass?"

"Or be damned! I will listen to any alternative suggestion as soon as anyone has one. Giles, your parents are not safe in Nice because the war is changing from day to day, and no one can say how long the Italians will be able to protect Jews against their big brother, Hitler. He will exert more and more pressure on them as he discovers how weak they are.

"Also, remember that Hitler has gained immense wealth by stripping the Jews wherever he goes and can practically run the war on what he has stolen from them! But he has just started to work on the Jews of France and hasn't gotten any of the Jewish assets from Italy. Petain is taking steps to preserve Jewish assets for France as they are stolen, by confiscation, to use in France. Their mutual hatred of Jews is a lot deeper than emotional hate. It's all about the bottom line!

"Must I remind you of the history of your Jewish people? Must I preach to you, the choir? Your people are a minority that are powerless and always hated in these countries, without a valid reason. First reason: because they supposedly killed or caused Jesus's death. And second: the logical view that Jesus died to save humans because of original sin, by the primary commission of evil, against

God's order given to Adam and Eve! Obviously one cause totally contradicts the other, but hate of the foreigners among us is such a pleasurable thing among the jealous and resentful that it never dies! And it gives a fine justification for stripping and killing them. And have you forgotten how, last summer, he related to you unprompted, how his life was saved by your father! And he clearly told you that he did so twice! He will not forget your father when confronted by him now! Nor, I think, condemn him!"

Then Etienne said, "In any event, I am requesting Marguerite to write to them immediately about all that I instructed her, and I shall make all preparations that are mine to do and so be ready when they return from Nice. If Gilbert and Clara are agreeable to carry out their end of the plan, I will map a route out of the country, if all succeeds to the point of carrying it out. When there is a response to her letter, then she and Beatrice need to leave for Nice."

Eleven days had passed since the letter was sent by Marguerite to Nice, and the response was positive, strongly positive. Two days later Marguerite and Beatrice left for Nice as planned. All details as perceived by Etienne were executed, including the support truck's performance on the return trip to Lyon, as contemplated.

Now both Gilbert and Carla needed photos for the passports since their originals were from the old state of France and might be questioned at the Spanish border. Their identity papers were from Vichy and contained a large letter *J*, which identified them as Jews and had to therefore be newly forged through Etienne, as with Giles ID and passport and also Elle's passport. Once the small photos were made in Lyon and given to Etienne, he would have the documents created for their signatures. Then the trip to Vichy, by Gilbert, could be taken as soon as he was prepared and ready! But first he had to be confronted with the plan----and the consequences of a failure!

Etienne's surreptitious organization, in which he was a small but efficient part, was, the "Conservation du Material," created by the General Huntziger's predecessor as minister of war and maintained by the "Chef D'etat-major de l'Armee" and a commandant under him. This group had growing tentacles into such areas as creating papers. Much could be accomplished from sympathy or by reward. Of course the thrust of sequestering 3,700 trucks and 80 percent more weapons than were authorized by the German armistice was providing for a suddenly enlarged force to be used to fight when the Allies invaded France for the war to free the country.

"We must have the pass we need under Petain's valid signature because he must be aware that he did it in case it is questioned," Etienne stated resolutely. "But unfortunately, it is said that his awareness is usually about two hours in the afternoon; otherwise, he is withdrawn and hovers frequently in his past. That is what I am told by one of his direct personnel."

" Because he may be somewhat alienated or actually in dementia we can not rely upon him supporting his act of having executed this form of passport for all of us and therefore there must be a nearly instantaneous departure for Spain from here. Our only delay must be the unavoidable time needed to reach the point of exodus at the Spanish Border. In short we must not be trapped in the Vichy area in case he takes action against us after we succeed in getting the documents signed."

LXXVII

NOW THAT ALL parties concerned were in Marguerite's manor house, it was time to meet with Carla and Gilbert to determine whether they were willing to follow Etienne's plan for Gilbert to meet with Petain, his possible nemesis.

It was time for the four of them to obtain the necessary photos at the kiosk hard by the St-Jean Cathedral near the Saone River. This would complete the paperwork, which would have to be finished by Etienne, who would also create the special visa or pass form for Gilbert to present for Petain's endorsement and to have applied the great seal of Vichy France.

All photos for the group had to be attached and stamped for each ID for each person, completed with the statistics of each with a stamped seal on the photos and ID and the "Great Seal of State" for Vichy, on the passports for each person. Etienne could accomplish that when he had the photos for each document and after he had entered all the Statistics.

This would have to be done before the meeting between Gilbert and Petain. Petain must not assume that Gilbert "took him for granted" but that the decision to grant him the visa or pass was spontaneously his. Etienne said that he rejected the idea of hanging around Vichy for a day or two. "Too much would be at risk. Petain would have too much time to change his mind or have it changed for him." But could the visa document be completed the very afternoon of the meeting? Only chance and the events of that day would tell. Carla, Giles, and Elle would be forced to wait in the manor house near Lyon and endure the tension, fear, and uncertainty until Gilbert and Etienne's return late that night.

It was Friday night, and Etienne was able to get to Lyon for forty-eight hours. Weekends were his possibility to leave Vichy, but it placed him under pressure when it was as frequent as recently. He was using Elle as an excuse, and if she would actually become pregnant, well that could be a problem, would it not? He remembered to bring the passport and ID forms with him for each of the four to complete.

If only the four of them could get them completed and the photos taken, so he could carry them back to Vichy on his return. Monday, on his return, would be the best day to connive the execution of the paperwork.

Etienne had asked the four principals to meet with him, together in the sitting room, for the explicit purpose of reviewing what had to be done by Gilbert in Vichy and determining whether he felt capable of making the performance and accepting the consequence of failure.

The sitting room was complete now. Giles and Elle, Carla and Gilbert, and Etienne were all there. Elle had told her mother that she and Beatrice were not to come because the meeting was for only those to be affected by the decisions to be made there. In other words, the meeting was "top secret." Marguerite was offended because of all she had done, to date, and had without doubt made it all possible.

Therefore Etienne met with her and thoroughly explained the risks to her and Beatrice if they knew "too much." They were being left here and must remain silent about all that occurred until the end of the war and the re-conquest of France by its old allies.

Even expressing that idea of re-conquest or what occurred here to anyone would subject Etienne to charges of treason and death and to the others here would mean German prison camps. At some later point, she must say that he and Elle never hit it off, and she never saw Etienne or knew of him after, and that her daughter, Elle, left for Marseille, with the intent of going to Morocco and

Dakar to practice her specialty for native children, possibly with a broken heart from her and Etienne's failed love affair.

She accepted the idea that she and Beatrice must stay behind and that her large Citroen would be used in the escape, with license changed to Gilbert and Carla's car, which she would use as her own unless hers could be returned to her by Etienne, if he could return to duty in Vichy after Spain was reached. Her vehicle would bear armistice army plates and probably staff flags on the fenders for the trip.

Etienne entered the sitting room and was immediately embraced by Gilbert. Then each stood a little apart from the other, holding on to each other's shoulders, and mutually looked into each other's eyes, without speaking, exchanging the deeply affectionate expression reserved for male family members who truly care for one another—for that was what they nearly were!

Gilbert and Carla, after the untimely death of both of Etienne's parents, who were friends brought together by Giles and Etienne's brotherly friendship in their school and seemingly everywhere, approached Etienne's uncle, his surviving relative and the archbishop of Paris, asking whether Etienne might live with them as they felt toward the boy as though he were a son. The archbishop was deeply touched by their endearment toward Etienne and believed sincerely in their honest affection and consequently made them a part of his private circle. But before that, he explained to Gilbert and Carla, over a meal, the impossibility of this by making a reasonable consideration of the facts.

"Although we are indeed all French, we are of different tribes and different religions. No French court would allow an adoption by a family of a differing religion. Of course, without an adoption, he could live with you as a family member, but how could you discipline your son and not be permitted to discipline Etienne? Thus he is treated as a guest in the house, not subject to your sway. How unfair this would be to both boys, causing differences. When it comes to matters of religion and observance, the differences could lead to differences between the boys and injure their friendship.

These are the most obvious of differences, but other unforeseen differences could arise. No, I must say no for these obvious reasons, but permit me to presumptuously insist that you continue your selfless kindness to my orphan nephew, continuing to treat him as your own, where your good judgment will lead you both, but I beg you to support me as his pater familias in all requirements to do with raising my nephew."

Now reunited, and in Marguerite's manor house, it took little time for Gilbert and Etienne to regain the warmth of family feeling between them. Gilbert handed him off to the waiting hugs and kisses of Carla, or "Auntie Carla," who spoke "funny French." Little Etienne had grown up, but Carla had a way of minimizing the changes. She gave a sort of scolding look and said, "After I hold you tight for a minute or two, then I will decide if you are all you pretend to be." After a minute or two of this charming interplay, Carla's spoof was ended, concluded with a kiss from Auntie Carla and a wink in return from Etienne!

Then when Carla and Etienne were seated opposite each other, Carla spoke first. "Etienne, Gilbert and I understand your plan to have Gilbert confront Petain and demand a passport out for the four of us based on the debt he owes Gilbert from the last war, but what gives you the confidence to believe that he is a gentleman and will react as one would? He no longer carries a restraint of any kind; he is a virtual dictator in this state of Vichy. Furthermore, he was not bred to follow that expected code."

"Carla, you're forgetting the code of conduct so stressed at St. Cyr during his four years as a cadet. You're also forgetting the warrior's code to never abandon or forget your fellow warrior who has proven himself by fighting for you or with you in the face of the enemy."

"I am a woman and am too practical to place my life or belief in such—forgive me for saying it—romantic nonsense! More importantly I visualize the following scenario: your expectations are denied, and then Gilbert is placed under military arrest and possibly you as well, if you are connected with this conspiracy to assist a former Jewish officer with evading the law! What immediate consequence would ensue? Next, under close questioning or torture, how safe will remain the people you leave behind in this house, and for how long would they remain so? In other words, do you have an escape hatch for us?"

"Allow me to answer you this way: I could not communicate the details of my plan in any tangible way, so the inferences told you by Marguerite, in her letter, had to be sufficient to get you to come and were clearly effected by telling you that Giles and Elle were here. How could you have done otherwise when you were in dread of what had happened to them as a result of the war? Seeing them had to be the most important issue in your lives! So I caused that to happen, you will agree?" All of this was blurted out, more or less, by Etienne.

"As for Nice," he irritably continued, "I can return you there in the same fashion I brought you here, in very short order. I understand that your apartment is paid for, and you were not to tell the owner anything about staying away more than temporarily.

"As for the others, the only thing that would bring trouble from Vichy here would be what was done by Marguerite when she bravely visited there to find me. All she did was leave a personalized note with Petain's office and her phone number and address with General Huntziger and the fact that she was looking for me as the child of an old family friend for a possible romantic connection with her daughter. She will say the romance didn't materialize and that she knew nothing further of me, after her daughter left for Marseille. Or if Elle is still here, working at the hospital and without Giles, then she will tell of her short love affair with me instead of Marguerite doing so," concluded Etienne. "With regard to Giles, he will immediately seek shelter with Archbishop Gerlier as the new monsignor and you, Carla, will join Elle in her department at the hospital as a new assistant administrator, a matter under her control."

Then he said to Giles, "Apparently you have not yet visited Archbishop Gerlier in Lyon. You need to visit the archbishop to explain who you are in order to give cover to my uncle in case the Germans follow up on the transfer of the monsignor here to this cathedral. This will give Archbishop Gerlier the opportunity to dispose of you in some way, if he is questioned about you. Further, as I have just said, you may desperately need him to shelter you if our plan with Petain in Vichy fails."

"As for protecting us when Gilbert goes 'into the lion's mouth,' I have someone in the CDM who will assure a change to a friendly guard arrangement in the Hotel du Parc and transportation out of Vichy to sweep us out of there after whatever happens in Petain's offices, good or bad! All this must be arranged on a careful schedule. Depend upon my accomplishing the completion of the IDs, which I shall take with me when I return to Vichy after this weekend."

"By the by, Elle, we had best do your ID again so that all IDs look the same, even though the dates of execution shall be different."

LXXVIII

THE FOLLOWING DAY, Etienne returned to Vichy with the necessary paperwork and photos to be forged into the forms needed to accompany the visa to be sought by Gilbert from Petain. All of this was accomplished by the secret organization within the armistice army, the "Camouflage du Material," or CDM. He was relying on them to arrange the guards on "the day" and to arrange the rapid escape out of Vichy on that day, as well.

That very same day, Elle drove the young monsignor, dressed in cassock and biretta, to the grandiose Romanesque-fronted Cathedral Saint Jean-Baptiste. Hard by the river Soane, in old Lyon and near the railroad station, it was, of course, enormous in size, and the interior reflected the different architectural additions since it was undertaken in the twelfth century. It had a fourteenth-century astronomical clock like none other. The church was originally intended as the *primatiale* cathedral in France.

All that said, the observant Giles, having spent time walking through, after alighting from the car and setting a time to meet in late afternoon, sought the archbishop, who was easy to find, in an office between the church level and its undercroft. Giles was wearing the dress oxford shoes called for with his cassock and biretta and had been most zealous in cleaning them after reaching the manor house the night of his arrival. They had been purposely heavily mudded before he walked in the snow at the train station area in Paris with the expectation that the Germans would not wish to dirty their gloves or uniforms in a close inspection. Lucien had removed and hollowed the heel of the left one in advance of his leaving and concealed a message therein, from Emmanuel to Gerlier, as follows, "Trust the bearer of this and his story," with a stamped, ring seal of the archbishop at the end. The two spoke over tea for two hours and agreed on a "fable"; this was succeeded by introductions to the church staff as a new monsignor "to work as an occasional assistant with outlying parishes in the area for a short time."

It was decided that he would visit the church daily for the period he was still there. When the visits stopped, the archbishop would understand that he was no longer in the area. In the meantime, he would provide any assistance that he could on the request of Giles.

Meanwhile, in a guest bedroom in the d'Hozier manor house, Gilbert and Carla were hotly discussing the burning issue of concern to everyone, including those two in the group not going. Everyone was effected by Gilbert's decision of whether or not to confront Petain face on. Carla was most apprehensive of facing down the most powerful man "in the kingdom." She began what seemed to be a closing argument against the defendant, Marshal Henri Petain.

"Had he not thunderously spoken of his attitude in October of his disregard for Jews and their property and lives? Would he, in reason, now ignore his own decision for some long ago, perhaps forgotten, obligation? Just because of some vapid code or other?"

Would a man who felt himself "the savior of the French people," thus as powerful as a God, be truly concerned whether or not his own God would feel him to be his equal in "omniscience and omnipotence"? In Carla's opinion this man was an egomaniac, who now fervently believed his own press, beginning with himself as the savior of France in 1916, as a result of holding the Germans at Verdun, and acting as a priest of the "Holy Army of France," since then warning the people of their danger from indulging in communist thinking, until his present redemption of them by the "armistice," which saved them from the slavery due them because of their own perverse self-destructiveness through their belief in

Russia and eventual communism. Furthermore, Marshals Joffre and Foche were long dead, and Petain, the lone seven-star survivor of the Great War, allowed as how he was their "Napoleon." And we all know the French always craved a godlike saint above politics. Unfortunately, the wrong marshal survived the longest!

There was little left for Gilbert to argue. The advocate had trained his wife, Carla, well! He had used Carla as his sounding board for his arguments over the years, "and the muscular strength that it gave to his jaw had lasted all of his life," to quote his automatic recollection of the words of Lewis Carroll, the author of *Alice in Wonderland*.

There was little to argue in defense of this obviously ponderous, slow-moving, quiet man who, through his stolid appearance, exuded great strength of purpose and quiet devotion and stratagem: which Gilbert always (reluctantly) suspected of being simple absorption in his own plodding self-determination, without cleverness or cunning but only a peasant slyness.

But Gilbert pondered and centered his defense argument, not on the defendant Petain but on his star witness giving substance to Gilbert's counterattack, to wit: "Etienne's position, whom we here believe in, is based upon his past performance, personal commitment, devotion, intellect, and planning. It requires us not to question his sincerity in this whole matter. To do so is absurd! To believe he would betray us in his planning or execution is unconscionable, and therefore I shall go forward with his plan, to the letter. And if it fails, it shall be a fluke of fate, not his intent or poorness of planning and preparation, but unavoidable!"

This came in the form of a loud announcement to Carla from across the room.

"I rest my case on our fine Etienne, not alone upon my power of persuasion in confronting old Henri Phillip, Marechal Petain. Carla, I have made up my mind. I'm going through with Etienne's plan. We are going on the offensive. And we are going as soon as he has everything prepared!"

Gilbert was both amazed and impressed with Etienne's assertiveness, his astuteness was far in excess of his rank and indeed was consistent with his strategical and tactical skills and were far beyond his years. Gilbert had gleaned this since he and Carla returned to Marguerite's chateau. Indeed, he felt that Etienne was capable of foreseeing confusion in his oppositions fixed posture.

LXXIX

ETIENNE REAPPEARED AT the d'Hozier manor house late the following Friday night, in a staff car to which he had ready access. He was ebullient about his success in completing all the paperwork, including the pass to be signed by Marshal Petain, when presented by Gilbert.

He was roundly greeted as he distributed the IDs and completed passports and noted good-naturedly that the only foreign country bordering on France now was Spain, but it seemed to be just the country that was needed. He also brought two French Beretta-style pistols for the two women to have on their person for the trip, with ammunition, also two short rifles to be placed in the luggage with ammunition, to be packed, along with the limited luggage. These would be placed in the trunk of the Citroen, along with all wearables and personal belongings. He also brought staff flags to display on the front fenders where and when needed.

Therefore, there was limited room for changes of clothes, requiring all to be dressed in appropriate street clothes but Gilbert, who would remain in uniform. Gilbert's uniform differed from an officer in the armistice army because he wore the kepi, which had been discarded for a beret, most likely because of the expense and unavailability of the kepi.

Giles, unfortunately, had only his black street attire and would appear as the priest that he never was. This "anomalous" priest would be carrying his holstered 1935s automatic with one cylinder (and two bullet magazines, which he smuggled in the bottom of his bag when he departed Paris, all unknown to Archbishop Emmanuel at the time) and, now, a bayonet, placed unsheathed and on the floor of the Citroen, next to him. Gilbert was armed with his loaded service pistol, which, of course, he could not wear into the Hotel du Parc when they made their visit to Marshal Petain in his offices.

They were all given to understand that no quarter was to be expected or given if they were interfered with in their intent to cross the border, to the south of Perpignan. The crossing was to take place at Cerbere on the coast just south of Perpignan. Etienne thought Perpignan would have some armed soldiers guarding the customs crossing and perhaps a German patrol hanging about.

Although they would have the pass from Petain, he didn't wish to have anyone second-guessing their written authority or other documentation, especially a German patrol, which the Vichy French allowed to roam the Pyrenees at will, to capture or kill Allied evaders, escapees, or political enemies attempting to flee France. Germans would not honor such a pass, even if purportedly from Petain's hand.

Etienne told the group to be ready and packed, and he would have arrangements already made for petrol tankers to meet them at three necessary places along their route to the southwest.

Carla and Gilbert stood together in a corner of the room. The years had almost grown them into a single stem, just holding each other in a silent embrace, in the symbiotic way of man and wife, fitting together in their private shell and mutually feeling the same agonies and doubts about their and their children's futures, from this moment forward. A single kiss on the lips and then, "Good-bye."

Giles and Elle each seemed filled with anxiety over the prospect of whether they would see a beloved father and an equally loved friend ever again. The die was about to be cast! Gilbert and Etienne were about to drive off for Vichy.

It should be noted that Etienne was wearing a Sam Browne belt with holster and sidearm attached and a Fourragere hanging from his right shoulder, and an armband below it, which established that he was the "officer of the guard," apparently, for the day of their trip to Vichy. This placed him in command of the military guards wherever posted in Vichy on this day.

"How clever of you to establish this," said Gilbert.

"Thank you," said Etienne. "This will establish our right to proceed directly to Petain's offices since all the guards on duty are under my command today. Also our vehicle can remain in front of the hotel headquarters. Remember, Colonel," he said with a shy smile, "in both tactics and strategy, there is always one more thing to do!"

The topic of conversation during the one-and-a-half-hour ride to Vichy consisted of Etienne listening to Gilbert's forthright justification for the Lamberts' pass to get out of France, which included an inference of the marshal's guilt, plus a healthy portion of personal obligation for the marshal's past debt to be paid as a matter of honor, both personal and military.

After that, and some bolstering remarks by Ettienne (which were in the nature of a coaching encouragement and not of valuable substance), the conversation turned to the Battle of Verdun and Gilbert's exceptional relationship with (then) General Petain.

"He was fifty-eight when he started the move upward to *chef de battalion*, and then he was quickly noticed after some solid victories and a notable analysis of reasons for French failure in the Champagne campaign. He was promoted to *general de brigade* and then *general de division*, and at Verdun he was *general de corps d'Armee*, a four-star position. The last two ranks are not true ranks but only based on the command that the general possesses." Gilbert wasn't sure that Ettienne was acquainted with the differences. "Anyway, he became commandeer of the Verdun campaign on February 25, 1916. I was an aide on his staff and became more relied upon as time progressed. It was on an inspection tour after his Second Army was brought up and he had been made commander of this front by Marshal Joffre on recommendation of General Castlenau that he drew new lines of resistance. On one occasion, by chance, I pulled him out of the line of ground fire just in time to save him, though, in doing so, I instantly exposed myself. Luckily it missed me as well!

"General Nivelle relieved him on April 19, but he returned in June. On June 24, I pulled us both out of a hollow we had fallen into. It was beginning to fill with phosgene gas, and we reached higher ground to our great, good fortune. These were just happenstances. I was not his chief of staff (this was Colonel Barescut) or Colonel Serrigny, in charge of operational execution—just one of his aides.

"Nivelle was known as the 'slaughterer,' and in June, as I said, Petain returned from his 'upstairs' command, perhaps because his 'Noria' method of feeding in and relieving troops, which kept our forces fresh, unlike the Germans, who were only relieved by wound or death. Later Nivelle managed to even replace Marshal Joffre as head of French forces."

After a short lapse in conversation, the subject turned to a lighter vein: the childish peccadilloes of Giles and Etienne, mostly acting together in harmless but amusing pranks from early childhood through the lycee years at Henry IV and the discovery of the mind-bending female sex.

The boys were, in the words of Etienne, visiting a new, strange, wonderful land where nothing but worthless worms and caterpillars seemed to inexplicably emerge as butterflies. Nubile, wondrous, breathtaking, unreal creatures metamorphosed from former, formless household pests called "sisters" or "neighbor-girls" of useless purpose. Now, the very sight of them aroused internal fires that consumed our boys as the proverbial phoenix bird.

They were exquisitely and repeatedly self-consumed by each sylph-like movement of these new creatures, each to be reincarnated from the ashes of their personal phoenix bird, in order to enable them to respond to each next movement or word or phrase from these wondrous creatures, causing the arousal of such palpating feelings as worship, devotion, fits of manly honor, formerly unknown sexual stimulation, and foremost of all, jealousy.

If this astounding butterfly flitted from one lovely flower to another, then the flower or bush was suddenly aroused against the other bush, who was a no less worthy companion, for all that. And poor Etienne confessed that he found himself now suffering alone while Giles had captured his very own butterfly of wondrous colors and talents.

LXXX

THEY DROVE PAST the Vichy opera house, essentially art nouveau in architecture and quite beautifully done, which was where the Estates General abjectly surrendered the liberty and freedom of the Revolution of 1789 to one-man rule. This was impossible to be done, according to the very terms of its constitution that created it.

Then they drove past the park and on until they reached the corner for a left turn and drove past the edge of the Hotel du Parc, to the corner where the flat-iron point of it joined the corner of the pavement; then their vehicle made a right-hand turn and proceeded to the entrance, below a large theatrical-style marquee hung above the entrance doors. There were two sergeants on guard at the entrance to prevent those without authority entry.

This hotel was the very "nerve center" of this new government called the "State of France," controlled and governed by Marshal Henri Petain, the shadow dictator allowed to control it with a prime minister and a shadow cabinet, but at the pleasure of Adolph Hitler. And, of course, the German army and government was in open control of the other two-thirds of France, including Paris and all the borderland that it wished to control or absorb into the German nation.

Etienne and Lt. Col. Gilbert Lambert parked the auto in front of the entrance after the colonel had secured his holster under his seat. Both officers approached the doors, where Lt. Picard, officer of the guard, accepted the salutes of the guards and abruptly stated that the colonel was to see Marshal Petain immediately, under his personal escort. "Clear our way, on your phone to the elevator, please!"

When they reached the marshal's suite, they both entered, and the lieutenant asked if the marshal was alone at the moment. The aide to the marshal said yes, but that Colonel Lambert was not expected. Lt. Picard then stated that the marshal and the colonel were old friends and that Lambert was the marshal's aide at Verdun in 1916 and to please notify the marshal that the colonel was here on "urgent and vital business" and simply announce the colonel.

Lambert simply followed in on the heels of the commandant-aide and closed the inner office door in front of the aide, as he stepped around and in front of him and coaxed him to step backward. At that moment, Lt. Picard was waiting in the outer office, along with the stultified aide, and he suggested that the aide sit down at his desk and wait for the marshal to conclude the matter with Colonel Lambert. The lieutenant had pulled the aide's desk phone to the edge, next to Lt. Picard's chair. The outer office door was closed so that Etienne could ward off anyone who knocked, wishing to see the marshal, until Colonel Lambert's business was completed.

In the scramble that was taking place at the marshal's inner door, between his aide and Gilbert, the aide's announcement was shakily made, in hesitant voice. The marshal made an automatic response as he rose from behind his desk, with the assistance of his walking stick, which he leaned upon more and more frequently to assist him in rising. "I do not wish to be intruded upon by anyone presuming upon my time! Commandant, whose face is that? Did you say 'Lambert'?" Then directly to the intruder he said, "Who are you? How dare you presume upon me without permission?" Then the marshal struck his other fist, the left one, upon his desk, in anger and emphasis.

Then, with a new dawning, the marshal almost physically drew back and in half recognition, loudly spoke a one word question, "Lambert?" And then in full recognition of this apparition from the past, he exclaimed, "Lambert! Lambert, it's really you! I'd still know you anywhere!"

"Yes, thank you, Marshal. It is I, after all these years! How many has it been—twenty-three or twenty-four at least? And you still remember me, sir?"

"Well, you have the same face, just some older. Besides, you remember that some of the staff thought you resembled me. That is a reason to if no other existed! What brings you too see the head of the State of France?"

"First of all, Marshal, allow me to congratulate you on becoming the personification of the new State of France. I wish to express my continuing high regard for your values and your reawakening and inculcation of the true values of the French people: 'Work, Family, and Fatherland.' It no longer fits—I mean, 'Liberty, Fraternity, and Equality'—since we are, shall we politely say, the 'subjects' of our overlords, the German people."

"Yes, it's true," said the marshal, "and it's good that you recognize our plight, and you need to realize that only through stringency and severe effort can the people become worthy partners instead of subjects, as you put it, of the German nation, our conquerors. I have been chosen and in fact am a volunteer to overcome damage and corruption caused by the workers and their sympathizers who have caused us to lose the war!"

"So then," said Lambert, "the lassitude and failure to prepare for a new type of war had nothing to do with it? Our fear of suffering the destruction and death of the last war had nothing to do with it?"

"Enough, Lambert! Enough!" Petain said with exasperation. A pause ensued during which the two men stared at one another, until Marshal Petain exclaimed with an imperial tone, "Then have you not come to serve under my command again, Colonel?"

"Why do you ask me that, sir?"

"Why else would you be here then? You were always faithful and loyal! In fact I remember that you saved my life—twice!"

"Yes, sir, so you told my son the last of May at a French cabinet meeting, which included some English cabinet ministers and other English officials. You remember: my son, a French second lieutenant, introduced himself to you, and you spoke with him briefly."

"Yes, yes! That is correct, and I shared something of the stories of your valiancy with him."

"And you told him if I or he ever needed you, to ask and you would respond to our needs!"

"Yes, yes! You correctly remind me of that, and in response to your need, you may again serve me in your rank—yes, as my aide, which I sorely need. And your son, as a second lieutenant in my armistice army if he desires! Further, Commandant Halevy may return with you if you know his whereabouts. He may assist you in your tasks. I've always understood that Israelites keep in touch with one another!"

"Well, sir, you have forgotten that you sent him on a personal mission to probe the enemy lines from which he never returned. His remains were never found; doubtless he was ground to dust by artillery fire as were almost all of the rest of our 360,000 French killed defending Verdun. Perhaps you and the French army, as well, were always a little unobservant where Israelite officers, as you call us, were concerned."

The marshal, taken aback, did not respond.

Then Col. Lambert proceeded, "Then, on October 9 of this year, you decreed a new statute withdrawing citizenship from naturalized Jews—pardon me, Marshal, Israelites—even those who were veterans of the war!"

"Lambert, you take all of this too literally!"

Lambert continued, "And in the same statute, you assumed the authority to confiscate Israelite property for the state. Further you declared that Jews may not be lawyers, doctors, teachers, professors, judges, or hold a position of government employment, and they may not be officers in military service. In fact that included some nine Jewish generals. Your statute makes such Jews—pardon me, Israelites—subject to being incarcerated in prison camps, to

The French Lieutenant and the King of Rome

be deported to German concentration camps and death. I therefore presume that my Legion of Honor and Croix de Guerre and clusters are property of the state and not mine, either to receive or retain! Am I correct in this?"

"Take care what you say to me, Lambert! If you and your son accept my extended hand now, none of these shall be invoked against you or yours. I, of course, am free to exempt you! To do so! No one may interfere with any of you or your property or your prosperity in the future!"

"Except, of course, you Marshal or perhaps your successor.

"Marshal, we are none of us like German Field Marshall Erhard Milch, the half Jew who is known as the 'half Jew Nazi.' The buddy of Herman Goering: he who decides who is a Jew and who is not. Hitler gave him a certificate that Aryanized him. Although he and his siblings are attributed to his mother's uncle, the incest is overlooked; anything will do as long as he is not a Jew. Still Hitler made him an Aryan, in contradiction to the incest uncle-father story. We shall not stand by while a government persecutes our coreligionists! We do not come to ask for such relief!" said Lambert.

"Well then, why are you here?" said Petain.

"To collect the debt you owe me!" said Lambert. "Marshal, I saved your life on two occasions at Verdun, which you readily acknowledge. Fair enough! Now as an officer and a gentleman, the code expects you to repay this debt freely. In this situation, it is without even a risk to your own life, or a cost to you, which would not be unusual under our priest-like values, as French officers.

"You may not release yourself by declaring me among the lesser persons, without any civil rights, as you have attempted to do, by your self-invoked anti-Semitic statute of last October. You could only be released by a uniquely higher authority under the code, and of course there is none in your domain! Your only higher authority would be Jesus of Nazareth, an Israelite, and I doubt that he would favor you n this instance, even if he could!"

"Yes, Lambert, yes, I did what was necessary to your people—for France and for the good of the French people."

"Yes, this is the way the French have always paid its Jews, with a knife in the back! Last time it was the Dreyfus affair, and now it's all French Jews! In any case, you, at your age of more than eighty-four years, may very well be dealing with Jesus shortly, if your religious beliefs are correct and mine are wrong. The gamble is yours to make! Either way, you're going to lose!"

"Hand me the paper, Lambert. I will sign it and seal it myself, and then you and yours shall leave France, immediately, however you can and with no further help from me. We are even. Ask nothing more of me or the State of France!"

"Here!" Gilbert said, as he leaned forward over Petain's desk, emphatically placing a sizable document before Petain, which purported to become a passport and stated that it was such, a passport for the following: "Colonel Gilbert Lambert and wife, Carla; Second Lieutenant Giles Lambert and wife, Giselle Lambert; and Etienne Picard, late second lieutenant of the armistice army of the State of France, herewith honorably discharged from further duty. All of the above individuals given right and recommendation to any nation of their free choosing under the order of and with the free recommendation of the premiere of France. To be given full freedom of entry.

Date_____   Petain, Premiere _____

Seal of the French State_____

LXXXI

ETIENNE AND GILBERT left quickly, passing the two sergeants stationed at the entrance, and hurriedly entered their staff car on the curb, where they had parked it earlier. They drove toward the staff car park, where they would leave it and transfer to Etienne's own Citroen for a fast return to Lyon and Marguerite's manor house.

They were thrilled at the success of their scheme, but Etienne worried about the evening change of the guard, which he had ignored. There would be confusion all over the military posting in Vichy because of his disappearance tonight. That thought was quickly followed by the realization that he was relieved of all responsibility by his discharge. Petain's order and passport was effective immediately by Petain's signature. Tomorrow's officer of the guard would just have to sort it out, starting with the realization of Etienne's absence tonight.

It was time to concentrate on their last ploy, the drive to Spain and crossing the Spanish border successfully. They had previously decided on the French town of Cerbere, which edged the Mediterranean, with its beaches commencing nearly at the very termination of the last lower hills, called the "Alberes Hills," of the Pyrenees. Customs there should only be a shack. Highway 114 became Spanish 252, which quickly joined A7 into Barcelona, which was less than 150 miles to the south of Cebere. Their goal was the British consulate in Barcelona and then hopefully British Gibraltar or Portugal.

There was thought to be a dangerous footpath across them from Cerbere that ended past the Spanish customs station. However, there should be no trouble with their crossing with both vehicles because of the exit visas from France, which Etienne had forged for all five of them. There were also the other documents with them, in the event that Petain's signed exit passport document was deemed to be insufficient by customs on either side of the border.

Their plan was to drive the next morning to Orange, missing Avignon and Petain's troops, which were heavily stationed there, then going west to Nimes, Montpelier, and then to Narbonne. There they were to meet their last gas tanker, to furnish them with more than enough petrol to reach Barcelona. From Narbonne they would continue heading south and avoid Perpignan by hugging the coast south to Cerbere and crossing there into Spain. Time, with necessary stops, should not exceed seven hours, and they should reach the border crossings well before 1600 hours, allowing time to deal with the officials on both sides of the border—that is, providing for no unforeseen interferences.

"But always remember," Etienne reminded them, "in tactics and strategy, both, look for one more thing that you may have overlooked in your planning! The shadow of the unexpected must be anticipated and dealt with to avoid disaster."

They were confident that they could deal with any French interference, but a well-armed German patrol at or near the border was a much different matter. Every one of them knew they must be prepared to use their weapons in advance of a direct German encounter. They would force their vehicles through the wooden boarder barriers, and all passengers would simultaneously fire broadsides or through the windshields and rear windows before any such patrol approached either car—especially if they were at the French border station. If it came to that, no one was to be left behind. The best shots, Gilbert and Giles, would each ride the front passenger seats, the old stagecoach "shotgun position," one in the front of each car. The first and heaviest auto would be driven by Etienne, and the other, by Elle. Gilbert would have a short rifle by his side; Carla would ride in the rear of the second car with her automatic and have a short army rifle next to her with a full clip. If combat came and there were wounded or dead, they still needed to end on the Spanish side of the border.

Gilbert would deal with the customs agent with all documents for everyone. He would have his bayonet sheathed and on the right side of his Sam Browne belt, available to cut any phone wires and dispose of the customs agent if he was troublesome. He was to do so quietly and quickly without any disturbance that might alarm Spanish customs nearby on the other side of the border. He, of course, had his fully loaded service pistol holstered on the left side of his Sam Browne belt.

The drive had been hard and intense. The roads were in poor repair and not an ardent concern of Petain's government. There were detours but actually very little traffic. They had traveled about three hundred miles from Lyon in about ten hours, which was lengthy but considering the road, not bad! After reaching Narbonne, they curved around to the south, closer to the sea. The Alberes Hills, the eastern foothills of the Pyrenees, began to spring up as they began to border the Mediterranean, which was on their left. The road was often treacherous, as it became twisted, with sharp descents at places, as it careened up and down, just barely negotiating the cliffs, with a series of rumpled ribbons of road, created by chance and not forethought. It was just hanging there! The road was above the sea and its beaches like a roller-coaster car before each descent. Only the brakes rendered the drivers the nerve to go on.

As they drew closer to Cerbere, they became more and more hesitant and concerned about what crisis it might present. They all wanted to believe that their nightmare would not occur—that a German mountain patrol would not be there. However, the more they thought about the isolation of Cerbere, the more they believed it was the very place they trapped most of their game. The isolation would draw the prey and its successful hunter!

LXXXII

ETIENNE SIGNALED A stop with his brake lights as he pulled under the shelter of the cliff created by one of the overhanging hills on his right. He could just make enough room for Elle, who was driving Etienne's car, under the same cliff. Etienne saw the stop under the cliff as a much-needed opportunity to get out and observe their surroundings. He called to everyone to maintain their positions except he and Giles, who were to do the scouting nearby, on foot.

This called for some surreptitious climbing on top of the cliff for each of them, observing as best they could. They moved in different directions, always seeking a rock, a tree, or a bush to somewhat obscure each of them from being standouts on the horizon. Giles called out to his companion, just enough to be heard by him above the howl of the wind sweeping off the cliff to the beach and sea below. The sea relentlessly crashed shoreward, in spite of the mountain wind hurling against it.

Giles's signal to him was clear. Giles was pointing westward and upward. There, about two higher hills to the west, was parked the silhouette of a German Kubelwagen, Germany's answer to the American Jeep. This was a four-passenger bucket-seated car, which had an underside that allowed it to go over larger rocks than a Jeep. Like the Jeep, it was unarmored, with no windows and a drop-down windshield. The two cautiously returned to their parked vehicles, informed the others of their possible plight, and decided to press on, hoping that there were no cutoff roads giving the Germans access to them or to cutting them off from Cerbere.

Unfortunately there was a narrow intersection with a right-angled road narrower than theirs that connected into their road. The Kubelwagen, apparently unaware of their nearby presence, made a right turn from it and to the front of the Citroen. This placed it angled and near the edge of the cliff. Etienne recognized his opportunity and took it, by accelerating the big Citroen and smashing into the right-turning rear of the Kubelwagen. He continued to shove it cliff ward as he turned along beside it, while his left wheels were continuing to push it to the edge and over the cliff, for a two-hundred- or three-hundred-foot drop to the beach below. He fought his steering wheel, hard right, as his front left wheel was fighting his left back wheel, to convince it to purchase some hard ground, on this joke of a roadway they had been on.

Elle had stopped about a car length behind and well into the worn car tracks of the road. Etienne's brakes were still functioning, and he could and did stop the car. He got out, looked down, and saw how close he had come to death with Giles his "shotgun." As he bent over, he wretched and vomited. Giles was out of the car too, shaky legged and leaning on the right front fender. The left rear fender was destroyed as was most of the left side of the Citroen, except the driver's door. His left rear wheel was not impinged by the destroyed rear left fender, neither was the mid body of the left side.

And Giles mumbled, quite inaudibly and ironically, in English, in the dialect and words of the half-track sergeant of the Welsh Guards, from seemingly so long ago, "Now, there are just four dead gents what 'ad a bad accident, on the road below. Too bad there ain't a Bobby around to maik a report."

LXXXIII

AFTER CARLA STOPPED sobbing and Elle stopped her tremors and was able to drive calmly, which amounted to approximately twenty minutes, they started rolling forward again. Gradually both vehicles advanced in speed. Before and below them, they soon saw what appeared to be the border-crossing shacks of both countries, just a matter of perhaps two hundred feet across from each other.

In fifteen minutes time, they were in front of the exit arm, which was dropped across the road in front of them. Gilbert alighted from his side of the car with everyone's total paperwork. The customs man arose from his chair with the intention of walking toward the cars, but Gilbert stopped him a few steps from his door. Gilbert told him that he had all the papers for everyone plus a passport for all of them, under the personal signature of Marshal Henri Petain and the great seal of the new State of France, awarding them all free passage out of the country.

The customs man was wearing the uniform of his service with the customs badge on his jacket and was middle-aged and appeared to be surly, probably because the colonel was in an obvious rush and customs people deal in frustration. In Gilbert's experience the customs service attracts negative personalities, of an officious nature and of passive aggressive temperaments. He felt their authoritative bent yields them the power to inconvenience anyone, no matter their status, unless of course, they perceive the situation as having an adverse consequence to themselves.

In the present instance, he told Colonel Lambert that he was closing in a few minutes and that he could not examine all of the papers until tomorrow morning, possibly early afternoon. The colonel showed him the great seal of state and the signature of the marshal clearing all persons traveling in the two vehicles. Their personal papers identified each of the persons on the marshal's passport. Col. Lambert made clear that they were on urgent business and could not return, but must have his clearance for the Spanish border guards now.

The customs man reached for his phone, and Gilbert grabbed the phone out of his hand and simultaneously called out, "Giles, come now and armed!" He unsheathed his bayonet at the same time and cut the phone wires and then pushed up the barrier lever in front of the Citroen. Giles was there in less than a minute, with his drawn pistol leveled at the agent's mouth, while Gilbert pushed the bayonet blade against his throat and asked him if he wished to have his throat sliced through the artery or a bullet through his mouth and then the brain. The customs agent was frozen, and his face was drained of all blood as he began to quiver in his chair.

Gilbert directed him to stamp a clearance form for both cars and occupants immediately, so that he might live beyond the moment. The agent did so with alacrity, still quivering all the while. Gilbert then told the agent that he would ride in the rear seat of the Citroen and accompany them through the Spanish barrier, carefully and *calmly* telling the Spaniards that these officers were on a special rush mission for Marshal Henri Petain, as Gilbert "flashed" the passport toward the Spanish guards, also that he wanted them to accommodate them in Barcelona by giving them the phone number and the address, if they had them, of the French consulate there.

"I advise you to say nothing that would alarm them. We do not wish to take your life or theirs if avoidable. If they delay us, it will be necessary," Gilbert told him.

"After the cars and occupants are clear of the barrier, we will free you, and if you complain or report any of this incident, we will have the three cars of armed guards following us, crossing here tomorrow afternoon, eliminate you per our orders from Barcelona. You may have your phone wires reinstalled after the three cars of armed guards have come through."

The two vehicles proceeded exactly as planned, and the French customs agent enacted his short portrayal perfectly, as though it had been rehearsed. Both autos arrived in Barcelona in less than three hours and found the British consulate another hour after.

Elle telephoned her mother which was very inconvenient because of the many phone trunk lines necessary, even though Spain, a neutral country was a near ally of Vichy. Elle "confirmed arrival of complete shipment of all plane tree saplings for the Bird Mercado on Las Ramblas, something very new for Catalunya. Next order will be date palms from Morocco for Sir Herbert Miles Road on the old Moorish-Iberian Coast. God's speed! See you after victory day!"

Finis

Made in the USA
Charleston, SC
21 October 2016